KUMAKANA
A GRONUPS TALE

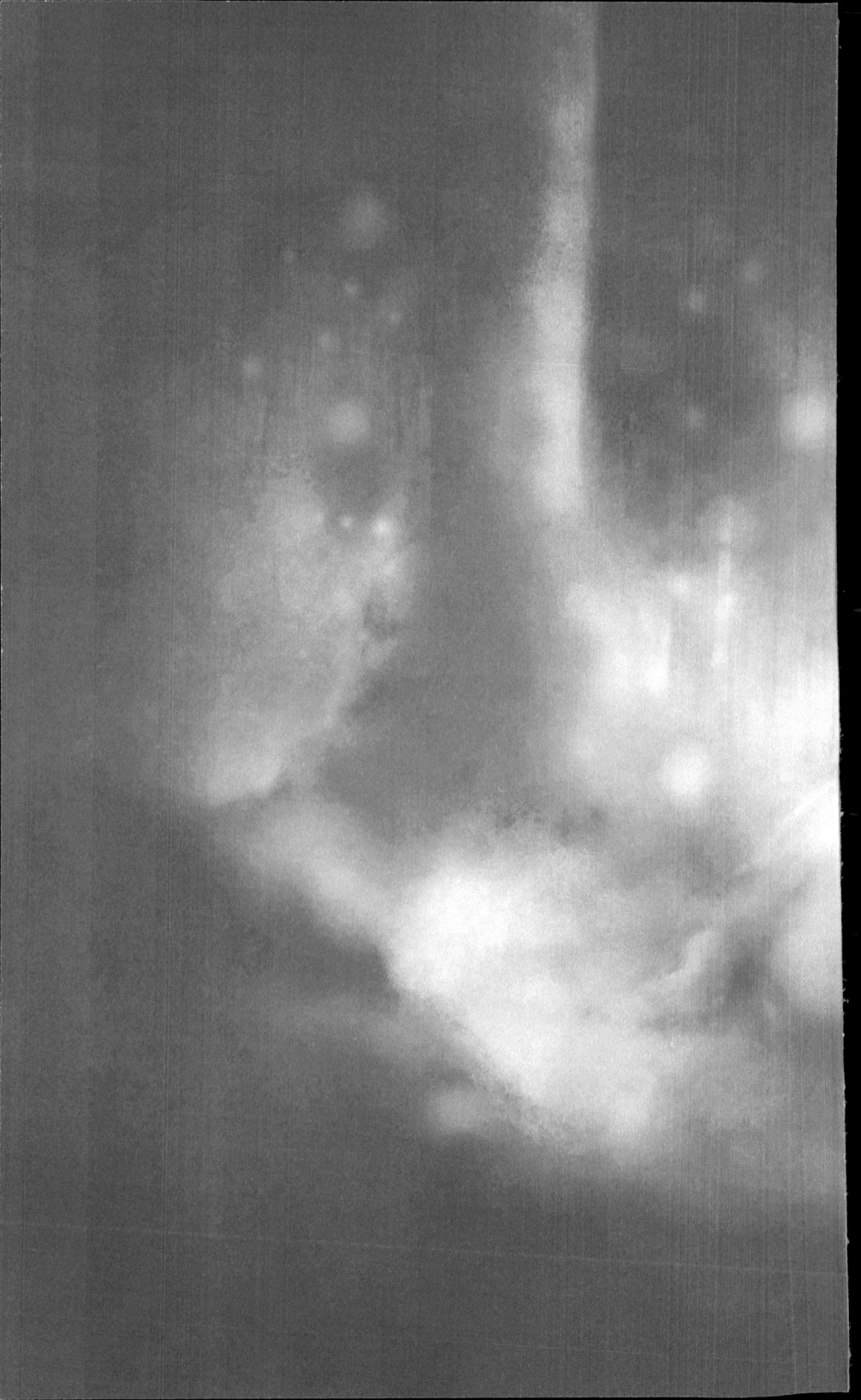

KUMAKANA

A GRONUPS TALE

Kevin Price

With illustrations by Judith Price

First published in Australia by Crotchet Quaver

Inquiries should be addressed to the publishers.

Crotchet Quaver
119 Ridgewood Loop Bullsbrook Western Australia 6084

Book Design and Typography by Logorythm

A CIP catalogue record for this book is available from the

National Library of Australia.

Hardcover ISBN: 978-0-9942115-2-1
Paperback ISBN: 978-0-9954086-4-7
eBook (kindle) ISBN: 978-0-9942115-3-8
eBook (epub) ISBN: 978-0-9954086-3-0

For those who believe there is always a better way

The Mountains

Valley of Six Curses

Ravine

Jerramunga's Journey

Valley of
Lengthened Years

Pool of Many Reflections

DENSE FOREST

KUMAKANA
FOREST

Kulwinkulkine

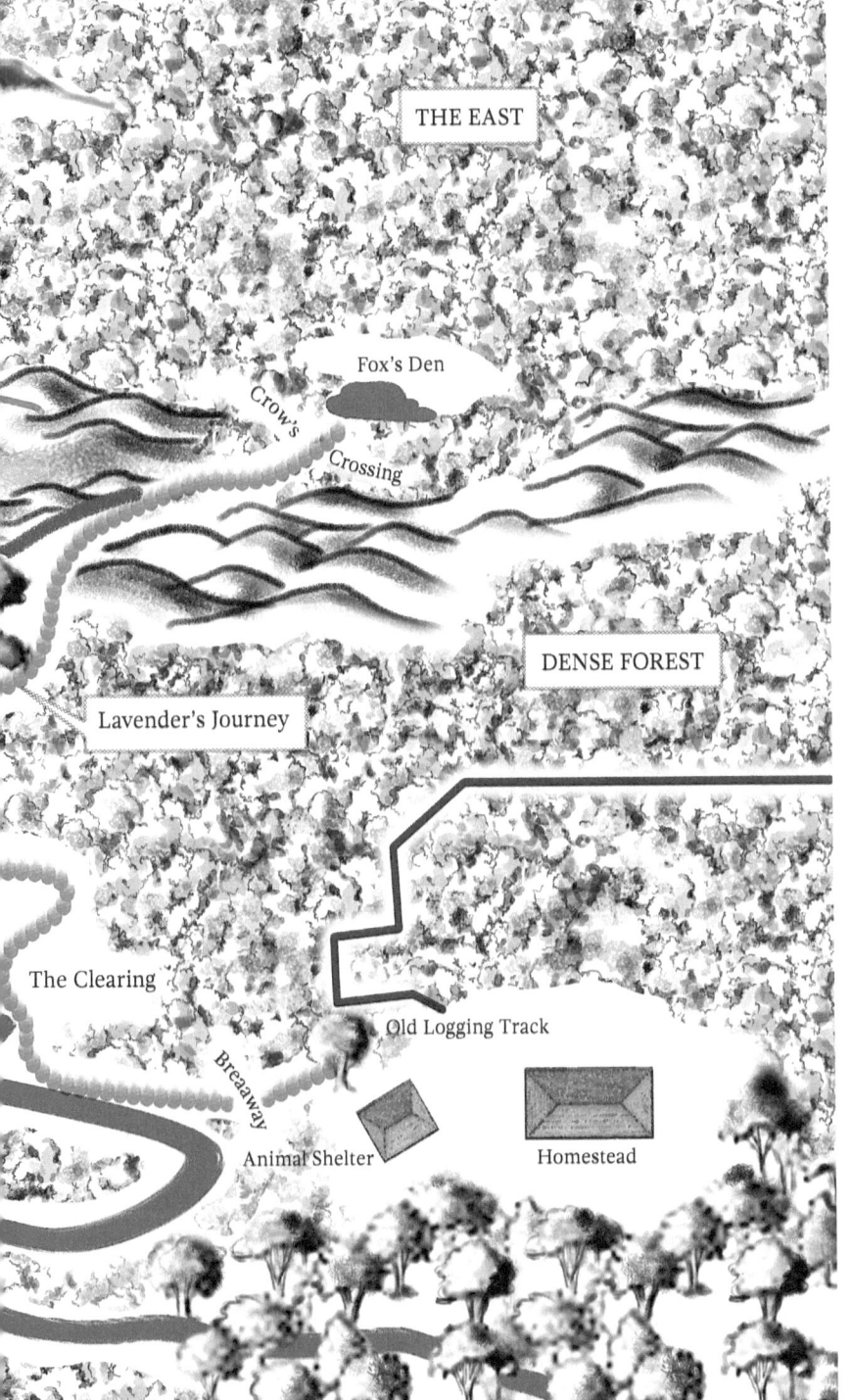

THE EAST

Fox's Den

Crow's Crossing

DENSE FOREST

Lavender's Journey

The Clearing

Old Logging Track

Breaaway

Animal Shelter

Homestead

INTRODUCTION

This story was produced on Aboriginal land. I acknowledge and recognise the strength, resilience and capacity of Australia's Indigenous people whose persons and spirits remain part of this country and without whom this work would be impossible.

I am not an Australian Indigenous person, and this is not an Indigenous story. It is, in fact, entirely a work of fiction. But, because this story returns to imagined concepts of a time before European colonisation—those referred to within as Enterers—there is a necessity to draw on publicly recognised beliefs of Indigenous people as a way of holding the effects of colonisation to account. The story recognises and acknowledges such cultural practice as part of its historic framework only in pursuit of a unique and original fiction. The characters, spiritual concepts and landscape are of my own imagining, inspired by my own walking of the country—which is how stories usually begin.

This story takes place in the present but you soon enough meet characters who have witnessed life come and go for millennia. In it I want to take you into a unique part of Australia and propose the idea that our bush animals have their own spirituality, ministered to by a special group of spirit creatures, and has been in existence since time, as we know it, began. For the non-Indigenous writer, this poses the problem of skirting 'cultural appropriation' because, quite clearly, writing in the language and culture of ancient European myths and legends is not going to produce a story true to my country. I appreciate and recognise that our Indigenous people's core belief systems stem from a deep and spiritual connection to the land, but that should not preclude my having similar reverence. The earth as mother and heaven as father is not unique to Aboriginal Australia.

I found the English language an inadequate vehicle with which to enter the ancient world of the Australian bush. Naming of our animals in English came much later than the animals themselves and consequently I found myself turning to words found in the language of local Indigenous people, collected and rendered into English by early European settlers. What struck me was the sheer musicality of the language and how the native sounds of the birds and animals in their utterances and movements are the canvasses upon which such identities were cast. It saddens me that these names are largely lost to our vernacular and replaced by wholly inadequate Anglicised ones, often celebrating the identity of the person who 'discovered' the animal. Earlier versions of the manuscript had far more Indigenous words throughout the text than can be found in this one, which confines itself to only a few animal, bird and reptile identities and colloquial expressions in an endeavour to establish a mood and soundtrack of the bush. (A word list with English translations can be found at the back of the book.) Were our society to cast aside some of the imported identities for our native fauna in favour of the original ones, I feel our language would be all the better for it, and our reconciliation efforts better empowered.

We all believe in something. I believe in story—its power to deliver an understanding and bring people together. This story seeks to blend adventure with magical realism, bring together humans and animals, Indigenous and non-Indigenous, the ancient and the contemporary ... in a world that does not exist, yet exists around us every day. I invite you to enter that world and let go your beliefs.

KP

CONTENTS

Part I
SPLITTING APART

Chapter 1

Lavender Jensen's imagination has a habit of being troublesome. Her mother has diagnosed it as a disease with more killing power than avian flu. Her father calls it imaginitis. Not contagious, although curable. Apparently.

But Lavender Jensen's imagination is not like a light switch to be turned off and on. It's her coping mechanism when other kids behave like dicks. Like when Selena Graham and her coterie of up-themselves-rabbits stuffed tissue paper in their bras to make it look as though they had bigger tits and Lavender said she only saw 'mobile mole dwellings'. The fight that followed brought on a firestorm of criticism from the adults in her life for what, when it was all said and done, were pretty mundane offences. Imagination to the rescue. It comes to the rescue when boredom threatens. It has been heavily indulged for the past few days.

She'd spent several days watching two magpies that perch high in the trees at the edge of the great forest, chortling back and forth like matrons snickering at the school gate. She'd formed the opinion that these two had a healthy business conjuring spells. Their tree—and those surrounding it—rises like a column in the rampart of a great fort, forming part of a landscape that sits idly, waiting, as the crackle of their leafy crowns tosses whispered incantations to the winds, passing on the myths and legends of dark days and forgotten languages. Lavender's mind had no escape from this bush bewitchery.

Under the direction of these two birds, hidden eyes watched her. Sly, spectral, movements crawling on her skin as they stared out from shadows that consume the light. Eyes sunken in the cheeks of hungry owners that slink through the understorey in search of food and sanctuary. The birds posted their twitter-feed of the goings-on in the murky depths of the forest in a cavatina so captivating that it generated an irrepressible urge in her to break the rules and nose around the void behind the giant trees.

They perched in the lowest branches of a high high karri tree. They changed their tune at every attempt she made to throw her ball. She was well aware that she was totally unco but did they have to be so snide about it? Everyone had to start somewhere. Just because sport wasn't Lavender's strong suit, at least it staved off the boredom. Just because *they* didn't understand didn't mean it was a complete waste of time. She shot them a glare and headed down the hill to retrieve her ball. Her last throw left it near a bit of scrub that was well wide and short of her target.

Lavender Jensen had limited tolerance of those who had limited tolerance—the kind who usually have something to fear. Perhaps the magpies felt threatened by her ball's awesome powers. That must be it! Because the ball had power beyond anything they could possibly know—ten times anything they had. Just wait, I'll show you.

She was thirteen years old. A single wave of glossy hair fell to her shoulders. The fine strands separated when the wind picked it up and the sun struck its ends, and brandished red and golden flashes among the Lindt-brown. She was midgety compared to her friends, and watched every day for the growth spurt that would see her catch up to them. Lately, though, she did notice that her jeans were shorter in the leg and her tops short in the arm. But not tighter around the chest. In her morning studies of her reflection in the mirror, she hoped her small breasts and too-narrow shoulders wouldn't get left behind when the spurt came. She was—at least according to her mother—beautiful, with eyes whose colour she was named after, her fine nose finishing in the slight upturn she'd inherited from her father. But her beauty was spoiled by a small population of itinerant pimples that had begun showing up on her chin and forehead. At first she tried to blot them with splotches of make-up, but it was always a shade away from her skin colour, spreading like a stain across her dial.

The forest surrounded a farm that was twenty-six kilometres by winding dirt road from Denmark. This pretty seaside hamlet on the south coast of Western Australia sported little more than bare commercial necessities and a smattering of tourist traps. The farm may as well have been a thousand kilometres from anywhere because it was completely surrounded by a forest about the size of the country of Denmark.

She'd been dumped here three weeks ago. Apart from her,

there was only her father. No friends within cooee. Where she lived normally, in a comfortable southern Perth suburb, the biggest shopping centre was only a five-minute walk away. Here, her mobile phone didn't have a signal, and there was nothing to do, except throw her ball or help her father in his displaced-animal shelter. Not that she minded being around animals—that was actually fun—but the daily slog of chores wasn't an ideal summer holiday activity—certainly not when you're a stone-age away from real living people.

She would need a lot of imagination to survive this summer. Not for the first time, a desire to disappear into the blackness of the forest swept over her. The magpies were strangely quiet.

She held her ball up at them as though it were a weapon, brandishing the eleven signatures that adorned it—the signatures of the champion Australian cricket team. Her grandfather, once an international cricketer, and ever since, an armchair expert, had given it to her.

'Eleven of the greatest ball magicians who ever lived,' he said. 'You know what that means?'

She shook her head.

'It's got all of their magic.' His eyes sparkled as he thrust it into her hands, his face bearing his lop-sided grin with its speck of white spittle nestling in the corner of his mouth that didn't open. 'It's their magic that makes the ball fly, and if you practise hard enough, you'll fly too.'

The word *magic* hooked her.

For as long as she could remember, she'd believed that magic solved problems. Her mother humoured her. Her father said she was suffering a bout of imaginitis. But she held to her beliefs, convinced that she felt the ball's magic every time she carried it. She could feel it pushing back as she squeezed it, its warmth radiating into her hand, urging her to carry on, to learn its great gift. She wasn't too sure about the flying bit—she imagined it often, soaring above the trees, dipping and rolling. But that was sure to take a lot of practise. First she needed to discover the spell to make the ball fly. At the moment all it did was dribble along and plop ...

Wait! That's it! The magpies are scared of the ball's flight magic. She lined up a throw toward the fence, closed her left eye, squinted with her right across the top of the ball, sighted one magpie's chest dead centre and willed herself to knock it off its perch.

The fence separated the forest from the farm. It ran east–west, plunging down a steep rise to a gully beyond sight, its top and bottom wires removed to allow animals easy passage. A firebreak—long overdue for grading—divided it from the trees. An old logging track, now partly regrown, started at the top of the crest and served as a dark doorway into the forest.

Her mother had told her how the trees shaped the forest—the karri, among the world's tallest, and the tingle, with its massive girth, one of the largest. She told her that their bark hid spiders with sixty-five million years of history. Some of these trees grew nowhere else on earth. But her mother didn't stop at that.

'There are secrets and legends far older than any recorded history,' she said. 'In an old language, this was called the *Kumakana*—it means the place of the great beginning. As far as forests go, this one is about as old as they get.'

Her mother was an animal-anthropologist and knew a lot about this stuff. When Lavender was little—several years before they'd bought the farm—she'd told her about the forest. Lavender's mother had been called to identify a large pile of bones that had been discovered in some hidden location deep within the forest's secret heart. It turned out to be a mass grave of Tasmanian devils—proof, among other things, that they once populated Australia's southwestern forests. The mystery, though, was why so many bones, and what caused the deaths.

The discovery created problems, though. Lavender had been dumped at the farm with her dad for these holidays because her mother had taken off to Adelaide to attend a conference on the Devil Facial Tumour Disease that was devastating Tasmania's devil population, threatening their existence. She didn't know when she'd be back. She seemed to think there might be a connection in her discovery that could lead to a prevention and cure. When there was science to get involved in, her daughter occupied some place far, far away. She wasn't a bad mother, just one whose priorities could change in a nanosecond. One minute Lavender was looking forward to a holiday just chillin' in her room, and the next she was removed to this remote outstation.

Her dad was tall, with that academic stoop that goes with the shape of a university professor. Wiry grey hair curled around his forehead like filigree, and he maintained his beard in a permanent three-day growth. His lips curled at the edges in a hard-worn smile that pinched miniature furrows from the corners of his almond-shaped eyes. His glasses perched well down his nose, affording his hazel eyes the choice of viewing over the lenses or through them, depending on his mood. He'd accepted a university research grant to establish his animal shelter, working to rehabilitate indigenous animals into the forest and reduce the impact of feral populations. It was important work and it dovetailed nicely with Lavender's mother's great find.

Her mother, though often here, had said quite emphatically that she didn't intend to live at the farm. She and Dad weren't separating, she'd said, just living in different places for a while. How exactly, Lavender wondered, was that not a separation?

At first, the discovery caused great excitement. But, about a year ago—around the time her dad got his grant and moved to the farm, her mother went quiet on the subject and wouldn't talk about it any more. The big find was suddenly hush-hush. Apparently silenced by something called *secret business*.

Her dad hadn't said much on the subject, which wasn't unusual in itself—he didn't have a lot to say on most subjects. The only thing he seemed really firm about was that she was forbidden to cross the fence—a rule she broke three days ago when she rescued a joey at the edge of the bush, an act of disobedience that brought on a hell-storm severe enough to melt a polar ice-cap.

What was she to do? The joey was injured. Isn't that what his shelter was for? But her father didn't see it all quite that clearly.

'It was dangerous,' he'd said, looking across the tops of his glasses.

She hit back.

'Dad, it's just bush. It's not likely to swallow me up.' She made an action with her arms, mimicking a hippo mouth chomping down on some poor insignificant creature.

'Yes I know it's just bush. But you can get lost in there—it's full of unexplored areas and hidden dangers.'

He tried to be rational. Firm.

She was anything but rational. Loud.

'Ugh! It's not like there are tigers waiting to pounce, or wolves ready to gobble me up on the way to Grandma's house, or three bears living in a cosy little cottage I'm going to stumble into—'

'I'm not talking about an imaginary world. This forest has very real dangers—'

'All I did was rescue an injured joey at the edge of the forest. I didn't even go in! You're acting like that was a bad thing.'

'It could have been if the mother was nearby. You haven't seen what a kangaroo can do—'

'Well, she wasn't. This time it's not *my* imagination running riot. You should listen to yourself!'

Anything he'd had to say after that was swamped by the wall of sound from the earbuds that she jammed into her ears as she stalked from the kitchen.

That was two nights ago.

Now, as she stood on the rise holding the bright yellow magic ball, she wondered about the magpies, and the eyes that stared out of the murk, and the shadows slinking between trunks, and the dissonant undercurrent of the forest's dangers. What made her father such a dick at times? She didn't need to be treated as a kid any more. He had no idea.

The earbuds were new and they rarely left her ears. It was her third set this year—the first had gone through the wash when they were less than a week old, and the second, within a month of replacing the first, crushed under the wheel of the car when dropped unseen from the back seat. Her father had bought these, threatening that it would be the last time. They were expensive, sat perfectly on her ears and sounded amazing. She knew he meant it.

And when she complained about there being no signal for her mobile, he simply pointed to the wall and said, 'There's a phone.'

'I can't text my friends on that.'

'Have a conversation.'

'Who has conversations? Dad, me and my friends don't have conversations, we text.'

'*Me and my friends?* Surely you mean my friends and I.'

Nitpicking about language was another of his favourite pastimes.

'No. I mean *me,* and my friends.'

Old people. Old ideas. Old beliefs. And she was stuck with them. For the whole summer.

Lavender Jensen hooked her hair behind her ears and bunged her earbuds into them. She hit the play button, cast a defiant look into the nearest karri tree, her yellow ball gripped tightly in her right hand, left the rise and headed past the house.

As she rounded the end of the house, another building, about ten metres from the property's boundary fence, came into view. Part of it was the remains of a single-roomed, stone logger's cottage, built some time in the latter part of the nineteenth century. It now had a new roof, a concrete floor had replaced its original earthen one, new internal walls divided an office, a locked medical supplies storage room and a surgery. There was a food store as well as six sheltered pens.

Chicken wire fenced the outside perimeter and cover. The entire complex, designed to accommodate a dozen or so recuperating animals—including birds and reptiles—measured about thirty metres by forty. This was her father's brand new, purpose-built animal shelter.

There were two ways to enter.

The original doorway in the stone wall led directly to the surgery. Lavender headed for a simple wooden-framed gate at the far corner. An ancient blackbutt stood in solitude about two-thirds of the way from the main house, the spiky grey fingers of its long-dead topmost branches stretched skyward above a wide and bushy skirt of healthy green leaves. A magpie sat motionless on a dead branch and watched her pass beneath.

She reached for the wire latch and was about to flip it open when something at her feet caught her eye. A bone about the length of a dessert spoon lay against the gate. She pulled the earbuds from her ears and bent to pick it up, leaving her ball on the ground.

It was thin and white, clearly old, but there was little decay. One end sported a knuckle. The other oddly rounded, as if it had been shaped by hand, and deep scratch marks patterned the length of it. She studied it, turning it over in her hand, trying to make sense of the markings, feeling the weight and running her finger along the polished length. How had it got there? The hairs on the back of her neck bristled and her gaze moved to the tree—and the magpie.

The bird eyed her but remained stoical on its perch. Pointing the bone at it, she sighted along its length like a gun barrel, made a sound she imagined to be a dull shot. Then she shrugged and, tapping the bone into her hand, disappeared into the enclosure. She didn't notice an object fall from her pocket.

The shelter only had one patient—the joey she'd rescued three days earlier.

She'd found it cowering beneath a bush at the edge of the forest, terrified, exhausted and bleeding badly from a gash in its right side. The right foreleg dangled and pain was obvious in its eyes. Her heart went out to the young kangaroo. She dashed back to the shelter, grabbed an old towel and rushed back through the fence. Her touch was feather-soft as she wrapped the towel around the animal and took it in. Her dad set to work straight away. She'd checked on her patient several times since that afternoon—feeding, watering, and holding one-way conversations.

She passed the pen and headed for the food store. Her dad was in his office working on his papers. She called to him as she reached for a container of kibbles.

'How's the joey?'

'Perked up a little.'

He didn't look up from his papers.

'Worked out what happened?'

'Fox attack I'd say.'

'How can you tell?'

'Canines. More than one set.'

'I've seen it,' Lavender blurted from the doorway.

Her father thought she was referring to the wounds and began a detailed explanation of the lacerations and contusions.

'No. The fox. I've seen the eyes,' she said.

He didn't reply.

'In the forest,' she continued, 'they watch me from the trees.'

Her father looked up from his work and stared at her over the lenses of his glasses.

'I've told you about going into the forest—'

'I didn't go in the forest.'

'I think your imagination's running away again. If you haven't been in the forest and you haven't seen the fox that looks at you from the trees, then how do you know it's there?'

'Don't know. It's just there—watching, smiling. Hiding in the shadows.'

'Are you sure it's not fairies? They're here too, you know.' He laughed. 'Anyway, more than one fox attacked that joey—he's lucky to be alive. I'll have to set out some bait.'

'What's bait?'

'Dried meat with a poison called ten-eighty. It occurs naturally in that plant—he pointed to a leafy branch on his shelf—doesn't hurt native animals, but kills the ferals.'

'That's cruel.'

'What is?'

'You can't go around poisoning animals just for doing what they do. Why do you have to control everything?'

'I'm not controlling things. I'm helping indigenous animals re-establish their range—'

'They'll work it out themselves, Dad, that's what animals do.'

'Lavender, you've got to realise something. Out here is the real world, it's not your fairy tale world. Animals aren't like the ones in books—'

'I'm not telling fairy tales, Dad. This place is weird. Magpies gossip about me, a crow watches me, and this joey came to me—'

'The joey was hurt. It was escaping a terrible life-threatening danger. Do you know how dangerous foxes can be? You were lucky this time, but you should have come to get me. Next time you may not be so lucky. You come and get me—understood?'

'Oh! You're such a control freak.'

She turned on her heel and headed for the joey's pen, stuffing the slim bone she'd found by the gate into her back pocket. She would have mentioned it, but after this last conversation, she thought it would lead to an accusation of some other fanciful crime.

To make the joey's pen more homelike, Lavender had added branches cut from shrubs and bushes, and spread a mixture of hay and sawdust around the watering bowl. Her dad told her to scatter the kibbles on the ground—he reckoned it was better than putting them all in a bowl because it encouraged the joey to scratch and use his injured paw. For the same reason, she wasn't meant to hand feed him. Anyway, he was too shy to take from her hand, although it didn't stop her trying. She'd left the internal doors open to give him the run of the whole enclosure, and, judging by the poo trail all the way to the gate, he'd made good use of it.

He was huddled in a corner of the pen. He looked *so cute*—Lavender's personal favourite phrase for describing any young animal—with his front paw bound to a splint and supported by a narrow sling fastened behind his neck. The bandages and sling were made from a special new biodegradable material, which disintegrated within a short time. Wild animals under veterinary care, her dad said, need to be kept in recuperation for as short a time as possible—especially a young one—and these new materials helped with faster rehabilitation.

The joey's eyes were large and dark as they regarded her from beneath long grey lashes.

She offered a handful of kibbles and talked softly, encouraging the animal to come forward and take a nibble from her hand.

She called him Cutie, but pronounced it more like *Koo-tee*, and followed the expression with five clicks of her tongue: *tch-tch, tch-tch-tchuk*.

The animal's ears twitched and turned at the sounds. He looked her square in the face as she squatted a metre or so away, but remained still on his haunches, his tail flat on the ground behind him. She was patient and totally absorbed in the ritual. She had come to cherish the time with him. She wanted this young kangaroo to be her friend.

That was the moment she struck upon the idea of music.

Perhaps he would enjoy some music—she had all of the latest hits—hip-hop, rock, and a solid collection of pop tunes. She reached for her earbuds but the only object in her pocket was the long, thin bone.

'Oh!' she exclaimed, as she searched the ground.

The joey came alert and stood erect at her exclamation. He retreated a step or two farther into the corner. Lavender left the pen and retraced her steps to the food store. It wasn't there so she continued back toward the front gate. What she saw sent her heart plummeting to the pit of her stomach.

Before her, a metre or so in front of the gate, the magpie was leaving the ground with the earbuds trailing like noodles. Lavender raced through the gate, scooped her ball and her phone up from the ground and called for the bird to return as it headed for the fence and the treetops beyond.

She reached back behind her shoulder with her right arm as she ran at full tilt, and flung the ball after the retreating bird.

It shot from her hand like a cannonball from the deck of a ship heading directly for the bird. The bird slid sideways mid-flight and ducked as the passing missile continued on its soaring trajectory across the face of the sun above the tree line, and was then lost to sight on its way down.

'Hell!' Lavender called after the bird, her voice coming on the top of a loud pant as she tore down the paddock. 'You were lucky this time.'

The ball returned to the ground, striking a rock with a loud hollow *plop*, then bounced over the fence, along the firebreak. By the time she reached the fence, the bird had disappeared into the forest, swallowed by the shadows. The ball rolled to a stop near the start of the old logging track.

She pulled up at the fence, angry and frustrated as she fought back tears. She looked through blurred vision back toward the animal shelter asking herself how she would ever explain the loss of a third set of earbuds ...

'Oh no!' she cried. 'Shit, shit, *shit!*'

In her haste to chase the bird, she'd left the gate open and, as she turned toward the shelter, the joey emerged, glanced briefly at her, turned his back and bounded around the shelter toward the fence.

'Oh, no! No!'

She raced along the fence, hoping to cut the young kangaroo off before he too disappeared into the forest. She slipped through the wire, the slim white bone gripped firmly in her hand. The wire twanged as she pulled away from it. At the same moment, the joey crossed to the firebreak. In a desperate race, she headed for the entrance of the old logging track. She would have beaten the joey to it had a fluffy brown blur not bolted up behind her and caused her to stumble.

She recovered and stopped, panting hard. Right before her eyes the vanishing bum of a puppy streaked away—a yellow ball in its mouth, tail wagging like windscreen wipers in a cloudburst, and a joey in its sights.

The joey turned into the old logging track. The puppy stopped for a second, challenged Lavender with a look, sniffed at the ground, and then disappeared in hot pursuit of the joey with her ball locked firmly in its mouth.

'Hey!' Lavender yelled, turning into the old track and sprinting after the dog. 'Stop, he's hurt. Bring back my ball.'

The pup was fast. It scampered beneath the prickly skirt of a *balga* bush and was gone before Lavender could catch it.

'Hell!' She slapped the side of her head as she puffed to catch her breath. She looked around.

Tall trees and dense scrub surrounded her. And her house was out of sight. The pounding blood in her eardrums gradually gave way to clumping sounds from the undergrowth deeper in the bush. She studied the prickly curtain of bush that the puppy ran beneath and listened.

'If this was a wand,' she said, pointing the bone toward the sounds, 'I'd turn you into a frog, zap Koo-tee back to the shelter, and turn that thieving magpie into a maggot. Damn it, look what you've done!'

The sound behind her came up fast.

She turned abruptly. A dark-skinned boy belted toward her through the long shadows. As she turned, her toe caught on a snaking vine and all that kept her from a nasty collision was the sidestep she took to keep her balance. He missed her by the mere skin of a grass seed.

As the boy swerved to avoid her, his sneakers found a bare patch of ground and he skidded, landing heavily, sprawled at her feet. When he righted himself he was breathless and red faced, sporting grazes on knees and palms, to which he gave only cursory inspections. Trickles of blood seeped into the wounds on his hands. He smeared them on his tee-shirt.

'Spot the dog?' he asked, breathlessly.

'Your dog?' she asked.

His smoky dark eyes regarded her. Then his brown features split into a wide boyish grin that she didn't appreciate.

'Your dog stole my ball and chased my injured joey—and you should look where you're going. You could've killed me.'

'You're standin' there like a bandicoot on a burnt ridge.'

'A bandicoot? I'm no bandicoot. What are you talking about?'

'Well,' he began, struggling to explain himself, 'when there's been a fire, y'get bandicoots and … Look, it's something my grandmother used to say…'

She observed him coldly.

He towered a head above her. His Harley-Davidson tee-shirt, black and loose fitting, was draped over baggy knee-length denim shorts. He wore his sneakers, scuffed and blackened, without socks. He studied her from beneath a strong brow, above which a shock of black hair exploded.

She pointed at the balga with the bone.

'You've chased my joey into the bush,' she said.

He looked at the bush. Then at her.

'I wasn't chasin' a joey.'

'It was sick, hurt—attacked by a pack of foxes. And now, your dog has gone after him.' She waved the bone in the direction of the balga bush, shrugged and turned away so he wouldn't see the tears welling in her eyes. She made to walk around the boy back toward home.

He stepped in front of her.

'Wait. How d'you know it's my dog?'

'Do you see anyone else here looking for a dog?'

'I didn't say I was *looking* for a dog—'

'But you are.' And she waved the bone at his chest.

'Hey. Watch where you're pointing that thing,' he said, turning toward the balga bush, leaning sideways as if it afforded him a better view. 'In there, eh? A joey and my dog?'

'Yeah I have to get him back. And my earbuds too.'

'He took your earbuds?'

'No, he took my ball and chased the joey. A magpie took my earbuds. But I have to get all of them back.'

He shrugged.

'What's so special about your ball?'

'It's magic.'

He looked at her as if she'd just claimed to have landed from the moon.

'What kind?'

'It's a yellow plastic cricket ball with all—'

'Not the ball. What kind of magic?'

'Air magic.'

He shook his head and grinned, and pushed his way past the prickles of the balga bush. 'That bone's likely to have more magic than your ball.'

'I think the magpie dropped the bone.'

'The magpie?' His brow furrowed as he looked at it. Then he flashed a grin and said, 'Well, come on then.'

Lavender turned back in the direction of her home.

'I don't know. I'm not supposed to be on this side of the fence.'

'Do you want to get your stuff back?'

And then he was gone.

He plainly meant that she should follow him into the forest. She hesitated. Already she'd gone further than she was allowed. But then she reasoned that she wasn't all alone. Not really. And life wouldn't be worth living if she went home without the joey and the earbuds. She alone cared about the ball. So she stepped past the balga, which gave her a sharp prick in the shoulder, and entered the forest.

She was confronted by a wall of springy ferns—the kind that snap back to their upright positions and slap you in the face after being pushed aside to pass through. A tangled web of vines snaked across the ground waiting on every step to trip her. She looked around but couldn't see the boy.

She sang out.

'Where are you?'

'I'm trying to get your ball. It's gone down here.'

Lavender picked her way through dense undergrowth, learning painfully fast which bushes had sharp prickles. Following the sound of the boy's voice, she came upon a clearing ringed by trees with trunks like stove pipes. He lay on the ground on the far side, one arm holding a squirming puppy, the other buried up to his shoulder, his face contorted like a sun-withered paddy melon.

'Hold on to Spot,' he called. 'Your ball's down here.'

'Where's the joey?' she asked, taking the dog from him.

Spot yapped and licked her face. She held him in front of her and scolded him. 'Did you put my ball there?'

A wounded look crossed the boy's face as he strained harder to reach a ball he could neither see nor feel.

'It must be half way through to China,' he grunted.

'How come the dog's name is Spot?' she asked the boy. 'He doesn't have any spots.'

The puppy was plain—leathery light brown all over, with a tiny white tip at the end of its tail.

'I've never had a puppy. Hello Spot. You're so-o-oh cuddly!'

Squeezing the puppy affectionately, she stepped around the boy to see where he was trying to reach the ball.

They were on top of what appeared to be a steep gorge. She

tightened her hold on a now resisting Spot, and craned her neck
to peer over the edge.

'I wonder where the joey is,' she said, her voice small and
distant as she searched.

She couldn't see the bottom, or even the sides of the chasm
below. Her gaze came to rest on a tree across the way and there,
sitting in plain view, was the magpie with her earbuds strung
from its beak. She pulled the bone from her pocket and waved
it at the bird as though casting a spell. As she turned from the
precipice to tell the boy, the ground beneath her feet gave way.

She began sliding, slowly at first, and then into free-fall. With
no ground left to support him, the boy was catapulted into space.

'Whoahh-aah!'

Their surprised screams were buried in the roar of tumbling
earth and rocks.

Lavender rolled and slid with the crumbling ground, falling in
a dizzy frenzy down a steep slope dotted with painful obstacles.
At some point she lost the dog and went on tumbling. Sharp
rocks scraped her arms and legs and loose stones pelted her in
the back and head.

Then she came to an abrupt halt.

When she landed, the ground wasn't as hard as she imagined
it would be. It was covered in a thick carpet of brown leaves
scattered over soft sandy earth. The boy had landed a split second
before her and she landed on top of him.

'Aagh—get off!' he cried, wiping a mix of spit and dirt out of
his mouth with the back of his hand.

Dust and grit rained about them.

'That hole went right through,' she told him. She stood and searched her legs and arms for signs of damage. 'I saw your hand—my ball wasn't there.'

He looked around. There was an edge to his voice. 'Where are we?'

Atnunga

Chapter 2

Atnunga was disguised as a gumnut. It was late afternoon and she was reposed among the flower buds high up in the canopy of a karri tree, swaying on the breeze. Below, the waters of the Kulwinkulkine tumbled along a rocky path seeking a greater destination.

A gumnut was Atnunga's preferred disguise. Her camouflage was achieved by folding her ears down and balling her body, leaving her wispy tail free for anchorage to a slim twig fork. Because her long fur's outer colouring had the same silver-brown tint as the karri's maturing seed-pod, it was impossible to tell that one gumnut in the bunch was not the genuine article.

Earlier that afternoon, she had enjoyed warming herself in the gentle spray of the southern midday sun, pushed to and fro by a retiring northeasterly bluster, a hallmark of early summer. She dreamt while she slept. Her dreams were of a happier and more peaceful forest, a time when the animals and birds had less to fear and nature was left to its devices. She dreamt of rain-filled rivers and mountains shadowing a flat timeless earth as a golden warmth ebbed and flowed on the wind's invisible motor. Her dream transported her back in time, when there was nothing but the wind—one moment an invisible wall, the next, a gentle waft:

a force as unpredictable as the ocean.

The icy gusts of the southern wind also ferried torrents of rain from the distant coast, blasting it through the leaves to be guzzled from the ground by the giants of the forest, its excesses left to swirl and froth and bubble along the paths of the streams and tumble into the mighty Kulwinkulkine. Then there was the easterly driven from the daily furnace and nightly freezer of the distant heartland to scatter its load of seed and spore so that life can begin anew. The wind carries life, inspires life, stirs life. The wind is life.

And as the winds are known to change, so must life.

The wind is Atnunga's transport system—though not in any conventional way, as a bird or a kite or a balloon might use it. Atnunga surfs the sound waves the wind creates, riding the pulses to any destination that sounds penetrate.

In her dream, a treetop rustle carried her through distant and wonderful times, until a cacophonous squabble on the next branch shattered it. She unfurled, opening first one eye, then the other; reverting bit by bit to her normal size and proportions.

At first glance it might be easy to mistake Atnunga for a mouse. But closer inspection reveals that she is not. No mouse ever possessed such beauty.

The subtle hues and lines of Atnunga's fur have all the colours found among the feathers of the birds. There are fine strands as black as the crow's back, others as gold as the ring around the parrot's neck. She has all the greens of the hundreds of parakeets, the brilliant reds of the fire-tail, the iridescent blue of the wren, and the browns and greys of the magnificent tail of the eagle. All lie in harmony, each for maximum effect in contrast and complement, each strand a masterful brushstroke.

Her head appears too large for her body. Her eyes bulge, bug-like, below a broad brow, but their spacing is perfect. Her face is somewhat beakish, with nostrils possessing an upward rather than downward tendency. Thin lips are stretched in a permanent smile, creasing outward into full cheeks. Her ears are on the largish side—rounded and tufted on top, unfolding like a pair of radar dishes that swing out as they unwrap from her face. Once vertical, they sweep constantly.

Squatting on her haunches with the length of her legs concealed beneath a skirt of fur, Atnunga studied the source of the disturbance.

As the din grew more raucous, a stick insect—which had only moments earlier been intent on a feed of yellow-mite eggs clustered to the underside of a leaf—scurried (if an insect shaped like a wooden spoon can be said to scurry) down the shadow side of the branch, and found refuge in a fork from which a dead branch protruded earthwards. The canny insect changed its colour from the brilliant green of the leaf to the brown-grey of the timber as it travelled. It disappeared completely in the cubby of the fork, its disguise so successful that, had Atnunga not seen it make its life-preserving dash, she would have thought it was no more than another loose piece of bark clinging tentatively to the mother tree.

Atnunga shot a dark and frosty look at the dream crashers.

A pandemonium of *dammalaks*—green ring-necked parrots—crowded her branch. The branch reeled against its own tension as the parrots juggled their positions, leaping off in turns and then wedging themselves back into their own bunch. They huddled, forming a tight scrum of intimidation.

On another branch, one that was a little more elevated, an equally angry flock of *gakkal-yakkals*—pink and grey galahs—were more spread out. Their white crowns raised and their chests barrelled.

Atnunga watched as abusive calls flew back and forth—parrot to galah, galah to parrot. Red flashes above the parrots' over-bitten beaks glowed against their black brows, and thick, gnarled tongues hammered out violent clacks. The galahs responded, stretching to their full extent, pushing their wings out and furrowing crest and chest feathers while snapping powerful beaks echoing like rifle shots at a firing range. They appeared larger, but the parrots were sleeker.

Atnunga recognised the dammalaks. But she'd never seen these gakkal-yakkals before.

'Hey-ey!'

Her screech framed a silence more ominous than the wake of a landslide. Everything stilled. The squabbling birds all eyed the source of the call.

'Atnunga! *Yay!*' a parrot exclaimed. 'Are we glad you're here.

We need your wise counsel.'

Atnunga grumbled. 'Disturb your own Gronup. Can't it wait until tonight?'

'Tonight? No way, there's not enough time to wait until tonight.' The bird bobbed up and down and shuffled up to the Gronup. 'You gotta help us now.'

Atnunga addressed the head parrot. 'You're Mal Aga, *Yoolinjah* of the Kumakana dammalaks, right?' The elder acknowledged the respect paid him with a short nod of his head. Atnunga continued. 'What do you want me to do?'

The parrot indicated his clan with his wingtip.

'You know my mate, Mal Ala? My sons and daughters?'

Atnunga nodded, greeting each of them, 'Yay, yay.'

'You know our nest in the dead karri near the Pool of Many Reflections?' He pointed a blue-black wingtip at two galahs. 'Well, today, these two moved in. Swooped and took it! And they're not even from the Kumakana. You gotta help sort this out, Atnunga.'

'That's tough. I sympathise, Mal Aga. But you know the rules. What can I do?'

'Hey, Mal Ala is already with egg!'

A male gakkal-yakkal fluttered across to the branch, landing with an upward swoop that sandwiched Atnunga between him and Mal Aga. He folded his wings and laid his crown feathers flat on his round head. Brown intense eyes with powder-white rims regarded the Gronup.

'He speaks truthfully,' the bird said, sounding like he had a quandong stuffed in his mouth. 'I am pleased to meet you, I am

Kal Barri—my mate is Kal Annie. I'm afraid she's with egg also.'

Atnunga responded using the common term for brother.

'Look, *koomboorlie*, I can't interfere. That's the law. If you invaded their nest, you have to move on.' She looked thoughtful. 'It's a bit late in the season for you isn't it?'

Kal Barri raised his beak.

'Well now look here, madam Gronup. How were we to know the nest was theirs? It looked deserted, a barren hollow, except for a layer of decaying wood dust, no scent around the entrance—'

Mal Ala shrieked, cutting in from across the divide.

'You don't know anything—do you? I put the wood dust there to decay. How do you think we keep my eggs warm? Moron!'

Mal Ala's attack brought a fiery response from Kal Annie.

'Huh! Typical! A dammalak can't even make a nest a home. Only a dammalak would bring up a brood in a dust bowl. At any rate, there's no sign that nest is yours; the entrance is not marked! Your name's not on it.'

Kal Annie pranced along her branch, flapping her wings and bobbing her head as she worked her beak into shrill calls.

Mal Ala spat back.

'Who the hell do you think you are? This isn't the jungle, Pinkie, it's the Kumakana. You can't blow in from snob city and just take something that's not yours. I inherited that nest from my mother. I was born there. She was born there. My grandmother was born there. My family's been born there for generations. And for your information, we dammalaks don't spit all over our doorways—we don't need to ... because we respect each other's space.'

Atnunga struggled to mediate calm between the squabbling birds. Nest invasion could cause serious problems. She'd seen minor territorial incursions lead to the wiping out of whole races.

But more than that, she was curious.

Gakkal-yakkals in the Kumakana were unusual. Their territories were much further north and east, though she'd heard that they migrated further south with each season. Yet Kal Barri and Kal Annie were mature birds, apparently elders of their family. And, judging by the number in their entourage, they had spawned several generations. Surely they have permanent nesting and territory.

'You didn't answer me. Isn't it late for your season?'

Kal Barri narrowed his eyes.

'Our airspace is the land to the east beyond the mountains, toward the sunrise.' Kal Barri indicated a distant mountain range on the eastern horizon. His eyes glazed over. 'But it's gone.'

'Gone? What do you mean gone?' Mal Aga demanded.

'Thunder monsters, bulldozers they're called, terrible things. They came and shook the earth and the air and flattened all the trees. And then there was fire everywhere. Hot flames leaping higher than the trees that stood before it, the smoke so thick we couldn't breathe.'

'And your Gronups?' Atnunga asked.

'Well that's part of the shame of it, I'm afraid to say ... we don't know. We thought we could find a sacred place to call them once we'd settled at the nest. You know how one needs to freshen up a little after long travel?'

A noisy ruffling of feathers and side-stepping erupted on the branch opposite. Atnunga waved impatiently at the dammalaks.

'Do you know any Gronups here?'

'No we don't, unfortunately. But we have heard of Babbildan Babbirra, and we know he is here somewhere. We've heard he has great magic. Maybe he can help.'

'Why would the great Yoolin-jah want to help you?' Mal Aga demanded, speaking of the Kumakana's supreme Gronup.

Atnunga motioned the parrot to calm down.

'Where's your spirit of accommodation, Mal Aga?'

She turned back to the galah.

'It's true that Babbildan Babbirra is very powerful, but I don't know if he can help you. He's got a lot on his plate.'

Kal Barri persisted, polite and firm.

'Do you know where Babbildan Babbirra is?'

Atnunga stared directly into the bird's powdery eyes.

'Yes.'

Her gaze shifted to Mal Aga.

'Of course, Mal Aga can invite you to tonight's corroboree ... as his guest, you understand?' The Celebration of Renewal was held every full moon.

'Will Babbildan Babbirra be there?'

'Possibly. But you might also find some local help. You could get word of an available nest. You might find some Gronups who aren't otherwise engaged. It's really a matter of fitting in.'

'Very well. What would I have to do?'

'Oi, wait just a minute white-eyes,' Mal Aga clipped, 'I haven't invited you yet. I have to discuss it with my family first. I'd be taking a big risk here ... could put everyone in danger. So, first we *yaller-yaller, twonk-twonk* and *chukkup* in the family. Then I'll let you know.'

Kal Barri's face remained impassive. He blinked.

'I still have the problem of Kal Annie—she is due to lay when the moon is full. And as you are aware, the three nights of the full moon begins tonight. She's anxious about shelter.'

'Well, I can't do anything about that,' Mal Aga said. 'All I know is you can't have ours. Mal Ala will be laying this full moon too!'

'I don't suppose you've ever heard of nest sharing?' Kal Barri suggested.

A cackle of laughter erupted on the dammalaks' branch.

Atnunga again addressed Kal Barri.

'If Mal Aga invites you to the full moon corroboree, you have to abide by the laws of the Kumakana. You'll have to sing and dance your story. You'll be shown a place where you can call to the spirits and your Gronups. But only a local yoolin, like Mal Aga, can invite you. And he's entitled to ask something of you in return.'

She looked hard at Mal Aga before turning back to the galah.

'We're all sympathetic to your situation. But if you can't secure a nest, Kal Annie may have to abandon her egg.'

A look passed between the two galahs.

Atnunga continued. 'Regrettable, yes. I wish it weren't so, but nature's only got so many sites, and if there are none, there are none. I can't interfere, though. Mal Aga and his family have to talk about any help they might offer. I suggest you talk about things with your family too. I'm sure it'll all work out.'

Before drifting away on a treetop rustle, Atnunga, deep in thought, watched Mal Aga and his family fly off to reclaim their nest, leaving Kal Barri and his clan perched in the dizzy heights of a giant karri tree.

Has to be an *Enterer* thing, she thought—the humans with ghost-like skin who came on a more recent tide. They have caused so much change in such little time.

She travelled as though aboard a roller coaster on invisible rails, eddying one moment on an up-note—bark flapping against the tree trunk, played by a breeze rushing through the leaves—and then, next moment, dipping on a paradiddle drummed by another loose piece of bark.

Her mind processed a string of thoughts in much the same way.

Do the Enterers not want the trees to stand in the forest? Do the trees stand in the way of the wood they bear? The air they clean? The water they draw? What Way can afford such tragic devastation? The gakkal-yakkals are not the first to come seeking refuge. She sighed deeply. Perhaps, she thought, drifting off in the direction of the Pool of Many Reflections, the corroboree tonight will offer a solution.

Lavender Jensen had no idea how far they'd fallen. The steep cliff with the sun behind it cast deep shadows into the forest. A dense, heavy gloom from the trees that towered above her smothered the ground. The air had the chill of a cave. It smelt musty and dank. In the silence she became aware of new sounds, introduced to her ear one at a time, building to orchestral strength.

From somewhere down the slope, a faint sound of running water reached her and, as if on cue, leaves rustled overhead, whipped by a chilly breeze from the same direction. Above her she could make out the cliff top, covered in shrubs and bushes. The sides of the gorge were sheer and impossible to climb. On top, trees spired, their tops lost to the sky.

She dusted herself off and turned to the boy.

'Hey, can you get up?' she said, and without waiting, walked off down the slope toward the sound of the water.

The boy had taken a nasty fall. Although he was badly shaken, nothing appeared broken. He rubbed his chest where she'd landed on him. A bruise began to show on his shoulder and a bloody scratch welled up on his face. He nursed a limp as he walked.

'Wait,' he called after her. 'Not that way.'

'Why not?' She stopped, studying dark shapes ahead of her.

'We have to go this way.' The direction he pointed followed the gorge wall as it disappeared into a shadowed slope and dense bush. The sun shimmered on the leaves of very tall trees, beneath which no light fell.

'Doesn't look like a way out,' she said and turned back. 'This way's better.'

'Wait. Where's Spot?'

'There he is.'

She pointed. Spot, his tongue pink and pulsing, was a little way ahead. The yellow ball lay at his feet.

'See, he wants to go this way. I think we should follow him.'

The boy's jaw dropped.

'Are you nuts? He's the one that got us here in the first place. He'll follow us if we go this way.' He pointed again along the gorge wall.

'I trust him. Anyway, I'm sure the joey went this way—and you said you'd get my earbuds back.'

'How do you know your earbuds are that way?'

'Because the magpie went that way.'

She pointed into the trees and took several steps down the slope, then stopped and turned.

'Look, you go your way if you want to; I'm following your dog.'

She turned and stalked toward Spot. He snapped the ball up and trotted off along a track etched into the undergrowth by hordes of small animals that traversed the ground by day and night.

Lavender trailed close to the pup. The boy raced to catch up. She was nimble and he was gangly. She climbed obstructing rocks with the ease of a seasoned abseiler. He tripped and got his feet stuck in small crevices. She deftly avoided the searing pricks from overhanging prickle bushes. He got snared. They made their way along the valley, snapping jibes at each other.

He told her his name was Jerramunga. He said he lived not far from her place.

'We've lived here since the beginning of time.'

She snickered. 'Yeah, right. You look like you've been here since the beginning of time. Are you Aboriginal?'

'Bibbulmun—my mum's people. My grandad's too. Everyone calls us *Nyungar*, but my grandad used to get really pissed off about people screwing the language. He always said that nyungar is man and by calling all of us that, it's disrespectful to the women—the *yorgah*. Anyway, my grandad taught me loads of stuff. He even taught me about tracking and how to find food. So all we have to do is follow the river, we'll be all right.'

She stepped past a tree, pushed a sapling back and turned to stare back at him. 'So you've been down here before?'

The directness of the question caused him to stop a moment just as Lavender let go of the sapling. It sprang back and caught him in the face, leaving a spray of red welts on his cheek.

'Oww! Well ... not so much down here. This leads into a dark place.'

'Are you scared? Is that why you wanted to go the other way?'

'I'm not scared,' he said. 'But there are scary things out here.'

'Scary, like how? Ghosts?' She fluttered her hands in front of her face. 'Whooo ...'

'I can't tell you.'

She looked at him, disbelievingly.

'Look it's secret business,' he said, 'I can't tell you.'

'Right,' she said.

She'd heard about this secret business before. People have a choice; they can tell you stuff they know, or they can keep it to themselves. Or, she thought, they haven't got a clue what they're on about, which is most likely what's happening here.

'Whose secret?'

'Ours ... our people ...'

'What's so secret about it?'

'It's just, well culture ... you know.'

'Culture's what you eat, how you behave, what you believe. Do you keep all that stuff secret too?'

'No. It's just ... well, if we tell our secret stuff no-one will respect it.'

'That's just dumb! If you want people to respect your culture you have to tell them what you want them to respect. If no-one knows about it, how can anyone respect it? That's the stupidest thing I've ever heard. If you're not going to tell me what the scary things are, then I'm not going to be scared—you can be scared all on your own!'

She forged ahead.

They walked until the sun dipped low and dusk began to fill in the shadows.

Beneath a sweeping sheoak, they came upon an old tree stump that covered more ground than a large water tank and rose almost as high as a house. The top was open to the sky, its circumference withered into spiky grey shards that fingered upward. One side split open in a triangle. The ravages of nature and years of termite excavation had gutted the inside to form a dark, cavernous hollow. Lavender wondered how nature could grow such a large tree. Perhaps it was too big when it stood.

She stared into the gloomy surroundings.

Before her were trees lost to trees, greens within green, browns within brown, blackened in fiery scratches poking beyond reach. Every tree had eyes, loopy eyes, droopy eyes, eyes with muddied mascara, eyes scalpel sharp—all looking without seeing, seeing through, seeing all. The trees held her attention minutely, quickening her heart rate until it matched the growing susurrus, racing into darker darkness.

His voice broke the spell.

'We can shelter here for the night.' With his head buried inside the cavern of the burnt-out stump, his voice reverberated, as if they were in a bathroom.

'I'm not going in there. It's creepy.'

'Well we've got to shelter somewhere—it's gonna be dark soon and it gets cold.'

'You can go in there but I'm not. It's bound to have spiders and bugs ... yuck!'

'Thought you weren't gonna be scared.'

'I said I wasn't going to be scared of stuff I don't know about— spiders and snakes are stuff I know about, and they are scary. So I'm not going in there.'

'Suit yourself.'

Jerramunga grabbed a dead stick from the ground, went into the tree-cavern and started raking out cobwebs and rotting vegetation.

'It's pretty cosy,' he called, settling himself down against a wall.

'That's okay, I'll stay here, thanks.'

Lavender scraped away grass next to the wall of the stump and sat down. She drew her knees up close and wrapped her arms around them for warmth. She watched the sky turn from the red and purple of the first sunset of the summer into grey shadows dragging a blanket of evening behind them. A stiff breeze whipped through the trees. She hugged her legs tighter.

A bunch of parrots chattered noisily in an old dead tree a little way up the slope. She held the slim bone in her hand, wondering how she could have possibly lost so many things that were dear to her in a single afternoon and be left with nothing but an old bone.

Is that what life comes down to when it's all stripped away? Nothing but bones? Wonder what my dad thinks? Wonder if he's even noticed I'm not there.

The parrot chatter faded into the dusk as different sounds emerged.

Gubba Gubba watched the spectacle of the final sunrays of

the day sweep into the sky. It was the perfect close to a perfect afternoon.

She'd spent the day disguised as a rock on the riverbed, pushed to and fro by the waters rushing into the Pool of Many Reflections. Like Atnunga, Gubba Gubba also enjoys the quiet rest that disguise provides. But unlike her elder sister—who loves the swaying forest canopy—her favourite place is at the bottom of the Kulwinkulkine, in the deep, where the perpetual rush of water through the rocks produces the most soothing sounds— thunderous and slow tumbling. Above, near the surface, they are frothy and roaring and fast.

Gubba Gubba and Atnunga are roughly the same size. But Gubba Gubba has larger ears. They swivel as if constantly writhen by the flow of water—even when she's on dry land. Her face is round, edged with coarse, white-tipped fur flowing around sunken cheeks, making her look like a barn owl. Her nose and mouth turn downward. The dark blue of her eyes shade unfathomable depths.

She was at the water's edge with a small group of friends, among them a frog, a pair of musk ducks, and Boo Ragoon, an old pelican. The sun's final rays were long and sparse, painting the horizon citrus orange, throwing long shadows that fused into darkness. A small herd of quokkas thumped down the path. The mob's elder halted them in front of the gathering.

'Yay koomborlie,' he said. Hello brothers. He drank deeply from the pool. A deft flick of his right paw wiped the few remaining drips of water from the tips of fur surrounding his mouth. He addressed Boo Ragoon, introducing himself as Wal Pole, asking about the children.

'Did you see a couple of koolongers come down here?'

'Koolongers?' Boo Ragoon grunted. 'What would koolongers be doin' 'ere?' Human children wandering in the forest isn't good for anyone.

'Won't be up t'any good,' the frog interjected. 'Humans've never done any good. An' them koolongers ... I could tell you some stories about them—'

The frog's memories took him back to when he was a tadpole in a muddy puddle, but his reminiscence was cut short by a quokka.

'I come from Rottnest,' he said, referring to an island off the coast. 'An' you ain't seen what koolongers c'n do less'n you been dere, koomborlie.' The quokka sniffed loudly. 'Awful! Place's swarmin' with 'em—old 'uns, young 'uns; dey everywhere dere. My good friend was kilt las' summer by a mob of Enterer koolongers—kicked like a football 'til he was dead. Dey jus' stood aroun' and laughed. Jus' stood around. No honour, koomborlie. No honour.'

The quokka took a drink from the pool.

One of the musk ducks whistled.

'Terrible. Terrible. Tourists are dreadful. Dreadful. But migrating down here won't help you, my word no. They swarm around here too. Swarm.'

'Too right, Mum,' her mate grunted.

'They're not all tourists,' Boo Ragoon the pelican said.

'Point,' the frog moaned, 'Point. Also got 'unters, tree cutters, river poisoners, salt raisers, dog breeders ...'

'But they can't all be bad surely. Surely,' the male musk duck quacked.

'Show me a good 'un and I'll show you the freeway south,' said the frog.

'Yeah, well dey got that now too,' Wal Pole sniffed, slipping backwards onto his tail. 'I reckon dey's born bad, koomborlie.'

'You can't be born bad!' the duck snorted. 'When you're born, you've only got a spirit and a Gronup. Spirit and Gronup. So you find your place in the Natural Order. Natural Order. You only turn bad if you reject your Gronup.'

'There is Don Canida,' the frog offered. 'And Snowqueen. If anybody's born bad it's them—they take the cake, I reckon.'

Boo Ragoon jerked up to stretch his legs and air his wings. He twonked.

'Yeah, yeah, you're right. They take more than the cake, but—but they're not human, and they ain't in the Natural Order are they?'

Everyone jumped backwards to avoid being clobbered by the great flappers.

'Maybe their spirits ain't like ours. What do you think, Gubba Gubba—do they have Gronups to help them with their spirits?'

'Goodness me, I can't say I've ever heard of it,' Gubba Gubba said. She turned to Wal Pole, smiled kindly and said: 'Where did you see these koolongers, dear?'

'We didn't actually see 'em,' the quokka replied, and then

pointed along the path. 'But dere's a scent all down this path 'ere. My brother ... he reco'nised it straight up—like he said, he's from Rottnest. Dey also got a scent of a *yirri-yirri*. Musta' passed round 'ere somewhere.'

The second scent he referred to belonged to a dingo pup.

A loud rustle issued from a reed thicket nearby. The group froze into a collective silence, each one tensed, ready to flock and vacate.

But they didn't need to.

Another Gronup emerged from the dense underbrush, his body longer and more wiry with shorter and coarser fur than Gubba Gubba's, every leap powered by legs that extended well behind him like a grasshopper's. The group relaxed once again.

'Hey, koomborlie, where'd you go?' Wal Pole asked.

The Gronup's voice thundered across the water.

'I was travelling on your *buddung-buddung-buddung*,' he said, sounding out the quokka's hopping motion. 'But then I saw this *kwenda* burrow so I took the underground—got a bit sidetracked.'

He looked around the group, and smiled broadly at Gubba Gubba. 'Hey, hey ... Gubba Gubba! How are you doin', sister? Long time no see!'

'Burra Baroona. My goodness! It's been such a long time—how long has it been? *Tdj, tdj*, my, my, it must be eons ...' She paused and studied the new arrival. Then she said, 'These travellers say they've scented koolongers along the track. Have you seen or heard any?'

'I almost made a stop at that old spirit place, the Clearing,'

Burra Baroona said, indicating a pear-shaped clearing a short distance downstream. I heard a *murna* I didn't recognise, but then I heard this here *beelarbonk's* wing-flap'—pointing at Boo Ragoon—'ba-da-boom! ... that got me—I came straight over here.' His fur shook and rippled the length of his body as he described the roller-coaster effect of the bird's recent wing stretch. 'What a rush!'

'Well I never ... What are you doing here?' Gubba Gubba repeated.

'Gotta see Babbildan Babbirra.'

'Oh, how exciting. Is there a new beginning?' Gubba Gubba was positively brimming.

'Beginning?' He gave a short laugh. 'I don't know about that. Ending, maybe.'

The group fell silent. Burra Baroona continued.

'You know how all beginnings start deep in the ground, right?' The group nodded.

'Well I've been in the east—that's where Wal Pole's clan's from,' he pointed to the quokka elder. 'Every tree in their forest has been pushed to the ground by monsters. Clans everywhere need urgent refuge.'

'We need a place t' call t' our spirits,' Wal Pole told Gubba Gubba earnestly. 'Be reunited with our Gronups.'

Burra Baroona continued.

'I thought Wal Pole could use the Clearing while I found Babbildan Babbirra. But I didn't detect any spirit presence.'

A long time ago, lightning felled a very large tree and opened the forest canopy to the sky leaving a huge stump behind. The cleared area around the stump became known as the Clearing.

Boo Ragoon twonked morosely.

'That was a great place for births and celebrations once. The spirits came all the time. My grandparents were born there. But now ... ah well ... see ... now I'm afraid that fox, Don Canida, has put paid to that. I doubt there's been any spirits there for a hundred generations at least. Just an old slimy snake, name of Cedric. He traps water rats for Don Canida so's he doesn't become dinner himself. He thinks no-one knows ... but I'm pretty sure everyone does. You'd only go to the Clearing now if you're on your way to somewhere else. Damn shame if you ask me. Not that you're askin', mind. But you wouldn't be safe goin' there now ... not with Don Canida round. Especially not tonight, full moon and all.'

The little quokka was curious.

'So, koomborlie, what 'appened?'

Boo Ragoon fell silent in reflection. Presently, he continued.

'When that tree came down, the grass and scrub had a field day. The birds loved it. It was alive with food, they sang and the colours were brilliant. Great place to grow up. See, the spirits created it, so it was sacred ground—anyone could go there and give birth and not have a worry in the world. It was maternity heaven for mobs. Yeah ...'

He continued in a more sombre tone.

'But then Don Canida and his mobsters moved in ... and they've got no respect for sanctity, them. So now it's riverfront housing for a fat nasty old *woggal*.'

Before the quokka could ask who Don Canida was, Gubba Gubba turned to Burra Baroona.

'You say you heard a murna you didn't recognise? How did it sound?'

'It was like a *widji* scratching,' he said. 'You know the way the old man emu goes *bee-an, bee-an, kurrdt-kurrdt doong-doong bee-an*. For sure, the footfall wasn't widji; but it was definitely a biped. And there was *goorr-da goorr-da, min-nie min-nie, goorr-da goorr-da, min-nie min-nie* all over the place. That, I'd say, was yirri-yirri for sure.'

The frog puffed his chest out.

'You could fly over the top and have a look at what's there, Boo Ragoon. Then if it really is koolongers, we c'n go scare 'em orf.'

'Bit late in the day for me,' Boo Ragoon twonked, looking directly at the male duck. 'My eyes ain't what they used to be. Better off with someone who's got younger and better eyes.'

'We could just go along the water's edge here, and then up the numbat trail.' Kul Yanobbin pointed across the rocks to the thinly disguised trail used by the local anteater clans.

'That's easy for you, koomborlie,' Wal Pole said, 'but in case you didn't notice, we're quokkas, not quackas.'

'You think of somethin' then!' the duck ruffled his feathers and waddled around in a small circle, only to return to where he started.

'We don' have to do anything,' the frog croaked, his voice dull and weary. 'Who's gonna care about a couple of koolongers in the bush?'

'What if dey're up t' no good,' Wal Pole huffed. 'Y'know, koomborlie, we gotta find a spirit place. Can't have koolongers wanderin' around. What if you Gronups 'ave a look first.'

'Oh goodness,' Gubba Gubba said, 'we can't get involved.' Her blue eyes rested briefly on each one in the group. 'But I suppose there's no reason why we can't all go up the path together and see what we can see.'

'Not me. I'm just gonna float downstream,' Boo Ragoon grunted, shaking his head from side to side, his foot-long bill coming within a wart of crowning the frog on the head.

'Ay, be careful with that t'ing!'

One musk duck got a brief nod from the other.

'We'll join you.'

He plopped into the water, and circles of waves rippled into the stream.

'I'm not keen about running into Cedric,' the frog moaned. 'I'll see ya's all later at the corroboree.'

One of the quokkas watched the frog disappear into the reeds.

'Not much adventure in dem guys, koomborlie,' he said.

The two Gronups and the small mob of quokkas worked their way stealthily to the edge of the Clearing and stood rock still, merging into the undergrowth to survey the scene before them.

'Oh look,' Gubba Gubba said. 'My goodness, what's *she* doing here?'

Just ahead, with her back to the group, Atnunga squatted on an old log lying a little way into the clearing. Gubba Gubba joined her.

'There're some quokkas here saying there's a scent of koolongers on the track leading down here,' she said. 'Have you seen anything?'

Atnunga pointed to the tree stump. Gubba Gubba followed the sweep of her hand and saw Lavender huddled against the outside wall.

As the Milky Way emerged and a blanket of darkness dropped over the forest, the murmuring reached Lavender's ears the way an aeroplane approaches from the distance. At first it was chatter hidden in the trees, like tinnitus. But before long, a giant sound canvas bore down on her, painted with all the songs and cries of the nocturnal, hiding all manner of animal and insect—all beyond her capacity to identify as friend or foe.

Pobble bonk and moaning frogs exploded like drums in a fuel depot contracting in the evening cool. Pelicans and ducks honked their bed-time announcements as they flew overhead, wings hammering against the sky. Nightjars cawed and gobbled and hissed and grunted. Wrens, robins and wagtails chirp-chirped and darted among the foliage, snapping flying ants from the air to feed to their young. Emus boomed and grunted greetings to each other. Mobs of kangaroos thumped among the trees.

Foraging woylies dragged their bushy tails through dried leaves, scratching at the ground for chunks of fungi and lichen.

Kwendas rustled beneath suckers, burying their long snouts in moist ground for juicy worms. Families of water rats trekked from the reed-beds to higher ground in search of flying insects. Dunnarts darted up and down tree trunks, snatching and scratching at lichen and moss.

Overhead, possums yanked at juicy leaves and young shoots, and hissed proprietary warnings at each other. Phascogales ripped the bark from branches and trunks, their masticated smacks and noisy sniffs devouring the ants and borers hidden within.

And occasionally—for the briefest of moments—the whole happy symphony was silenced by a low hoot from a watching barn owl, only to return to full tilt seconds later. Somewhere upstream a curlew wailed like a baby crying for its mother in a wilderness of the dark and unknown.

The volume and the intensity notched upward as the falling darkness drew them closer and the shadows claimed the light. New shapes emerged on gnarled tree trunks around the clearing— haggard and vile faces with bulbous noses, misshapen eyes and gawping mouths.

Everything moved.

The breeze sniped and snatched at her hair and neck as its chill penetrated beneath her clothes.

She told the boy her fears.

'It's safer in here,' he said. 'It's warm. It'll be all right in the morning.'

'How do you know that?'

'It's what my mum always says.'

'But she's not here.'

'Yeah, I know—it's just something she says.'

'You think she'll be out looking for you?'

'Nah.'

'My dad'll be having kittens by now.' She fingered her phone. 'I'd call him, but there's no signal out here.'

'Yeah, it'll be okay. Trust me.'

Those magic words, she thought as she crawled inside and sat next to him. I've heard them before.

She was in two minds about the boy, not knowing whether she actually could trust him. So far he'd shown her scant evidence that trusting him would get her out of this mess, but she had little choice in the matter. They had to stick together. All the same, she thought, a magical rescue of some sort wouldn't go astray.

'What about your dad?' she asked.

'My dad?'

'Yeah ... you talk about your grandad and your mum, what about your dad?'

'I don't know him.' There was an edge to his voice.

'Are you angry at him?'

'How can I be angry at him? I never met him.'

'How come?'

'Dunno ... when I was born, he was gone.'

'What, like magic?'

'Magic?' he challenged. The whites of his eyes shone in the dark. 'Like your ball's magic?'

'No, more like, you know, abracadabra and poof ... we're out of here.' And to demonstrate, she waved the bone she held in her hand the way she'd seen in the movies.

'That's just made up stuff,' Jerramunga said. 'Real magic doesn't work like that. I know about magic—'

'Sssh! Did you hear that?'

Her frightened whisper cut him off.

'What?'

He tightened his grip on a heavy stick he'd found and kept by his side.

'What did you hear?'

'Voices.'

'Could be Gronups,' he said warily, crawling forward on all fours and craning his head through the opening. He strained his eyes into the gathering darkness surrounding the tree stump.

'Eh? No, I don't think they're grown-ups. They'd have torches and they'd be calling out—not hissing like cats.'

She pulled him back inside the tree stump.

'Not grown-ups! *Gron*-ups,' he said, emphasising the shorter sound of the word.

'Gronups? What are they?'

'Monsters. Big, hairy—really, really scary spirit creatures. They can trick you because they talk in voices. They live out here in the dark forest.'

'Have you ever seen one?'

'No-one has ... at least no-one who's ever lived to tell.'

'If you've never seen one, how do you know they're monsters? How do you even know they exist?'

'My grandad said. I told you ... we've lived here since the beginning of time. He knew all the stories of this place from way back in the Dreaming. He was Ngungakatta. It means man of great wisdom. He knew everything about everything ... Gronups and all the spirit creatures. We don't want them to see us or they might use their magic on us.'

'Thought you said magic was just made up stuff.'

'What you were talkin' about is just made up stuff. Gronups have bush magic, the most powerful of all magic. They control everything—the wind, the sounds, the water ...'

The boy's voice trailed off. Lavender assumed it was because he feared monsters. The discussion stilled her. She was frightened but was determined not to show it. She listened closely for sounds she'd recognise, wondering which were the fearful Gronups. She felt shadows moving among the trees. She elbowed the boy painfully in the ribs and whispered her suspicions to him.

'Cats? Where?'

'Over there,' she said, pointing into the scrub along the river edge of the clearing.

'Cats aren't that scary—are they?'

His hand tightened on the waddy by his side.

'I thought you knew the bush?'

'Yeah. But not cats.'

'I think they're talking about us,' Lavender whispered urgently.

'That's dumb. Cats can't talk.'

'Sssh! Listen. Look! What's that up there?'

Jerramunga followed her pointing finger to a tree overhead.

He could make out a pair of orbs on a lower branch glowing, the image of coals in a dying fire. He strained his ears to filter the noises, thinking that some did, indeed, sound a lot like urgent hungry hisses.

He put one arm around the girl's shoulders, with his other hand he gripped the waddy by his side so tight his palm ached. He began rocking and launched into an incoherent chant.

Lavender listened closely.

'What do the words mean?' she asked.

Jerramunga thought for a moment.

'It's secret. I can't tell you.'

'Oh ... that again. How come?'

'Because that's the law.'

'That's stupid. There's no law about keeping secrets. Whose law is it anyway?'

'It's our law. If I told you, I could be in big trouble.'

'But there's no-one here, except us. How do I know you're not turning me into a snake?'

He laughed nervously.

'I hate snakes. Hope there's none around here. Anyway I told you, magic doesn't work like that.'

'Ah, so it is magic!'

Jerramunga relaxed his grip on Lavender's shoulders.

'Look,' he said, 'it's something my grandfather taught me. I can't tell you.'

Gubba Gubba

Chapter 3

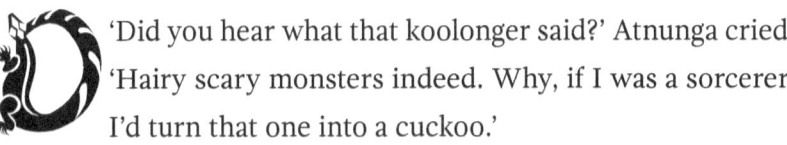'Did you hear what that koolonger said?' Atnunga cried. 'Hairy scary monsters indeed. Why, if I was a sorcerer, I'd turn that one into a cuckoo.'

Gubba Gubba laughed. 'Oh my goodness, Atnunga, if only you were a sorcerer, the Kumakana would be completely free of trouble. Point your bone and anyone who doesn't agree with your way of thinking ... *poof!* Gone. Just like that! Oh what a wonderful way to fix everything. Yes, everyone could sit around all day and preen. They'd look so pretty. Oh my, they'd starve of course, but that's okay, because they'd all look pretty.'

Burra Baroona, having snuck up behind Atnunga, grinned. Atnunga shot a dark look at Gubba Gubba.

'And what would you have? Everybody falling over themselves to be kind to the next one. It's dingo eat dingo in this world, sister. The big fish eat the little fish. But instead, in your world, the big fish would say to the little fish: "Oh excuse me, I hope you don't mind, but I'm a bit peckish, so I'll just have you for a snack." Little fish says: "That's quite okay, open wide and I'll just swim in. Bon appétit." No chase, no sport, no spirit. So much for fish being brain food.'

Burra Baroona coughed. The ground shook.

'Hey ... excuse me ...'

'Burra Baroona! What are you doing here? Is there a new beginning?'

'Nice to see you too, Atnunga. I see you two are getting on well, as usual. What's the situation here?'

'The situation?' Atnunga pointed to the nearby tree stump. 'There's two koolongers in that tree stump over there with a yirri-yirri. The little one talks of magic. And the other one calls us huge hairy scary monsters.'

'Oh my, how awful for them,' Gubba Gubba said. 'They're just koolongers. Obviously that one is misinformed. But they can't see us can they? Goodness me, Atnunga ... you can't you expect them to know.'

'Koolongers grow up, you know. They shouldn't make things up,' Atnunga said.

'Yes ... yes, they do. Oh my goodness they do. But did you also hear what else that koolonger said? His ancestor was Ngungakatta. What do you make of that?'

'Not a lot,' Atnunga replied. 'How does that make any difference?'

'Surely you remember Ngungakatta—the great spirit-master of the Originals? He helped restore the Natural Order when the dingo first came. Oh my, he was a great force indeed.'

'Of course I remember him. But who's to say how many offspring he has? Just because the koolonger says his ancestor is Ngungakatta, it doesn't mean he's got Ngungakatta's magic.'

'Yes, true. But what about that song? That's the crossing over song. Oh my, Burra Baroona, you must remember that!'

'Yes, Gubba Gubba, I do. Interesting. Perhaps Ngungakatta taught the koolonger the song for his own protection.'

'But why would he pass him that song?' Gubba Gubba mused. Then she said, 'Oh, I nearly forgot—I must tell you, I got an oracle in the tortoise shell today.' The markings on the shell of the long-necked tortoise were known to tell the future.

'Oh?' Burra Baroona's golden eyes brimmed with curiosity.

Atnunga rolled her eyes and waited impatiently as Gubba Gubba continued.

'Yes—oh my, it was most unusual now that I think about it. It said that return would come to the Kumakana—the turning point. That must be why you're here. And, you know, that koolonger may very well carry the spirit of Ngungakatta but not know it. I feel there's more ... do you sense it?'

'Sense what?' Atnunga demanded, still thinking about how she might set the record straight with the koolonger.

Burra Baroona answered for Gubba Gubba, identifying the special spirit he sensed. 'The little one is *wallagudgal*, a pure spirit.'

'Wallagudgal?' Atnunga mocked her brother yoolin. 'You can't know that! And what if she is? What's that got to do with Gubba Gubba's crazy oracle?' Atnunga often labelled Gubba Gubba's oracles as nonsense.

Burra Baroona looked into Atnunga's eyes.

'Maybe it's not nonsense. If you put the oracle together with the song, it could mean a lot. I have some experience with wallagudgal.'

He went on to explain.

'Wallagudgal is a spirit that looks neither above nor below for the meaning of the time—there is an opening to the heart—it hasn't been shut off by rejection or hardening. If Gubba Gubba's oracle is correct, the way the light of a new beginning can enter is through the heart of a wallagudgal. If that koolonger is wallagudgal, then it is possible that the oracle will come to pass. There's no telling what can happen.'

'Maybe. But we don't actually know if she is wallagudgal—how can you tell?'

'I can tell,' Burra Baroona said. 'It's a little unorthodox but you will soon know.'

'Let me guess—you're going to make yourself appear as a hairy scary monster,' Atnunga said, and laughed lightly.

'Tell me,' Burra Baroona asked, 'who would best know the spirit of Ngungakatta?'

'Babbildan Babbirra,' Gubba Gubba replied. 'My goodness, yes ... yes. It was he who brought Ngungakatta to the Valley of Lengthened Years long ago.'

'Then you need to tell him about this. If this is the primal point of such an oracle, we must take advantage. The great master needs to know.'

'Babbildan Babbirra's got enough problems of his own,' Atnunga protested. 'And, in case you're not aware, the Renewal corroboree is tonight.'

'Babbildan Babbirra has to know about this, Atnunga. As

Gubba Gubba has just said, this could be a turning point. And if Babbildan Babbirra knows the spirit of Ngungakatta—'

Atnunga cut him off.

'Look, do you really think two koolongers have the power to change anything? Look at them. They huddle in that old stump like a couple of frightened echidnas.'

Burra Baroona reminded Atnunga of her earlier words.

'Koolongers grow up.'

Atnunga conceded the point.

Burra Baroona continued. 'Besides, Atnunga, the form of the final tree is always inside the seed ... even when it's borne on the wind. When moisture penetrates the seed, it sprouts. When earth nourishes the seed, it grows. But if, as a young sapling, it is denied enlightenment, it grows bent and deformed. Here, we have the chance to nurture the saplings, who can then plant seeds with new form.'

Atnunga couldn't argue with the logic. Burra Baroona's specialty was to know when something new is being given form. She knew that Gubba Gubba, by seeing into the heart of a situation with the greatest clarity, knew the meaning of the time. If it turned out that she was right, then perhaps disasters such as the one she'd heard of from the gakkal-yakkals could be prevented in the future.

But what if they were wrong?

In a valley, not far from the Clearing, Babbildan Babbirra, Supreme Leader—Yoolin-jah—of the Kumakana Gronups, paced a well-worn path around a sacred chamber secreted in the heart of a massive tingle tree. His long gangly legs and the portliness that rode above them, gave the Gronup elder an unusual swagger—a combination of purposeful stride and leap.

His reverential position had been imposed on him when the spirits created the Natural Order. He wasn't asked. He wasn't voted for. He wasn't appointed. The occasion lacked any public celebration. All that was deemed necessary was a pronouncement.

'Babbildan Babbirra,' they said, 'the Natural Order in the Kumakana is in your hands hereafter.'

Then, as promptly as they came, they left him to preside. There was no instruction manual. No rule book.

He protested. He didn't believe that the Supreme Leader's appointment should be permanent. He'd even dared to suggest at one point that such an important position should be elected.

They scoffed at the suggestion.

'If we agreed to that, we'd have to change the courses of nature every time a Yoolin-jah was elected just to meet the promises made during the election campaign. That's a ridiculous idea. The Natural Order can no more be a democracy than the wind can have a heart!'

The spirits haven't stopped joking about it since.

But his protests didn't stop there. He'd argued that the position carries a responsibility too great for one Gronup to bear for all time. He suggested appointing someone else after, say, a few hundred years.

'At least I could rest and retire.'

But his words fell on deaf ears. The spirits had nature worked out right down to the last detail. And there was no mincing their words when they told him that the appointment of Yoolin-jah is part of that detail.

'It's not something that can be changed. The magic is in you— not in the position of Yoolin-jah. It is your nature that holds the fabric of the Natural Order together. If we changed that, we'd have to change the Natural Order. And that's not possible.'

Eventually, they did concede that the responsibility was great. They agreed to form a council of yoolins to share the load— although they insisted on making the appointments because they claimed to know which natures would be most beneficent as the Yoolin-jah's helpers.

The end result is not a perfect system, but it is a system nevertheless.

Babbildan Babbirra stopped mid-lope at the southern end of the chamber. He stood straight and tall, scratching the top of his head lightly with the clawed nails of his right hand. He looked around his great room—the secret meeting chamber—and absorbed the shapes of the shadows, marvelling, not for the first time, that only because there is light, can there be dark.

A paradox, he thought. To have one, you need the other, even though they appear to be locked in eternal struggle.

He sighed and clicked his tongue against the roof of his mouth and stared deeper into the room's shadows. They were fluid and indistinct, created by a reflected and filtered aura of a dying day, their edges fuzzy and centres lightless—much like his percipience of late. Many times he has found answers to great and difficult problems in those shadows but today, such answers eluded him.

The secret chamber is the bowels of the burnt-out centre of a huge tree with a massive split in its substantial girth—a cavernous room secreted above the apex of the split. The tree itself stands in the exact aural centre of the valley, its openings—one facing directly north, the other directly south—acting like two giant ears into which all the sounds of the valley pour: streams of a mighty river of life. Everything, from the softest whisper rustling the tops of the valley giants to the explosive smack of the loudest thunder is heard in the Supreme Leader's sacred chamber with the clarity of crystal.

He knows every sound in the forest like the fur of his beard. The rumble of the emu calling for a son she has never seen. The five-thudded crunch from the kangaroo's walk, tail dragging as he grazes among the fresh sprouts. The call of the cockatoo, loud and clear on the wind as it rustles the treetops and the spiky anteater's scritch-scratching as he carves an adit for his sticky tongue to snake through the tunnels of the termite mounds. These are the sounds of life.

Babbildan Babbirra picked up his long feet and loped the curve of the western wall, circumnavigating a large eight-sided object that dominated the room—an altar shaped like a sword. The ancient altar is used in meetings of council, forged from all the elements on earth when time itself began. Each face is defined by the nature of its material and the complementary nature of the attending council member. No side is the same length or elevation as any other. Images and markings that show the complete organisation of nature are inscribed into its surfaces.

These are the markings that the eight Gronup yoolins use to determine the meaning of the time.

Babbildan Babbirra looked across the altar to where Gubba Gubba sits in council. He smiled as he conjured the image of her wise face, grave and blue-eyed, bringing forth proclamations from the spirits of the running waters, casting warnings of impending dangers, and then how simply seeing the goodness of things leads to escape. If I am the soul of life, he thought, she must be the heart.

Hers is the lowest surface and the only convexly curved one in the raised altar. It appears as a single growth ring plucked from a giant tree. A complex grain pattern flows from its centre, a map of nature's nerve system branching like a network of rivers gouging deep canyons through mountains, fingering into the plains. Babbildan Babbirra studied the pattern for a moment. But as he turned away, his heart skipped a beat.

There was a movement.

He turned back and stared hard into the surface. It was unmistakable. Although it was as slight as a cricket's breath, there was movement. Like the first dewdrop rolling down a leaf, it was a mere trickle. His eye traced it to its beginning—in the centre where the grain contracts to a single point. He concentrated, looking for the direction of the flow. But it stopped before he could be absolutely certain. He continued to stare at it for a long moment, willing it to move again. Stubbornly, it refused.

Babbildan Babbirra lofted himself and stroked his beard, studying pockets of shadow seeking refuge in the great room's walls. Only one explanation seemed plausible.

Gubba Gubba has received an oracle.

That decided it.

It was time to call a council meeting. And what could be more perfect than a council meeting on the night of the Renewal?

In a hollowed-out fork of a dead karri tree, on the bank of the Kulwinkulkine, above the still waters of the Pool of Many Reflections, a family discussion had concluded. Mal Ala, the parrot, had been convinced by her two daughters that she should offer to share her nest with Kal Annie, the galah. Although breaking with convention, the daughters had convinced her that it was the modern way.

'You could come to an arrangement of sharing the brooding, and then you could spend a day with Mal Aga every once in a while—or come seed cracking with us.'

'I always wondered what this secret business was,' Mal Ala

said to her daughters. 'He takes off with his cronies and leaves me nest-bound during brooding. Who knows what they get up to?'

'Well you can find out,' one daughter suggested. 'And once the babies hatch, Kal Annie can share feeding duties.'

'Hey this could be a whole new concept in day-care!' the other daughter chimed in. 'And you'd be free to go to the Renewal corroboree for new feathers and colours before fledging. You'll be the envy of all the dammalaks.'

Mal Aga voiced the occasional objection, but otherwise sat quietly during the discussion. He knew better than to disagree when his mate and their daughters were in full voice.

But he was uneasy.

'What do you daughters know? You're fledged a mere two seasons, sheltered and protected. You don't know anything about the ravages of life! And you, Mal Ala, what are you doin'? You can't just start something totally new ... something totally unheard of. You've got to consult your Gronup before you start meddling in stuff that could alter the course of nature!'

'Oh Gronup shmonup, Mal Aga. You heard Atnunga. I don't know why you're getting your pectals in a twist. Where's your spirit, fer *Yurlungga*'s sake?'

He shook his head, scratched his brow with his left foot and bowed out of the debate. Once she'd invoked Yurlungga, the great creator, there was nothing he could do to stop her.

Nature must take its course.

Don Canida rose from a dry sandy bed of leaves and twigs after a day-long slumber. He stepped around Bella Canida, his mate, who opened one eye to observe the movement, sighed gently, and closed it again. He deftly avoided the mauling of his ankles by the ferocious troop of pups he'd fathered six weeks previously, and padded outside to relieve and refresh himself. Like many of the forest's inhabitants, Don Canida preferred to sleep days and hunt nights.

He stood by the waterhole watching the dusk turn to dark. The senior members of his hunting party joined him in dribs and drabs. With a family numbering in the hundreds, organisation and discipline were vital for survival. His hunters operated in small packs, systematically working separate parts of the territory.

Their quarry was mainly small ground animals: rabbits, bandicoots, numbats, small kangaroos and other tasty marsupials. Many choices, mallee fowl for example, had now dwindled to the status of rare delicacy. Aggressive indiscriminate hunting and a rapidly growing family had made Don Canida a lot of enemies.

His closest and most trusted lieutenant was Eddie Vulpré, who sidled up to his leader's shoulder.

'Hey boss, what's on tonight, eh?'

'Well now,' the senior fox said, grinning, 'I hear tell they've got a new nesting of woylies up near Dooledup Rock—been a while since we had a feed of those.'

'Mmmm. One ah' muh' fave'rits.' Eddie Vulpré salivated noisily at the prospect.

'Seems woylie's getting a bit rare these days boss,' Red Cliffe, another of the lieutenants said, as he joined them. 'Are they out of season?'

Don Canida shook his rangy head and looked pensively down upon the crowd gathering around the water hole.

'Red, my boy, nothing is out of season to the King. They just keep running further into the forest, or seeking higher ground where they think they can escape us.'

Suddenly upbeat, he added, 'Of course they don't realise how futile it is because they can never escape the supreme hunter, can they ... huh? Waddya say Red?'

The two lieutenants grinned widely and shook their heads vigorously.

'I ... er ... 'eard that the old *gnow* Ma Lisse has got a new nest down near the Christmas tree grove, Boss,' Red Cliffe told them. Her chicks were one of Red Cliffe's favourite snacks.

'Well this is good news. Offer her some protection. Are you going in for the eggs, or waiting for the births?' Don Canida asked.

'Heh, heh. I know who would like us to wait for the births,' Red Cliffe joked. 'Fresh chicks would be a fine thing, especially if you were a cat, eh?'

Don Canida laughed.

'So we're in for a little omelette tonight, then?'

'Could be, boss. Yeah my informant tells me she's laid ten.'

Don Canida grinned, nodding his head.

'This is very good, Red Cliffe. Who's ... er, who's your informant?'

'Ah well, boss, y'know ... that'd be tellin' wouldn't it? Y'know privileged information and all that ...'

Don Canida's eyes narrowed. The snap of his jaw stilled all movement around the water hole. Sly eyes cast cautious glances toward the leader and his lieutenant.

'Privilege! You snivelling cur. Your only privilege around here is the privilege of membership of this family. I too, have informants. Little dogs like you don't keep information from me. You know the penalty for deception. And you will tell me now, exactly how many eggs that old fowl buried in that sand pit of hers, or else you will be cast out to take your chances with Snowqueen.'

Red Cliffe's tail dropped between his legs. His eyes searched the ground. There was no escape. The prospect of being cast out was more frightening than if Don Canida had threatened to take his life. Death would come of course, but it would be the slow agonising death of loneliness.

'Yeah boss. I ... er ... I believe there's maybe more eggs perhaps five more.'

'Hmmm. And your informant is?'

Red Cliffe looked around to make sure no other foxes were in earshot. Then he moved close to Don Canida and whispered in his ear. Don Canida nodded, satisfied, before abruptly dismissing him with instructions to take all the eggs and the male fowl.

'You know, Eddie,' he said turning to his first lieutenant, 'we must do something about the honesty of our troops.'

Eddie Vulpré laughed.

'Don, they're foxes. They're liars, cheats and lethal—if they were anything else, they might as well be pussycats. Don't want that, do you?'

Both foxes laughed heartily.

An explosive chittering descended from the branches of the tree overhead.

Don Canida rolled his eyes and whispered out of the side of his mouth, 'Here we go. It's the Preacher and his flock.'

He cast a sweeping glance over his troops.

'I don't mind them taking the ticks and fleas off my back, that's fine, but gee whiz, they do go on about joining the Natural Order and all. That's a bit much.'

'You want me to take care of them for you, boss?'

Eddie Vulpré grinned.

'Just humour them. This guy, Willie Abrup, reckons we're all sinners. Keeps sayin' the world's gonna end tomorrow, and we can only be saved if we join the Natural Order. Goes on something terrible about the great Babbildan Babbirra showing us the Way. And the mighty Atnunga providing us the wind of life. Must be on commission, because they keep coming back. And, you know, I keep telling them the same thing. *We* are the Natural Order. We are the supreme hunters. We are the kings of the forest. Still, I hate the ticks and fleas ... uh-oh ... here he comes.'

The flap-flap-flutter of wings carried the wagtail down from the tree. He perched on a rock in front of Don Canida. Two acolytes joined him. Each fanned their tails as they sermonised.

'*Sweet pretty preacher, sweet pretty preacher, sweet pretty preacher.*'

Willie Abrup fluttered closer and looked directly into Don Canida's eyes.

He swayed his black-cloaked body from side to side, his long black tail feathers pointing straight out the back swinging left and right, white vest puffed and prominent. His white eyebrows accented what could have been interpreted as a frown of disapproval as he looked, cold and unblinking down the straight lines of his pointed beak.

'We come in the name of the great Atnunga, who gives us the wind and all that is borne upon it,' the bird trilled.

'*Sweet pretty preacher ... sweet pretty preacher ... sweet pretty preacher,*' his companions chorused as they flew sorties onto the backs and shoulders of Don Canida, snapping fleas and ticks from his fur before darting swiftly back to the rock where they swayed and chorused their refrain before descending on new targets.

'Atnunga be with you always,' Willie Abrup intoned, snapping a flea from Don Canida's ear.

'Yeah, yeah—where would we be without good old Atnunga?' Don Canida asked, more for the benefit of the small audience of foxes standing nearby than in response to the bird in front of him. He'd heard it all before. 'Does Atnunga bring me gifts of savour and succulence? Or does she merely tempt me with all the aromas?'

'Atnunga *is* a gift, Don Canida. Atnunga cools you when the great fire in the sky is too hot. Atnunga spreads the bush's voice— the *murna*—before you, warning you of danger to your life, long before you can see it. Atnunga immerses you in the songs of life, so that you may sing with them. Is Atnunga not the greatest thing?'

Willie Abrup's beak snapped loudly in Don Canida's ear, cracking the back of a flea before it disappeared down his throat.

His companions worked enthusiastically, all the while singing their chorus, '*Sweet pretty preacher ... sweet pretty preacher.*'

'I've never seen this Atnunga,' Don Canida told Willie Abrup. 'Why don't you bring her to meet me?'

'First you must join the Natural Order. That is the only way to meet the great Atnunga who is with you always.'

'O-o-kay. What do I have to do, you know, if I join the Natural Order?'

The banter was well practised. Don Canida had gone through it many times. The longer he played the game, the longer Willie Abrup and his acolytes stayed harvesting the blood-sucking parasites embedded in his skin.

'It's simple, Don Canida. All you have to do is give up your evil ways, respect the lives of the young and unborn, hunt only those animals who are intended for you, and be hunted by animals whom you are intended for.'

'But we're not intended to be hunted by other animals. We're the supreme hunters. The supreme hunters can't be the hunted.'

'We all die, Don Canida. That is part of living. If you accept that your spirit lies within the earth, when you die that spirit will recycle and become part of the living heritage of your line. Your line can only live on forever through death. Dying is the end that makes everything new again.'

'That's ridiculous. When you're dead, you're dead. Finished. Surely the joy of living is to take as much life as you can. That's what makes us so strong. And if the spirits are in the earth, what's all that up there?'

Don Canida pointed to the first of the evening stars emerging in the fading light of the day.

'Those are the sky spirits. You can never reach them.'

The fox smiled. 'Everyone knows all the spirits are up there. That's what happens when you die. Death is the end of life, and you become a spirit in the sky. A strong spirit is one that takes plenty of life with it.'

'The sky spirits are the human spirits. A fox will never become a human.'

Willie Abrup's eyebrows expanded to their full extent.

Eddie Vulpré sneered, 'Yeah right, like we really wanna do that!'

'So ... what happens if we foxes don't join this Natural Order?' Don Canida asked. 'Not that I think there's anything wrong with my own order, mind.'

'Your order, Don Canida, is an order of greed and self-preservation. The Natural Order is one of sacrifice and spiritual everlasting. You can see the difference.'

Willie Abrup launched into his sermon.

'If you continue in your way and stay outside the Natural Order, you will eventually hunt all the animals until there are none. When the animals are all gone, the Gronups will also be gone. Without the Gronups, there will be no-one to minister to the spirits. Your spirits, which are now wayward, will be lost forever because your survival will depend on self-preservation.

'You will be forced to eat your own kind. First, the young and weaker members, then ... well I'm sure you can imagine what comes next. You'll be forever looking over your shoulder, wondering when your own lieutenants are going to turn on you. Is that the sort of life you think your pups should look forward to?'

Don Canida's eyes narrowed for an instant, the fur on his shoulders briefly stiffened; then flattened again. The birds put some distance between them and the foxes.

There was a change in the atmosphere.

'This cock and bull story is just to save your own feathers. Look ... how tough can these Gronup fellas be if they depend on guys like you to spread the word? Your stories don't scare me. Besides, what's wrong with the colours and markings we've already got?'

Don Canida lifted his nose to the breeze and sniffed. He turned to Eddie Vulpré, his grin revealing deadly white fangs.

'Last time they were here, they said some guy named Babbildan Babbirra is the king of the forest. But we both know that I'm King.'

Eddie Vulpré dipped his head. Don Canida faced Willie Abrup.

'If this guy, Babbildan Babbirra, is king of the forest, how come I've never seen him?'

'If you join the Natural Order, you will see him.'

'Well, to hell with him. And to hell with this Atnunga guy. And to hell with all of your make-believe demons. We're foxes, and foxes are the supreme hunters, and if this Babbildan Babbirra really exists, if he's really the king of the forest, then you tell him from me, he'll have to prove it face to face!'

He turned to his offsider.

'The moon is good tonight, Eddie. Let's go out there and bring back a decent feast for the whole leash, eh?'

Don Canida led his lieutenant down the incline of the rock, as the three birds relocated to a perch on a nearby tree.

'That went well,' Willie Ton commented, stropping his beak against the branch, to clean off the remnants of his meal.

'Yeah, I think you really got to him with the self-preservation stuff,' Willie Ams chirped. 'Maybe he's beginning to see the light.'

'The day that guy sees the light will be the day the widji flies,' Willie Abrup said, referring to the great flightless emu. 'Even the fish that swim the Kulwinkulkine are less obstinate than that one. And let's face it, as far as swimming against the tide goes, they take line honours. But this one ...'

He shook his head sadly as he watched the foxes melt into a formation and assemble around the waterhole.

Don Canida surveyed the heads of his hunters awaiting his instructions.

'Things are going to start changing around here tonight,' he said, slightly louder than under his breath.

Eddie Vulpré watched him climb to the top of a large boulder to address his troops, more than a little curious about what he'd just overheard.

Burra Baroona

Chapter 4

The wind that eddied across the Pool of Many Reflections penetrated the tall timbers foresting the steep bank on the far side of the river. The breeze carried a subtle but distinctive scent that piqued the instinctive curiosity of Snowqueen—a large, but by no means ordinary, cat.

Snowqueen leads the Moggy Maulers, a lawless clutter of cats terrorising the Kumakana, leaving swaths of death and destruction in its wake. Her leadership style is as ruthless as her butchery.

She was with her current beau—and there have been many—a big ginger tomcat, who goes by the name of Bluey. He stands a full head taller than she, sports big square shoulders, a broad chest and legs like fence posts, has a foul temper and is constantly at the ready to fight to the death any cat silly enough to defy Snowqueen's orders or challenge him for her attentions.

They were prowling the bush, hunting for a succulent feast of quail or potoroo to take home for the pack, when they were drawn by the scent on the opposite side of the river.

The tree beneath which the children and Spot had found refuge almost spanned the river, its branches mingling with trees on the other side, bridging the gap for arboreal creatures.

One main bough passed almost directly above the old stump. The unfamiliar bouquet drifted up, but any hope of a clear view was obstructed by lower foliage. Snowqueen stretched along the branch to listen and study.

Bluey crouched, ready to spring into attack.

'The scent I am getting, my Queen, I have smelt that before,' Bluey purred.

To Snowqueen, it had a distant sense of familiarity, but she was unable to put a claw on it.

'Well, what is it?'

'When I was just a kitten,' he said, looking longingly at his tail, which was a few inches shorter than nature originally intended, 'this big ugly brute with teeth like a crocodile came up behind me and ...' Bluey's eyes glazed over as the pain of the memory flooded his mind. 'Well, it's a short history.'

His brow dropped and flattened across the bridge of his nose. His expression hardened like flint as he spat the words.

'It's a dog.'

'Don't be an idiot; I can smell the dog. I know what dogs are. No. This is a different scent, and I think I should know it ... I've smelt it before. Go down there and tell me what you see.'

Snowqueen pointed to a lower bough that passed to one side of the old stump, a vantage from which he would be able to see into it.

There were two ways Bluey could reach the lower branch. A sensible cat would simply walk back to the tree trunk, climb down and make his way out along it. But Bluey wanted his queen to appreciate his athletic prowess, so he crouched deep into his haunches and, with a mighty spring, sailed off into the air, dropping the two or so metres between the branches. He knew from the instant he launched that he'd executed a perfect leap and, knowing this, he puffed his chest and looked to see that Snowqueen was watching him.

He should have been looking where he was going.

His claws were extended their full length to make certain of a perfect anchorage in the old timber.

Only it wasn't wood.

It took a split second for Bluey to realise that he had sixteen curved claws, sharp as embroidery needles, embedded to their hilts in something much softer than a tree branch. But before he could recover, or lose his balance completely, the 'branch', as fast and fluid as a stockwhip, wrapped around him, and then wrapped again and then a third time around his neck. An old scaly head swung into view before his bulging eyes.

A pair of unblinking yellow eyes wide with menace considered him for a second or two.

'That was excruciating,' Cedric, an old carpet snake, hissed. 'When they s-said there's no gain without pain, I certainly didn't suspect I'd get stuck with you ... ha—s-stuck with you ha, ha ... Understand?'

'No. Ugh, aah, wait,' Bluey gasped, 'you don't wanna eat me. Aagh. Naah. Not so tight.'

'Says who?' Cedric asked. 'I wouldn't s-say pressed cat's the most s-succulent spread—gives me dyspepsia—spot too acidic.

But never s-spy a gift horse in the mouth and all that s-stuff. Anyhow, what's a smelly feral like you doing in this neck of the woods? It's the wrong s-side of the river, isn't it?'

Bluey could only manage a grunt and a wheeze as his breath was squeezed out of him.

Cedric didn't notice Snowqueen approach along the branch.

'Er, Mister Cedric, excuse me, but I think you shouldn't be too hasty about Bluey here,' she purred. 'I'm quite sure you wouldn't enjoy him.'

Cedric snapped his head around, involuntarily squeezing Bluey's ribs as he did so.

'Aaah!' Bluey's cry faded into the tree.

'Oh-oh, yay, Miss S-Snowqueen. I didn't see you about. S-s-stupendous night. Is this prickly squire yours?'

If he had been wearing one, and had the hands to do so, Cedric would have doffed his hat.

'Yes, he's mine. And yes, he's a shifty moron. But he's useful to me, so I'd be much obliged if you'd just uncoil him. Now, if you don't mind.'

Snowqueen dipped her brow and tilted her head coyly. Her eyes softened.

'I'm not so sure that's in my best interests.'

Snowqueen stretched along the branch beneath Cedric's head. To see one cat or the other, the snake had to turn his head through a hundred and eighty degrees, which was difficult because a large portion of his body was being used to keep the squeeze on Bluey.

She lazily scratched the branch, and then with four fully

extended claws from each front paw, scored a set of deep cuts in the timber along either side of the big snake's belly. A ripple of fear travelled the length of Cedric's spine. His scales rattled as he snapped his head up high and looked down into Snowqueen's eyes. There was more hiss and malice in her voice than Cedric had ever heard, even from a snake.

'No problem. Have him. Crush him now. Crush him into pulp. Then eat him. And when he reaches about here'—and with one finely honed prong, right at the point where the snake's belly curved away from the branch, she scratched the surface of Cedric's scaly skin very lightly toward his chin—'I'll make a fine incision about so-oo long and remove him.

'Oh, he'll be dead, I know. And that's bad luck for me ... worse for him. But you'll still be hungry. And you'll have a belly ache so bad, you'll wish you were dead too.'

Snowqueen drew herself up until her eyes, narrow crimson slits that they'd become, were level with Cedric's. Cedric's already cold blood turned to ice.

'So, my dear Cedric, unless you want to live out your retiring years on a diet of flips made from the plover eggs that the kookaburras reject, then I suggest you release him right now. Accept his apology and we'll just move forward—as a certain ginger friend of mine used to say.'

Cedric was snookered.

He knew there was no way he could tackle both cats. And he also knew from Snowqueen's reputation that she was as good as her word. He uncoiled.

Bluey stretched and stroked along the branch, and prodded and padded his more tender spots before rounding on Cedric, claws fully drawn, back arched, ears flat, and his whiskers stretched so taught they could be played like a harp.

'Why, I oughta tear you from end to end,' he spat.

'Bluey!' Snowqueen's shriek stopped him cold.

'Oh, er yeah ... sorry I jumped on you,' he mumbled. 'I ... er ... I don't know what I musta been thinkin'.'

'Now let's all settle down, eh?' Snowqueen said, squatting back on her haunches as if she'd just returned from a stroll in the park.

'What I'd like to know is what's going on in that old tree stump down there?'

'Same goes for me,' Cedric said. 'I snuck out for a s-slither along the numbat path'—he referred to the trail that ran along the water's edge—'and when I came back, these two koolongers and a yirri-yirri had taken over my place.'

'Koolongers?' Snowqueen tasted the word, drawing it out in an icy smile that showed the full length of her front teeth. She stretched in the direction of the tree stump, savouring the nuance of the word.

'What are koolongers, Mister Cedric?'

'Surprised you're not apprised of that snippet, Snowqueen. They're human kittens. Koolonger is the Originals' word, but the Enterers call them children.'

'I've heard about them,' Bluey butted in. 'I heard the Siamese twins talking about 'em one day ... strange skin ... a bit of fur on top ... funny lookin' paws—I ain't never seen one, but hey—

somethin' sure smells nice.'

'Yes. I know something of Enterers and their kittens,' Snowqueen said, the vague memory of rejection finally associating the scent. 'They ... should make good eating, these koolongers; don't you think?'

Her curiosity was stimulated by the aroma wafting from below, now fuelled by the prospect of revenge for past sins.

'I suspect so,' Cedric answered. 'Take a fair crowd of you to down one. My interest's more in the yirri-yirri. That's just about sufficient sustenance for all s-summer. Tastier than Bluey I'd say. Sss, sss, sss!' Cedric's joke was lost on Bluey.

'Hey!' Bluey arched before catching a warning look from Snowqueen.

Then he said, 'Those koolongers do smell good though. How big are they?'

'Concentrate, fool,' Snowqueen snapped. 'What's the dog doing?'

'Hah! Dog? That's no dog, it's just a pup. I think it thinks it's keeping watch, but I c'd take it out with three paws tied behind my back. Want me to?'

Bluey was never one to pass up a chance to impress Snowqueen with his fighting skills. But she's not easily impressed.

'No, you moron. Cedric can have the dog. Those koolongers look like an admirable meal for our clutter ... the sweet one particularly.'

'I reckon my Queen. I c'n smell dumplings with sugar an' spice an' all things nice.'

A large drop of saliva rolled off his tongue, was caught by the breeze and fell on Spot's nose.

Spot's reaction was instant.

A growl sounded deep in his belly as he looked up and saw the cats.

'You idiot!' Snowqueen swiped Bluey across the nose with a lethal talon. 'Instead of drooling all over them, think about how we lure them across to our side of the river.'

She turned to Cedric.

'Do these koolongers have any weapons?'

'Can't s-say really—it's not something I've got the guts on,' he replied. 'I'm more inspired to give them a miss, 'cos they're not the same as us. To start with, they use two limbs to walk on. Say ... have you heard the story of how we woggals lost our legs? No? It was back in the—'

'Some other time, Cedric. Right now, I'm more interested in tonight's dinner ... and I rather fancy what's down there. Now, what was it you were saying about weapons?'

'Er, s-sorry where was I? Oh yeah ... they use these s-second two limbs to transport stuff, but there's no claws or fangs or poisons. These are still younglings too. S'pose if you got all the Maulers down here, you could chase them across the river. And leave me the yirri-yirri.'

'Why don't we kill 'em now and while you keep watch my Queen I'll go an' get the Maulers. We can eat here,' Bluey suggested.

'Are you nuts? Do you want to start a war? This is Don Canida's side of the river. We kill here and in one whiff he'll be on to us quicker than you can say a rabbit's in the hole. He might be an old fox, but this is not the place to start a territory war. We must somehow chase them to the other side and kill them on our own turf.

'And, anyway ... Cedric?'

Snowqueen's change of tone made the old snake recoil.

'How is it that Don Canida lets you occupy such a fine piece of riverfront property? And for so long? This must be prime hunting ground, even for an old fox, wouldn't you say?'

Cedric's tongue flicked nervously between his teeth, and his head swayed like the squashing and stretching of a spring.

'I ... er ... lease ...'

A chorus of kookaburras laughed out across the treetops, leaving Cedric's words hanging in the air like a lonely sock on a clothes line. The first one sounded from a distance down river. The last from a tree directly across the Clearing. A sequence of others connected the first and the last the way lines connect dots in a picture. To Cedric, any kookaburra call is ominous, but a string of them is enough to shake the very limb upon which he was coiled.

What rendered him speechless, however, was something completely different.

In the same instant Snowqueen questioned his relationship with his landlord, he noticed—for the first time—three Gronups on a log observing the tree stump.

And, as if that wasn't enough, he'd caught the unmistakable

scent of Don Canida on the wind.

'Uh-oh,' he whispered. 'I s-smell turbulence.'

'What?' Snowqueen demanded, suddenly suspicious.

'Do you know what it means when the kookaburra laughs?'

Bluey scoffed. 'Snakes like you run like hell ha, ha ... At least you would if you had legs.'

'Worse,' Cedric said, raising his cold eyes to Bluey's. 'When the kookaburra laughs, there's a monstrous storm a-stewing. And that trio of Gronups sittin' on that log there mark the s-start of it.'

Bluey's back arched, his hackles combed like a Chinese fan across his broad ginger shoulders. Snowqueen narrowed her eyes and flicked her tail across the tree branch. The tip tightened into a shepherd's crook.

'Gronups? Where?'

'Sitting on that log.' Cedric craned his neck in their direction.

Snowqueen followed the snake's gaze and stared hard into the night.

'I can't see anything. Which log?' she demanded, baring her teeth.

'What d' you mean you can't see? Sitting there right in front of my place. Three of them. Yoolin too.'

Cedric identified the Gronup elders.

The fact that Snowqueen couldn't see Gronups incensed her. To know that a creature existed but to not be able to see it or smell it or, more importantly, taste it, was more than she could stand.

'What do they look like?'

Cedric was curious now. He could see Snowqueen was rattled.

'You can't see them?'

'Of course I can't see them you stupid woggal. What do you think I've been saying?'

'So plain a blind snake wouldn't miss them ... straight in front, sticking out like dog's balls.' He softened his tone. 'Ah, so you don't accept the Natural Order ...'

'Now you're getting it!'

'But your coat always looks so stunning—who does it?'

'I do it myself.'

'Oh ... I see. When was the last time you saw a Gronup?'

'I wouldn't know one if I bumped into it in the middle of the track!'

'But surely they've asked you to share the Way?'

'Not directly. They used to send these stupid chitti-chitti around to try and talk us into accepting 'the faith'. It was all right for a while because they made quite good eating, but then they stopped coming.'

'I see. Would you like a description?'

Snowqueen nodded. Cedric seized the moment.

'Well ... they're long streaks of majesty, shaggy, with sizeable incisors sharper than an echidna's quills. That one's staring straight at you.'

'But it can't see me—right?'

'She can see you sure enough. Gronups see all. Hear all.'

Snowqueen shrank visibly into the shadows of the tree branch.

'What're they doing?'

'Just observing. Seem to be sorely interested in what's going on at my place. Doesn't make sense. The last thing Gronups want anything to do with is human. Uh-oh ...'

'What? What? What is it?'

'Straight up, see? Surely you can see him.'

Snowqueen followed Cedric's gaze and watched as Don Canida emerged from the shadows, followed closely by two of his lieutenants.

As the fox walked toward the tree, he cast a baleful stare at the branch above, and motioned for his lieutenants to watch the cats. He continued toward the old tree stump.

At another gesture, two more foxes moved silently forward from the opposite side of the clearing and sat a few metres away on the other side of the branch.

The three Gronups watched.

Don Canida, and the ruthlessness with which he controlled and protected his territory, was Kumakana legend. A simple flick of his forepaw could spell death for an animal straying or poaching. How many foxes were hidden in the underbrush was impossible to know.

A stranded silence fell over the Clearing.

Gubba Gubba and Atnunga had sent Wal Pole and his party off to hide in the next valley. The quokka had melted into the ferns, a faint musky scent the only evidence that they were ever present. In the trees above, the dammalaks sat silently, watching through heavily lidded eyes. The chirigers—blue wrens—hid among the sharp spines of the long-skirted balgas. No-one made a sound. The murna died, leaving only the rustle of leaves on the breeze.

The three Gronups watched Don Canida approach the stump, noting the sentries posted around the perimeter.

'Babbildan Babbirra still hopes to get him to join the Natural Order,' Atnunga told her comrades. 'The chitti-chitti reckon it's hopeless, but still they persevere. What do you think, Gubba Gubba? Will he ever accept the Natural Order?'

'Oh my goodness, I doubt it. I believe he has no reason to. They are a law unto themselves, that lot. And, you know, Don Canida may seem to be the worst of them, but he's not the only one. There's Snowqueen up there, and as you well know Atnunga, her clutter's not only a terrestrial terror. Mark my words—she has the potential to be far more evil. Thank goodness she's not as organised.'

'No argument from me there,' Atnunga said, looking directly up at Snowqueen. 'What's she doing here anyway?'

'Hoping to turn the koolongers into a meal, I'd say,' Burra Baroona said.

'Oh my goodness, we can't let that happen,' Gubba Gubba said, looking from one to the other.

'Do you think Don Canida's got other plans in mind?' Atnunga jibed.

'Well he doesn't know they're here,' Gubba Gubba replied.

'Yet!' Atnunga said, ruffling the fur along her back, the waves calming her nerves.

'Then we have to help them,' Gubba Gubba said.

Atnunga looked at her, perplexed.

'Gubba Gubba, you know and I know that interfering could make things worse. We can't interfere. It's up to them to alter their spirit, not the other way round. We both know that we may never be able to connect with Don Canida, or with Snowqueen—if we could, it would go a long way to restoring balance. But there's another problem you seem to have forgotten ...'

'What's that?'

'Bad enough we're trying to deal with the evil of Don Canida and Snowqueen, but have you forgotten who brought them here? The Enterers themselves. They've got to stop causing all this destruction. That's the real problem!'

A wide grin split Burra Baroona's face as an idea lit the depths of his mind.

'Perhaps tonight, the tables will begin to turn.'

He explained his plan to his two companions.

Atnunga's concern darkened her face.

'It's a bit risky isn't it? You don't know if the koolonger is a descendant of Ngungakatta. And you certainly don't know if the little one is wallagudgal.'

'I'm not going to interfere with Don Canida or Snowqueen. I'm not going to give them anything they haven't already got,' Burra Baroona insisted. 'I'm just going to level the playing field a bit. Besides, it gives us the chance to test the spirit of the koolongers. And I'm telling you, I'll know straight away if we have a wallagudgal among us tonight. It would help to know that wouldn't it?'

Atnunga was sceptical.

'How will we know?'

'Watch and learn.'

'And if they're neither?'

'Nothing ventured, nothing gained.'

Atnunga and Gubba Gubba agreed to Burra Baroona's plan and, as they watched Don Canida approach the tree stump, he began to twitch. His snout quivered, wavering like he was trying to hold back a sneeze. The radar dishes that were his ears swung—turning and steadying, turning and steadying—until they locked, tuned into some hidden frequency. He fixed a stare on the stump and his eyes projected a dark fire; as dark as that from deep in the earth.

Above, Cedric nearly fell from the tree.

Right before his eyes, one of the Gronups hovered above the log, lit up like a candle, eyes beaming as its fur-tips struck a golden glow. Curiously, nothing around it caught the light. It appeared to shine nowhere. It cast no shadow. The snake looked sidewards at Snowqueen and Bluey. They couldn't see it. Neither, he noticed, could any of the foxes. This was worth hanging around for.

Don Canida approached the stump deferentially, craned his neck and peered in. For those observing, it gave him a new presence. When he saw two children and a pup sheltering in its shadows, he spoke with an affected concern for their situation.

In Don Canida's book, good manners are the key to control. And in control is exactly how he likes to be.

'Well now, this is a fine place to sleep, isn't it?'

His voice, nasal and whiney, cut through the night like a chainsaw at a baby shower and barrelled around inside the stump, hung for a second and then fell away to the night murna.

Spot leapt from Lavender's arms and launched a noisy assault, yapping and growling. Lavender wasn't sure that she'd heard correctly—perhaps she was dreaming. She grabbed Spot and moved close to Jerramunga.

He drew his club up in front of him.

'Someone's out there,' he whispered. 'I think they've found us.'

'There's a torch,' she said, looking at the log. 'They've found us.'

'I don't see a torch,' Jerramunga said.

'There.' She pointed, watching the glow from the log brighten.

'You're imagining things.'

If he could have seen her face, he'd have thought she was about to clock him. Her whisper was harsh. 'There, on the log ...'

But her claim died out when she realised the glow, although bright—and becoming brighter—wasn't illuminating anything. It seemed to be coming from a small animal but nothing around it caught the light. That's just weird.

Looking straight at it, she said, 'But someone spoke—you heard that, right?'

'Yeah. I think I was dreaming—'

'But I heard it …'

Jerramunga raised his voice a notch above the whisper.

'Wh-wh-who's there … Who said that?'

Don Canida came around to the front of the opening, into full view. Spot emitted the most menacing growl he knew. The fox looked first at the girl, then at the boy.

'Me,' he said, directing a sharp growl at Spot, which made him yap even louder.

'But … you're a fox,' Lavender said, astonished.

'Yes,' Don Canida replied smoothly. 'European Grey, to be precise.'

'You're kidding?' Jerramunga's eyes stretched as far as his lids would allow.

'No. Although there's quite a story—my ancestors were sent out here by mistake—'

'But, foxes can't talk. I gotta be dreaming!' Jerramunga slapped the side of his head.

The sound of the slap sent Spot into action. He leapt from Lavender's grip and lunged at Don Canida. In a blinding swipe with the back of his paw, Don Canida sent him flying through the air. Jerramunga, his eyes already white with fear, gasped as Spot slammed into him.

Don Canida flashed his teeth, the menace of his growl directed at Spot. After a moment his eyes softened; he pinched his cheeks into what was as close to a smile as a fox is ever likely to get.

'I must admit,' he said, looking from one to the other, 'I'm as surprised as you. I've encountered your kind many times, but I didn't know you could actually ... talk ... not properly I mean. But this is good. Maybe we can share some stories eh?'

Jerramunga pulled his waddy closer to his side.

Don Canida saw his action.

'I don't mean you any harm. My boys and I'—he looked over his shoulder—'found you sleeping here. It's not a safe place you know.'

He paused and pointed his nose at Spot, who was now sitting on Jerramunga's lap, licking his paw and wiping his face. Spot growled in his belly, lifted his head and pushed into the safety of his young master's lap.

'I'm sorry about the yirri-yirri there. I don't think I hurt him, just surprised him is all. Anyway, as I was saying, this isn't a good place to spend a chilly night. It crawls with danger. It's a good thing I came along when I did. You see those two cats up in that tree?'

Don Canida sat on his haunches and pointed his snout at Snowqueen and Bluey.

Lavender and Jerramunga both looked hard at the shapes of the cats in the branches. Although their shapes were only silhouettes against the night sky, their eyes emitted a distant meteoric glow.

Lavender gasped.

She looked sideways at Jerramunga, who stared hard into the tree above. Her gaze shifted to Spot, his head cocked slightly to one side, curiously looking straight ahead to the fallen log. He whimpered, licked his chops and settled quietly in his master's lap.

'Yeah, you see them,' Don Canida continued. 'Well they're sitting up there with the old woggal whose home you're camped in.' He saw Lavender's confusion. 'That's right, woggal—you know, python—a mean and nasty piece of work named Cedric. He's up there with them, no doubt planning your demise. Make no mistake—they're not the kind of cats you want to meet in a dark alley. And they've got hundreds of mates. And that snake'— he dropped his voice and lowered his head—'well, I can tell you I've never met anyone meaner. And if I know old Cedric, he'd have his eyes on the yirri-yirri here for dinner. And you two?—looks like you've been paw-picked for the Moggy Maulers' table—worse than pirates on the high seas, that clutter.'

Jerramunga pushed hard against the back of the stump, his knuckles white from the vice-like grip on the stick by his side.

He was shaking.

Lavender couldn't take her eyes off the fallen log, where she'd glimpsed the glowing Gronup. The menace of Don Canida's words didn't register in her mind. She strained to see, and although not certain, she thought she could make out three small shapes.

'We got lost,' she said, dreamily. 'We fell down a hill and couldn't get out again. And then it got dark. I heard them up there but ... there were so many noises.'

Don Canida lowered his head and looked directly into Lavender's eyes.

'It's the murna. But you don't have to stay here. You can come to our place where it's warm and dry ... sleep the night, and then we'll get you back to your own place at sunrise.'

'My dad's gonna be really pissed off at me,' Lavender said. 'What's the murna? It sounds ... spooky.'

'Aah well ... yes ... it would be, I suppose. To us, the murna means life. To others, it means death. How to explain? Oh yes, I guess you could call the murna the rhythm of life. So the murna is the spirit voice speaking—one of the great laws of the land. We know it as *Atnunga*. Perhaps a little foxtrot will help you understand.'

He barked out a sharp order and silently, in the penumbral light of the new evening, a circle of foxes formed round them.

Lavender led Jerramunga out of their refuge.

She stared again at the log where the glowing figure had been, but there was nothing. A mob of foxes formed a ring around them, silent shadowy forms of different shapes and sizes, so many that they were nose to tail and a complete circle. More foxes waited outside the circle while Don Canida stood in the middle and faced the children.

He was smaller than many of the others, but his presence was commanding. Like a conductor rapping his baton, he swept his paw. The crackling creaking buzzing chirping moaning sounds that were hidden in the forest suddenly arranged themselves into a dark rhythm. The pulse gathered momentum, drumming through the trees.

DOmm-td-de-d-d-d
DOmm-td-d-duh-eh-da
DOmm-td-de-d-d-d
DOmm-td-d-duh-eh-da...

Lavender was spellbound. The ring of foxes pranced around four quick steps forward, a turn to the left, a dip, then two steps backwards; forward again, a turn to the right, a dip, two backwards steps and a turn. As they danced, they chanted:

Bada-dah-duh, dur-uh-du-dah,
Dah-duh-durdle-lurdle-duh;
Bada-dah-duh, dur-uh-du-dah,
Dah-duh-durdle-lurdle-duh.

Don Canida broke into voice.

What you hear, I'm talkin' about
Tails, long and stout—
Tales in the understorey
Tell me what's going on.
Like the three-toed widgi—
The tallest of the tall ones callin',
Calling for her young
'Cos she ain't never seen her son.

'N if you listen to the crawlin'
Creepin' where the leaves're fallin'—
Crawlin' up and down the spine,
The bush has come alive.
Could be yongar walkin'—
Hunchbacked, pentapedal stalkin'—
Walkin' on all five
'Cos he don't stand to tan his hide.

The murna rumbles down under
And the murna calls right out of the blue
There's a murna soft like rain,
And another one like thunder ...

And the murna on the wind
Called the great dalagooroo-ooo.

What you hear among the leaves,
High up in the tallest trees—
Chatterin' n cacklin'
Where the wind is blowin' through.
Sits a golden-banded dammalak,
Crackin' seeds to know her luck,
Seeds to feed her brood
'Cos they'll soon be shootin' through.

'N if you listen all around—
Tune in to the underground;
In the sub terrain y'c'n hear
'Bout the things that're goin' down.
A prickly old echidna scratchin',
Sticky tongue bent on dispatchin'
Every giant mound—
Returning wood back to the ground.

The murna rumbles down under
And the murna calls right out of the blue
There's a murna soft like rain,
And another one like thunder ...
And the murna on the wind
Called the great dalagooroo-ooo.

There are things you have to know about the laws of the land:
A murna travels faster through the rocks than through the sand,
And a murna in the bush is worth two more in the hand—
But if you wanna survive the night, you have to listen to all you
can!

The murna rumbles down under
And the murna calls right out of the blue
There's a murna soft like rain,
And another one like thunder ...
And the murna on the wind
Called the great dalagooroo-ooo.

The sounds faded to the silence from which they'd come, leaving only a chilled wind whistling through the clearing. Lavender stared at the log, but saw nothing as Don Canida's lackeys melted once more into their sentry posts around the perimeter.

He approached the children, grinning as he looked from one to the other, his head cocked to one side, ivory teeth gleaming wetly in the dark. An uncertain look passed between Lavender and Jerramunga. Spot growled and earned a sharp look for his trouble, then whined softly and sat between the girl and the boy.

'As you may have gathered,' Don Canida said to them, 'it's not safe for you to stay here. The murna is strongest when the moon is full, and it's quite unpredictable. Our place isn't far so it won't take long to get there. Like I said, I don't mean you any harm and you'll be safe there.'

Applause rained down from the tree above. Snowqueen's shrill voice cut through the evening air as sharply as a finely honed axe.

'Very nice show, Don Canida. Very, very nice. But you don't fool me. Oh no ... not me ... with your fancy footwork and magic tricks. And you ... you koolongers, you shouldn't be fooled either, he's foxing you about his intentions. And about ours. Mark my

words—you go with him, you'll never leave. But, I've got to say
... that's a very good trick with the wind, Don—very, very clever.
You'll have to tell me how you do that one day.'

Her tone changed, and she addressed Lavender as though
reporting a weather forecast.

'We were only trying to help Cedric. We haven't seen you
around here before and we don't chase strangers off—that
wouldn't be polite. But heed my warning. Be careful of that old
fox. He might be inviting you to dinner, but you won't be his
guest.'

Don Canida stood up, an imperceptible nictation summoned a
dozen lieutenants to his side. He called up to the tree above.

'Enough of your catty clap-trap, Snowqueen. Come on down
here where we can talk it over.'

'I don't think so Don, I've seen the way you talk things over.'

Snowqueen howled loudly. Another howl from across the
river answered almost immediately.

'What's she doing?' Jerramunga asked, hefting his waddy like
a drum major's mace.

'Calling for reinforcements. And if we don't move pronto, this
place'll be crawling with mean, nasty, hungry cats.'

The fox quickened his voice.

'I think the best thing is for you come with us, at least you'll
be safe from Snowqueen and the Moggy Maulers.'

As he summoned his pack to form up around them, Lavender
looked once more at the fallen log. Spot trotted toward it, sniffed,
wagging his tail furiously.

'Did you see?' Lavender asked Jerramunga in an urgent whisper, searching the space.

'See what?'

'Just there on that old log ... where Spot is sniffing.'

'See what?' the boy demanded.

'A little animal. On that log there, just before they started singing. Weird looking, like a mouse, but floating. And glowing. I thought it was a torch, but it didn't light anything up—just for a second. Then I thought I saw it again, just normal in the dark, with two others but I'm not sure. I can't see it now, but I think Spot can. It looked straight at us, and smiled. Are you sure you didn't see?'

'Look, talking foxes and cats is all freaky enough,' he said. 'I didn't see any glowing animal ... maybe you're imagining it.'

'Imagining? Look! I don't *imagine* things—'

Jerramunga looked at the log and cut her off. 'Well I don't see anything!'

He scooped an excited Spot into his arms.

'Come on boy. This place is creeping me out.'

Don Canida turned to one of the foxes standing guard a few paces from the old log.

'What's the child talking about?' he asked, quietly.

'No idea boss,' the other replied.

'She says she saw a glowing animal on this log, did you see anything?'

'I've been here all along, boss. If there was any animal here, y'd be savouring its flavour by now.'

'Well what was the yirri-yirri sniffing at?'

'There's a bit of quokka scent. They've been gone a while, but it's still pretty fresh. So I dunno ... beats me, Boss.'

'Hmmm. So it seems. If you want to stay alive through this night, I suggest you keep your eyes open. Am I clear?'

'Perfectly. But I tell you there was nothing...'

'Enough! Let's move before the moon comes up.'

Cedric had watched the exchange from above with amusement. Being considered mean and nasty by Don Canida was something of a compliment. The Gronups were still on the log, where they'd been all along. The pup saw them. But Don Canida didn't—or couldn't. Nor any of his clan.

So, the foxes are as blind to the Gronups as these stupid cats.

Obviously humans can't see them either. But the small one saw the one that glowed—if only for the briefest of moments. His tongue flicked excitedly in and out of a wide fangless aperture. Most unusual, he thought.

Then he whistled aloud.

'Ah yes-s. When the kookaburra laughs ...'

His smile faded quickly, as his thoughts came back around to his own situation.

Had the Gronups seen him consorting with the cats? What if they'd heard him tell Snowqueen about his arrangement with Don Canida?

Guilt flooded the length of the snake like a strawberry milkshake sucked through a straw.

Burra Baroona had been watching Cedric and thought it curious that two such natural enemies should be sharing a branch. But just as enemies may unite in the face of a common foe, so might they unite in the prospect of common prey. He made a mental note to find out more about Cedric later. That was one old woggal behaving very suspiciously.

He had no doubt that all of them thought of the koolongers and the yirri-yirri as meals. He was certain that the young one was wallagudgal—she'd seen him when he'd tapped into their unconscious minds.

But the other one hadn't seen him. And this puzzled Burra Baroona because somehow his speech and hearing had also altered. Surely though, if he carried the great spirit of Ngungakatta, then he too should have witnessed the Gronups. But just as there's always more than one road home, there are other possible explanations. Perhaps he doesn't carry the spirit after all; perhaps his spirit strives for heavenly enlightenment, the same as other humans.

But that still didn't explain how he could understand the fox.

He turned to Atnunga.

'I'm curious about the fox's song. I got the impression that he knows about you, yet he obviously lives outside of the Natural

Order?'

Atnunga laughed.

'The chitti-chitti have been trying to convert Don Canida for such a long time, they've had to invent stories to help explain the Way. Although they do it for Babbildan Babbirra, they do it in my name. But Don Canida is an unbeliever. Anything that he cannot explain, he attributes to me—apparently even the murna.'

'But that wind that he conjured at the end. What dark art—?'

'Coincidence, I'd say. Come on, let's go and rouse Babbildan Babbirra. I think you're right—he needs to know about this. But don't be too hopeful.'

A chain of kookaburra laughs saturated the valley and the three Gronups dissolved. Their destination—a mysterious dark valley and a meeting that could possibly alter everything.

Cedric watched them evanesce into the trees, his stomach churning with more than just a little nervousness, icy blood pulsing loudly beneath his scaly exterior. Humans and animals being able to converse together could be a very bad sign. And Don Canida had not, technically speaking, collected any rent this night.

He watched Don Canida marshal his forces. With two foxes escorting the children and the pup, they set off along the trail.

Snowqueen stepped out along the branch, her silhouette clear against the penumbral sky, the fur on her shoulders at full attention, her back arched in defiance of Don Canida's claim over the children.

She screamed after the retreating fox.

'Don Canida, if you harm as much as a hair on their heads, you'll pay.'

But the scream was lost to an empty forest.

She turned on Bluey, who had his back arched and his half-tail standing stiffly, as tall as it reached.

'This is war!' she thundered. 'Round up the Moggy Maulers. We attack the foxes' dens before they make a meal out of those koolongers.'

'But, my Queen, are you sure about this? We can always get something else to eat.'

'You idiot! There's enough meat there to last all of us a week. Not messy eating either—no fur, no feathers. That is *our* meal, not his. How could you stand by and let that fox make me look foolish? He's stolen our dinner and I won't stand for it. Tonight we teach Don Canida a lesson. Then we'll enjoy a feast like we've never had before and celebrate the biggest takeover in Kumakana history.'

Bluey was stirred by the fire in his queen's eyes.

As she stared cold and hard into his face, he dropped his tail and lowered his body on his shoulders and hips, shrinking inside his gigantic frame. With a sidelong glance at Cedric, he turned tail and padded back along the branch to the other side of the river.

Cedric laid his head flat on the branch, drooped his long coils either side like the slack hawsers of a ship in a still harbour, cold unblinking eyes staring blankly at the angry white cat.

'I hope you know what you're doin' Snowqueen,' he said. 'I

think there might be big trouble afoot here tonight.'

'You're damned right about that,' she said.

And with a slash of one powerful paw, she raked the branch in front of Cedric's nose and strutted off after Bluey.

The sough of the gentle breeze through the leaves joined the roar of the Kulwinkulkine as it tumbled across the rocks to where it lapped among the reed-covered shallows at the banks of the Pool of Many Reflections. The peaceful rhythm surrounded the old python as he slithered down the tree to the familiar safety of the ground, thinking about hibernation.

'Such a shame I have to last the summer first,' he muttered, stretching his way toward the water's edge to slake his thirst.

Chapter 5

Babbildan Babbirra reached the decision to call a council meeting at the same moment Atnunga and Gubba Gubba arrived in the meeting chamber. The Yoolin-jah regarded the sudden arrivals with amusement. They could bring news of great importance.

'Atnunga, Gubba Gubba. Welcome, welcome. Are you getting ready for the Renewal?'

One arm swept a gesture that indicated the valley as he beamed at his visitors.

Gubba Gubba proceeded toward her place at the altar. 'There is something amiss in the forest tonight; the rhythm of life is not in harmony.'

Babbildan Babbirra nodded. 'Don Canida no doubt?'

Atnunga regarded him through big round eyes, the deep furrow burrowing into her brow added emphasis to her words. 'It is much more than disharmony. The still waters of the Pool of Many Reflections are deeply stirred. Feathers are ruffled by an ill wind.'

'What evil is that cur up to now?'

'It is the doing of the Enterers, not Don Canida,' Atnunga said.

Babbildan Babbirra noticed Gubba Gubba gazing intently at

her place in the raised altar.

'You are sure this disturbance does not have anything to do with Don Canida?' The senior elder scratched his head with the prong of his index finger.

'Quite sure,' Atnunga said, her gaze boring into him. 'Why should it?'

Babbildan Babbirra was pensive.

'If it has nothing to do with that evil beast, then I'm not sure I can be of much help. Is it not something you can sort out yourselves?'

Gubba Gubba spoke quietly from the northern end of the altar.

'Yoolin-jah, I have seen an oracle from the waters of the Pool of Many Reflections. It was inscribed on the shell of Goo Malling, the long-neck yoolin. The numbers coincide with this full moon. It showed an image of Ngungakatta, the great yoolin. And it told of a new beginning—a turning point.'

'Ngungakatta?' Babbildan Babbirra looked sharply at Atnunga. 'Is it his spirit that has stirred the waters?'

Gubba Gubba continued.

'Just so. I think it's the Enterers.'

'You think it's the Enterers who will bring the turning point?'

'Well that might be so—but what I mean is, it's because of the Enterers that Burra Baroona is here.'

'Who?'

'Burra Baroona. He came from the east. He found us near the Pool of Many Reflections. He has come to seek an audience with you.'

'What brings him here? Is he here now, with you?'

'He is, Yoolin-jah. And his coming is like the thunder when it shakes the ground beneath our feet.' Gubba Gubba rolled her arms above her head. 'He cast magic upon these koolongers like I've never seen. Magic that showed us where the spirits lie, where all the great beginnings are, from where he arouses things. He came from the east. And he seeks an audience with you, Yoolin-jah.'

Babbildan Babbirra shook his head and sat heavily at the altar, confused. This was what happens at council meetings too. Discussions go round and round in circles. It doesn't matter what the subject, nobody ever seems to be able to get straight to the point.

But is this possible? Out of the blue, after all this time, Burra Baroona returns to the Kumakana.

He addressed Atnunga again. 'If it is because of the Enterers that Burra Baroona has returned, tell me what you know about them? From the beginning.'

'I know nothing at all,' Atnunga responded evenly. 'I was disturbed earlier by a gakkal-yakkal family arguing with a dammalak family over nest invasion. The dammalaks have their nest in an old tree on the steep rise above the Pool of Many Reflections. When I went to investigate, two koolongers and a yirri-yirri came along the track from the east to the Clearing.

'I think they lost their way. They sheltered in an old stump—the home of the woggal, Cedric. He was nearby.'

'So Burra Baroona came with them?'

'I don't think so. He says he came from the east. Well that's also where the gakkal-yakkals came from—'

'And the quokkas—' interjected Gubba Gubba.

'Did the koolongers come from the east?' Babbildan Babbirra asked.

'How could we know that?' Atnunga shot back.

'I'm just trying to get it clear in my mind,' the Yoolin-jah explained. 'How is it that two koolongers can disturb the deep waters of the Pool of Many Reflections? Or kick up an ill wind?'

'On that we're not really sure,' Atnunga said. But one of them told the other one that Gronups are big, hairy scary monsters. I think the water spirit must have been angry—that koolonger was telling grotesque untruths about us.'

'What are you going on about?' Gubba Gubba fanned the air in wide strokes. 'Goodness me, this has nothing to do with all that!'

She turned her attention to Babbildan Babbirra.

'It's true the larger one did tell the smaller one that Gronups are hairy, scary monsters, but he also said his ancestor was Ngungakatta.' Gubba Gubba stared Atnunga directly in the face. 'And at the time you seemed to think that was important—remember?'

'Then they are Originals, not Enterers?' the Gronup elder asked, his eyes flashing.

'Oh my, my ... that is not clear to see,' Gubba Gubba said, from the opposite end of the altar. 'But the mere mention of the great Ngungakatta is cause to consider that there may be more here than meets with the eye.'

'And the oracle?'

'Well yes ... I saw the oracle before the koolongers came—earlier in the deep currents of the pool. I also felt something odd about the smaller one's spirit, which Burra Baroona showed us to be wallagudgal—'

'Hah,' Atnunga snapped, 'wallagudgal!' She appealed to Babbildan Babbirra. 'She doesn't realise just how dangerous these Enterers are. Why, the gakkal-yakkals I met today told me that their entire forest in the east was destroyed by them.'

Gubba Gubba roared, her voice filling the space. 'Yes that is what Burra Baroona told me. He travelled today with a family of quokkas that also came from the east, and whom I also met. And they, like the gakkal-yakkals you speak of, have lost their homes and are seeking shelter here in the Kumakana. Their homes are shattered, split apart. I fear that these are but two examples of a great many families. It is merely the tip of the tingle tree. But as you know well, in the sequence of all things—it is from splitting apart that a turning point arises.'

She took a moment and several deep breaths to calm down before continuing.

'I do not believe that the koolongers in the Clearing have anything to do with the destruction of the forest in the east ... goodness me, no. Burra Baroona proved that the small one is definitely wallagudgal, and a wallagudgal could not do anything like that. But the events are inextricably linked.'

'So,' Babbildan Babbirra said, in a soothing, melodious voice, holding his hands in front of him to once again restore the atmosphere in the meeting chamber. He extended a clawed finger for emphasis.

'We have two koolongers, presumably lost in the forest, and we are debating whether that is of concern to us.'

A second finger shot skywards.

'Gubba Gubba has received an oracle telling us that on this full moon the spirit of Ngungakatta will return to the forest and bring with him the light of the new beginning.'

A third finger uncoiled.

'You overhear a koolonger say his ancestor is Ngungakatta, but you cannot say definitely that the child is an Original, yet he calls Gronups huge hairy scary monsters.'

A forth finger extended.

'And Burra Baroona, our eighth yoolin, thunders in after I don't know how many lifetimes of absence and tells us to be prepared for a massive number of refugees from the east where things have been split apart by Enterers. He then confirms a wallagudgal spirit is wandering about in the forest. And after all this ...' Babbildan Babbirra's face clouded slightly, and his eyes took on a new depth as his fifth finger extended. 'You say this has nothing to do with Don Canida. I must call a council meeting. And now that Burra Baroona is here, all the yoolin must attend. Send Wonaiea to watch the koolongers.'

Both Atnunga and Gubba Gubba reacted.

'Wonaiea!' they exclaimed in chorus.

'But Yoolin-jah,' Gubba Gubba protested, 'the koolongers have gone.'

'Gone? Gone where?'

'They have gone with Don Canida.'

Babbildan Babbirra's stomach churned as he took in the full impact of Gubba Gubba's words.

Don Canida has just been delivered the feasting opportunity of a lifetime. And there are mobs of animals wandering the Kumakana on the night of the Renewal ceremony, all separated from their Gronups, and not a spirit in sight.

Why is it that when things can't possibly get any worse, they do?

He turned to a small recess and extracted a long thong attached to eight unusually shaped discs. The carved wooden objects nestled next to each other at one end, leaving a long string which Babbildan Babbirra held at the other. He began to twirl it slowly, at arm's length, gradually increasing speed. As he did so, the discs spun rapidly on their cords, each emanating a low, yet differently pitched roar.

Babbildan Babbirra increased the speed at which his arm whirled about his head. The volume of the roar filled the chamber and thundered out into the valley, saturating the forest air. So present was the sound that it penetrated the trees, rocks, waters and earth in complete complement to the evening chorus.

As it reached its climax the council members began to arrive, surfing the sound of the strange instrument from wherever they'd spent their day and, as each of the yoolin took his or her place at the altar, the sounds gradually diminished.

When Unkurta had arrived, all that remained was a single

hum resonating at such a low pitch that it was barely audible. Just as Babbildan Babbirra turned to silence the remaining spinning disc with his hand it stopped. He struggled to remember the last council meeting when the bull roarer fell silent of its own accord. Usually it had to be quieted manually. As Burra Baroona, without being bidden, took the eastern position at the altar—the one that had remained vacant for the longest time—there was no question that any of the participants would not be in their proper place.

Arunga, the youngest sister yoolin, directly opposite Burra Baroona, in the west, was the first to notice.

'I knew you'd come,' she said quietly, her face beaming the great joy she felt at seeing a full complement at the altar.

On one side of the Clearing was the base of a steep and thickly wooded rise. The other edge led to the river which, after roaring across a mass of rocks, spread out into the Pool of Many Reflections—so named because, when the night is dark, the stars become a rippling mass of fairy lights reflected in its gentle waters. The giant river cedar that gave Snowqueen, Bluey and Cedric their vantage, grew out of the river's edge at the point where the pool began. At the far end of the pool, the river's course entered an abrupt gooseneck and huge boulders impeded its flow, gated its progress, forced the waters into a powerful funnel.

The children had come upon the Clearing at the stalk end of its pear shape. The tree stump that gave them shelter stood in the middle of the neck. Other than the path from which they'd entered, Lavender could see no way in or out. There was only the steep rise and thick bush on one side, the river, a huge cliff and tall timbers on the far bank. But Don Canida urged them toward the rounded part of the pear shape. She scanned the bush edge and eventually saw what had been hidden to her only moments before.

Just beyond the clearing, obscured by dense shrub, lay a small, tree-lined path of well-worn animal tracks. They filed into the path and almost immediately followed a sharp turn right.

They twisted and turned along the track for a short distance. Lavender and Jerramunga often needed to duck below low-hanging branches and ease their way around the prickle bushes. Soon, they entered another clearing, smaller than the one by the river, and on higher ground.

This clearing was almost perfectly round and formed a depression in the ground with rocky edges growing a thick scrub of sheoak and myrtle, its floor carpeted with emu bush—a dense shrub that covers the ground in smoke-coloured waxy spines. The depression was a dimple the forest giants looked down upon.

Don Canida drew the party to a halt in the centre. Dark shapes skulked around the perimeter, Lavender clutched Jerramunga's hand. She gasped. He'd seen it too. Instinctively, he drew his waddy up in front of him. Spot had also become aware of the moving shadows and, at Jerramunga's movement, dropped the ball between his master's feet and growled.

Don Canida turned about, taking in the whole group.

'It's all right,' he said, reassuringly. 'They're with me.'

Hand in hand, the children, and Spot, who was again stretching his rubbery jaw around his now precious yellow ball, walked cautiously forward and stood closer to Don Canida. Foxes of all sizes padded toward them, their shadows cast long by the golden light of a newly rising moon.

Some stood loose-jawed, pink tongues pulsing to a hidden rhythm, piercing yellow eyes cast steadily on the children and Spot. Others sat back on their haunches, mouths closed watching and waiting patiently for an order. Some patrolled the outside of the group, pacing one way and then, with a sly turn, the other. Others simply lurked, more shadow than flesh and fur. There were too many to count. Lavender bent down and scooped Spot into her arms.

'What are they going to do?'

Her voice was barely audible above the sounds of the bush night.

Jerramunga paused, his concern clear in his lack of words. 'I don't know. What do you think they want with us?'

'That fox said we'd be safe,' she whispered, 'but I don't think Spot trusts him.'

'It seems it's either these guys or the cats,' Jerramunga said. 'Let's see where they take us.'

He watched Don Canida take one of his lieutenants aside, and said: 'Wonder what that's about?'

Lavender watched and strained to overhear, but the foxes were beyond earshot.

'Eddie,' Don Canida murmured privately, 'take a couple of the boys ahead and let Bella Canida know we're coming, and that we have ... guests. They can prepare the top den for them and then, in the early hours we'll have a special feast.'

He smiled reassuringly at Lavender, but when he turned away his tongue flicked wetly over his teeth, his eyes gleaming like stainless steel in a butchery.

He lowered his voice even further.

'Tell her we will have the sugar and spice stew from the old recipes, with dumplings made from snips and snails, garnished with puppy dog's tail. But it may be some time before we arrive. We'll have to take the longer path—around the Valley of Lengthened Years. And I'll need a butcher crew on hand.'

Eddie Vulpré, smaller in stature than Don Canida, and darker, with a long nose that curved slightly upward when he opened his mouth, was the most trusted of the henchmen. His beady eyes were set back in his forehead, high above full whiskered and rounded cheeks. They narrowed into piercing slits as he took the meaning of Don Canida's words, grey eyebrows arching on his forehead with full understanding.

'Sure thing, Boss. Be careful going that way—that valley's a bad place ... especially tonight. You'll have to beat the moon, because once it's over the trees ...'

'I know, that's why most of the boys are coming with me. But you're right—the moon is already on the rise.'

'Another thing, Boss,' Edie Vulpré motioned for Don Canida to follow him a little way up the slope, 'some of the boys smelt fresh quokka back in that clearing—quite a lot of it too. I reckon a party ought to track it down—we haven't had much of that lately.'

'Good idea—I'll see to it.'

Eddie called two of the foxes to follow and together they slunk off into the woods. Lavender watched him jump a log and disappear into the night. She then saw Don Canida call one of the foxes from the outer ring, who, after a few words, took a cluster of the shadows back along the path they'd come.

'Now ...' Don Canida turned to the children, a wave of enthusiasm lifting his voice, 'Eddie has gone off home to let them know you're coming, and to make sure there's somewhere warm and dry for you. We have to have a proper reception for our guests. But first, introductions ...'

He extended a paw toward Lavender.

'My name is Don Canida, what's yours?'

'Lavender Jensen,' she replied, taking the paw tentatively.

'And yours, Sir?' Don Canida inquired of the boy.

'Jerramunga,' he said to the fox, not taking his paw. Turning to Lavender, he whispered, 'I don't think I trust him either.'

'Hey, you forgot Spot!' she said.

Don Canida looked confused. His eyes momentarily narrowed and glinted, cold and steely, as he studied the boy. He'd caught the undercurrent of his whisper and was slighted by the fact that he had not shaken his paw. He turned away and saw the little dog in Lavender's arms. Suddenly he realised what she meant.

He smiled at her.

'I'm sorry ... the yirri-yirri here is called Spot? Well, how do you do, Spot?'

The little dog attempted a yap behind the ball plugging his mouth, but be managed only a sound like the first part of a hiccup.

Don Canida watched Lavender as she stared into the bush where Eddie Vulpré had left the clearing.

'We won't be going that way,' he said to her. 'Our dens are a little way off, over that hill.'

He indicated a direction through the trees and a peak that was visible above the treetops.

'But the going that way is tough. The hills are steep and the valleys deep, and the bush gets pretty thick. So we have to take an easier path—a bit longer, but easier. We have to get going though—the moon is on the rise. Come, I'll guide you.'

Lavender put Spot down and followed the fox as they set off along a narrow rocky pathway that took them up a steep hill toward the rising moon. For a pack of such number, they travelled surprisingly quietly and quickly through the trees and scrub, stopping occasionally to check a scent or confirm the safety of the source of a sound on the wind.

Following his boss's orders, Rusty Steyne led his party back to the Clearing. They quickly picked up the quokka scent on the path leading down to the river. Cedric felt the steady rumble of their gait as he slid from the river bank. He took refuge in a hollow log and watched them turn toward the gooseneck in the river, where the water roared into the valley beyond. The pack beat a steady pace, their noses barely off the ground, concentrating on their objective in the way of an elite search-and-destroy squad.

From a perch high above the fork in the path, two more pairs of eyes, one red-rimmed, the other white, watched in silence as the deadly parade nosed ahead.

'The Natural Order is under serious threat,' Babbildan Babbirra said, beginning proceedings. 'There are two koolongers in the Kumakana. One appears to have descended from the great Ngungakatta. The other is wallagudgal.'

'Is Ngungakatta coming to aid us as he once did?' Unkurta inquired.

'Oh my, we're not sure of that,' Gubba Gubba declared. 'But what I saw in the tortoise shell today was a turning point—the waters are predicting it.'

'Let's not get ahead of ourselves,' Babbildan Babbirra said, regaining control. 'Although that would explain the movement I saw earlier at your altar ... But, truthfully, there was no actual sign that Ngungakatta's spirit is present, was there? After all, he's never really heard from the spirits.'

'True, Babbildan Babbirra, true. But I wonder,' Wollerta asked, 'has anyone ever actually heard from the spirit of Ngungakatta?'

Atnunga chimed in, sharply.

'It's got nothing to do with us. The koolonger can't possibly be Ngungakatta. He said that Gronups were hairy scary monsters and if he was Ngungakatta he wouldn't say that!'

A Mexican wave of head-nodding swept the room.

Then Gubba Gubba challenged Atnunga.

'You know, the great Ngungakatta could have hidden the truth from his offspring to protect him and us. He could, after all, see much into the future of things.'

Wollerta, passive and gentle, took control.

'Were the koolongers in the Clearing by accident? They were there indeed, and you heard Ngungakatta on the wind. Can we assume that this is the sign you speak of?'

'What is accident if it is not chance, Wollerta?' Gubba Gubba demanded. 'My goodness, how long has it been since chance met nature's needs?'

'You mean, like when the dingo first came?' Unkurta asked, his enthusiasm sparked.

'Oh goodness, no, Great Uncle, nothing like when the dingo first came.'

'Well that's when Ngungakatta came. You remember, Babbildan Babbirra?'

'Indeed,' Babbildan Babbirra said.

Unkurta continued to pursue his line, turning again to Gubba Gubba, who was seated at his immediate left. 'And what of Don Canida?'

'Don Canida invoked his own witchery.' All eyes suddenly shifted to Atnunga.

'What happened?' Unkurta asked her.

'The koolongers went with him.'

'They *what?* Why did they do that?'

Gubba Gubba swept to the floor. 'He called upon his own spirit. They danced and he used the murna. Then, suddenly, a wind swept through. He also uttered Atnunga's name in vain.'

'Where are these spirits of Don Canida?' Unkurta asked.

Arunga, the reflective one, supplied the answer. 'They are sky spirits Unkurta. He believes his ancestors are up there. He prays to them at the lake. He believes their reflected movements are messages to him.'

'Why did the koolongers go with him?'

'They were scared of the Moggy Maulers,' Gubba Gubba replied.

'So what's his game?'

'Dinner, I should suspect.' This from Burra Baroona.

'That may be unfortunate, but, as another has already asked, what's that got to do with us?' Old Wonollee asked, shifting slowly in his seat. 'It's nothing to do with the way of the Natural Order and it's not something that we can interfere in, so why are we here?'

'That's what I'd like to know,' Atnunga seconded.

'Because the other koolonger is wallagudgal—the young one ...' Babbildan Babbirra told the court.

'Wallagudgal? How do you know that?' Old Wonollee asked.

'Because of Burra Baroona,' Gubba Gubba told him.

Unkurta looked across at Burra Baroona. 'What did you do?'

'I tapped into the koolonger's mind and gave credence to her belief she could understand and be understood.'

'That's interference,' Old Wonollee admonished.

'No it's not. It's something they already have. They have a word for their visions. It's like seeing things, and she can do it by the spadeful. Unkurta, you were there before the beginning of all things. Surely you, of all yoolin, should know this. They see, therefore they are.'

Old Wonollee leant forward onto the altar and held his hands before him, as though pleading for sanity. 'We all see things, Burra Baroona. But that's not the same as seeing what you can't see. Or you seeing what I can't see, eh? Hrmph ... I don't know anything of this. Does anyone else here know of this?'

Six heads shook slowly and simultaneously.

Burra Baroona stood and moved to a position higher up the wall of the chamber. The low octaves of his voice thundered into every crevice.

'But it is true. Not for all humans. Some even call it a sickness. But I've seen it—it's a spark within the mind. It is the heavenly flow that fills the mind when realisation hits. It is the picture of all possibilities. It is the magic of the wallagudgal. With this unseen-seen thing, much can be achieved.'

'Where did you learn this, Burra Baroona?' Babbildan Babbirra asked, curious as to why the spirits had left him in the dark about something so potent.

'I studied it in the spirits of the wallagudgal. But you have all seen it before. Ngungakatta used it when he helped bring the dingo into the Natural Order.'

Unkurta addressed Burra Baroona, who remained perched high up on the wall.

'I don't remember you being at that event, Burra Baroona. But we all know that if it hadn't been for Ngungakatta, the dingo might have destroyed the Natural Order. And what is most significant about that event—and what we have here tonight—is that it was only through chance that Ngungakatta showed us the way. He never mentioned this ... vision thing.

'And for the first time since Yurlungga divided the spirits and rose into the sky, the spirits of the humans and the spirits of the Natural Order had a connection. A peace lasted a long time and we learnt much about the human spirit. And because the sky and earth spirits reached a peace, the rain came, the drought ended and life flourished. That is, until the Enterers came. But nowhere is there this seeing thing that you can't see. Yet you say it is part of the spirit of the wallagudgal. The spirits have not bothered to let any of us know about it! Next you'll be telling me that Don Canida possesses this this magic.'

Unkurta sat back with a heavenly flourish.

'But Don Canida did not come from the Originals,' Babbildan Babbirra said.

'True Yoolin-jah,' Unkurta responded, quickly, 'but, like the dingo, he came by chance. And he has caused great damage to the Natural Order. As did the dingo. He and his kind. Snowqueen and hers. But the danger is not of their making.

'Since the Enterers came, no humans share our corroboree, no humans protect our sacred places, the fish and the tortoises are choking on the cloudy poisons in the streams, there is less forest, more scrub and weeds. And in what does remain, our charges have fewer nesting sites, less protection from Don Canida and Snowqueen and their mobs.'

Unkurta looked around, locking momentarily on each pair of eyes. Then he continued.

'So many things have changed in such a short time, but the effects are not so different from when the dingo came. Remind us of the first meeting with Ngungakatta, Babbildan Babbirra. Maybe Burra Baroona can discern what role these visions played and how they might have something to do with two koolongers in the Kumakana tonight, and Don Canida. Burra Baroona, you said they had a word for it—what is this word?'

'They call it *imagination*.'

Burra Baroona resumed his seat in silence. He was anxious to hear the story.

Babbildan Babbirra followed his pacing trail around the altar as he recited the detail of the great drought that, long ago, had descended on the land and brought hardship to all creatures. And how, of all the magic men in all the human clans, there was only one who saw a way to prevent complete annihilation of the Natural Order. But in his vision, he was alone.

Babbildan Babbirra entered his fifth circuit of the floor.

'Somehow the spirits answered the call and they called upon me to meet with him. And so I did. His name was Ngungakatta and I saw a terrible fear of the future in his eyes. He believed there must be a way. I told him how, for a long time, the Gronups beseeched the dingo to join the Natural Order. It was then that he showed me the way ...'

Old Wonollee stirred and looked directly across the altar at Unkurta. It was as if he were contemplating the view from the highest mountain top, his craggy features deeply reflective.

'Pardon me for interrupting Yoolin-jah,' he drawled, 'but is Unkurta suggesting that the koolongers are in league with Don Canida?'

'In league? No I don't think so,' Unkurta answered.

'Why do you think they are not in league?' Babbildan Babbirra asked him.

Unkurta studied his place at the altar. A long, intensely black claw on his right forefinger traced a creamy green seam. A visible trail remained where the heat of the finger melted the condensation on the freezing surface.

'The fox travels with his companions but there is no bond between them,' he said.

'Then why would they go with him?'

'Oh my, Yoolin-jah,' Gubba Gubba cried, 'they were afraid. Snowqueen and her sidekick were watching from the tree that stretches across the river at the Clearing.'

'Surely, with his greater numbers and organised army, Don Canida would be more of a threat to them than Snowqueen?' Unkurta prompted.

'Don Canida can be very persuasive,' Gubba Gubba replied. 'Snowqueen sent out a call for the Maulers. I've seen them reduce a body to bones faster than the bite of the sou'westerly can nip down a kwenda burrow. Don Canida convinced the koolongers that they were in great peril if they stayed where they were. And they were too.'

'We shouldn't be interfering in this matter,' Babbildan Babbirra growled.

'Why not?' Arunga, the joyous, asked. 'What do we have to lose? If what Gubba Gubba says is true and we learn more about this seeing business, then this could be the chance to bring changes.'

'The changes we need are far bigger than can be achieved by two koolongers here tonight, younger sister,' Babbildan Babbirra said, his tone lowering the temperature several degrees.

The Gronups fell silent, only the sounds of the murna from outside could be heard. The eyes of all the yoolin finally turned expectantly to Burra Baroona.

'I beg your pardon, most revered Yoolin-jah,' he said, addressing Babbildan Babbirra, 'it is clear that the coming of Ngungakatta to the Kumakana was such an event that it altered all of life on earth. But the coming of a wallagudgal is an altogether different matter.

'A wallagudgal has the same significance as that of a butterfly passing wind in a distant land across the great blue water. Such a small matter can affect the clouds and the rains in our valley. We cannot possibly know what can be achieved by two koolongers—especially if the one carries the spirit of Ngungakatta and the other is wallagudgal.'

'A fine point, younger brother,' Old Wonollee grunted, shifting in his seat. 'We don't know the effect of this—good or bad ... hrmph? Here, Don Canida, there, the Enterers. Do the koolongers go with Don Canida against their will? Maybe. Maybe not ... we don't know. We don't know if it's significant. Babbildan Babbirra is right to be suspicious. Gubba Gubba right to take the oracle seriously. But'—he looked hard at Burra Baroona—'hrpm ... we must be sure. A mistake could risk the Natural Order. Consider the consequences carefully, no matter small or big.

'We could do great damage if they're in league with Don Canida and we reveal ourselves to them. A clever trick could deceive us. Hrmph ... great care is needed.'

In the silence that followed, Babbildan Babbirra looked from one yoolin to another. The auspiciousness of the moment was not lost on any of them. Seat shiftings, ear scratchings and whisker flutters were signs that each wise and ancient mind recognised this great moment.

Babbildan Babbirra also recognised new potential for a much greater catastrophe.

For many generations, the great clans have occupied territories in the Kumakana and new population pressures could bring new disasters. It was clear that Babbildan Babbirra couldn't allow just anyone to inhabit the Kumakana Forest.

'So, we know the young one is wallagudgal,' Arunga was asking, 'what can that mean to us?'

Burra Baroona, his voice canyon deep and rock steady, replied: 'The spirit of the wallagudgal is not like that of other humans. The koolonger will not look to the sky-world for the meaning of the time, for hers will not be a spirit that clings like fire to the soul, burning upward. Nor is it a spirit of the Natural Order. But, because it is a joyful spirit all the same, it will seep downward like the lake, to bring great joy to the heart.'

Arunga was overjoyed. 'It is a long time since we had such a spirit in the forest. But what good will it be?'

'That, we will not know until we can see the spirits in opposition, my younger sister.'

Burra Baroona's announcement aroused the council to the shocking reality that they could be completely wrong and completely right at exactly the same time. He continued.

'The spirits of the sky-world and of the earth-world are the opposite of the other. But even when there is opposition, there can still be agreement and respect for the dependence one life has upon another. There was a time when the spirits were locked in conflict—the one trying to destroy the other—but if either the sky-world spirits destroyed the earth-world spirits, or the other way round, they would both lose, for each is dependent on the other. That is the way of everlasting life, and everlasting life is the quest of all spirits.

'When others are looking to the heavens, the wallagudgal will see the earth. When others are looking at the earth, she will see the heavens. A pure spirit sees the truth instinctively because it does not let the one interfere with the other. This is a great power and it will show itself at the right time. You will see.'

'How can we be sure that she will not meet her peril before that time?' Gubba Gubba asked, 'given that we are prevented by the natural laws to intervene.'

'We can do nothing,' Babbildan Babbirra re-affirmed. 'Even though they are koolongers, they will one day be grown. If we act prematurely, and expose ourselves to them before they have shown us their spirits, we could be letting loose a greater terror than Snowqueen is to the *mardo*.'

Babbildan Babbirra studied the growing division in the council.

'Because we don't yet know their spirits, we don't know their natures,' he said, quietly. His voice rose. 'They could be like the Enterers who flattened the forest in the east. Or those who brought animals that turned wild and became Don Canida and Snowqueen. Or those who hunted the dingo with their bang-sticks for attacking the grass-eating animals they brought for their food.'

He strode to the end of the chamber and turned, sweeping his arm across the council as he pressed on.

'They cannot know of our existence. If they knew, they would destroy the Natural Order. The bond that connects us to all the animals is fragile enough. Already we're powerless to stop many of them sinking toward extinction. For one thing is certain—the sky-world spirits will stop at nothing to learn the secrets of the earth-world spirits.'

He bounded to a position halfway up the wall, drew breath and dropped his voice.

'However, there may be a turning point. If so, that is most fortunate. But the dangers are real. We must take proper care to avoid invoking consequences that we cannot abide. We must see their spirits and be sure of them before such a gathering together can be sanctioned.'

He watched them all from above as silence followed him into the upper reaches of the darkness.

Burra Baroona displayed no emotion at Babbildan Babbirra's pronouncement. His position was clear. He was bound to abide by the decision not to interfere. But it didn't mean he couldn't keep an eye on things.

Mal Aga and Kal Barri flew close to each other, zigzagging between branches in the upper reaches of the riverbank's giant trees, the only sound coming from the soft beating of their wings as they tracked Rusty Steyne and his party's deadly path.

Five foxes moved quickly and silently through the understorey, their lethal intent clear to the observers. Mal Aga had seen it before. Somewhere ahead would be quarry, and he felt duty bound to warn them if he could.

The two birds had been discussing the finer details of the nest-sharing arrangements, Mal Aga just about to issue an invitation for Kal Barri to attend the Renewal, when the foxes passed beneath them, silencing their chatter.

This gakkal-yakkal is a strange bird, Mal Aga thought as he led the reconnaissance through the branches. Clearly more concerned with the nesting needs of his mate than reconciling with his Gronup. Like every bird and animal, he knew that the

Kumakana must provide for refugees. In their discussions, Mal Aga reluctantly, but hospitably, offered to share his family's nest until a suitable one was available. He was dumbfounded when the gakkal-yakkal suddenly flew off to inform his mate before discussing the details.

And when he returned, there was little gratitude—simply an announcement that Kal Annie had moved in and was quite settled.

Mal Aga, though disconcerted, kept his cool and brought up the subject of the gakkal-yakkal's estranged Gronup, hoping to lead the conversation to a point where the gakkal-yakkal would undertake his spiritual responsibility. But then the silence that preceded the foxes reached them.

Odd too, Mal Aga thought, as he ducked beneath another branch, how Kal Barri seemed to the skies a little too interested in this particular deadly activity. At least he'll see what happens to a spirit that is not guided by a Gronup.

The surprise of the attack was complete.

Wal Pole was the only one to escape the slaughter, owing his life to the fact that he had momentarily separated from the clan to scout ahead.

Rusty Steyne and two of his party emerged from the shadows, striking at the centre of the small gathering of quokkas with all the deadly dispatch of a dugite. Between them, within seconds, they tore gaping holes from the necks of three, and completely removed the heads of two before any realised what was happening.

In panic, two quokkas hopped immediately into the bushes at their right, straight into the waiting jaws of another fox. Both were dead within seconds. The remaining two quokkas stood mesmerised—one having sufficient presence of mind to thump the ground with its tail and send a warning signal to any who may still be alive and not caught in the deadly trap. Three thumps were all it got before it was pounced upon and executed.

Wal Pole got the message. He couldn't look back. That would mean certain death at the paws of savages who did not respect the natural laws. He rushed headlong into the forest, choosing pathways that looked to afford the quietest passage through an increasing density of understorey. He pushed his little body to the limit, bounding breakneck as bushes whipped at his face and tore his forepaws.

As he moved higher and higher out of the valley, away from the river, the trees grew taller and the forest thickened. He had no idea where he was going or what dangers lay ahead. The only thing that mattered was to find a safe and sacred place where he could call upon his spirit to reunite him with his Gronup.

Mal Aga the parrot studied the scene below. Nine carcasses lay scattered around a small clearing surrounding a granite outcrop. The foxes had closed in on their prey without warning. The quokkas had been disguised against the grey of the rocks, and Mal Aga had not seen them. Rusty Steyne and his death squad didn't need to see them. They'd caught the scent downwind.

Nine carcasses and five foxes—what's the plan here? Mal Aga wondered.

A sudden movement from one of the corpses caught his eye. A juvenile quokka hopped a few short steps from the dead form of the mother who had been carrying it in her pouch. A few short hops and that was that. It was snatched from the ground, shaken violently, squeezed like a rag doll between powerful jaws, the cracking of tiny bones reaching into the tree above. Another young fox grabbed at the lifeless form and the two of them entered into a tug of war until it was torn to bloody shreds. Mal Aga blinked several times, but he could not tear himself away from the scene below.

Revulsion raked his body. What's the sense in that? These demons can't carry or eat what they've already killed—why simply snuff out a life?

He watched Kal Barri, who looked impassively at the scene from a nearby branch. Each fox took a carcass and headed one after the other up the incline until all disappeared into the bush. Four dead quokkas, each with gaping chunks torn from their flanks, and the scattered remains of the juvenile were left in the clearing.

'The *wardongs* will have a good breakfast,' Kal Barri said, cocking his head to one side as though aiming a camera and snapping images of a murder of crows feasting on the remains.

'Perhaps. But one without honour,' Mal Aga choked, standing on his left foot to scratch his ear with his right.

'What is honour when you have an empty belly?'

'No-one in the Kumakana has an empty belly.'

'That might not be true for long, my green-feathered friend.'

And with that, the gakkal-yakkal launched himself into the air and flew at speed through the trees toward the higher reaches of the forest.

Mal Aga watched him go. He ruffled the golden band of feathers around his neck and lifted his shoulders to air his converts before laying them flat over the bases of his primary flight feathers—the ritual of an automatic flight check before speed flying.

Babbildan Babbirra

Chapter 6

Koopoo stood erect, his huge frame supported by the tripod of two of his hind legs and a massive tail, his highly tuned ears over two metres above the ground. He'd just received a message on the bush telegraph, a ripple through the ground.

The bush telegraph was his preferred way of gathering important news. A system that keeps both the source of the message and its content hidden from all but the sender and receiver—a secret code handed down over many hundreds of generations and available to all clan leaders. It's how they advise each other of impending dangers and successful food discoveries.

This one, however, told the giant kangaroo that he was about to receive a visitor.

His visitor emerged from the scrub, frightened and shaking, glancing furtively about before advancing in cautious hops. At each pause he studied the unfamiliar territory, as though contemplating the safety of continuing toward the waiting kangaroo.

Koopoo pivoted on the hinges of his huge hips and assumed the five-limbed posture he used when grazing. His visitor stopped a forepaw's length away, directly in front, squatting on his haunches, exhausted. Their eyes were level. Koopoo looked kindly upon the newcomer.

The quokka introduced himself.

'Yay koomborlie. I'm Wal Pole, Yoolin-jah of a clan from the east. But now I'm alone. The rest of my clan who travelled with me ... have all been killed—murdered—yes murdered, koomborlie ... by the demons who haunt the understorey ... in a valley alongside the Kulwinkulkine ... beyond the hill that rises in front of the sun ...'

The quokka's eyes conveyed his sorrow and the guilt he carried.

'I ... I ... escaped koomborlie, only because I was separated from the clan to scout for a sacred place where we could call to our Gronups. We were separated when the Enterers destroyed the land to the east ... wiped it out ... completely. We came to seek refuge ... travelled with a great Gronup yoolin ... Burra Baroona— he led us to a place he called the Clearing ... but when we got there we met some locals who said the spirits had left because of those filthy curs—the ones who attacked us. We were sent along the track to the valley where the casuarina trees grow and that's where ... where ...'

Wal Pole's breath failed him. He sat back on his haunches, the rims of his eyes red, the centres blank. He clawed at his moustache in short nervous gestures, not knowing what impression he'd made on the one crouched attentively before him.

'Seems to me, my boy, you need something to calm your nerves. Here, come with me ...'

He led Wal Pole toward a cluster of small bushes. The quokka bounced behind him. Koopoo indicated a bush with a waxy smoky green leaf.

'We find chewing on a bit of this lightens the load a little. Sort of takes your cares away.'

Wal Pole chewed a small green leaf from the end of a bushy branch. The taste was salty and acrid. It suited his palate. The bitter juices of the leaf instantly refreshed his mouth and cleared his airways. He took a larger twig of leaves and sat chewing for several minutes. Before long he began to relax, gradually tuning in to the activity of his surroundings.

Koopoo watched, smiling, from a short distance. *A most interesting plant. It has a calming effect on marsupials, yet other creatures cannot tolerate it. The Enterers call it box poison.*

A rush of wind over his head alerted him to the descent of a shadowy form. A large black cockatoo glided into the wispy branches at the top of a nearby bottlebrush, perching precariously on a flimsy stalk. The bird fanned his tail displaying a flash of brilliant red feathers.

'Aah—Karra Katta,' Koopoo said, a gentle chuckle shaking his beard, 'what brings you out at sundown?'

'To see you, of course, Koopoo. What other reason could a bird as great as me give up his most important hour?'

The bird spat out a length of flower stem he'd cut from the tree.

'You flatter me, O great flying fire in the sky.'

The kangaroo loped closer to the bottlebrush, the flowers of which were now suffering a brutal attack from the cockatoo's secateurs.

'Hey you should leave some for the bees you know.'

'The bees have plenty, these are for the ants.'

Another cone of crimson dropped uselessly to the ground. The bird cocked his head and looked steadily at the fallen flower. His crown ruffled, and he clicked his tongue noisily against the inside of his upper beak.

He fanned his wings and tail, glided gracefully to the ground, landing a wingspan or two in front of Koopoo, his back to the quokka. The kangaroo's great tail lay flat on the ground behind him, his forepaws resting in front so they could easily scratch at his shoulders and rump where the fleas and ticks competed for the warmest and juiciest parts of his flesh.

He looked directly into Karra Katta's eyes, listening carefully to the raspy words of the great black bird.

'And there is no question of this?' Koopoo finally asked.

'What? There's always a question, isn't there? I can only speak of what I saw and heard. And if you ask me, there's something very fishy going on.'

'Which direction did they take?'

'That's the fishy bit. They came up the track away from the Kulwinkulkine, this side of the Clearing. If you ask me, they are going to cross the Valley of Lengthened Years moonward side of the tingle tree.'

Koopoo was thoughtful for a moment.

'Now why would they do that?'

'Beats me. But that's why I say there's a feather short somewhere. I thought you ought to know about it.'

'And you are quite right, my old friend. The question is—who else knows about it? And who else should know about it?'

'The Gronups know about it.'

'Do they indeed? Which Gronups?'

'Well the whole council by now, I should think. Atnunga and Gubba Gubba were there. And one I'd never seen before. Had a voice like thunder.'

Koopoo looked quickly around at the quokka, now lying on the ground under a bush, fast asleep.

'That would be Burra Baroona—travelled with our little friend here. Maybe he also knows something about it.'

'Oh yeah?' Karra Katta studied the sleeping form. 'Who's he?'

Koopoo told the bird the quokka's story.

'Aah—' Karra Katta croaked, realisation dawning. 'So that's where they went.'

'What do you mean?'

'I saw him send them back—I didn't know where they went. But there is one other odd thing you know ... at the same time, he also sent off a small party separately, led by that snively little lieutenant of his. I was a bit preoccupied so I didn't notice which way they went.'

Koopoo thought a moment, and then told Karra Katta what he wanted the bird to do.

As soon as Karra Katta had taken to the sky and faded away into the dark, Koopoo thumped his tail several times on the ground. His mob, which was spread widely around the scrub, gathered round and prepared for travel.

Koopoo's mob was one of the largest in the Kumakana, perhaps second only to Don Canida's, numbering in the hundreds. He usually spent the early part of his days lying under a bush with one or another of his mates and young offspring nearby. As the sun began its descent into the late afternoon, he would lead the mob to a safe grazing ground. While the females and joeys grazed, he liked to engage in sparring sessions with some of the young boomers.

He won his position of Yoolin-jah seven mating seasons earlier in a brutal and bloody fight. Every season, he's had to defend it in the same way.

So far it's been easy enough. He's big and talented and a skilful fighter but, if today's training sessions with one or two of the young boomers were any indication, he will face an unwinnable challenge soon enough. Perhaps not this season, but maybe the next, or the one after. Still, that is soon enough, he thought, stealing a fatherly look at the joey his latest mate had recently weaned, the one they named Koo Tea—*the one of the one.*

Koopoo kept a watchful eye.

Koo Tea had been missing for two days after being stalked and set upon by foxes. His mother had taken him away some distance from the grazing ground to start him on his way of life without her. Don Canida and his hunting party had separated him from his mother, but he'd escaped, wounded, and headed for open ground. The Enterers had taken him in, caged him, but he was resourceful. He'd escaped, wounded and tied up with cloths.

Not everyone is as fortunate.

Koopoo looked at the quokka nearby, now roused from his nap, rested and calm. He shook his head at another example of mindless slaughter. Action needed to be taken against the foxes. The cats too. Snowqueen and her Moggy Maulers also needed to be brought into line.

His thoughts returned to the present.

Tonight is the Renewal ceremony, a coming together of scales, fur and feathers. Not before time either, he thought, picking at a patch of matted fur on his rump, and scratching away at the ragged ends of his ears.

'Time I had a new suit,' he mumbled to himself, looking around.

The assemblage was complete.

Koopoo looked upward. A falling star cut through the darkening sky. The only impression it left behind was a trace. Good enough, he thought, and thumped his tail solidly on the ground three times, rousing the mob into action.

Led by the *whamp-b-whamp-b-whamp* of Koopoo's massive tail drumming the ground and driving his powerful body across metres of earth in single easy leaps, the huge mob bounded purposefully toward a night of great entertainment and wonder. Wal Pole travelled in the middle with the younger kangaroos. None questioned his inclusion. Birds and possums that were scattered among the treetops stopped their chattering and watched the heaving procession pass beneath them.

Don Canida commanded a furious and punishing pace along a winding narrow path. Lavender needed to rest. The rocks and sticks of the forest floor bruised her feet and scratched her legs and Don Canida had either not heard her requests or ignored them. So she grabbed his tail and yanked.

Hard.

He yelped and instinctively turned to snap as he skidded to a stop. She made her complaint heard and Don Canida, although reluctant, agreed to a brief rest. They'd descended into a valley where the air was damp and cooler. Lavender felt the gloom of the slope envelope them. She noticed that the trees were different. Overhead, monstrous canopies obscured the stars and connected heaven and earth. Towering, gnarled trunks wore dark shadows of ghostly faces.

Don Canida scattered sentries among them.

'Where are we?' Jerramunga asked, gaping at the trees.

'Passing the Valley of Lengthened Years,' Don Canida replied, tense and nasal. 'Once we're through and go around the other side, we'll be safe in our territory. But it's not safe here. We've got to be gone from here before the moon clears the horizon.'

'What happens then?' Jerramunga asked.

Don Canida's yellow eyes narrowed.

'The sides of this valley come down.'

A falling star skidded across the sky. Lavender and Jerramunga saw it together.

'*Yantamurra!*' Jerramunga said on a breath.

'A falling star,' Lavender informed him.

'Yeah. That's what I said.'

'No you didn't. That's not what you said.'

Before Jerramunga could answer, Don Canida jumped up and shoved his snout as high into the air as he could reach. He tested each direction, and then turned toward the children and snarled.

'Okay you've rested enough. We've got to go. Now!'

The children got to their feet and once again began threading through the trees. This time, the pack closed in tighter around them.

Karra Katta's large form, pitch and ghostly, landed on a low branch of a Christmas bush. He snipped a branch of flower to raid the seed vessel, which he cracked open and then spat the shell out onto the ground. He clicked his tongue in rapid succession against his upper beak. A dark shape loomed from behind the myrtle—a bulky, feathered barrel with a craned neck and two lanky legs. The head attached to the craned neck darted left and right until it stopped, and two beady eyes regarded the cockatoo.

'Well, Karra Katta,' the emu boomed, 'why all this cloak and dagger stuff?'

Karra Katta delivered Koopoo's message.

'Sounds like good sport, Karra Katta. What's in it for me?'

'June Dalup, surely to be of service to the Gronups and your spirit is reward enough.'

'Very well. Tell him, this bird has flown the coop. He'll know what that means.' The great emu watched the cockatoo leave. 'He really thinks I'm gonna fly.' She laughed. Then she called her flock together.

'To the Valley of Lengthened Years for the ceremony,' she said. 'But first, a small detour.'

Karra Katta headed northeast to the beginning of the Valley of Lengthened Years. Flying just below the treetops, he traced a path back toward the Clearing until he saw them racing through the valley. He looped around and backtracked a little before taking up a position high in a karri tree, directly in their path.

Lavender felt danger. She felt it in Don Canida. She felt it in the foxes surrounding them. The pace was furious and the prickles, springing ferns and low branches painful. Don Canida kept looking to his left, where the valley was darkest. He sniffed at the wind as it eddied through the trees. His fear had become her fear. And the more furiously they went, the more frightened she became.

When they hit the valley floor, the entire pack was brought up suddenly with a raucous screech that knifed like the screams of a hundred children through the darkness ahead. So sudden was the halt that Lavender barrelled straight into Don Canida and sent him sprawling into the fox in front of him. Both ended face down, in the dirt.

'What was that?' Lavender's whisper amplified in the silence.

'Gronups?' Jerramunga said. It was both a question and a statement.

Had a bolt of lightning struck the pack the effect of his utterance would not have been any less. Don Canida's eyes narrowed into slits the colour of embers.

'Gronups!' The word caught in his throat. All the other foxes froze, rooted to their places like the trees that had stood there for hundreds of years.

Spot dropped his ball and peeled off a series of excited yaps, his rapid barks firing lonely echoes from the sides of the valley. Don Canida glared at the puppy, who then gobbed his ball and retreated to his master's ankles.

The foxes sat stock still in the black of night, their legs folded like deckchairs beneath them.

A short distance ahead, in the crown of a giant karri tree, a solitary black cockatoo cocked one eye at the confusion on the ground below, chuckled quietly, and leapt from his perch into an easy flight toward the darker reaches of the valley.

'How come they're so afraid?' Lavender whispered to Jerramunga.

'Silence, you fool!' Don Canida snarled, toothily. 'Do you want to get us all killed?'

Lavender was shocked by the sudden anger. The silence allowed her to hear something else behind them. From high up on one side of the valley, a barely audible rhythm like distant heartbeats thrummed into her presence. It grew louder with each beat and it was soon apparent that the rhythm came from hundreds of individual thumps, not in unison, but a distinctive meter nonetheless. It bore down on them.

Crashing branches and swishing leaves produced a sibilance that bounced from the trees and coupled with the thunderous rumble below—a powerful breath-catching syncopation building toward crescendo.

Lavender stared into the dark, and clutched Jerramunga's hand in a sweaty vice as the pounding walloped toward them.

She couldn't see Jerramunga or the mask of fear he wore as they waited, huddled behind the girth of a massive tree, obviously capable of standing its ground regardless of what monstrosity was bearing down on them. Nor could she clearly see the shadowy forms of foxes—their camouflage resembling just another bush in the night forest.

As the sound reached its deafening peak, a shaft of moonlight snapped on, as bright as a stage spotlight. It pierced the treetops, lighting the ground around them. The moon had breached the valley horizon. And, like stage footlights, it diffused through the dew on the leaves and melted the dark, throwing spectral grey shadows all around.

And then sound swallowed them.

With the moon at their backs, a mob of kangaroos stampeded straight for them, tearing between towering trunks and bounding clear over tall shrubs, agile and fast.

The moon lit Don Canida's terror-stricken face.

He was rock still with his ears and hackles fully erect, one paw lifted and his head stretched forward as if immediate attack might be called for. His tail was raised, nose pointed, lips drawn taught, his ivory canines, appearing too long for the jaw that contained them, exposed. Without moving a muscle, he watched every movement around him.

Spot watched the passing parade with great excitement. He stayed by his master's feet spinning rapidly in tiny circles, tail wagging, ready to join in the chase. Jerramunga grabbed him and passed him to Lavender.

'Hold him tight,' he said, as loudly as he dared above the din.

She grabbed the puppy and Jerramunga wrested the bright yellow ball from his mouth.

'Just don't let him go, okay?'

Lavender could only nod.

Jerramunga waved the ball in front of Spot, let the pup lick it several times, and then with a mighty heave, threw it as far as he could at the backs of the kangaroos. Spot fought Lavender's grip as the ball sailed past the trunk of a large tree into the bush where it bounced off a tree and crashed through leaves and scrub.

'Hey!' she snapped. 'That's mine. What'd y' do that for?'

Don Canida glared at Jerramunga.

'Come on,' the fox snarled, 'we've got to get out of here now! Gloves! Cornelius! Lead on ... come, move!'

'What about Spot? He'll want to get—'

'I'll take him,' Jerramunga said, cutting her off sharply and reaching for the dog.

'But my—' Lavender stared defiantly at Jerramunga.

'Look, Spot can't carry it and keep up, okay? So leave it!'

'Come on!' Don Canida snapped. 'We can't waste any more time. The moon's almost above the horizon.'

The pack set off at a furious pace, heading for the top of the opposite valley wall. But they hadn't travelled far when the scream knifed through the heart of the night again and silenced the forest once more. Don Canida's tail stiffened, but he didn't stop. With added determination, he increased the pace, heading for the safety of his territory.

A sound like thunder shattered the air. Deep and guttural, it rose from the earth and rolled from the trees before them. The foxes froze at first; then scurried for the nearest shelter as a new pump of swishing and clumping advanced upon them.

Then, out of the murkiness, a flock of emus pelted down the side of the valley—each bird, a live quarter-tonne torpedo propelled by raptorial three-toed feet, ripped through the underbrush at a frightening speed, dodging the forest giants with uncanny accuracy. A clangourous haka boomed off the trees as the avalanche poured, helter-skelter, toward the valley floor.

The two lead foxes never saw what hit them. They were passed like soccer balls between June Dalup and her running partner, June Dana, then kicked back into the pack and trampled into bloody pulp. Don Canida scrambled behind a fallen log, leaving Lavender standing fully exposed.

Jerramunga held Spot tightly and grabbed Lavender's tee-shirt, pulling her back against the trunk of a giant tingle tree. She stood, trembling, watching warily as hundreds of emus stampeded past, dragging a powerful wind into their wake, certain their booms were laughter.

Waitjd! Waitjd! Waitjd!

When it was over, an angry and frustrated Don Canida got to his feet and called his lieutenants to form a protective ring around him and the children. With one fox limping severely, and two others lying dead in crumpled heaps, the party continued its journey. Slower now, and a little more cautiously.

Babbildan Babbirra had the full attention of the council.

'The spirits complain that there has already been too much extinction. If the Enterers persist, they say it will accelerate. I don't need to remind you that every extinction takes the Gronups who minister to that kind with it. Without Gronups the spirits weaken, and so it goes, until all life has gone. *Poof!*

'We must find a solution before the situation reaches a point from which there will be no return. Time is running out.'

A buzz ribboned around the chamber. It quietened as he continued.

'Where lies the Way? What can bring the Enterers to hold themselves in check? Can a single wallagudgal give us hope? If not, then what other Way is there? If we can't find the Way, we will be at the mercy of the sky-world spirits. And Don Canida and his kind will rule the Kumakana. It will be left to the laws of the jungle.

'Humans have learnt to control some of the secrets of nature. And what have we done? Stood by and watched as they cut the karri and the jarrah, destroying the means of life for many of our flock. Is it right that we should stand by, watch and do nothing?'

Babbildan Babbirra swept his right hand in emphasis as he turned his back on the council.

Burra Baroona's voice boomed in response.

'When they push the forest to the ground to make way for their houses and build shelters for their gleaming metal machines, they call it development. They dig huge holes in the ground and take out the rocks and call that development. They build poisonous lakes, pour excrement on the ground, wash it into the rivers and choke the fish—they dam the rivers and draw upon the hidden energies of the earth to reach the places where the sky-world spirits live. They call this development too.'

Babbildan Babbirra once again faced the assemblage.

'Apparently their quest is to dominate all and master that which ultimately cannot be mastered,' he said.

'Is this the way of the sky-world spirits?' Wollerta asked.

'Obviously Enterers misunderstand the purpose of nature,' Unkurta rumbled, his round eyes gleaming from an obscured position he'd taken on a ledge high up the wall of the meeting chamber. 'They've got it so wrong. Do they assume that in all of nature that one action causes only one effect? And that one effect is the result of only one action? They take what they can use and they transform it into other forms, yet they put back only the waste, which nature is powerless to transform again into useful material. They are destroying nature. And if they destroy nature, they will ultimately destroy themselves.'

'We can't wait for that to happen,' Arunga reflected. 'They'll destroy all of us first.'

Burra Baroona looked directly at the joyous one.

'True Arunga. It would split the Natural Order apart. But the light cannot be extinguished altogether, for as the final fruit decays, so does new life sprout—there may be wholesale destruction, but the Natural Order cannot be utterly destroyed.'

'The spirits reckon that if they could reach the sky-world spirits and explain the problem,' Babbildan Babbirra said, 'the spirits of the humans could be influenced to alter their own nature.'

Unkurta dived in, waving a hand in dismissal.

'That's ridiculous. When Yurlungga divided the spirits he created a chasm with no ford—the earth-world spirits cannot communicate with the sky-world spirits.'

'They want to try,' Babbildan Babbirra insisted. 'Was not the Natural Order established so all can exist in harmony with nature? In nature all things may seem to flow to a perfect goal, but it isn't so. Nature cannot be perfect. Perfection was never sought until the Enterers came. Originals didn't seek perfection because they knew that such an idea does not accord with nature. The idea of perfection ignores the element of chance.'

Babbildan Babbirra looked to Gubba Gubba at the far end of

the altar. She was deep in concentration, following his thoughts. She looked up.

'It is nature's way that every diamond has its flaw,' she said. 'Goodness, yes! It's not just we Gronups who bestow recognisable individuality upon others—nature does too. Chance is a most unusual phenomenon. Chance belongs to the spirits. It is that moment when the spirits influence nature.'

Old Wonollee, turning his bulk, entered the discussion like one observing a great landscape from a lofty height.

'A chance meeting between Originals brought the dingo. Chance brought drought. Only a few remained. Chance brought Enterers. Has chance intervened again? Is it chance that Burra Baroona observed the wallagudgal?'

Wollerta, always the level-thinking member, turned her question to the leader.

'Why is it not possible for us to appeal directly to the natures of the koolongers and ask them to draw our plight to the attention of other Enterers? And to the serious consequences that might follow? If the bigger one carries the spirit of Ngungakatta, and the other one is wallagudgal, and because they are young, they might have the power to make a difference.'

'The humans' spirits are different to the spirits we minister to—' Unkurta said.

'For one thing,' Burra Baroona cut in, 'they don't take shape at birth.'

Atnunga agreed. 'Not only that, the spirit of one is often penetrated by the spirits of those that surround the one. Nor are they fixed in nature. They can be hard or soft, firm or yielding, light or dark ...'

'Hrmph ... even in the same spirit—firm toward one thing, yielding toward another,' Old Wonollee offered.

'*Our* spirits don't take on such complex and unintelligible forms. They're always joyous and seek only unity through fellowship of all the animals,' Wollerta said.

'Two differences,' Unkurta said. 'Innocence is unique to them—present in all but rare exceptions of newborns. And their spirits can be transferred—throughout life and through death— from one to another. Our spirits can only recycle.'

After a sufficiently reflective moment, Babbildan Babbirra broke the silence.

'It is time for us to make a judgement on this situation. Wollerta, if you would begin please ...'

Each of the yoolin concentrated on their respective positions at the altar as Wollerta, who ministers to those who are mothers, made her pronouncement, her voice lilting like the undulating hills and valleys of the earth.

'I feel the presence of the two spirits of the koolongers through the earth. If one carries the spirit of Ngungakatta, it is a spirit of the old beliefs, one that long ago crossed to the spirit world. The koolonger carrying this spirit is not old enough to have been instructed in magic, so there is no way of knowing the current nature of the spirit. It may be strong, but it is also possible that it may be changed. I fear a changed spirit as powerful as Ngungakatta could be of great danger to us.

'The younger one is pure her spirit is unrestricted. It has been a long time since a wallagudgal wandered among us.'

Babbildan Babbirra took up the commentary, his brilliant tones filling the chamber with melody and counterpoint. 'Perhaps she is without the many prejudices that we have seen in so many Enterers. But can this spirit encourage the Enterers to put right what has been wrong for so long?'

'I fear these koolongers are in mortal danger,' Burra Baroona thundered. 'How can it be arranged that the spirit of Ngungakatta ensures the protection of the wallagudgal?'

'The problem is, we can't be sure of the nature of the spirit of Ngungakatta,' Gubba Gubba said, reiterating Wollerta's point.

'Perhaps we can challenge his will and test his spirit without interfering,' Unkurta suggested.

Wollerta didn't dismiss the suggestion. 'Risky. We'd have to arrange for the spirit to be compromised in some way, shown that there are alternatives, and that the one he chooses will show us the true nature of his spirit. Perhaps he can be forced to choose a path that causes him to express his beliefs.'

'The will to change must come from within,' Babbildan Babbirra said, reminding them that they could not directly interfere.

'Yes,' Wollerta agreed. 'But we can alter the conditions ... cause the koolonger to question the old beliefs and reveal his true nature.'

Old Wonollee, like a mountain shifting to see the sunset after looking at the sunrise, looked across the altar.

'We've had this trouble since Yurlungga divided the spirits. It is dangerous for humans to cross ... we must bridge the abyss or the animals will perish before a hundred more years pass—and us with them.'

He studied each of the faces and then lowered his voice, appealing to the council.

'Take advantage. Reach the wallagudgal. Give that spirit power and courage to alter the course ... hrmph? This is a rare opportunity for a new beginning—why else would Burra Baroona be here? We must take extreme care—exposing us could turn out badly.'

He faced Babbildan Babbirra.

'Doing nothing could be worse, I fear. It's vital that conditions are right. Changing the Ngungakatta spirit may be as difficult as changing the desert into forest ... hrmph? Wind and water change the stone, so the pure and innocent can influence the old and weathered, but great care must be taken. Hrmph ... consider the wrath of our own spirit masters if we get this wrong.'

Babbildan Babbirra took it all in. He considered his council.

Arunga, placid and a deep thinker, reflective and joyous, and Atnunga with all the penetrating powers of sight and sound had both yet to contribute. The silence admitted only the sounds of the bush as they all waited patiently.

Atnunga broke the silence.

'When the wind is over the water, the surface ripples. Waves are sent ahead. The wind carries the moisture, mounting and dispersing, filling the clouds and they move and collide and grow sodden. Rain falls, the lake is changed, it grows to fullness.'

She consulted her place at the altar.

'We must gather the spirit Ngungakatta in a wind of change and encouraged the koolonger to receive it, altered and refreshed. It can be done. But it must be from within.'

Arunga was the last to speak before Babbildan Babbirra pronounced judgement.

She smiled.

'The still surface of a great lake can be influenced by a small pebble dropped into its shallows. A wallagudgal is such a pebble. Nothing takes as great a pleasure from everything that it sees and touches and hears. It can be a path to the spirit of Ngungakatta— the wave that moves ahead of the wind.'

Babbildan Babbirra contemplated and then raised his arms to indicate a decision that included his consideration of all contributions.

'Burra Baroona was not wrong to give the koolongers the power of communication with the animals of the Kumakana if, as he says, he used this pre-existing power. To a koolonger, it will be natural, although unusual. The wallagudgal in her innocence will influence the older one. In turn, he will show whether he has the spirit of Ngungakatta.

'In the face of adversity, he'll make a choice. He will recognise the fears of his adversaries. And we'll know the truth when he takes action. The Kumakana will provide the grounds, but we cannot interfere even if things go wrong and the spirit of Ngungakatta fails to show.

'We must first see the sign that he distinguishes between the darkness and the light, then we can manifest the image of approach. Through the image of the unexpected we will receive the wallagudgal, acquaint her with the sayings and deeds of the past so she is enlightened to the nourishment of the Natural Order. And when the one with the spirit of Ngungakatta stands facing the abyss, when he prevails and has success in his heart, that ancient spirit will shine brightly in his soul. He will see that all life is conditioned and unfree. Then our coming to meet will be safe.'

The meeting came to an end with a declaration that much had to be done to make ready.

Babbildan Babbirra watched the others leave. The strains of an old blues refrain came to him. He sang it when he needed clarity.

You can turn to the mountain side,
Seek protection from the wind
Stand upon the brink of doom,
Let the rain fall upon your sins
But if you don't respect your source of life,
How can you say that you've lived?
It couldn't be any other way—
We're all someone's next of kin.

The third incident happened just before they reached the top of the hill. The severity of the slope, clusters of prickle bushes, and pebble gravel underfoot slowed their progress. Lavender slid on a patch of loose stones right when the hair-raising scream split the night sky. Her blood turned to ice and she involuntarily grabbed Don Canida by the tail and yanked it.

He yelped and skidded to a halt.

Which saved his life.

The snake slithered downhill, past the exact spot where Don Canida would have placed his front right leg had the girl not brought him up sharp. It was a smidgin short of two metres in length. And deadly as hell.

And then the sound came.

A chorus rose from the bushes like rain drops falling on leaves. When Lavender's eyes found its source, she froze.

A carpet of scales, slithering and glinting like gold in the orange moon glow, filled the path a little way in front of them. Hundreds of snakes sped into the valley, paying little attention to the travellers, who were, all but one, rooted to where they stood. One fox leapt this way and that, snapping violently at the snakes. It seized a snake just behind the head and dispatched it in one powerful crunch. Its reward was the deadly injection of two fangs in the backside. The bitten fox yelped and turned in circles, stepping on more snakes and collecting more venomous injections.

'Stand still,' Don Canida hissed, as though his speech had been infected by the passing parade. 'If you move even a muscle, they'll get you.'

Lavender heeded the fox's words. So did Jerramunga, holding Spot tightly. The tide of death swept down the hill, receding into the night.

After the sound subsided, Don Canida lowered his nose to the ground and sniffed long and hard. He rested his cheek on an exposed rock. Moments later, he declared it safe to continue.

Once they made the top of the hill, the going became easier. With the moon now above the horizon, Lavender could see the way ahead. The trail was more travelled, clearer of trees and scrub. Don Canida fell back and walked at her side, appearing as though he was once again in control.

He was now in his own territory.

'Not far,' he said.

Lavender's limbs felt like they belonged to some other body. Her fears threatened to overwhelm her. A solitary tear rolled down her cheek. She tasted its salt and fought against its followers.

'Was that the murna?' she asked, her voice soft and distant.

Don Canida mumbled incoherently.

Lavender, took it for confusion.

'I mean those things that happened—first the kangaroos when they came from up the hill—the ground shook and rumbled like an earthquake—it was so loud. And then the emus sounded like thunder; and those snakes—' She gave an involuntary shiver. 'I thought it was rain. And that scream from the sky ... What was that?'

Don Canida looked at her out of the corners of his eyes.

'I ... yeah ... that's the murna all right ... that's ... that's about ...'

'Was that scream from a Gronup?'

'There's no such thing as a Gronup,' he growled, nastily.

Lavender was unfazed.

'So what about the one that goes *dal-a-goo-roo-oo*?'

'Trust me, little girl,' the fox said, carefully, 'if you ever hear that one, it'll be the last sound you hear.'

The party was now travelling at a steady pace, spread out along the path and dispersed through the trees on either side. Occasionally, a fox would dart into the bush in pursuit of a small animal and rejoin the pack bearing a carcass in its mouth. The moon at their backs cast long silver-blue shadows before them. Lavender began to worry about getting safely home. She asked Don Canida how he was going to get her there.

'It's no problem. I know where you live.'

'Really?'

He smiled. 'You see that white rock on the other side of that valley there?'

He pointed to a white cliff-side rising out of the trees some distance away. When she nodded he continued.

'That's my place. And you see beyond there, where the trees are taller?'

Again she nodded.

'Well that's the river. The road crosses the river around the other side of that hill there, so your place would be—ah—let me see ... yes just around behind that smaller hill over there. So, you and your friend here—uh what's his name again?'

'Jerramunga.'

'Yeah ... him ... so you can have some rest and then join us for a magnificent feast. And just before the sun comes up, we'll take you back home. How does that sound?'

'Maybe my dad's out looking for me.'

'I thought of that. You remember I sent some of my boys off in a different direction when we set out?'—she nodded—'I asked them to scout around and see. They'll let me know if they come across anything and we can get you together. Sound good?'

Lavender nodded, her fears dissolved in the fox's kindly words.

A large black cockatoo with tail feathers glowing like wind-blown embers sank beneath the treetops of the Valley of Lengthened Years and glided to the ground. Atnunga listened to Karra Katta's words with amusement, interrupting only to clarify a point. A moment later, the big bird lifted from the ground and rose like a jumbo jet through the tops of the forest giants.

Atnunga, elder sister of the Gronups, was delighted with the way things were turning out. She went looking for Old Wonollee, the elder brother, and found him checking supplies for new suits at the re-furring station. Together, they made for the food centre—he'd ordered a special concoction of fruits and seeds and he wanted to be sure that they weren't eaten before the party started.

Atnunga shared her news.

'Seems the koolonger may have passed his first test,' she said.

'Set a course for the future?'

'It doesn't confirm he has the spirit,' Atnunga said, dryly. 'It's a start though. Karra Katta triggered some interesting events. If he satisfies the challenges to come, I think we can accept that he has the spirit. If not, there is no more we can do.'

'The Kumakana will long remember tonight,' Old Wonollee said, and smiled.

'Let's hope so, old one.'

Atnunga darted off to inspect the feathering centre, leaving Old Wonollee alone with his thoughts.

If the spirit of Ngungakatta returned, could they channel the wallagudgal? He shook his head to clear dark thoughts. Don Canida is formidable. Escape will not be easy.

The thought of two young koolongers against such a cunning predator disturbed him deeply. Has Atnunga set up a test, or has she sealed their doom? With her, one couldn't tell. She didn't exactly embrace the oracle. Nor Burra Baroona's test of the wallagudgal.

To Old Wonollee, Babbildan Babbirra seemed to care little about the possibilities. But then, perhaps his indifference had a purpose. Surely Babbildan Babbirra could see the split in the council. Some saw Gubba Gubba's oracle as the Way. Others were swayed by Atnunga's argument that it wasn't proved. But sometimes opposition is exactly what's needed. That was some magic Burra Baroona performed, though. This *imagination* thing could be very useful.

Or very dangerous.

From the corner of his eye, he saw Babbildan Babbirra

making for the amphitheatre where the songs and dances were performed. The backstage area was below, through the opening of the tingle tree in the south. Babbildan Babbirra, a gifted songster himself, inspired much of the music of the Kumakana, but it was rare to see him backstage—which is exactly where Old Wonollee watched him go.

Part II
RETREAT

Arunga

Chapter 7

'You can rest here awhile,' Don Canida told them. 'Refresh yourselves. Our home is just up that next rise.' They'd come upon a water hole in a large rocky outcrop. The water was clear and fresh, but no visible stream fed it. Jerramunga rushed to the water's edge, leaving Spot and Lavender to follow. The long walk had driven up a mighty thirst. He scooped handfuls of water and drank rapaciously, savouring its taste as it cooled his parched mouth. He washed the grit of the journey from his eyes, splashed water over his face and stood to survey their whereabouts.

The waterhole was as big across as a swimming pool. It was heart-shaped, sitting between an outcrop of huge granite boulders and a miniature beach of fine white sand that flecked and glittered in the moonlight. The boulders climbed sharply in massive chunks. Behind them, a steep hill rose, dense with tall timber. A grove of paperbark and sheoak trees grew to the curve of the tiny beach. Opposite, some tall, straight salmon gums disappeared into the starry sky.

They'd approached the waterhole by climbing a small hill, emerging from the scrub through a thicket of sheoak and tall bony trees. Jerramunga looked back in the direction they'd come from. He could see the ridge of the hill that separated them from the valley where the kangaroos had stomped through.

He wondered if it was Gronups.

Since he'd been a small boy, his grandfather had told him stories about the Kumakana Gronups. Scary stories.

'Kumakana means comrades in spirit,' his grandfather had once told him. 'It is time and place as one thing, and great spirits come together for a big corroboree. They sing and dance and sort out the problems of the world. All life begins in the Kumakana. So it is there that the Gronups guard the spirits of the animals. It has the biggest magic in the world.'

A cold shiver descended Jerramunga's spine as his mind returned to the present. The pit of his stomach weighed heavy. He'd never been here before, but something was disturbingly familiar about this place.

This waterhole was obviously part of Don Canida's territory. Skeletal remnants of meals—once furred and feathered creatures—littered the ground. Foxes milled around in small groups, picking at bones here and there, slinking to the water's edge for a drink, observing others as they licked their paws; watching dutifully with sly eyes. Don Canida had left the group in the charge of Eddie Vulpré, who was already waiting at the waterhole when the party arrived, while he went off to, as he put it, 'Check that everything was ready for our guests.'

Lavender, cradling Spot in her arms, approached Jerramunga. The pup growled and snapped at foxes that came too close.

'We have to get away from here,' Jerramunga whispered.

Lavender followed his gaze and her eyes fell upon the scattered remains of what were once animals.

Dread passed through her.

'I have to pee,' she said.

Jerramunga took her hand and led her to a thicket of low shrubs. Four pairs of dark menacing shapes silently loomed in their path. Jerramunga stared into the smouldering eyes of Eddie Vulpré and the others of Don Canida's goons.

'Where're you goin'?' the fox snarled.

'She's going behind that bush to pee,' Jerramunga shot back at him. 'Unlike curs, she likes privacy.'

He took Spot from Lavender.

'Go on,' he said gently, and urged her behind the bush.

He stared straight into the yellow slitted eyes of Eddie Vulpré and, loading his voice with as much venom as he could muster, said, 'We'll wait here.'

Eddie Vulpré lay down, his stomach on the ground, and watched the bush that offered Lavender her privacy. His offsider, Rusty Steyne, had his back to Eddie Vulpré, and sat on his haunches leering hungrily at Jerramunga and Spot. Several others lurked on the flanks. Jerramunga retreated to the base of a sprawling marri. He leant against the rough bark and watched the two foxes. From his point of view, they appeared to be one two-ended, two-headed fox.

He laughed silently. Imagine these two Einsteins in one body, he thought. They'd run round and round in a circle, each tail chasing the other head.

His thoughts turned to escape and he studied his surroundings as his grandfather had taught him—listening, looking, smelling.

Then he heard something odd.

If there hadn't been a lull in the breeze that rustled the leaves overhead, he might never have heard it. But it was unmistakable. A sound he'd heard many times.

With a fluttering low pitched whistle, the gumnut shot from the tree like a bullet and struck Eddie Vulpré behind his ear. He flicked his head around at Rusty Steyne and snapped viciously at him.

Rusty Steyne looked bewildered.

'What's the matter with you?'

Eddie Vulpré snarled and turned his head away.

A moment passed before another gumnut flew from the tree, striking a stinging blow on the very tip of the ear. He rounded on the younger fox.

'Hey! Quit it, will ya?'

'What?' Rusty Steyne whined. 'I didn't do nothin'. What're ya pickin' on me for?'

'Yeah, well just don't do it again.' Eddie Vulpré looked toward the bush hiding Lavender and raised his voice. 'Come on, girlie. Hurry it up will ya!'

This time two gumnuts screamed as they rifled through the air striking Eddie Vulpré on the tips of each ear. Jerramunga almost felt the pain.

Eddie Vulpré yelped, leapt around and lunged viciously at Rusty Steyne, his long fangs sinking deep into the other's throat.

Rusty Steyne yelped and arched his back. He pushed Eddie Vulpré around in a tight circle, dipped his head and twisted his neck out of the grip of his opponent's powerful jaws. His counter-attack erupted in a blur of fur and saliva. Rusty Steyne lunged and missed. Eddie Vulpré had ducked and, his head low, bit viciously into Rusty Steyne's leg.

Eddie Vulpré twisted away from the attack, feinted his way around Rusty Steyne's flank and struck violently at his jugular. Rusty Steyne sidestepped the lunge and swung his backside into Eddie Vulpré's midriff, tossing him like a sack of cotton waste into a bush and then pinned him to the ground, his teeth closing in on the exposed neck.

Lavender had run from behind the bush a split second before Eddie Vulpré crashed into it. She skirted the fighting foxes and found Jerramunga gawking at the life-and-death struggle playing out before him.

Spot yapped at his feet.

'What happened?' she asked.

'I dunno ...' He broke into a quiet giggle. 'Some gumnuts flew out of this tree and hit that ugly little brute on the ears and they started fighting. Boy, they must've hurt.' He grinned and looked up into the tree. 'I dunno how it happened, but now we can get away.'

'How?' she whispered.

'We gotta go. C'm on.' His face suddenly clouded over. 'Didn't you see the bones around the water hole? These foxes are planning to eat us.'

'No way!' she cried.

'Way. We've got to go back to that valley. That's the only place we'll be safe from them.'

Eddie Vulpré escaped Rusty Steyne's deadly attack at the very last second. It cost him a piece of his right ear, but with lightning reflexes he delivered a crushing bite to the hindquarters of his younger adversary.

The fight rolled and snarled and snapped its way along the bush edge, a fine mist of blood and saliva sprayed the air. A growing audience gathered, yapping and growling encouragement and discouragement at one or the other of the combatants.

Jerramunga scooped Spot into his arm and pulled Lavender by the hand behind a tree and along the edge of the bush, putting the waterhole between them and the melee.

They made their way back to the path unobserved.

'How do you know where to go?' Lavender asked, as they ducked into the grove.

He pointed to the ground. 'We came in on this path. Look over there … we came down that hill … the valley is on the other side.' He looked back toward the water hole. 'I don't reckon they'd dare go back there.'

'But how do you know it's safe for us?'

'I don't. All I know is they won't go back there. That old fox was scared shitless when he heard that scream and the kangaroos went past. Come on!'

As they dashed into the forest a blood-curdling scream sounded behind them. There was no mistaking the silence of victory that followed. Jerramunga wondered which fox had won. Either way, it wouldn't be long before they'd be missed, and the foxes would be hot on their tails.

Don Canida heard the commotion from his den, a cave set in a limestone cliff a short distance from the waterhole. Foxes fighting among themselves wasn't unusual. At first he didn't take a great deal of notice and went steadily about his business. But as the sound of the fight intensified, it occurred to him that attention to the children might be distracted.

Or worse—they could be the objects of the fight.

He sprinted back to the waterhole, arriving just in time to see Eddie Vulpré deliver his coup de grâce to Rusty Steyne's neck. He could see no sign of the children. His angry scream penetrated the noise of the pack, masking Rusty Steyne's dying howl.

The silence that Jerramunga heard was not the silence of Eddie Vulpré's victory, but of Don Canida's anger.

'Who's guarding those koolongers and the yirri-yirri?' he seethed.

His steaming eyes looked from one fox to the next. As his gaze fell upon each of them, they either lowered their eyes or slunk away.

'You stupid, stupid curs! Eddie Vulpré, I'll deal with you later.'

Eddie Vulpré licked his wounds as he presided over the carcass of his conquest. He eyed Don Canida with the cold disappointment of not having been congratulated for his victory.

'I ... I ... got distracted, boss. I'll make it up to you.'

'I don't want you to make it up to me, you idiot. I want *them!*'

He turned to address the other foxes.

'Sniff around and tell me which way they went. Eddie Vulpré and you other boys, take this carcass back to the dens. The vixen can prepare it. You—' he pointed to a skulk of other foxes, 'wait here with me. Now move!'

The group dispersed.

Four foxes circled the water hole one way, another four the other. Eventually, they determined that the children had left along the same path they'd come.

'Right, you follow them. I think I know where they're going. You others come with me. We'll circle around and head them off at Crow's Crossing.' He paused, making sure he had every fox's attention. 'When you catch up to them, just bring them back here. Do you understand?'

The parties left the waterhole in their different directions, one leash following the trail, Don Canida with a smaller troop heading in a more direct path for the gully where the crows feasted on the foxes' leftovers.

The foxes sent to follow the children entered a dense thicket of tall trees. They were brought up with a round turn when a hail of gumnuts pelted them from above. A huge nut struck the leader on the nose. Before his howl faded, a shower of sharp spines embedded in the rump of the trailing fox like needles in a pincushion.

The pack circled and snuffed about.

The unseen snipers fired a barrage of gumnuts, followed by a spray of prickle leaves that whistled and lodged silently, like shiruken, in the flesh of their targets. The foxes were forced back to the waterhole where another surprise awaited them.

Sitting on a log near the water's edge, licking her forepaw in long strokes like a painter working a masterpiece, was Snowqueen. Bluey, and a substantial gathering of mean-looking, scruffy felines closed in on either side of the pack of foxes.

'Well, hello boys,' Snowqueen purred.

'You!' one of the foxes snarled, 'why, I oughta' tear your head off.'

'Hey! Hey!' Bluey brandished a finely honed set of claws, the fur on the back of his neck lifted to resemble the back of an echidna. 'I'd watch my mouth, if I were you.'

More cats materialised from the bush. The foxes were surrounded and grossly outnumbered.

'Where's your boss?' Snowqueen asked.

'Go to hell,' one of the foxes shot back.

Bluey's paw arced over the fox's face so fast that even a crow would have had trouble seeing it. Four bleeding scratches ran the full length of the fox's snout. He howled.

'The lady asked you a question, furbag. I suggest you answer it.' Bluey's menace was crystal clear.

One of the smaller foxes was clearly shaken by the turn of events.

'What are you going to do to us?'

'That depends on what you tell me. I'll ask again. Where's your boss?'

'Crow's Crossing,' the fox whimpered.

'Crow's Crossing, eh? What's he doin' down there?' Bluey asked.

'Gone to head off the kids.'

'Kids?' Snowqueen asked.

'Yeah, er, koolonger ...'

'So they're still alive?'

'Yeah ... 'spose. We were gonna get 'em from behind, until you fleabags hid in the trees and attacked us,' another of the foxes growled.

'Whaddya talkin' about?' Bluey spat. 'We don't hide in no trees pal. If we want a piece of you, we do it right here on the ground.'

'Well if it wasn't you, who was it?' the fox snapped. 'Peltin' rocks at us, and needles and gumnuts.' And to prove his point, he extracted a missile from his hindquarters.

'Don't know,' Snowqueen said. 'Don't really care. We're wasting time. We've got to get to those koolongers before Don Canida does.'

'What do you want with them?' It was the fox who'd told Snowqueen where Don Canida had gone.

Bluey bared his teeth.

'What do you reckon, you moron? Dinner—same as you.'

'Come on,' Snowqueen bristled, 'let's go.'

Bluey stalked around the foxes.

'What'll we do with these mangy curs? Get the twins to cut

'em up for curry?'

'Leave them,' Snowqueen ordered. 'We've got bigger fish to fry.'

She nosed up to the smallest fox and stared coldly into his eyes.

'Perhaps you'd better go back to your den and start deciding who your new leader is going to be.'

Bluey sidled up to Snowqueen for a quiet word.

'But, my Queen, they might round up others in their pack and bring them after us.'

'You have a point Bluey. But time is wasting.'

She turned back to the fox.

'If any of you foxes even think about playing hero and following us with any of your buddies, you can be certain you'll be the first to die. What's more, I'll do it myself. Are we quite clear on that?'

The foxes knew they had a rock on one side and a hard place on the other. Left to ponder their fate by the waterhole, they decided to stay a little longer.

Lavender and Jerramunga made rapid progress. A gentle breeze blew in their faces. Jerramunga reckoned if they kept their faces to the breeze, they'd soon be climbing the hill that led to the valley. Spot led, nose to the ground.

'When we saw that falling star, you said, "Yantamurra,"' she said. 'What does it mean?'

Taken a little by surprise, Jerramunga mumbled. 'It sort of means falling star, but it's like the spirit of the falling star too.'

They plodded on. Then she said, 'So what happened to your father?'

'Told you, I never knew him.'

'Yeah but something must have happened to him.'

'He was white. He never came back.'

'White?'

'Yeah, whiter than you.'

'Who said I was white?'

'Well, you look—'

'Looks aren't everything. You're not exactly *black*.'

A silence hung in the air between them. Jerramunga broke away from the path and climbed a stump to check their direction. He moved ahead and they continued walking in silence, until Lavender spoke again.

'Anyway, I'm not white, I'm Asian.'

Jerramunga remained silent, striding purposefully ahead.

'Well my mum is, at least. I dunno about my dad, he could be anything ... Afghan, Irish who knows?'

'Still white,' Jerramunga said, stopping and turning toward her. 'Still invaders.'

'Excuse *me!* Do you reckon your mob came out of a rock or something?'

'My mob? My mob came from here. This is our land.'

'Who says?'

'My granddad. He was an elder of his people here, and before him his grandfather and before him his grandfather too. He was Ngungakatta, which means wise man of the land. He told me stories of the land, some from a long time ago, way back in the Dreaming, where we came from.'

'Your people still came here, even if it was a long time ago.' She walked beside him, matching his pace. 'And guess where they came from?'

'No. We've always been here.'

'Always here ...' She scoffed and looked at him, threw her hands in the air and stalked ahead.

'This is why we have secret business,' he called after her.

'Yeah, "secret business"—so secret you don't even know the truth. I 'spose yantamurra is secret business too?'

'I dunno. All I know is that Ngungakatta said there's a star for every living person. That's where your soul is kept. Everyone's got one. And when you die, your star falls. So when you see a falling star, that means someone has died, and you're seeing their soul leave heaven and return to earth. And the wisdom that person got while he's been on earth enters the spirit and mind of the person who sees the falling star.'

Lavender stopped and looked at him. 'So who gets the wisdom when we both see the falling star?'

'I dunno. I guess we share it.'

'Did you get any?'

''Spose. But you don't know what you get. It's not like you suddenly know a whole lot of stuff. It's a spirit thing, it grows in you—' Jerramunga put his hand out to still Lavender.

He'd heard a noise. The breeze had stiffened and chilled. 'Sssh. There's something ahead of us.'

He cradled a stout piece of tree limb about the size of an axe handle, gathered Spot with his free hand and passed him to Lavender. 'Keep behind me and hold Spot.'

She tore a switch from a low-hanging branch and they inched forward, treading warily and listening hard for signs. But whatever Jerramunga had heard wasn't making any noise now. Spot growled low in his belly and wriggled to get free.

They emerged from the trees into a dry rocky gully. The soft blue moonlight drew shadows across the path and disappeared into the black bush on the opposite side. Crepuscular streaks smeared the rocky way across.

Jerramunga pointed.

'That's where we came down. We've got to go up there past that rock, up the hill and down the other side. Then we'll be safe.'

But the rock he pointed at stirred, stood up, split into several forms, some of which moved purposely toward them. One headed straight for them; two others split left and right. Spot growled.

'So.' Don Canida broke into a hideous smile as he faced them. 'We've been waiting for you. It seems you don't care for our hospitality. I must say, I find that somewhat disappointing, especially after all the trouble we went to.'

He stared up into Jerramunga's eyes. 'That's not very gracious behaviour, is it?'

Jerramunga extended his arm, raising his club level with Don Canida's chest. Lavender stood close behind him.

'Go away you creep!' he fumed, 'or I'll bash you one with this.'

Don Canida bared his teeth, saliva glistened wetly in the moonlight. Lavender, nervously watching the other two foxes pace the ground, swung her switch; it whistled through the air.

'Listen, boy.' Don Canida's nasal voice added a new degree of chill to the atmosphere. 'I could kill you here and leave you for the wardongs. It wouldn't matter to me.' He lowered his voice to a half whisper. 'Or I could let you go. It's her I want, she's the one. Sweet smelling, delicate bones. Pure. Innocent. Make the finest stew. So what's it to be, boy?'

Don Canida looked past Jerramunga to Lavender. 'You die here, now. Or you go and leave her with us.'

Lavender emitted a frightened gasp and gripped Spot so tightly he yelped. 'What's he mean?'

'He's trying to trick me,' Jerramunga replied, his gaze fixed on the eyes of the fox. 'But he's not going to.'

He leant forward and poked Don Canida in the chest with his club. Don Canida sidestepped, snarled and tried to grab the end of it. But Jerramunga was too quick for him, lifting it above the fox's head before he could close his mouth on it.

'I'm telling you fox, leave us alone or I'll use it.'

The club whistled as it cut an arc in front of Don Canida.

The fox's eyes narrowed into amber slits. He pulled his jaw back to reveal the full menace of his teeth and the cavernous mouth beyond. The fur on the back of his neck stood erect; he pawed the ground, making little boxer feints left and right.

'Have it your way, boy!'

As Jerramunga launched his club at Don Canida, he shouted to Lavender.

'Run! Run now! Head for that path, follow Spot and keep going. Don't stop. Don't look back. Spot, find the ball; find the ball. Follow him. Find the ball, Spot! Go. Go. Go! I'll catch up.'

He swung his club hard and caught Don Canida full in the chest.

The fox reeled sideways. Lavender dropped Spot to the ground and burst through to the other side of the gully, running as hard as she could. A fox on Jerramunga's right started after her but the full force of Jerramunga's club struck the animal on the side of the head. The fox grunted as it crumpled, unconscious, bleeding, to the ground.

Don Canida recovered quickly from the initial attack and advanced toward Jerramunga. A third fox held his head low and ran like a greyhound at a rabbit for Jerramunga's left flank. Several others formed up around him. Jerramunga swung and caught the advancing fox on the snout with the tip of the waddy. It howled to a halt, shaking its head, rubbing its snout with its forepaw. Don Canida took advantage, uncoiled like a spring, catching Jerramunga off balance.

The boy crashed to the ground. Teeth punctured his arm. The waddy fell free. With his free hand, he grabbed at the fox's lower jaw and wrenched it free of his arm, holding on with the tenacity of a pit bull as Don Canida shook his head. Fighting the crushing pain of powerful incisors against his fingers, Jerramunga pushed harder and rolled to the side, twisting the fox's neck. Don Canida tumbled to his side and Jerramunga fumbled desperately for his lost club with his free hand, finding the foreleg of another fox instead. He ripped with such force that the leg dislocated at the shoulder and the fox rolled away howling in agony.

Jerramunga once again scrabbled for the club. His fingers found their quarry just as the fox that had taken one across the snout advanced again, revenge burning deep in its eyes. It lunged for the boy's face. In one movement, Jerramunga released Don Canida's jaw, grabbed the club and rolled into the path of the advancing fox as it leapt for his throat. The fox overshot and crashed into a rising Don Canida.

Both foxes sprawled into the dirt.

Jerramunga jumped to his feet and dashed toward a large rock jutting from the gully. The foxes snapped dangerously at his ankles as he clambered up the smooth weathered surface. They were left circling the base as Jerramunga stood and steadied himself above them, wielding his club at any attempt to follow.

Don Canida snarled an order to one of his offsiders. 'Get up there and get him.'

The fox climbed up from behind Jerramunga, first using smaller rocks as stepping stones, and then cracks and crevices in the surface of larger ones as footings. He had to leap across a gap in the rocks to access the one upon which Jerramunga stood.

The club whistled through the air.

The fox howled as excruciating pain flooded its brain and a left foreleg dangled at an odd angle. The sound, with rifle-shot clarity, cracked through the gully. The fox lost its footing and slid into the crevice between the rocks. Jerramunga, no thought to mercy, brought the club down on the fox's head in two smashing blows. The foxes trailing behind stopped in their tracks.

Jerramunga breathed hard, looking down at the base of the rock where Don Canida's henchmen circled. Don Canida stared up with cold death frozen in narrowed yellow eyes. Jerramunga hefted his club and returned the stare, his arm bleeding and sore, his shoulder muscles stiffening from exertion. He gripped his club tight, and searched for avenues of escape.

Out of the dark, a voice he recognised interrupted the silence.

'Well, well, well ... look at what we have here.'

Snowqueen leapt from a tree behind Don Canida as Bluey and a small army of Moggy Maulers materialised out of the shadows and stood by her side. Don Canida's remaining hatchet team had parachuted into a slipstream of shadows. Only his injured mobsters remained with him.

'My guess is you wouldn't be referring to three holes in the ground, Snowqueen,' Don Canida said, managing a smile as the cats cluttered around him and lined the perimeters of the bush.

'We only need one for you, Don. What happened to the rest of your bully boys?' Snowqueen made a show of looking in all directions. 'Don't tell me boy wonder has beaten you down to just one?'

The cat moved in close to Don Canida.

'You're alone, you know.'

She sprang onto a nearby fallen tree and stretched her paws out in front, pulling each one back with the rhythm of a butcher sharpening a knife. Once every few pulls she paused and held her paws, one at a time, to inspect the claws and the fine points at their tips. When she decided no more was necessary, she drew herself up to her full height and walked between Don Canida and the rock on which Jerramunga stood.

'Don't count on your back-up team, Don, they're not coming. They've gone back to the waterhole to decide who's gonna be their new leader.'

Don Canida moved only his eyes.

'Well, Snowqueen. Perhaps you needn't be too hasty, maybe we can ... negotiate. Cut a deal, you know ...'

'I don't know, Don. What have you got to bring to the table?'

'There's the boy here ...'

'Yes ... there *is* the boy here'—the cat smiled, glancing at Jerramunga—'but he's not yours, is he? What I want to know is what you've done with the other one? The sweet one. That, I think, is a far tastier morsel.'

She raised a paw to her forehead in mock disappointment. 'Don't tell me you've already ...' She searched his eyes. 'No. She got away didn't she?'

Bluey's impatience got the better of him.

'Let me do this guy, my Queen,' he snarled into Don Canida's face.

'Yeah, you and whose army?' the fox snapped at him.

'Whoa, whoa,' Snowqueen said, her tone calming, 'we're not finished negotiating yet, Bluey. Don, where *is* the other one?'

'She escaped with the yirri-yirri when this one attacked us.'

He pointed with his snout. 'She went that way. I'm sure you can catch her if you hurry.'

'No!' Jerramunga screamed from the rock above. 'You leave her alone, she's gonna find the Gronups.'

'The what?' Snowqueen spat. 'What makes you think those demons will help her?'

Jerramunga's blood turned to ice at Snowqueen's reaction.

The cat continued. 'I warned you earlier about these foxes and you didn't take a blind bit of notice. What do you think now?'

'I think,' Jerramunga said, shifting his grip on his waddy and swinging it in front of him, 'that you're no better than he is, and it wouldn't matter which one of you we end up with—you both think we're dinner.' He looked back into the forest where Lavender had gone. 'Well, I'm here to tell you that ain't gonna happen. Gronups might be demons, I don't know. I've never seen one.' He pointed his club directly at Don Canida. 'But I do know that he's scared stiff of them.'

'You don't know what you've done, boy,' Don Canida snarled.

'What I've done, *fox*, is save a girl from your stink!'

Jerramunga counted fourteen cats.

An excited shout went up from behind.

'Hey there's a dead fox here!' A large, scrawny tabby with a face that looked like it had slammed into the back of a bus had wandered into the crevice between the rocks. The cat tugged violently at the carcass, trying to pull it free as a flurry of cats rushed in for a piece of fresh meat.

'Get back here!' Snowqueen screeched at them.

But the Moggy Maulers, while loyal to their leader, are not known for their discipline. Snowqueen and Bluey were now the only ones with their attention on Don Canida and Jerramunga.

Don Canida saw that the odds had shifted in his favour. He wasted no time.

He lunged for the back of Bluey's neck. Bluey was quick. He ducked. Don Canida's jaws closed on no more than loose skin and fur. But, not one to yield even the slightest advantage, the fox held tight, shook the cat like a rag doll and flung him through the air. The battle-hardened Bluey had barely landed on his feet before launching a full frontal attack, teeth bared and claws extended into wolverine barbs.

Snowqueen slunk to Don Canida's flank. But the fox that Jerramunga had clubbed earlier regained consciousness and entered the fray. His powerful jaws locked around Snowqueen's hindquarters, lifting her clear of the ground as his teeth drove deep in a bone-crushing, nerve-killing clamp.

A Siamese cat at the fringe of the feeding frenzy saw her leader's plight and leapt to the rescue A fully extended set of claws hooked into the corner of the fox's jaw, tearing the flesh clean up his cheeks. The fox howled as blood gushed from the wound. Snowqueen was freed. The Siamese worked quickly and severed the artery carrying life to the fox's brain. He was dead before he hit the ground.

Jerramunga studied the scene below him.

Bluey was locked in a deadly battle with Don Canida. Snowqueen, licking her wounds, was trying to restore sensation in her legs. The Siamese was presiding over her kill. A flood of cats from the other fox carcass raced to share the bounty.

Jerramunga jumped from the rock and ran as fast as he could down the gully to where Lavender had entered the bush. He heard Snowqueen's scream before he reached the path.

'Get after him you morons. Don't let him get away.'

A clutter of cats swung into action behind him. He turned and brought down his club furiously. A sickening smack sent one flying back to the middle of the gully. It landed with a thud and didn't get up. He kicked another hard in the midriff before it could sink its claws and teeth into his leg. It sailed straight into a tree and honey-dribbled into a glob at the base. The remaining cats chose to return to their feed.

Jerramunga ran with all the haste of a cut cat along a trail he could hardly see. Branches whipped his face and sharp prickles tore his legs as he made snap decisions about which path to follow whenever the trail split into two. It was soon after one of these decisions that he failed to see a low overhanging branch. His head struck the branch with a loud smack. A lightning bolt of pain rocketed through his skull. He reeled, lost his footing at the edge of a jagged cliff and fell half the height of a house to a scrubby ledge, where blackness engulfed him.

Lavender was exhausted. Brutal scratches scored her legs and arms, muddy tear tracks streaked her cheeks and her parched lips had the puffed-up appearance of bardi grubs. Spot's quest to recover the yellow ball had been unrelenting. He hadn't slowed until they were deep in the valley. When he found it, he snapped it up, bounded back to Lavender and dropped it at her feet.

'Oh Spot, you are such a good dog. Now all I need is my earbuds and to get back home somehow.'

She cuddled the little dog, almost squeezing the life out of him as she sat heavily at the base of a giant tingle tree.

A chorus of noises had travelled with them.

When they crossed the hill, a passing parade of cockatoos, big and black, wheeled across the face of the moon screeching their way into the treetops. Crickets and cicadas ground their jaws to the rhythm of her footfall. Distant thumps and nearby scratchings rumbled through the underbrush. But no yapping came from behind. For the whole journey she dreaded any signal that Jerramunga had lost the battle and the foxes were in pursuit. The air cooled as they descended into the valley. It tasted fresher. The moon brightened as the trees loomed large and their canopies thickened far above, where a breeze soughed and sighed and descended in gusts to rustle the lush understorey.

Lavender sat close to where the mob of kangaroos had thundered through earlier in the night. She marvelled at the enormity of the trees surrounding her. Trunks as big as giant power pylons stretched across the land, their towers reaching beyond vision and their split bottoms forming tunnels as big as the underpass she used walking to school. The ground around her was carpeted with decaying leaves, bark and discarded wood.

A heady scent of eucalyptus filled the air.

The image of a smiling Jerramunga popped into her head, a boy she'd never seen before today, yet he had saved her life. He insisted she leave, at his own peril. Spot curled up in her lap like a living teddy bear.

'If I believed in God,' she said to him, as she drifted into sleep, 'I'd beg for Jerramunga to be all right.'

Don Canida limped, bloodied and sore, to the lapping edge of the waterhole. Eddie Vulpré, with a cat's whisker of time to spare, had arrived with a large troop of foxes, sending the Moggy Maulers retreating into the night.

One eye was almost closed and blood flowed from a cut in the soft part of Don Canida's belly. Fortunately, Bluey hadn't found his mark. Had he, Don Canida would be dragging his entrails behind him. But even though his wounds were serious, his pride had suffered the bigger hiding.

So far this night he'd lost more good members of his leash than he cared to, along with the opportunity to enjoy a meal that very few foxes get in a lifetime. He was angry with himself. He was angry with Eddie Vulpré. He was angry with the boy, Jerramunga. And he was angry with Snowqueen and her clutter of flea-ridden bandits. But his anger was far greater at the Gronups, because, even though he didn't believe in them, he somehow knew this was their doing.

He stood in the shallows of the waterhole and let the cool water soothe his feet. It stung his lacerated belly. He drank in long languid laps, his tongue scooping the water from the surface and trickling its cool wetness down his dry throat. He watched the ripples his lapping tongue left behind spread out across the pond. In the movement, he saw the reflection of revenge. And oh, how sweet it would taste.

The old fox drank deep before making his way to the top of his favourite rock, where he rested and made plans, unaware of a pair of sharp, red-rimmed, black, beady eyes watching from the tree that towered above.

Wollerta

Chapter 8

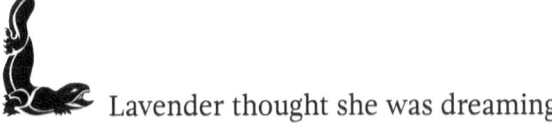 Lavender thought she was dreaming.

As she blinked into wakefulness, she found herself surrounded by animals chattering in low voices. Two bandicoots—*kwendas*—fussed and ferreted around her, covering her with leaves. One of them standing very close. She knew it wasn't a dream when the furry little animal's pointy pink nose nudged her neck just below her ear and removed a line of small black ants threatening to invade her hair. The rough, cold, tip of the nose roused her.

'Oh dear,' the bandicoot said, its whispery voice leaving a shrill whistle in its wake, 'we thought you'd get cold. You don't have much fur and it and gets very chilly here. Dotty and I covered you with these leaves. Are you all right, dear?'

She cleared sticks and small debris from around Lavender's head and every so often drew whole lines of ants into her mouth like a miniature vacuum cleaner.

'We didn't want to wake you,' the other one wheezed—the one called Dotty—snapping up another line of ants. 'But you are at the entrance of the Valley of Lengthened Years. What's your name, dear?'

'Lavender.'

'Oh, what a pretty name,' the first one gushed, repeating it; tasting its sound. 'Lavender. Lav-en-der. Lav-En-der! Oh, you can say it so many ways. My name's not so pretty ... I'm just Plain Jane.'

Lavender sat up and leaned against the bole of the giant tree rubbing the sleep out of her eyes.

She smiled at the little animal. 'But you're very pretty, Plain Jane. I haven't seen anyone like you before. Do you live here?'

'No. We live on the other side of the valley—we've come for the Renewal. Are you going too?'

'I ... I don't know. What's the Renewal?'

A mallee fowl clucked from behind a small forest of bracken and waddled to join the two bandicoots. As Lavender watched the plump bird approach, she peered into the darkness of the forest surrounding her. Hundreds of shining eyes stared back. Plain Jane scowled at the newcomer, with her brown eyes bulging and flashing, her long tail feathers taking the rhythm of a conductor's baton.

The hen stopped in front of Lavender. 'It's secret business, is what it is. And it's no place for the likes of you.'

'Oh how rude,' Plain Jane said. 'That's a terrible thing to say, Ma Lisse. You take that back this instant! The Renewal corroboree is the most fantastic thing, isn't it, Dotty? Everyone comes to sing and dance and listen to the stories.' She turned to Lavender. 'It's how we share our knowledge among all the animals. The Gronups give us new coats and colours, and sometimes stripes and spots.

And afterwards we all look like bright new gum leaves.'

Dotty chimed in. 'Yes dear, everyone comes to the Renewal. Sometimes even visitors from other places. That's what we thought you might be doing here.'

Ma Lisse rounded on Plain Jane, her flightless feathers ruffled from neck to tail.

'Look, you bug-sucking, big-mouthed, bandy-tailed, nosy little creep, this is our corroboree. It's secret business. It's got nothing to do with this Enterer. What possible purpose could she serve anyway?'

'It doesn't matter why. She's lost and needs our help,' Plain Jane scolded.

'Help?' Ma Lisse snapped. 'Why give her help? How much help has her kind given us? Anyway you should know, Naraait saw her pass through here earlier—and she wasn't alone ...'

'How do you know that?' Plain Jane demanded.

'Deary Ree told me.' Ma Lisse's tone rang with contempt and patronage. 'And she found out because Tiltili told her, and Toota told Tiltili. And Naraait told Toota. Herself.'

'I can just imagine,' Plain Jane retorted. 'What exactly was it that Naraait said she saw that she told Tiltili, who told Toota, who told Deary Ree who told you?'

'No. Naraait told Toota. It was Toota who told Tiltili, not the other way around.'

'Well it sounds like a chiriger whisper to me. Starts as one thing, ends up completely different. So ... what did she say?'

Ma Lisse pointed at Lavender. 'She came past here before the moon came over the valley wall, with another koolonger. And she said Spot was with them too.'

'Spot was with her? Oooh, I didn't know that. Dotty, did you know that?'

Plain Jane was mystified by this snippet of news.

'Well indeed I didn't know that!' a surprised Dotty exclaimed. 'I thought he was out ferreting for ants, and all the time he was with her. Just wait till I get my claws into him!'

Lavender was suddenly concerned. 'Where is Spot? Spot's not here.'

'There, there, dear,' Plain Jane soothed, 'why would you be wanting to see Spot?'

'Spot's my friend,' she told them, her jaw set firmly forward. 'He helped me get away ...'

'See, I told you,' Ma Lisse clucked, smugly.

Lavender, surprised by the tone of Dotty's shrill voice and confused by the fact that everyone seemed to know Spot, turned to Dotty. 'Do you know Spot?'

Plain Jane answered for her friend.

'Know him? Why of course we know him. The question is how do you know him?'

'He stole my ball this afternoon. That's how come I got lost.'

'He what?'

Dotty spat the words and rose indignantly on her haunches. 'Spot would never steal anything. He's just not that sort of 'coot.'

'Well he did,' Lavender said, indignantly. 'And then he ran into the forest with it and that's when Jerramunga came.'

'Well, we'll just see about this!' Dotty turned a full circle in a single leap and bounced off through the crowd only to reappear within a few moments, driving another bandicoot ahead of her, prodding its backside with her long snout and whipping it across the rump with her sharp claws.

'Now I want the truth you lying, good for nothing, lazy old 'coot. Have you been stealing things and spending your afternoons with this ... this ... this ... koolonger?'

'Ow. Ow. Cut it out you crazy female ...' the smaller bandicoot tried to make his protests heard. 'What on earth has got into your pouch?'

Lavender could hardly believe her eyes.

'Who's this?' she asked.

'Who's this? Who's this?' an angry Dotty chanted. 'First you accuse my mate of stealing, and then you say he's your friend and he helped you get away. And now you don't know who he is? Don't you play games with me!' Dotty's eyes flushed crimson as she rose on her hind legs and waved her front paws about in wild sweeps. 'Or ... or ... or you'll be very sorry.'

She rounded on her mate again.

'And that goes for you too Spot. You'd better tell me exactly what's been goin' on. Or you won't get the chance to be a father.'

The penny dropped.

On hearing that Spot was also the name of Dotty's mate, Lavender burst out laughing. It was easy to see why. Spots covered his whole body, as they did Dotty's, only his were in more beautiful patterns, in shades of brown and black and grey on a mat of soft fawn. When Spot the bandicoot, attempted to explain to the irate future mother of his young that this had nothing to do with him, neither Dotty nor Plain Jane nor Ma Lisse seemed to see any humour in the situation.

'This isn't the Spot I mean,' Lavender said, catching her breath. 'Spot is a dog, a little puppy. He was here with me, but now I don't know where he is ...'

An awkward silence followed, until Dotty, very quietly, said: 'Oh. Oh dear me. Oh how foolish I feel.'

And then she disappeared quietly into the crowd.

'Never mind, never mind,' Spot tut-tutted as he followed hard on her heels.

Lavender searched the ground for her yellow ball, wondering what had become of Spot, when a large grey kangaroo approached in a strange five-legged crawl. She could see a joey trailing her, keeping shyly behind the older animal, but there was no mistaking the bandage wrapped around its paw. The joey made further attempts to hide from her view behind the older kangaroo, now standing between an embarrassed Plain Jane and an indignant Ma Lisse.

'I saw this koolonger before the moon came over the valley wall,' she told them, nodding toward Lavender. 'And it is true, there was another one. And a yirri-yirri. But,' she said looking directly at Lavender, 'they were with Don Canida and a bunch of his thugs. Koopoo says he had a report that they were in danger—I don't know about that, but I do know that she had my Koo Tea locked in a cage beyond the forest.' The kangaroo inclined her head at the joey behind her, and then stared hard into Lavender's eyes. 'Tell me, how did you escape Don Canida?'

'He was hurt ... I found him at the edge of the forest—'

'Don Canida was hurt?'

'Not Don Canida, Koo Tea' She pronounced it _cute-ee_. 'He was hurt, he'd been attacked. I needed to help him.'

'And you do that by locking him in a cage?' Ma Lisse had taken a step closer to Lavender, and she fairly spat the words out.

Lavender stood her ground. 'I took him to my dad—he knows how to fix things like that, he's a retired veterinary science professor—'

Ma Lisse pounced on Lavender's words before the kangaroo could react.

'Well, we don't care about veteran-trees or whatever you say he is—you have no right to lock an important member of this community in a cage.'

Ma Lisse buried her beak in the ground and flung a spray of earth at Lavender. 'You have no business here. You should go back where you came from.'

She turned to the others. 'I think she's a spy—why else would she have been with Don Canida.'

Lavender wiped the grit from her face.

'That awful fox said we'd be safe with him but all he wanted to do was eat us. He ... at first he was nice, but then he was horrible. And now I don't know where Jerramunga is. Jerramunga told me to run away while he fought the fox with a stick. Now I don't know where he is.'

Plain Jane muscled her way in front of Ma Lisse before the mallee fowl could attack again.

'You were with Don Canida?' She was gobsmacked at the prospect. 'Uugh, that's horrible. Oh, you poor, poor dear.'

The kangaroo also moved between Lavender and Ma Lisse. The mallee fowl tut-tutted as she waddled off a short distance and stood, glaring at Lavender, who by now had backed up against the tree trunk.

The kangaroo spoke kindly. 'I know about Don Canida. And yes, you are right—he was the one who attacked my son, Koo Tea. But you must understand how worried I was when I found he'd been locked away.'

The kangaroo pressed on. 'Who's this Jerramunga?'

'He's my friend. And Spot's his puppy. He said he would come to this place when he got away from the foxes. He said we'd be safe from the foxes here. But I think he's afraid of Gronups.'

'Well, he's right about one thing,' a voice boomed from the darkness behind the kangaroo. 'You're safe from Don Canida here—at least while we're all here. But that could change when we enter the Valley of Lengthened Years.'

A huge kangaroo emerged from the darkness and towered above them, scratching his rump as though treasure were buried beneath the fur.

'About time things got under way isn't it Janey?' he said to Plain Jane.

A deep throaty voice came from around the tree beyond Lavender's vision.

'Yeah, what's happening? I thought you 'coots were in charge of this shindig.'

'Hey ...' Koopoo grinned broadly, looking around the tree for the owner of the voice. 'Is that you, Burra Coppin?'

He took a couple of short hops in that direction.

'Yeah, Koops ... how ya' doin' koomborlie? Been a long time. They hangin' well?'

Lavender heard a series of slaps and thumps.

'Yeah, good,' she heard the kangaroo say. 'It's good to see ya' man. You got your horn too ... Long journey?'

'A killer,' the deep voice grumbled. 'All the way from the Snowys. Had to take the underground across the plain. But that's cool. So what's happening here, man? Let's get cookin'.'

'Yeah, well, it seems there's a bit of problem. There's a koolonger on the other side of the tree ... appears she got snared by a rogue fox we got around here. She got away but now she's sitting here blocking the entrance. The amazing thing, man, she can talk!'

'What? You mean proper talk? Like you and me are talking now?'

'Yeah ... Pretty wild, ay?'

'Talkin's one thing man. The question is, can she sing?'

Four slow, heavy legs thumped their way round the base of the huge tree and Lavender found her eyes fixed on the shining eyes of a big, rotund, black-faced hairy-nosed wombat. Slung across his back was a long, well used, intricately carved didgeridoo.

'How're ya doin?' he said. 'I'm Burra Coppin ... Burra "C", they call me. Koops says you're holdin' up the works here.'

'Sorry, I didn't know. My name's Lavender, this is Plain Jane, and I don't know your names ...' Lavender's voice faded as she indicated the kangaroo and the joey.

'Oh, yeah,' Burra Coppin said, 'I know Koorda—Koop's mate. Good to see you again Koorda. Hey who's this little jumper? You were just a glint in your old man's eye last time I was here. And nice to meet you Plain Jane—are you the one in charge of this knees-up? Is it time to get on with the show or what? Seems the moon's pretty right about now.'

'Well I don't think *she* should see our secret business,' Ma Lisse clucked sharply. 'It's not right.'

'Well we can't just chase her away,' Plain Jane snapped, 'she's lost and lonely, and she's been through a terrible ordeal.'

'Yeah lady, where's ya good neighbourly manners?' Burra Coppin asked. 'Say Lavender, can you sing or dance? 'Cos that's all ya have to do around here. And boy, do we need some new material ... Hey, Plainy Janey, let's get cookin' huh?'

Spot had stayed awake, on guard against anything that might threaten them, lying with his chin on his forepaws, yellow ball in front of his nose and one eye open, absorbing the sounds and smells around the tree. The tree was alive, humming. He left the sleeping Lavender, grabbed the ball and nosed his way around it.

Every few paces, he dropped his ball to snuff the forest floor, hitting on hordes of ants, bugs, grubs and insects occupied with nature's recycling. Some proved to be tasty morsels, others forced a grimace. A centipede came from nowhere and locked its pincers onto the septum of his nose. Spot shook his head violently and sneezed. He knocked his ball. It rolled around the tree and perched precariously at the lip of the gaping cavern formed by the tree's split trunk, unsure about whether to enter the void or stay outside.

As Spot dived on the escaping ball, a bobtail lizard blocked the path, brandished its inky tongue, and hissed at him. The pup skidded and jumped back, landing at the edge of a small precipice. Still watching the lizard, he tumbled backwards, fell to the bottom and impaled his rear end on the spiky back of an echidna industriously mining an anthill.

Spot scrambled back to the top and sat down to lick the needle wounds around his bum and watch his ball. He caught sight of a pair of eyes in the dark of the tree-cavern. The bobtail gave the ball a lazy couple of licks with his big blue tongue, then picked up his dinosaurian feet—one by one—and plodded noisily across the tree-cavern's adit. The lizard's tail-swing knocked the ball down the slope into the cavern, where it disappeared in the dark.

Spot trotted up to the tree and poked his nose inside. The ball was a metre or more beyond, taunting the little dog to enter and snatch it up. But Spot had learnt—*pup who throws caution to the wind gets yelping dog in return.* So he waited until his eyes adjusted to the dim interior while his nose explored the scents. He stepped in—nose pointing, forelegs reaching ahead in soft pads, tail sticking straight out behind like a ship's spar.

Each slow step forward finished with a forepaw lifted ready for a hasty retreat. Inch by inch, he advanced on the unsuspecting ball. Once within snatching distance, he waited. Something had changed. The forest noise had attenuated—someone had lowered the volume—and the gloom inside lightened. He looked back to the entrance. Odd how it seemed farther away. He shook his head and returned his attention to the ball, ready to snap it up and beat a hasty retreat to Lavender.

But he didn't.

He bent down to it, and then suddenly drew back in alarm.

Sitting on top of the ball was a small furry animal about the size of a mouse. It was odourless, had a huge grin and large round eyes that held the little dog spellbound. Spot closed his mouth, cocked his head to one side and whined. A few seconds passed. Then he saw images in his mind. His young master was in trouble and needed his help.

Spot knew his duty.

With a surge of will, he snatched the ball and bolted from the tree-cavern. As the pup swooped, the creature on the ball leapt straight up and landed—with no more impact than a flea—just behind Spot's left ear and clung to his neck fur as Spot wheeled around and hightailed it into the moonlit forest, totally oblivious of his passenger.

'Seems you've had a pretty rough night.'

Don Canida didn't recognise the squawking voice. He looked sharply up into the tree next to the rock that he was resting on and came face to face with the hooked beak and red-rimmed eyes of Kal Barri.

'I've had rougher,' Don Canida said.

'They're tough to deal with, cats.'

'Tough? Cats? Sure, when there's one of you and twenty of them.'

Don Canida made a show of licking his wound so he could turn his back on the bird. Kal Barri moved to a branch at Don Canida's side.

'That ginger Tom nearly had you licked on his own. I've seen how they do it.'

Kal Barri swept his head into the air.

'Seen how who does it?'

'Cats. I've seen them take out fellows as big as you. They're good at it.'

Don Canida stood and snarled at the bird.

'Good at it? Now listen here ... what are you, some kind of cat lover? What do you want?'

'I want to help you get rid of them.'

'Get rid of who?'

'My clan's moving into the Kumakana. We don't want cats around.'

Kal Barri scratched the side of his face with his left claw. Don Canida turned his back on the bird again.

'Listen pal, if you want to live in the Kumakana, that's your concern. Snowqueen's Maulers are likely to be the least of your troubles.'

Kal Barri fluttered to the ground in front of Don Canida, although a safe distance away.

'Yeah, but she's not the least of *your* troubles is she? I saw how they got you in a head-to-head. He got you to attack. That was your mistake, you know.'

'Look, I don't know what you're doing here. But I've got better things to do than listen to you beak on about a spitting contest.'

'Spitting contest. Boy, have you got some issues. He out-stepped you, he out-lunged you ... and he outsmarted you when he did that jaw-locking thing and rolled under you. You didn't even see it coming.' Kal Barri bobbed up and down excitedly, as though watching a live replay. 'You need to pick fights with those who can't fight back.'

Don Canida snarled and crouched low to the ground, his teeth level with Kal Barri's head. 'You need to stop pestering me and go tend to your flock, or whatever it is you do with your time.'

'What I need to do, Don Canida, is find prime nesting sites for my clan here in the Kumakana so we can breed and be tended by Kumakana Gronups. We can help each other.'

'I wouldn't bother. There won't be any Kumakana Gronups after tonight.'

As a lone traveller crossed the crest of the hill on the far side of the valley, a tap-tap-tapping from behind a snotty gobble tree stopped him. He remained motionless before cautiously lifting his head as high as he dared and peering about. His tongue flicked rapidly in front of his mouth, but the wind blowing at his back didn't reward his olfaction. Another vibration resonated beneath his belly. Taking it as a warning, the traveller slithered off the path, retreating to a refuge from which he could assess any potential threat.

He mounted an old log near the snotty gobble tree to gain a better view. As he rounded it and appropriated a weathered branch that stretched skyward, Cedric came face to face with Snowqueen.

'Aah, Missster sss-Cedric. How nice to see you,' the cat purred.

'Well … yes. It's nice to see you again so soon, Snowqueen. I thought I heard someone tapping.'

'Me. I wanted to get your attention.' Snowqueen smiled. 'Got a moment for a little chat? I have a proposition for you.'

'I'm pretty busy. What do you have in mind?'

'We've just had a discussion with our good friend Don Canida.'

Bluey sidled along the top of the log behind Cedric.

'He wasn't feeling well when Bluey left him. But—and here's the thing—that stupid fox let those koolongers escape. First the sweet spicy one … apparently she ran off with the yirri-yirri while the other faced Don Canida and his pack. He killed one of them, and we're thankful to him for that—not bad eating, young fox— but while we were negotiating with Don Canida, he got away.

Injured a mauler in his escape too.'

'They went to the Valley of Lengthened Years,' Bluey chimed in. 'Wouldn't be where you're headed by any chance, Cedric? Some corroboree or such?'

The silence dripped on the breeze.

'Well I gotta get some new scales fitted and stuff, yeah. Are you guys going?'

Snowqueen purred.

'You know as well as anyone that our clan haven't been invited to that little hootenanny since the mardo complained about being hors d'oeuvres. Before my time, but still I never really understood it.' She grinned at Bluey. 'What's the point of having a party if you can't eat the tasty bits?'

'Yeah, my Queen, the tasty bits ...' Bluey licked his lips, the motley fur on the back of his neck ruffling slightly at the memory.

Snowqueen continued.

'So, Cedric, the Moggy Maulers are taking over the territory along the river where your place is. Now, we know how much you like living there and—don't misunderstand me—we want you to stay. We don't want to chuck you out on your ear. Ha, ha—on your ear—ha, ha, that's funny isn't it Cedric? You don't have any ears. So we couldn't do that. But there's something you have to do for me.'

Cedric met Snowqueen's eyes.

'What could I possibly do for you, Snowqueen?'

'I want that koolonger—the young one. If she is at the Valley of Lengthened Years, and I'm pretty sure she is, bring her to me.'

'That could be extremely dangerous, Snowqueen. If the

Gronups find me even trying to do something like that, they'll turn me into something lower down the food chain. Or worse, they could banish me like you. No, I don't think I can do what you ask.'

'Cedric, I'm not asking. If you don't do it, the only part of the food chain you will be, is the part that feeds the helmet orchids around here. You get my point?'

Snowqueen scored a deep set of parallel lines into the side of the log. The raking sent a ripple of shivers down Cedric's two-metre spine.

'Okay then, but I still don't know how I can do it Snowqueen.'

Cedric bowed his head as he contracted his length along the upper surface of the log.

'Persuade her,' Bluey growled from behind.

'We'll wait for you in Willow Hollow. I'll expect you with the koolonger well before the sun comes up,' Snowqueen said with finality.

As she watched the snake slide into the undergrowth through the buttercups and blue damperia, she reflected briefly on her banishment from the Renewal. Not being able to hunt what, where and when you want is no way for a cat to live.

'Come,' she called to Bluey, stepping sprightly off the log, 'let's go catch us some woylies on their way to the corroboree. I feel like something rare.'

Beyond the hill separating the Valley of Lengthened Years

from Don Canida's territory, the mighty Kulwinkulkine winds into a loop, its course marked by thick woods of Warren cedar and river banksia and steep slopes forming gorges and breakaways hiding behind majestic jarrahs and sprawling marri gums.

Two possums were crouched in deep discussion with a big black cockatoo on a branch of one such marri, a tree heavily laden with budding new fruit due, any day, to explode into white scented flowers. The cockatoo leapt from the branch and soared through the trees toward the valley, its flight as effortless as a paper glider.

On a narrow rocky ledge, about five metres below the branch lay the prostrate form of Jerramunga.

He stirred. But with his returning consciousness came pain—waves of it travelling the nerve highways from different extremities of his body. He felt Uluru growing on his forehead, where he'd thwacked the tree branch. A stab of pain shot up his arm as he moved it. The deep gouges left by Don Canida's deadly incisors were clotted with a mixture of congealed blood, sweat and dirt. His fingers were stiff and slow to move.

He checked his legs.

Although they moved okay, his left hip hurt. He rolled a little as he strove to sit upright. Suddenly there was no ground beneath his legs. He grabbed around for a secure hand-hold, found an exposed tree root and hauled himself back to the safety of the ledge.

Ignoring the pain, he tried to figure out where he was. Above, he could see the dark outline of the brow he'd fallen from, but he could see no way to climb out. The wall was as black as a coalface, the moon still casting long shadows.

On the opposite side of the chasm, moonlight shimmered off the treetops. A faint sound of trickling water far below reached his ears. In the grey umbra, he could just make out the brink of the ledge he was on, but could see nothing in the inky depths beyond. Nor was any detail obvious in either direction along the ledge. He rubbed at his sore shoulder and searched his mind for escape.

His thoughts drifted to Lavender and Spot.

He reflected on his flight from Don Canida, silently thanking the cats for their timely arrival. Once the moon was higher, he might be able to see a way out. Until then, rest was the best answer. He studied the black rock face then leaned back into the wall of the abyss.

How come the animals could talk? And how come he and Lavender could talk to them, but not Spot? Weird. He studied the stars and remembered what he'd told Lavender about yantamurra.

I wonder why they all want to eat her, he thought. Not that he was disappointed that they didn't want to eat him, but it was curious. She was a nice enough kid—though she had some pretty strange ideas, and was a know-all, but she was a girl after all. He hoped she'd reached the valley safely.

But what about Gronups? A shiver skated down his spine. Maybe the stories his grandfather had told him weren't all true. His grandfather had often teased Jerramunga. Maybe they were just stories.

Unkurta

Chapter 9

Jerramunga sat in the dark, contemplating the stories his grandfather had told. Although he had great respect for them and the histories of his people, he was sceptical about gods and spirits. But it was hard to disbelieve them completely. The mention of Gronups certainly sent Don Canida into a frenzied fear.

He looked up and was surprised to see that the moon was now overhead, flooding the rocky chasm with soft golden light. The small shrubs that clung here and there to the cliff walls threw ghostly shadows onto the ledge. More small shrubs and sharp protruding roots were visible on the wall.

He'd fallen onto what appeared to be the widest section. It petered out about four metres in one direction and continued at about the same width for some distance in the other before falling sharply where the wall turned a corner. He searched for hand and foot holds among the small crevices etched into the granite and limestone by countless seasons of rain and wind. It was while he was studying these gouges that he felt a presence above.

Two large eyes, glowing like stop lights, regarded him from the shadows of a tree. A second pair of eyes matching the first swung into view. Jerramunga's gut turned liquid as he stood and stared.

Spot charged through the bush. Smaller animals heading in the direction of the Valley of Lengthened Years scattered as he careened along the path. He was still unaware of the passenger clinging to his neck, bouncing and swinging wildly as the little dog wove through the understorey. His jaws were locked tightly around the yellow ball. He sniffed periodically at the ground, separating Jerramunga's scent from other animals travelling the path.

The traffic thinned once they crossed the brow of the hill. His passenger was almost thrown clear when Spot skidded to a halt. He spun round and round like a top, snuffing maniacally at the ground. He dropped the ball, sniffed out a perimeter as he turned in circles, and then snatched up the ball again and tore off along a path leading away from Crow's Crossing.

He hadn't travelled far when a foreign whiff caught his nose. He turned his head in the direction of the scent without breaking his step, which was unfortunate.

He hurtled headlong into an adolescent fox.

The jolt sent Spot's passenger straight up into the air and clear over the top of the fox. The ball flew from Spot's mouth, struck a tree, bounced back into the path, rolled over the edge of a small mound, and disappeared under a prickly water bush.

Spot recoiled, and was about to pick himself up, when the fox bared its teeth and snarled. Three other young foxes, one of whom had recovered the yellow ball, joined them. Spot was surrounded and trapped.

'In a hurry, yirri?' the fox Spot crashed into sneered.

Spot whined and locked eyes on the yellow ball. Another fox snarled.

'Hey yirri, my brother asked where you were goin'. That means you give him an answer.'

He shoved Spot hard in the midriff with his nose, pushing him back into the fox he'd first collided with.

'Stop runnin' into me.' And the offended fox pushed him roughly into the fox opposite him.

He pushed Spot into the fox carrying the ball. 'Watch where ya' goin' ya' mangy mongrel.'

Spot lunged for the ball, but he was too slow. With a deft flick, the young fox flung it on to another, who caught it and dropped it on the ground. Spot whirled around and leapt. But the young fox snatched the ball off the ground and flung it on to one of his companions. He let the ball drop between his forepaws.

'Want the ball?' he said, looking intently at Spot. 'Can't have it … it's ours now.' Then he addressed his mates. 'Hey this looks like the yirri-yirri Don Canida said was with those koolongers at Cedric's—the ones who escaped.'

All four foxes closed around Spot.

'If we brought that sweet one back, we'd be heroes,' said a fox standing behind Spot.

The leader put his nose to Spot's.

'Where is she, yirri-yirri? The sweet one. Tell us or we'll pull you apart by the legs.'

Spot growled. The foxes laughed.

'It doesn't matter anyway,' the leader continued. 'Don Canida's gonna wipe 'em all out as they leave their stupid corroboree tonight. We're not supposed to know, but I heard Eddie Vulpré talking.'

The fox behind Spot asked, 'What are we gonna do with the yirri-yirri then? Eat it?'

'Good idea,' another said, 'I haven't had dinner yet.'

The Gronup who had ridden on Spot's shoulder had heard enough. He flung himself onto the ball sitting between the fox's legs. Spot saw him and cocked his head. His ears lifted and a vision flooded his mind.

He darted between the fox's legs and knocked the ball clear with his nose, and raced out from under the young fox in the opposite direction.

The fox impulsively followed the movement of the ball, realising, too late, the pup wasn't with it. Stunned, he spun about and lunged after Spot, jaws wide and drooling. He snapped them shut and felt his teeth sink deep into flesh. But the howl of pain that shot up wasn't the yirri-yirri's. The knowledge that he'd snared the wrong prey came from the searing pain of needle-like incisors ripping down his own flank. Two foxes, both chasing Spot, collided, each biting deeply into what they mistook to be Spot but turned out to be the rear end of one and the flank of the other.

One young fox held back while the fourth circled to face Spot, lips taut, teeth bared and jaw a whisker shy of the ground. He eyed Spot hungrily, ready to pounce.

Spot maintained a steady gaze on the flexing muscles of the larger animal's forelegs. An almost imperceptible dip revealed the pounce an instant before it happened. Spot rolled to the right, regaining his feet as the vaulting body landed on the ground he'd vacated. He leapt and sank his teeth deep into the soft hollow where the fox's foreleg joined its shoulder. With the tendon secure in his grip, he shook violently until it tore. The fox collapsed, screaming.

The gang leader snarled. One fox standing back from the fray called to him.

'Hey, Greaser, maybe we should leave...'

'What? No way, Junior. We'll be the laughing stock of the leash.'

The fox who'd been bitten by Greaser stared at Spot, and swaggered toward his leader. 'He just got lucky that time. I ain't gonna let 'im get away with it.'

As he circled, Spot turned with him.

'Anyway, it's more like a rat than a yirri-yirri. Looks like a rat. In fact, I think I'll have it for a' appetiser. Anybody gonna join me?'

He padded closer.

Junior protested again.

'You guys ... I don't think you quite understand. I don't think this is really a yirri-yirri. I don't think you should mess with him. I think you should leave him alone. We oughta' get back ...'

'Leave him? Listen, Junior, you might be the next Don, but this is one rat I'm gonna make a mess outta.'

The fox lunged for Spot.

Powerful jaws cracked together. And before he could even consider how he'd missed his target, he was flying, somersaulting, turning end-on-end through the air.

Spot had again watched and waited. As the fox dropped into his pre-lunge, Spot somersaulted to land flat on his back beneath the belly of the fox. The fox was already in flight as Spot kicked sharply upward and propelled the larger animal, jujitsu style, through the air. The flight ended with a sickening thud as the fox plummeted head first into the trunk of a jarrah.

Greaser burned. He lunged.

The little dog sidestepped and delivered a sharp nip to the fox's left fetlock. Greaser went face down in the dust. He rose up and came at Spot, jaws wide and fire in his eyes.

He never got to close his jaws.

Spot snapped up a short stick from the ground, twisted sideways and popped it into the fox's mouth. It lodged vertically between upper and lower jaw—exactly the right length to keep them at maximum gape. He could neither close them nor open them wider.

He was defeated.

The Gronup stood on an old tree stump and watched, glowing with pride as the foxes limped noisily through the undergrowth. He heard one say, 'I did try to warn you.'

Spot's bright pink tongue pulsed over his glistening white

teeth, spraying drops of spittle onto the yellow ball nestled between his legs.

'Won't be seeing those canidas around here for a while,' the Gronup said.

Spot leapt to his feet, circling the path and sniffing wildly. An exclamation from the Gronup stopped him in his tracks.

'Oh no! We have to stop Don Canida! Come, yirri-yirri. Can't waste one second.'

Spot whined as the Gronup leapt onto the ball and stared into Spot's eyes, his voice soft and gentle.

'It's vital we return to the Valley of Lengthened Years at once. If Don Canida does what that punk said, then everyone in the forest's finished. Your young master is safe for the moment, but your young friend could be in great danger.'

An image of Lavender filled Spot's mind. He saw her sitting beneath the giant tingle tree surrounded by the animals of the Kumakana. A more disturbing vision crashed into his head—an army of foxes ghosting through the trees.

Within seconds, Spot and passenger were hurtling through the bush again, the yellow ball securely ensconced between rows of needle-like teeth.

A shock of thunder stilled the chatter of the animals who had gathered around Lavender. It split the air, bounced off the valley walls, reverberated among the trees and rocked the ground.

Numbat, bandicoot, bilby, quokka and potaroo stood with their ears at attention, radars seeking the source. Birds of all feathers sat watching through the trees.

Plain Jane led a company of bandicoots, beating the ground with their tails. Other tailed animals, small and large, joined in. Before long the entire crowd moved in a foot-stomping, thigh-slapping pulse.

The heartbeat of the Kumakana emerged as Lavender examined the trees.

Above her, flocks of wrens and robins, wagtails, miners and parrots lined the branches, their silhouettes haloed by refracted moonbeams. It was the most beautiful sight.

They broke into song, their sweet voices filtering through the trees, symphonising with the percussion rising from the ground below. Higher in the trees, magpies, kookaburras, crows and cockatoos built the chorus into a chant, flooding the treetops with a metronomic repetition that drummed into the night.

Kum-Ka!—Kum-Ka!—Kum-Ka!

Burra Coppin led a group of ground animals, his nose firmly pressed into the end of the hollow log he carried. His cheeks ballooned as he filled his strange instrument with air, his pursed lips generating a deep growl inside the tube, its percussive shots punctuating the treetop chorus.

Brightly striped goannas moved into the circle flicking their long tails producing sharp cracks that split the air like gunshots. Pairs of mallee fowl strutted forward, each one carrying a stick in its powerful beak, striking it against its partner's as they faced each other like jousting knights. The young bucks of Koopoo's clan slapped their thighs loudly with their forelegs. Possums shook dried branches of leaves and gumnuts, splitting the time into beat-parts across the top.

As the tune passed into the next movement, a group of cranes, emus and wedge-tailed eagles sang a walking bass melody.

Kum-Ka!—Kum-Ka!—Kum-Ka!

Above them, magpies and parrots lilted through a scale, resolving an octave above its starting point.

Kuma-kana!kuma-kana!

All the parts came together and an atmosphere of heady, mesmeric funk, enhanced by the reverberation of the valley, enveloped Lavender. Melodies rose and fell in counterpoint, each a separate sound and rhythm—together, a perfect orchestration.

Blow—sniff—sniff—blow
grunt—sniff—grunt—blow
Breath—breathe—breathe—breath—breath—breathe

Awestruck, she watched the large circle of animals and birds multiply, weaving in and out of the trees. The bandicoots and their relatives, some in pairs, some in family groups, others by themselves, formed a separate inner circle, each one joining in the chant at a convenient coda as they fell into formation and danced.

Forward—back—sideways—rest—forward—forward—back—
sideways—rest—forward ...

They stepped, hopped and jumped, pink and brown snouts lifting and dipping, tails swishing and sweeping.

Then they turned. Inward with a dip, an accented shuffle, a change of footing from back to front, and then sweeping their snouts to the heavens, a loud sniff like a cymbal crash, an outward turn and jump—they landed together in a jarring stomp.

All in perfect time. A single weaving mass.

As the rhythm drummed into the night, Lavender failed to notice a huge black crow on an old stump in front of her until a conga line of animals formed behind it. There was no mistaking the presence of this new character as it gazed intently at Lavender and gestured with its broad black wing. It was at once a welcome, and a motion for the orchestra to bring the sound level down.

The crow began to sing.

Deep in the heart of the Kumakana Forest,
'Neath the towerin' spread of the tingle tree.
There's a party tonight in the southern moonlight;
A murna in the forest spreading out on the breeze.
Kumakana Gronups in the shadows of the night,
When the sun's gone down and the moon is bright.
Callin' everyone to the tingle tree ...
For a hootin' tootin', boot scootin', knees-up, chivaree—
Hell raisin' jamboree, corroboree.

A chorus of voices erupted from the trees.

Wombat's blowin' on a didgeridoo,
Cockatoos crowin' in a crimson hue,
Thigh slappin' toe tappin' big red roo
And the brolga's stomping with the bald emu.

Lavender watched the emus and cranes dance a strut and stomp. The rhythm mellowed and the crow took up the second verse.

All through the night y'c'n hear secret business—
Hollerin' bull roarin' ceremony—
Featherin' cockatoos and furrin' kangaroos,
Stripin' bandicoots in a busy, busy bee.
Kumakana Gronups gonna work all night,
When sun's gone down and the moon is bright.
Callin' everyone to the tingle tree
For a hootin' tootin', boot scootin', knees-up, chivaree—
Hell raisin' jamboree, corroboree.

Hundreds of birds and animals added their voices to the chorus rhythms and harmonies.

Wombat's blowin' on a didgeridoo,
Cockatoos crowin' in a crimson hue,
Thigh slappin' toe tappin big red roo
And the brolga's stompin with the bald emu.

Emus and brolgas again led the dance to the crowd's chant.

Kuma-Ka! Kuma-kana!

The crow picked up the bridging verse.

Long ago, it was Dreaming back then,
Only spirits roamed the earth, no animals or men.
In the Kumakana Forest, so dark you couldn't see,
Yurlungga brought the light, said 'it's time to set you free—'

A curlew stepped forward and wailed out a brilliant solo, which was followed by choruses and chants and solos from different members of the ensemble, the dancing driven into wild frenzied movements around the circle.

Wombat's blowin' on a didgeridoo,
Cockatoos crowin' in a crimson hue,
Thigh slappin' toe tappin big red roo
And the brolga's stompin with the bald emu.
Bobtail lizards singing the blues
And Kumakana Gronups are doing it too.

Lavender was lost to the beat and its kaleidoscope of patterns. She wanted badly to take part in the whole strange affair, the shuffles, lifting and dipping—so badly that she didn't see the creature that first materialised in the circle.

Or the one that followed it.

Not until there were several of them did she notice the additional presence. It was the way they multiplied so quickly that she noticed first. Then she saw that they were the only ones not dancing.

Where were they coming from?

Aha! The gumnuts lying around the ground magically transformed. Some appeared to emerge from small stones. As she looked harder she saw some materialise from knots and scars in the trees, and others from within the fur on an animal's back. Wherever the moon shadow came in contact with the trail of lines and spots created by the dancing bandicoots, whether it was gumnut, rock or scar in a tree or fallen log, another tiny creature would appear.

It took only seconds—although time seemed suspended—for masses of tiny creatures to fill the circle. Some were mouse-like, similar to the ones she had seen earlier. Others were stretched and spindly, with sparser fur, and still others were smaller, like dumplings. They could have been ants pouring from a nest onto spilled honey, popping up, jostling—expanding until the bandicoot circle burst.

In their dance, the bandicoots stepped archly over the shadows spilled by the trees as they blocked the moon. When the conga line formed, a writhing sinew of hops and scuttles gloved the fingers of the rhythm perfectly. Far above, the stars winked their approval.

Lavender circled the tree in search of where the animals went. It had swallowed hundreds, yet none emerged from the other side. When she peered inside, she saw their fading forms melting into the dark.

She sat at the base of the tree, her mind agog at the magic of it all, when a familiar yellow ball crashed through the leaves and branches above her and plopped to the ground at her feet.

It broke the spell.

A bounding, leaping, licking, yapping Spot dashed straight through the circle of dancing animals, tail wagging furiously, and plonked an enormous lick on Lavender's face. A silence settled over the remaining animals: the kind of silence invoked by a conductor rapping his baton on the rostrum at an annoying error from a rehearsing kettle drummer.

Plain Jane scurried across to Lavender, her eyes black and angry at the sudden meltdown. She hissed loudly at Spot. But Lavender, overjoyed at Spot's return, ignored the angry animal. It was then that she noticed Spot had a passenger.

The Gronup on his shoulder grinned. Plain Jane rounded on the little Gronup.

'You!' she shrieked. 'I might have known it would be you. Can't you get anything right?'

The Gronup opened his mouth to speak, but immediately closed it again, shrugged his shoulders, and turned to face Lavender, his smile wide and charming. His eyes were the roundest and brightest she had ever seen. Black folding into black, depths of which she had never dreamt, surfaced with more glisten than polished rosewood. Behind them, as though cups framing ebony marbles, two ears billowed, pointed and pixie-like, big enough to cover the whole of the dumpy little body—an in-built tent.

He folded into a squat on Spot's shoulder, his thick tail curled like a possum's at the end, and his long hind feet hugging the curve of the puppy's neck.

'Spot, where have you been?' Lavender asked.

Plain Jane ferreted restlessly at her feet. None of the other animals from the dance remained. Lavender peered around through the trees.

Spot licked Lavender's hand in response, and pushed the yellow ball at her with his nose. The Gronup on his shoulder smiled wanly and barrelled his chest.

'This,' Plain Jane announced, swiping her paw, anxious to be the one to inform Lavender of a history she apparently needed to know, 'is the cause of more disasters in the Kumakana Forest than anything the spirits have ever been known to throw at us. Fire, flood, winds, predators—none of them can hold a candle to this guy.

'Lav-en-der,' she continued importantly, 'allow me to introduce Won-ai-ea.' She pronounced it as if he had only one eye and one ear.

'If he's supposed to be flea-in' n' tickin', he's spot'n' 'n' dot'n'. If he's s'posed to be furrin' or featherin', he'll be stripin' or tipp'n. He's hopeless. Mostly he's asleep under some gumnut, or hiding in a karri knot singing some stupid country song about loves and leaves. When he's assigned to doin' ground animals, he makes an entrance like he's at a rodeo. Last time he dropped from the tree— and you can only do that if you're assigned to birds or possums, or maybe some lizards or other sleepy tree dwellers. But, as you'll come to know, life is finely balanced in the Kumakana. You might as well drop a bomb as make an entrance like that!'

She threw a dark glare at Wonaiea.

Lavender had no idea what was going on.

Wonaiea's hind legs unfolded and his body assumed its full height. About that of a small mouse.

'I *am* Wonaiea.' He bowed to Lavender, careful to give full weight to the pronunciation. 'I'm a spotterer. And I'm the best spotterer there is. There's nothin' I can't spot ... even this little fella ...'

He stretched like an elastic band around in front of Spot's face. Spot let fly with a full length of tongue in a wet lick, but Wonaiea deftly avoided contact. He furrowed his brow.

'And I know when I spot trouble. And it's trouble I spot. So we can't hang around here all night, can we? Got secret business to tend to. So ... what are we gonna do? Lavender, you need to come with us.'

Lavender's recent experience with Don Canida was still vivid in her mind.

'Where do you want to take me? I think I should wait here. Jerramunga said he would find me here. He was worried about Gronups.'

'But the Gronups are here,' Plain Jane said.

Lavender looked anxiously around, but could only see moonbeams and shadows among the trees.

'Where?' she demanded.

'Here. Me. I'm a Gronup,' Wonaiea said, and grinned at her. 'That's what I'm called: a Gronup. That dance you just saw called all the Gronups. Don't they have Gronups where you come from?'

'No. Jerramunga told me Gronups were big hairy scary monsters.' Lavender set her jaw forward, practically accusing Wonaiea of not being what she thought he should be. 'You're not.'

Plain Jane saw her frustration and tut-tutted. 'There, there dear. Why don't you come with us to the party now? You can rest, have something to eat and drink. Wonaiea will look after you.'

'How do I know I'll be safe?' Lavender challenged. 'That awful fox said we'd be safe with him, and all he wanted to do was eat us. And now I don't know where Jerramunga is.'

At the mention of his master's name, Spot whined and rubbed against Lavender's leg.

'Fox?' Wonaiea said, 'You'd compare us to a fox? What fox is that?'

'She was captured by Don Canida,' Plain Jane said. 'Terrifying. But never mind, no-one can harm you here, the yoolin don't allow it—which is why Don Canida and his bloodthirsty thugs aren't allowed at the corroborees.'

'Who's Jerramunga?' Wonaiea asked, scratching pointedly at his ear.

'He's my friend,' Lavender replied. 'And Spot's his dog. He fought Don Canida while I escaped. I hope he's all right.'

Wonaiea sat, thinking deeply. Then, without warning, leapt to the ground and folded himself into a ball, covering his body completely with his ears, tent-like. He looked like a leaf over a small rock—a piece of forest debris. A soft and rapid rattling Lavender thought was loose bark fluttering in the wind came from his tiny tipi. A moment later, he unfolded again, grinned at Lavender and bounded up the tree trunk into the leaves.

'What's he doing?' Lavender asked Plain Jane.

'Who knows?' she replied. 'No-one ever knows what he's doing. But, if I were to guess, I'd say he's probably trying to find out where your friend is.'

'Wow, can he do that?'

'Like he said, he's a spotterer, he can spot anything. That's why he's called Wonaiea.'

If she'd known what to listen for, Lavender would have heard a burst of whistles coming from the tree. But they mixed with the sounds of crickets and cicadas at work high above.

And then Wonaiea was on Lavender's shoulder.

'I have just had a word with Babbildan Babbirra—he's our Yoolin-jah—he knows what is to be done to restore you to your family. He said you are welcome in the Valley of Lengthened Years, where you'll be safe. Come. I am to take you to meet him. He has business he wants you to take back to your world.'

He gestured to the giant tree's cavern, where the animals had disappeared.

'Come on. Your friend is safe for the moment. We'll receive news of him soon.'

Jerramunga could now see that he had to climb a vertical wall that was three times his own height.

The crevices in the face of the precipice provided provable purchase until he'd climbed about a metre, where progress halted. He was on his third attempt and it seemed he'd made more progress than the first two when a soft plop sounded on the ledge below. He froze. Then he lost his grip and slid back to the ledge. He stood still. The rasp of his breath and blood pounding at his temples masked all other sounds. But he could see nothing. Again, he turned his attention to the wall.

He voiced his thoughts out loud.

'What I need is something that I can climb up.'

'I know just the thing,' a small voice said, behind him.

Jerramunga jumped in his skin, whirled round, and came face

to face with a possum.

'Did you just say that?'

'Yeah. Me an' Stretch up there bin keepin' an eye on you.'

He pointed to the tree above.

'Rough when you don't got the climbin' gear, hey? Not like us see ... born to abseil ... up 'n' down's easy. But you bipeds ... Well, anyway, we gotta get you outta here 'cos you don't wanna be around here when those foxes get back on the war-path. Once is enough with those mongrels, eh?'

Jerramunga stood agape.

'You know about that?'

'Yeah. Watched the whole thing. Boy what a fight! You sure did give that ol' Don Canida something to think about. *Wap! Bam! Pow!*' Standing on his hind legs, the possum mimicked the boxing actions of a street fighter. 'Name's Squash, anyhow. And my mate up there, that's Stretch.'

Jerramunga looked up but saw only the glowing coals of a pair of eyes.

'How can I get out of here?'

'Well if you hang on for just a minute, I think we can help. But also, I think we need to attend to some of those wounds you got there.'

'Wounds? Nah, I'll be right.' Jerramunga moved his arm and winced at the stiffness.

Squash turned his face up toward the top of the cliff and screeched loudly. It bounced off the valley walls in a ghostly repeat. Jerramunga's heart thumped. Squash noticed the boy's fright.

'Ah, sorry mate—just had to call in some helpers. I'll be right back.' And he scampered up the cliff face and disappeared over the lip.

Squash reappeared a few moments later as a branch from a fallen tree inched its way over the edge of the cliff. As Jerramunga watched and listened to a small army of possums, quokkas and wallabies, heaving and shoving to Stretch's commands issuing from the tree above, Squash appeared by his side and spat loudly into his paws and held them out to Jerramunga.

'Here,' he said, 'smear this on those bites on your arm, it'll numb the pain and prevent any infection.'

Jerramunga looked suspiciously at the masticated gunk, swallowed hard and scooped it onto his wounds. The effect was almost instantaneous as the anaesthetic took hold. A moment later he was able to move his arm with ease, and reach up to catch the tree branch as it toppled from its moment of fulcrum and slid down the cliff face. It crashed into the ledge end-on and began to topple away from the wall.

Jerramunga grabbed it like a caber, but it had already passed its point of balance and he had neither the strength nor size needed to prevent it from falling. Determined not to lose it to gravity, he gripped it as tight as he could and dug his heels into the hard rocky ledge. The midpoint of the pole struck the outer edge of the ledge with a jarring thud and drove the lower end into his armpit. Fighting off the pain, he hugged it and, using a crevice as he walked it backwards, levered it onto the narrow ledge.

He wiped the sweat from his eyes. His breath came in short rasps as he studied the top of the cliff in search of somewhere to anchor the pole.

There must have been a hundred pairs of eyes shining down at him.

'Thanks a lot guys,' he called as he lifted the narrow end of the branch and pushed it up the wall as high as he could reach.

Several times he found a place to rest the top, but when he moved the bottom, it crashed back down, jarring his arms and shoulders each time. He was close to tears when Squash split the air with another shrill scream.

The end of a thick and leafy red coral vine snaked its way down the cliff wall. Jerramunga tied one end to the pole, and he hoisted it back up the wall. At a signal from Squash, the team at the top of the cliff took up the slack. Jerramunga pushed the bottom into place and Stretch, in the tree above, cajoled the team. The pole moved toward the top, where it locked into a small crevice at the lip. The bottom was anchored against a large boulder. Jerramunga tested it for security.

It would hold. But would it take his weight?

'After you, Squash.'

The possum bowed, leapt onto the log and ran swiftly and easily to the top.

'Come on,' he called back to Jerramunga.

'Yeah, it's easy for you. You got claws and you weigh about as much as a parrot feather. Still ... here goes.'

Jerramunga grabbed the pole above his head and pulled,

gripping tightly with his feet to push up. In the fashion of a tropical coconut harvester, he pulled and pushed his way toward the top of the cliff.

About halfway, he felt the pole bend, creaking and cracking in noisy protest under the strain of his weight. He prayed silently, but kept going. When the top was almost within reach of his hands, he looked down. The narrowness of the ledge below raised a sweat in his palms. The moon now illuminated the shadowy depths of the gorge. It was a long way down.

Above, a weighty quiet had fallen from the trees. A moment of vertigo struck, and sweat dripped into his eyes. He returned his attention to the task at hand and doggedly clawed his way toward safer ground. He drew level with the ground at the top. And froze. He'd been too preoccupied with the effort of the climb to notice that his helpers had all disappeared. The yellow eyes of a familiar face looked at him over the precipice.

'Well, I'll be a dingo's uncle. Look who's here,' Eddie Vulpré said.

Jerramunga's stomach turned.

'What do you want?'

'Well, for starters, I think we, you and me, have a little unfinished business.'

The pole protruded only a few inches above the cliff. The fox placed a paw on top of it and pushed. The pole swung a little way out and away from the edge. But Jerramunga's weight quickly brought it back. The fox pushed again, harder this time. The pole once more returned to the edge. This time, it bounced out of its crevice.

Jerramunga tried to find something to grip at the cliff's edge. But the fox snapped at his grappling fingers.

Another violent shove and the pole swung out into space, hesitating for a moment before returning to the cliff face, bouncing to the left. Jerramunga could see the danger of sliding away, sideways.

He would be fox meat if he didn't think of something, and soon.

A feathering whistle sounded above his head. A gumnut struck Eddie Vulpré behind his left ear. The fox snarled as he turned round seeking the perpetrator.

'Who did that?'

Mutterings and low growls emitted from those around him. But there was no admission of guilt.

Jerramunga sniggered.

Eddie Vulpré snarled at Jerramunga and rushed to push the pole with both paws and his complete body weight. A barrage of gumnuts, stinging nettles of balga spines and spiky discs from waterbush shot through the air. They found their marks. Eddie Vulpré looked up at the tree above him. A waterbush prickle embedded itself within an eyelash of his right eye. He yelped and brushed violently at his face with his paw, driving the spike deeper, opening a bloody wound. Another barrage rained down, forcing the foxes to find cover in the bush.

Jerramunga hauled himself over the cliff top.

A substantial guerrilla force of possums had taken up positions in the branches above him. A brave but foolish fox turned toward Jerramunga but a fusillade of missiles sent him cowering back to his pack. Eddie Vulpré lay on the ground at a safe distance, furiously licking his paws and wiping his face below his eye.

Jerramunga found a suitable weapon of axe handle proportions. He called out to Squash.

'How many of them are there?'

'I don't know. But they're all around us.'

'Where can we go that's safe?'

'We gotta get to the Valley of Lengthened Years. They won't go there. But it's over the other side of the hill and I reckon we're gonna' need some ground reinforcements. We can hold them off from here because they can't get behind you; but I think we'll be in big trouble if we try to move.'

Jerramunga leaned against the trunk of the tree, thinking. There has to be a way out. Surely, it can't be too hard to outfox a few foxes. He watched Squash and Stretch clamber down the tree.

'You two were back at the water hole? That fight between those foxes ... You started that? And that scream as we went through the valley before the kangaroos came?'

The possums grinned.

'That's a neat trick you do with the gumnuts. How do you do it?'

Stretch answered.

'Easy. Take a good sized gumnut—all the better if it's been hanging a while and become weather-hardened ... and chew it off so that there's a sharp bit of stalk left here see, then roll it into the end of your tail like this, line 'em up and ...'

Fwooft!

The possum's tail snaked through the air like a stockman's whip. A gumnut flew from the tip at great speed and struck the nose of a distant fox. A blaze of missiles from above followed.

The foxes kept their distance.

Jerramunga laughed, impressed. He was still chuckling to himself when a yelp from somewhere in the bush stilled the air. Eddie Vulpré and the other foxes nearby pricked their ears, sniffed the air and melted silently into the scrub. Squash hissed and two possums followed them from the treetops. One returned a few minutes later. Squash scampered up the tree into the leaves.

He returned in a moment.

'They've scampered. But we may have bigger troubles.'

'What could possibly be bigger trouble than that mangy crowd?' Jerramunga asked him.

Squash replied quietly.

'How 'bout an animal that can rip the heads off a couple of foxes in two easy bites.'

Stretch darted a body length or two up the tree. 'Hey you bat-eyed scat-rat, don't kid around like that!'

'You think I'd make jokes about something like that?' the other possum snapped.

He turned to Jerramunga from the safety of a branch above the boy's head.

'If I were you boy, I'd get some claws and start climbin' up here fast.'

Jerramunga brandished his waddy in anticipation.

'Well I'm ready, whatever it is,' he said, with more courage than he felt.

'Mmm ... after seeing how it dealt with those foxes, I'm not sure how much good that toothpick's gonna do you.'

Jerramunga looked at the jarrah branch he held in his hand. What animal would consider a waddy bigger than a man's arm a toothpick?

'But I think we're gonna find out about now!'

Jerramunga and Stretch followed Squash's gaze.

A shadowy form moved confidently toward them in a stiff, rolling gait. It was a big animal. A long tail, thick at the base, rode horizontal like a steering rudder. It tapered out more than half a metre behind its rump. At the other end, a wolf-like head, broad as a bear's, sat stoically on a thick round neck. Its bright eyes were pale yellow, set in tear-drop cavities along the skull. Round ears that looked too short for such a big, intelligent-looking head bore forward, sweeping the aural landscape left and right as it progressed.

The animal padded steadily, sniffing earthy sites and airborne scents as it progressed, long shanks driving huge paws to the ground at each step. It was a tribal sort of rhythm. It sniffed the base of a nearby tree and, apparently satisfied that the tree needed it, lifted a right-side hind leg forward, tilted awkwardly, and issued a brief but steady stream of urine onto the bark. The task completed, it sniffed the base of the tree again and, secure in the knowledge that the mark had been made, continued directly toward Jerramunga.

It paced a wide circle around the tree and stopped, looking directly at the possums above Jerramunga's shoulder.

Jerramunga blinked to make sure he wasn't seeing things.

The animal's jaw was huge, easily big enough to take his head in one bite. It ran well back into the skull. The moonlight added menace to the stripes that crossed and fanned out along the snout. Dark bands marked its lower back, spreading from muscular flanks on each side. It easily came up to Jerramunga's waist—a good four or five hands in horse measure from the ground to the ridge of its back.

'Yay, koomborlie,' the newcomer said, in a deep voice, accented with age.

'Yay, koomborlie,' Stretch said, quickly. 'What can we do for you?'

'Seems I've got myself a bit lost, eh. I'm going to a meet at the Valley of Lengthened Years. I asked this cur back there for directions, but he thought he was a bit tough see ... anyhow he didn't answer and his mates surrounded me and wanted to play tough ... I had to deal with them. But I still don't know where I'm goin'. See, it's been yonks since I've been there and my memory's not as good as it was. You guys point me in the right direction, eh?'

'Are you alone?' Squash asked quietly, peering around.

'Yeah.' The animal looked around, as though checking. 'Yeah, I am as a matter of fact. I got a bit sidetracked, lookin' at the scenery—I haven't been roun' 'ere for a while and there's lotsa' good stuff to see. Them snarly critters were a bit funny though, had to give 'em what-for ... he-he ... know what I mean, eh? Left a head or two for the wardong.'

Jerramunga smiled.

This animal was a sheer brute. Forelegs like fence posts and a face like a wolf from hell. He liked him immediately. Ten Don Canidas couldn't take this guy.

'I know exactly what you mean,' Jerramunga said, glancing sideways at the possums beside him.

The animal jerked his head to one side and furrowed his brow. 'You c'n talk?'

Jerramunga grinned and cradled his waddy, hoping the move didn't appear threatening.

'Yeah,' he said. 'Amazing isn't it?'

'Too right. Not that I've been roun' too many like you, mind— you are an Original, I take it? But I've never heard one talk since ... ah don' matter, most of your type haven't exactly been very friendly toward us the past few dozen generations. But look ... hey ... I'm open ... you never know ... maybe things c'n change.' He paused. 'You been invited t' this shindig too?'

'No. But I think my friend is waiting there for me. I hope!'

'How come you're going to the Renewal?' Stretch asked, from above.

'Ah, well now, seems there's a bit of a to-do, a long story, maybe not my place t' say. Perhaps you ask the Gronups.'

'The Gronups?' Jerramunga asked.

'They run the show,' Squash told him.

'They run the show?' The boy echoed. 'What do you mean, they run the show?'

'I take it you've never met a Gronup,' Stretch said, and laughed.

'No. And I don't think I want to.'

'Oh. Why's that?' Squash asked.

'I've heard they're pretty scary. And that ... if a man disturbs one he'll die from bad magic.'

Squash looked at Stretch, and they both looked at the visitor for a long moment before Squash turned back to Jerramunga.

'I think it's probably safe to head for the Valley of Lengthened Years now. We'll all go together and we can tell you some things about Gronups on the way.' To the wolf-like animal, he said, 'By the way, I'm Squash, my mate here's Stretch, and they say this young fella carries the spirit of Ngungakatta.'

Jerramunga was shocked at the recognition of the title.

'That's what they called my grandfather. My name's Jerramunga but, not Ngungakatta.'

The wolf-like animal responded.

'Ngungakatta is an old and respected spirit of the land. What Squash's sayin' is you got wisdom and courage. Anyhow, my name's Dan Daragan. I'm one of a very small family. You may have heard of the Nannup tiger ... anyhow, pleased t' meetcha, Jerramunga. Ah, hang on ... can't go without a pee.'

Knowing exactly what this meant, both possums leapt to the ground and led Jerramunga along the path. Dan Daragan walked around the tree sniffing at the ground where the trunk erupted.

He stopped on the windward side, did his unusual leg-lifting three-legged squat and directed a stream of piddle to the tree trunk. When he'd finished, he sniffed at the miniature rivulets tracking their way to the ground.

'Yup! We'll call this one the tree of the quiet lake,' he said, as he trotted up to the small band of travellers. 'Now, young fella. About Gronups ...'

Part III
THE RECEPTIVE

Old Wonollee

Chapter 10

Don Canida was in a black mood.

Eddie Vulpré stood before him with two offsiders who'd survived Dan Daragan's attack.

'What do you mean bit their heads off?'

'Just what I said, Don Canida. I've never seen anything like it. For a start it was a good three or four times the size of any of us. And it jumped from one side to another, like its legs were loaded springs. Our guys didn't stand a chance. With one snap, it simply took their heads off.'

Eddie Vulpré shook at the memory.

'Why did it attack?'

'I'm not sure. I heard it ask the young one if he could direct it to the Valley of Lengthened Years. Next thing I knew the two young ones were lying dead—headless.'

'So. Is it Canida? A dog of some sort?'

'Gee boss, I don't think so. It looked way too different. It's got a tail like a yongar's, but it sticks straight out the back. And then its face. At first it looked like some sort of dog, but when it opened its mouth ... I never seen a dog with a mouth like that. Ugh!'

Eddie Vulpré sat on his haunches with his tail hugging his feet.

Don Canida drifted into thought.

Since announcing his war plans to the leaders of his hunting parties, he'd sent each of them to find out where the animals would be leaving the corroboree. Two teams had returned— Eddie's, which brought disturbing news of this giant fox-killer and his brother's patrol that reported the Moggy Maulers massing near Willow Hollow at the far end of the valley. Don Canida thought this occurrence strange, but he was pleased because it meant no interference to his planned theatre.

'Maybe these so-called Gronups are bringing in some muscle,' he said. 'But he must be as thick as a wombat skull to ask a fox for directions. Still, you morons could've got some useful information instead of getting team members killed. It's been a pretty expensive night so far!'

He needed someone inside the Valley of Lengthened Years. A spy.

Jerramunga absorbed what he'd learnt about Gronups as they walked. The story his companions told was remarkably similar to his grandfather's, which made him wonder why his grandfather had led him to believe that Gronups were bad spirits.

'The original creator must have been the same for men and animals,' he said.

'Of course, it had t' be,' Dan Daragan replied.

'Then why is there so much trouble in the world? Surely, if we all came from the same original spirit, we should be able to get along peacefully.'

'Is it so in your world?' Dan Daragan asked, rising to the boy's enthusiasm.

'No. My world is divided. There are the haves and the have-nots.'

'Which group are you in?'

'Me? I'm a have-not.'

'Tell me, what is it that you have not and others have?'

'It is a long story, Dan Daragan,' Jerramunga said, after a small pause. 'I'm not sure you want to hear it.'

'Oh I've got a willin' ear and we've still got a way t' go. You might as well tell, pal.'

The big animal grinned.

Jerramunga began.

'Well, there are three things: money, land and status.'

'What are they?'

'Money is what people use to get things—stuff—from one another. Like, if we want to get food, we exchange money for it—if we've got any of course. In our world, your worth is measured by how much money you've got. If you've got none, you're a nobody. Money buys influence and influence brings status.'

'How do y' get this money?'

'Well see, that's the hardest thing. My grandfather used to tell me that before whitefella came, we had no need of money. Blackfella didn't have to own the land, because blackfella was a part of it—'

'Wait, wait, wait,' Dan Daragan interjected. 'Who's this whitefella an' this blackfella?'

'Well, you know how things changed when different humans arrived—the Enterers?'

Dan Daragan nodded.

'Well the blackfellas are the Originals. They were my ancestors—at least on my mother's side. They held corroborees and danced and sang their stories so that everyone knew about everyone else.

'Well, see they didn't use money. They took from the land only what they needed to put in their bellies and traded things with other families. Food and land were shared among the people.

'Whitefellas are Enterers. They took the land and put fences round it and said, "This 'ere's mine." Whitefella cut the trees so he could trade the wood with other whitefellas. He burnt the bush so he could grow food that he traded with other whitefellas. All these things he trades for money. With money, he buys a flash house, a flash car and he gets status among other whitefellas.'

They plodded in silence for a few moments before the Nannup tiger spoke again.

'So when this whitefella took the land, what happened to the blackfellas?'

'The spirits told blackfellas they were *custodians* of the land—that it had to be cared for and nurtured so that it could care for all of us—humans and animals, like our *mother*. We didn't own it, we shared it. But the whitefellas chased our mob off it 'cos blackfellas' old way of life was different ... They all lived in a group and looked after a part of the mother earth. They read the sky and knew the signs of where the food was and the water, and they gathered and hunted, and shared. The old people got looked after properly, and the young ones had to learn the Way.

'But whitefella said, "You can't live like that." They said, "The land belongs to us now." And when a blackfella sees one of them whitefella's sheep, he thinks this must be good tucker, so he spears it and takes it home to his family, to share. But whitefella gets angry and says, "You stole my sheep," and he punishes blackfella with his gun, or hangs him from a tree or locks him up away from his mob.'

The Nannup tiger licked his chops loudly and said, 'Yeah, I've tasted their sheep. You're right it's good tucker.'

Jerramunga laughed. 'Yeah, and look what they've done to your mob.' His tone turned sombre again. 'But that's what whitefellas do. They made blackfellas live on worthless land near their towns. They didn't share. They said, "You have to live like us." But blackfella's got no voice in the whitefella's world—no status.

'Now, blackfellas want a share of the land again and a voice in running the country and even though whitefellas know that stealing the land and the children, and locking up blackfellas was wrong, when he says sorry, he says it wasn't his fault—it's history. But my grandfather said the day would come when they have to recognise the Originals, give blackfella a proper voice, and protect the earth.'

'For such a young fella, you seem t' know a lot about your

past. How do y' know all this?' Dan Daragan said.

'My grandfather told me many stories. His people came from this forest. He was a great man. His grandfather was too, and his grandfather before him. He was teaching me but he died last year before I learnt many of the things I need to know.'

'I know of Ngungakatta—he is a great spirit,' Dan Daragan said as they lumbered along. 'But y' shouldn't worry, boy, you've got something no whitefella can ever have. You got the Ngungakatta spirit. And that's greater than this thing, money.'

'But he died before he could teach me all the things I need to know.'

'Ngungakatta is inside you, boy! All y' grandfather was teaching you was how you can get to it. The Way of the Great Spirit.'

'But that's just it, I don't know how!'

'Grrrraaa!' the Nannup tiger growled. 'Know, know! Everyone wants t' know what they think they don't know. But y' don't know what y' don't know. And you're never gonna know what y' don't know y' don't know. Even when y' do know something, y' don't know if it's what y' wanted t' know, because y' don't know what y' don't know. What's the point of worrying about what y' don't know? Foller y' heart, boy. Just do! Don't worry about know.

''Ere, let me tell y' about the greatest thing Ngungakatta ever did ...'

Dan Daragan launched into a story of a time long past, when his family was the top predator of the forest.

'A drought was upon us, lasting many seasons. The meat eaters were in a competition that only one'd survive. The dingo—y' know him? Well he had an advantage. He was faster'n my clan and bigger'n the Tassie devil ... yeah, so, what food there was, that dingo got it first.

'See, after the dingo came and joined the Natural Order, Ngungakatta came to a corroboree to see if there was a way we could all help each other. He asked the Gronups t' get in touch with the spirits of thunder and wind and rain. But those spirits said they were in opposition t' the spirits of fire and the heavens, and that they had t' wait. There was nothing they could do.

'The animals and the Gronups were worried about how t' survive. Every day starvation killed more victims. The dingo knew that if they ate their fill there'd be nothin' left 'cept their own babies. The humans had to travel great distances t' find little to eat. Their songs were full of misery instead of joy. When a family came on the grounds of another family, there was nothing t' share. The only solution was for all t' agree to limitations.

'Ngungakatta painted a picture on a stone where the corroboree was held. He drew the dingo 'n the kangaroo, the wedge-tail 'n the emu, the Nannup tiger 'n the possum, the wombat 'n the Tasmanian devil 'n the tortoise. Any'ow, he drew them sittin' round a lake, showing us that life, like the lake, occupies only a limited space.

'He said, "When water flows into a full lake, its overflow damages other things. Because a lake can only hold so much water. But when y' look at the river, y' can see that water is inexhaustible—it has no beginning and no end, always follerin' a

path of lowest resistance, filling up all the holes, and then flowin'
on. And it flows only toward that which is wet. Water itself hasn't
got form. It's the edges and limits of the lake that give it form.

'He said, "This is how we can understand limits. Everything
has limits."

'His drawing showed that limits must be set. And then he
showed us how the markings on the tortoise's back show the
differences between the animals. And with that knowledge, how
each of the animals can see what he needs.

'So ... while the dingo's got the speed and agility t' out-hunt my
tribe and the Tassie devil, he doesn't have endurance. He can't
travel long distances without water. But the kangaroo can go all
day with little water. Something had to give, some sacrifices had
t' be made. It was agreed that my mob, the devil and the wombat
would seek out new forests, limiting competition. That's how we
survived the drought.

'A few families—mine was one—stayed behind, living in a part
of the forest where the dingo and the humans agreed not to hunt.
We agreed not t' grow any more'n our total number.

'Eventually the drought passed, and the forest began t' grow
again, rewarding those who'd limited their range and their loyalty.
Everyone lived in abundance, but those who left the forest at that
time never came back. Those few of us who'd stayed were in our
own protected places. During the hard times when the forest
couldn't feed everyone, our spirits were all needed t' keep the
balance, otherwise there was no-one t' keep the dingo in check.

'See, Ngungakatta showed us that when there're no limits,

everything dissolves into chaos. Can you imagine a river without its banks? Without limit to its depths? Left unchecked, the end would defeat the beginning.

'The corroboree was secret because bold ideas can only come t' fruition if they're handled carefully. Only the leaders from nine animal clans, the eight Gronup yoolin and Ngungakatta himself knew the details. So while my mob, the Tassie devils and the wombats have been in the Kumakana Forest since, it's a secret. That's the only way life can stay balanced.'

Jerramunga had hung on every word, his attention held so powerfully that, without realising it, they'd reached the Valley of Lengthened Years.

They stood beneath a huge tree.

Jerramunga stared at branches stretching into a shadowy void, scratching at a sky dripping with stars and the golden spray of the full moon directly overhead. With Dan Daragan's story still spinning through his mind, he took in the awesome expanse of the tree, looking first at the heavens and then earthward where he noticed the split trunk. The timber broke apart, triangulating from an apex high above him. Each tangent, blackened and ragged, struck the ground so far apart you could drive a truck through the gap. He was looking at the tree through which Lavender had passed only a short time ago.

He inspected the clearing and saw nothing but shadows thrown by the giants of the valley against a brilliant moon. Dan Daragan stood silently. A rustle in the leaves above them preceded a *thumpity-thumpity* descent down the tree trunk. Squash and

Stretch leapt to the ground at his feet. They scurried across the clearing and were swallowed by the darkness.

A resonant moaning drifted through the trees—faint at first, rising from deep within the earth and, as it grew steadily louder, Jerramunga recognised the sound.

'*Woondah!*' he said, 'the sound of the calling.'

He reached around his neck and extracted a short carved piece of wood that hung at the end of a leather thong. His grandfather gave it to him when he was very young.

It was shaped like a long gum leaf, about a pencil-length from end to end, and the width of a fifty cent piece at its broadest. It had been carved long ago from a piece of mallet tree, dried and fired to preserve its qualities. One edge was longer than the other. A ridge crossed its face, connecting opposite corners to create nine facets. Each facet had a different animal's image branded into it. Red and yellow dots and small quartz crystals wove a mosaic between the facets in decreasing circles until it finally resolved as a single dot. The back was slightly concave and carried no ornament.

He untied the double loop of the leathery string. It felt warm and vibrant. He dropped it to his side and rotated his arm, the centrifugal force pushing the bull roarer to the extremities of the orbit. It began to spin at the end of its thong. He increased the speed of the twirl, forcing the instrument harder against the wind pressure, and the expertly crafted vane pumped a roaring pulse into the air around him.

Woondahrrh—woondahrrh—woondahrrh ...

Smothering everything, Jerramunga's bull roarer mingled with the sound from the forest. Its power engulfed his body and mind, his sight lost to all but darkness. The moon shadows swirled about him, brilliant shafts of moonbeam scattered into the trees, reflected by the quartz crystals of the magic stick. A stroboscope flashing around him transformed his surroundings. When the darkness lifted, he wound the woondah to a stop.

He stood before a strange tableau.

Dan Daragan was there. So was Stretch. And seven other animals. The largest kangaroo he'd ever seen, a bronzed broad-backed dingo, an emu, a wedge-tailed eagle, a hairy-nosed wombat, a long-necked swamp tortoise, and an animal about the size of a bull terrier, but black with a brown, bear-like nose and white stripe across his chest—the Tasmanian devil. It was the same collection of animals that Dan Daragan said was at the great corroboree all that time ago.

None made a sound.

They sat in a spooky quiet, all eyes on Jerramunga as he felt his bull roarer. It was unusually hot and he was suddenly drawn to its ancient carving. He gasped.

The scene before him was the same as the one carved on the ancient talisman. It all made sense now—the story of Ngungakatta, the bull roarer, and his grandfather's lessons. He looked up and stared into Dan Daragan's old eyes. For an instant, between blinks, he imagined he saw the eyes of his grandfather in them.

Then it was gone.

Chapter 11

The world that Lavender emerged into was completely different to the world from which she had come.

The shadowy blue of the moonlight was gone. This light was golden, softer, diffused, scattered shards spraying dew-misted leaves like a theatre stage. Every colour was visible in equal balance—green melding into green, bright and verdant against olive and eucalypt, sun-kissed orange and blue-veined lichen punctuating brown and burnt tree trunks that rose like capital letters from their depths. Gum-tree flowers, radiating red with bright yellow stamens, delicate spider orchids—pink, blue, white, yellow—and the rose of the pink bunny and fairy orchids ... it was an artist's palette in the master's studio.

Lavender's young mind mopped up detail after tiny detail.

Birds and animals in their hundreds mingled in the most unlikely groups: running, gambolling, scampering and jumping, or lazing in mixed knots. Cacophonous chirping, grunting and squealing filled her ears as the parade hobnobbed like a family at Christmas.

Wonaiea led her deeper into the throng, his effortless bounding brisk, glissading in twists and turns through the masses.

They passed congregations of marsupials, birds, frogs and lizards chatting. He stopped once in a while to make sure Lavender and Spot didn't get lost in the crowd.

Lavender had no idea so many different birds and animals could be gathered in the one place. When they stopped, she sat on a fallen log and studied the scene, at a loss to identify many of those surrounding her.

Spot dashed off after a gang of young brush-tailed phascogales. They swished their feather-like tails in his face and then raced up the trunk of a tree or along the branch of a shrub beyond his reach. The little dog scooted around the trees and shrubbery yapping after them, his pink tongue pulsing as he sniffed at their trails.

Lavender was fascinated. She'd never seen such strange animals. They were about the size of an outstretched hand, trailing a tail like a long leaf of black banksia. Their ears had strange serrated tops protruding from bald heads. Snouty faces with dark eyes that glistened at every movement around them. She watched them race up and down the tree trunks and along the branches of shrubs, agile and fast. They had Spot running in circles.

A bright blue wren flitted onto a branch near Lavender's shoulder and launched into song. It chirped several times, as though warming up. Then, to an unknown cue, it counted, '*brrt, brrt, brrt, brrt,*' and broke into song. From the top of its scale, its cavatina trilled to its lowest note and back again in waves of growing intensity. Lavender craned her head and met the little bird's gaze as its eyes sparkled in the moonlight. She studied its plumage.

A dark line of red-black feathers led from the beak, encased the eye and followed the crown of its head. Above the line, the feathers were dark blue, almost inky, short and neatly brushed backwards. Below the line, above the throat and around the neck, they were the light blue of the dawn sky. The throat feathers, dark purple-blue, brushed downwards until they struck a red-black band that ran from wing to wing around the bird's chest. The tail feathers stood erect and wagged in time to the tune. They were iridescent blue with tips of purple.

The song came to an end and the little bird plucked a long tail feather and placed it in Lavender's hair. Then it flew to a perch on an old balga stump, where it took its encore.

'*Chira-chira-chira* ...'

'What a beautiful song,' Lavender called out. 'Thank you. What's your name?'

Wonaiea explained.

'That's Chad Stone. He's a chiriger and has just welcomed you to the Renewal corroboree.'

Wonaiea excused himself to attend to some important matters and left Lavender sitting comfortably on the fallen log in the care of Plain Jane and her friends. Animals, birds, frogs and lizards gathered around her. Her heart was filled with an unusual joy, the emotion that comes of spending time with friends. At her shoulder, Plain Jane was pointing out this one and that one, providing commentary on who they were and what they did, along with tidbits of gossip that may or may not have had the basis of truth.

The next thing she knew, a long line of large leaves, one following another, was snaking toward her. It wasn't until the first leaf reached her feet that she saw, beneath each leaf, a small army of caterpillars bore the load. Each leaf held another object on top.

A rush of air swept overhead and Lavender looked up as a black cockatoo, its wingspan as wide as the stretch of her own arms, descended. It stood—a little unsteadily, Lavender thought—in front of her, bobbed its head up and down, cocking one eye, then the other, all the while scratching at the thick carpet of leaves and debris on the ground. Finally, it walked drunkenly toward the snake of leaves, fluffed its wing-feathers, and then lifted its tail feathers off the ground only to drop them back down again. It repeated this action several times until it seemed to give up. The bird eyed the approaching line of leaves, turned about, almost toppled, then strutted toward Lavender.

It stretched to its full height in front of her.

A long beak curved deep into a chin of downy, dark grey feathers that graduated around its face and neck to a sudden white patch on its puffy cheeks. A pair of black beady eyes was centred inside brilliant yellow circles. They had baggy concentric lines etched beneath them that somehow explained the cockatoo's unsteady vigilance as it studied the girl in front of it.

The first of the marching leaves drew to a halt in front of Lavender. A second leaf halted behind the first. The third fell into place behind the second. The fourth began a new line. Each leaf joined the parade in a well-ordered formation until a spread of food lay upon a leafy table before her.

The bird whistled, bobbed its head, whistled again, and then addressed Lavender in a voice with more screech than new chalk on a blackboard.

'Welcome to the Valley of Lengthened Years,' it said, hiccupped and continued, 'I'm Ngo-lak Bungal. And it's my pleasure to bring you food, refreshment and entertainment to help make your night as—ah—comfortable as possible.'

Lavender studied the bird with amusement. Clearly, it had already found much pleasure in the refreshments. Ngo-lak Bungal continued.

'I'm your mate of d-d-d, er d'otel tonight. And if there's anything you need ... these two will see to it.'

A pair of pigmy possums swung down from the branches of a nearby snotty gobble tree and scurried across the ground onto Lavender's knee.

'Bella Warra and Mum Darda at your service,' one said, fitting a paperbark napkin over Lavender's knees, and laying out her table on the flat rock in front of her.

'Tonight we have some of the finest fruits of the forest. First, a crisp salad of fresh-picked sweet yellow buttercups served with a sprinkling of white wedding and topped with a lightly peppered sword sedge and holly flame-pea dressing.

'For your main course, in the second and third rows'—the possum indicated two lines of leaves—'we have freshly pulled

succulent baby onion yams marinated in a dark grass-tree sauce
served with sautéed berries from the red coral vine, pea flowers
and potato orchid petals, with a side serve of our chef's home-
made pickle of liverworts, lichen and karri damperia.

'For dessert we have emu plum pudding and quandong,
drizzled in sugar orchid custard. To drink, may I recommend the
blue fairy with the buttercups, and the clubbed spider with the
onion yams? And we have a lovely sweet mignonette to finish.
Bon apétit.'

The little possum raised itself on its hind legs, and snapped
the claws of its forepaws three times, producing three distinct
and sharp cracks.

Then Mum Darda whistled sharply and the first three rows of
leaves moved forward. She scooped the first one away from the
caterpillars. It was piled high with a stack of yellow petals. She
held it level and sprang to the setting. A brigade of miniature
possums moved the small portions of food from the backs of the
caterpillar train and passed it on to the next while Mum Darda
dressed the setting before Lavender. When she'd finished, Mum
Darda beckoned her to partake.

Lavender tentatively lifted one of the morsels of buttercup to
her mouth. It tasted wonderful. She ate hungrily as servings of
the delicious food snaked through the trees to settings and groups
of animals all around her. Ngo-lak Bungal directed operations,
squawking at the caterpillar lines and waddling drunkenly
between groups of guests.

A huge feast was soon under way.

A continuous stream of animals entered and left through the trunks of the tingle trees that ringed a large area of level ground in front of her. It had eight sides, all of uneven lengths, marked-out with ochres of different hues and unfamiliar symbols. As Lavender ate and drank, a dark shadow fell. The markings on the trunks glowed like ghostly icing on a huge cake. All noise ceased. Not one leaf rustled. Not one footfall sounded. Nobody chewed.

Then, the loudest thunderclap Lavender had ever heard split the air and shook the earth. At the same time, a streak of lightning lit the symbols around the ground. Mantles in a huge lamp glowed and fused and a white river of light surged through a gully of shadow. The image, although as transient as the silence and the thunderclap, was frozen in an instant of light.

One pattern of light swirled through the arena and linked each symbol in an unbroken chain. Another snaked in a sequence with a definite beginning and end. There was a fluid oval and a pointed star of light. Each only lasted a split second but the effect on Lavender's mind was as permanent as a photograph. A snapshot of all life. Somehow she knew it was just for her.

Then the crow whose song paved the entrance through the tingle tree appeared.

He was a large bird with a powerful, sharp and pointed beak, his colouring so black that he wore an ebony sheen in the dark, matched only by the glow in the centre of his eyes. Eyes of stone cold marble. He cocked his head first to one side and then the other, as if to get a clearer view, or to confirm that what he saw from one eye was the same as what he saw from the other. When he spoke, his voice was deep and croaky like a crow's call, but his tone was soft, gentle, oddly poetic.

Welcome to our sacred ground, my name is Wardong Warn Bro—
All these gathered here around, are all folks that I know.
My family is the wardong, but I know you call me crow,
For it's me, who, every morning, sings to bring the sunglow.

I'm not the type of wardong who flies the line straight;
They're my cousins, the Ravens—Thorpe, Wood and Gate,
And there are other cousins I have—out east in hotter, bluer skies,
The ones who're flying backwards to keep the dust out of their eyes.

Now my master, and may the spirits bless him for being true,
Babbildan Babbirra, he is called, has asked me to show to you
The Kumakana and all its wonders, a side of life you never knew
And explain our corroboree, the story of how we renew.

But before our stories can begin, there are things we must know
Like the name that you've been given, and the roots from which you grow,
And how it is you are placed with us in this sacred ground tonight,
For this is a dark and deadly place, and you are one who is of the light.

So, please, tell us now—and tell it loud so all in here can know—
The name that you've been given and the seeds from which you grow.
Come forward into the light and address all the folk you can see;
Dance or sing the story of your line, and draw for us your family tree.

Warn Bro beckoned Lavender to join him in the arena. She took tentative steps to the edge, where she felt herself touched by the soft light. She moved to the middle. The dark of the centre swallowed her. The eyes of the audience examined her. At first her voice was lost deep in her throat, overshadowed by her beating heart. But she took a deep breath and let it pour out.

'My name is Lavender. I live in the city, but my dad's got a farm and I'm staying with him. I got lost in the forest before the sun went down and he's gonna be really mad at me for that. And because some magpie pinched my earbuds—is he here? 'Cos I've got things to say to him ...'

She looked around, but could only see darkness.

'Anyway, then my friend's dog, Spot, pinched my ball—Jerramunga, that's my friend—well he wasn't my friend at first but now he is because he fought Don Canida ... but I don't know what happened to him. Do you know? Wonaiea says he's all right, but I need to find him. Anyway, then I woke up under that great big tree and Plain Jane and Dotty were there and then you came and sang that song and, and then Wonaiea brought me in here ...'

Her words petered out.

'Anyway,' she said at length, 'please tell me what the corroboree's for?'

The crow strutted forward.

Our corroboree
Young Lavender—
Ball and earbud chaser—
Is when the forest folk all come and gather,

And all night yaller-yaller.
Each bring their tales and singing sticks,
Their share of joy and woe
And talk among the folk who gather,
Friends of wing and scale and toe.

A corroboree
Is their song; their dance,
An ancient art in rhyme.
It's a way we look at things that have passed,
An interpretating time.
For once you know what's gone before,
How the winds've honed the stone,
Then you'll know all that is to come,
And the road the futures roam.

A corroboree
Is a magic art
Where the sorcerer prevails
And snakes and lizards twist and weave
And spin their likely tales.
Dammalaks fluff and chirigers puff
And widgis stomp the ground
And among the murna of the night
Spirits and spirits abound.

A corroboree
Is a sign of change
Of cycles and sequent time
When a council sits and plans ahead
And the yoolin judge on crime.
And the sacred ground feels the thousand feet
Pound upon the earth

And beneath the pounding rhythm
The spirits bring forth the birth.

A corroboree, Friend Lavender
Ball and earbud chaser—
Is when the folks all come, gather round
Chukkup and twonk and all night yaller-yaller.
It is to celebrate all life itself
Births and deaths and in-betweens
And to bring about the new beginning
That follows the end of every scene.

Warn Bro stepped back as his verse came to an end. The shadows swallowed him. Plain Jane led Lavender back to her seat on the fallen log. The light darkened and from the depths of the arena came a new rhythm.

Boondah, woondah, boona-dah-da; tap-tap-tap
Woondah, boonadah, tj-tj-tj!
Boondah, woondah, boona-dah-da; tap-tap-tap
Woondah, boonadah, tj-tj-tj!

A dark shape—marginally lighter than black—walked into the arena on four stout legs. It was as long as a big dog and barely visible on the darkened stage. An intricate pattern of bands and spots covered its back. Trailing behind was, what looked to Lavender, a long whip-tail. It danced around the arena, side—forward—backwards—side, pausing at each symbol along the edges, standing erect on its hind legs before bowing deeply.

When it finally found the centre, only the dots and stripes that accented its facial features could be seen glowing in the dark. The apparition was intriguing and grotesque. The rhythm swelled and

a length of brilliant orange light snaked from its mouth toward
Lavender. A dark, sonorous voice boomed.

*There are stories that tell of how the world began ... And then
there are stories that tell of how all living things grew into what
they are today.*

The rhythm pounded into the night.

*Your eyes cannot see how dark everything was before there was
light, but such darkness did prevail, for there was no sun to
light the day, there was no moon to light the night, and there
were no stars in the sky-world. And in that darkness, all the
spirits were held prisoner. Though they had done no wrong,
neither had they done right. Ever since the beginning of time,
they had done nothing other than roam the earth and bump into
each other.*

*'What is the purpose of this?' they asked. 'For what reason do
we roam? What is our function?' One day the greatest of all
spirits summoned them to gather round.*

*'I am Yurlungga,' the Great Spirit announced. 'You have asked
many questions, and I am here to tell you that you are soon to be
released.'*

*When they were released, half were taken into the sky and the
other half buried in the earth. Together, they were to bring life
to the earth.*

'What is this life?' the spirits asked. 'What form shall it take?'

*'Life is change,' Yurlungga told them. 'And change is life. It will
take the form of those who can walk upon the earth, swim in the
seas and fly through the air, and these forms will be visible to all*

others.

'First there will come the change of the dark to the light; then
will be the change of dry to wet. After that will come the change
of the small and insignificant to the great and mighty, from
which will come the change from the old to the new, and finally
the change of the soft to the hard, which in turn will renew the
light. This is a cycle of change.

'But a cycle of change must also have a sequence of change. The
great and mighty can be cut down by that which is hard; the
hard can be melted by the light; the light can be smothered by
the wet; the wet can be muddied by the renewed, and the new
can lose all its goodness to the great and mighty.

'The cycles are immutable, but the sequences are yours to
control. And as one will act upon the other, it will create
balance. It is up to you to maintain the balance: that is your
purpose.'

And then Yurlungga left them to wait in their world of
darkness, until the time came when they would be released.

Boondah, woondah, boona-dah-da; tap-tap-tap
Woondah, boonadah, tj-tj-tj!

The pulses of the rhythm faded into silence. Then new sounds,
like the roar of wind and the pulse of falling rain, came.

Dalagooroo-oo, dalagooroo-oo ... Gab-bi-gab-bi-Gab-bi-gura-jyt
Dalagooroo-oo, dalagooroo-oo ... Bid-ji-bid-ji-Bid-ji-roon-go,

Although the air was still, the rhythm conjured a howling gale
that thrashed through the trees, drove heavy rain onto the leaves,

forming rivulets that poured in aerial streams to the ground. The air chilled and Lavender once again sensed movement within the dark arena. The rhythm of the rain pounded on.

Dalagooroo-oo, dalagooroo-oo ... Gab-bi-gab-bi-Gab-bi-gura-jyt
Dalagooroo-oo, dalagooroo-oo ... Bid-ji-bid-ji-Bid-ji-roon-go,

A cacophony of kookaburras broke the spell. A single call in a low register purred out, followed by a cackling staccato.

Dalagooroo-oo, dalagooroo-oo...
Goor-goor-goor...
Gab-bi-, gab-bi-, Gab-bi-gura-jyt
Ga-ga-ga-ga-ga...

The area was sprinkled in red, yellow and white dots, each one pulsing in its place. As the rhythm bore on, more dots joined the chain. The image of a wriggling snake emerged.

A chorus of whispering voices rose from the depths of the arena.

Yurlungga, Yurlungga,
Move to the left, move to the right.
Yurlungga, Yurlungga,
Make the mountains, make the rivers.
Yurlungga, Yurlungga,
Rise from the depths, rise from the soul.
Yurlungga, Yurlungga,
Bring the warmth, take away the cold.
Yurlungga, Yurlungga,
Give us the light, take away the night.

The dots vibrated faster, squashing and stretching and blurring and then fusing into a single line, spiralling into a tight curl. The rhythm pounded. The tight spiral became a brilliant ball, shot into the sky and exploded to drip among the stars.

Tumultuous applause rose from the audience. Lavender was awestruck. She turned and shouted to Plain Jane over the roar.

'That was fantastic.'

The bandicoot was on her hind legs clapping her forepaws and cheering.

The applause eventually died down, the arena darkened again. Lavender's insides were aglow as silence descended on the corroboree.

Don Canida passed through a treeless limestone outcrop beneath the moon's muted hue and entered the Gully of Six Curses. The trees that lined the perimeter kept the centre hidden from view. But they were dead trees. Petrified. Unmoving relics of a time long past, permanently calcified, untouched even by termites. The gully had no water running through it, nor any evidence of an underground source near its surface. The surface was crusty and crumbling underfoot with ridges, sometimes sharp, sometimes chalky, where shales of mica formed and strange fungi took root and died shortly after. It was a dead place in which everything fossilised before it atrophied. Its trees hosted no life. Snakes sometimes crawled through but they never stayed long.

The outcrop in the centre housed the entrance to a cave

system, a labyrinthine network of tunnels and deep, underground lakes. The caves were etched into the land from the coast, burnt through stone like acid through cloth.

To enter, Don Canida had to negotiate a narrow path between six calcified boulders, giant ping-pong balls rooted in place, named by the forest occupants who had refused to go there for millennia.

The first, the largest stone, served as a visual deterrent to anyone wanting to enter. Parents would tell their children, 'That boulder marks an evil place. Never go there.'

According to legend, a spirit came to the land and made his mark upon the soil there. He announced that if anyone should ever wish to bring the wrath of the spirits upon another, they should stand on this rock and shout their curse to the wind. The curse would be borne through the trees until it reached the ears of the one who was to be cursed.

Many had come and stood on the first of the devil's stones but, as they shouted their wish to bring evil upon another, they were consumed by the rock. Its size grew as more layers were added to its surface.

A second, smaller rock stood behind it. It had been cast at the first from heaven, a censure for trickery, a curse upon the first rock.

Next to this was a third. It was a similar size, but flattened like dough thrown against a kneading board. Ejected from a nearby mountain in a torrent of fire and thrown at the second rock, it missed its target, leaving a narrow passage between the two. You couldn't pass without touching the sides of both. The third stone became, forever, the curse of the profane oath.

A fourth boulder, this much larger, sat in the path at the end of the passage between the second and third. It was round with sides so smooth and slippery that it could not be climbed by anything—not a rock wallaby, a lizard or even an ant. Should the smallest of wrens so much as attempt to alight on it, it would slide off. This fourth stone was the curse of the evil evoked.

The fifth rock was a flat slab with the largest diameter of all. Its surface was coarse, like a rasp, with so many channels carved into its sides that any water that fell on it instantly drained away. It met the ground in smooth cemented joins, so no moisture could gather beneath. This was the curse of blood flow.

The one remaining rock stood at the entrance to the cave.

It is smaller than the others, a pebble compared to some. It stands freely on its narrow edge like a wheel. It is said that it shifts position of its own volition, sometimes leaving the opening clear, other times closing it completely.

According to the legend, if those who wish to enter the cave face a closed entrance, they can only move the stone if they wish in their heart a terrible evil, calamity or injury upon others. If this is the case, the stone will move at the slightest touch. If not, no amount of force can shift it.

Don Canida faced a closed opening.

His tail had brushed the second and third rocks as he passed. He was touched by the heavenly stone and had issued a profanity. Now he nosed the circle of stone in front of him. It rolled easily to one side.

The ultimate curse was his to command.

The cave was dank and musty, and the air carried the stench of guano. No light penetrated from the outside and, as he ventured into the cavern, the stone at the entrance rolled back across the opening, barring all but the smallest of exits.

Don Canida waited a moment at the top of the narrow pathway that led down into the cavern to let his eyes adjust. The walls sweated water that emitted a faint phosphorescence. The pathway to the floor of the first cavern was not well trodden. It fell steeply but Don Canida knew the way.

He came upon a level floor. The stench of decay was stronger and, guided by the scent, he tracked around the edge of the still waters of a deep pool. He strode carefully though an opening into a low, narrow passage. It rose steeply at first, then fell again as it twisted left, right and left before widening. The ceiling lifted away and he was in a huge underground chamber.

The roof was far above, near the surface of the earth. Don Canida knew there must be another entrance through the ceiling, for the air was fresher—even though the smell of rot surrounded him. In the dim light he saw an accumulated mass of small bones and feathers beneath a ledge. He sniffed his way from one pile of dead animal bits to the next. He was satisfied that he was in the right place.

He called out.

Shocking reverberations of his own call answered, striking back with an intensity that folded over onto itself. Short repeats one upon the other bounced off the walls, floor and ceiling. When they died away, a ghostly silence and the metronomic drip of calcified water was all that remained.

He smelt fresh blood.

But still he was made to wait. He knew that impatience would get him nowhere. A moment later a high-pitched scream sounded from somewhere near the ceiling. Like his call, it too bounced around the chamber, forcing the fur on Don Canida's back to leap involuntarily to attention. Powerful wings beat the air above him and a high-pitched cackle laughed in his ears.

'Timing, Don Canida. Timing is everything!'

The screechy tones were painful to the fox's ears.

'I heard you coming. But even though you expected me to be here, my little pause made you just uncertain enough. Timing, you see, if you know how to use it, it can work wonders. Did the stone open by itself, or did you have to move it?'

'Well now, that would be telling,' the fox replied, sitting back on his haunches.

'It's a silly question anyway. Who would you have cursed?'

'I curse the Gronups.'

The hollow echo of dripping water filled the chamber as, drop by drop, stalagmites grew on the floor. Don Canida let the weight of his answer fall. At this delicate point, the first to speak will have the disadvantage.

He, too, knew the value of timing.

The dark and heavy silence continued while Don Canida waited. Eventually, it was broken by the shrill voice above him.

'The Gronups cannot be cursed—they are agents of the spirits.'

'Then,' Don Canida said slowly, 'all the animals of the Kumakana must be cursed.'

'*All* the animals?'

'All, except the bats. And the foxes, of course.'

'Aah, yes I see,' returned the voice, softening slightly. 'Could be very expensive, Don Canida.'

'Whatever the price, I will pay.'

'But how, if the price is too high?'

'What price could be too high to rid the forest of those demons?'

Don Canida snarled toward the overhang, still unable to see the owner of the voice.

'I didn't think you believed in them.'

'I don't. But all the forest does. It would be better all round if they believed in me.'

'Hmmm. I see. How exactly do you propose to bring down your curse?'

'I thought that was your job.'

'Perhaps. What I mean is ... what exactly you would have me do? Then I'll give you a price and you can figure out how you're going to meet it. Of course, now that you've entered here with a curse in your heart, you can't leave without setting it in motion ... unless you want to suffer your own curse. Or you choose to leave by the curse of flowing blood.'

Don Canida snarled. The voice continued.

'Yeah. I presumed that would defeat the purpose. So ...

enlighten me ... what are your plans?'

Don Canida explained what he'd encountered earlier in the night, and the solution he proposed. When he finished, he stood and stretched his hind legs, waiting for the response from the darkness.

When it came, it was a shrill cackle.

'Preposterous, Don Canida. Preposterous. Leave here at once and bear your own curse upon yourself. Unless of course you wish to drown in your own blood.'

Don Canida was shocked. He had not expected such rejection. He snapped at the dark ledge.

'You snivelling inverted rodent. How dare you insult me? We share the same blood lust, we have the same needs. You will regret mocking me. Tonight, the rivers of this forest will flow with the blood of all who live in it. I, and my family, will consume all the meat and you will starve. It will be an agonising end— long, slow. How many more losses do you think your species can sustain? After tonight, it will not only be you who's finished, it will be your entire species. You will go the way of the dragon.'

'Your threats are idle, Don Canida—and meaningless. But you have alternatives. You should be aware of them, for the price of this curse is well beyond your capacity to pay. You must be very sure of your commitment.'

'What choice?'

'Well, you could join the Natural Order ...'

Don Canida spat. 'The Natural Order? The Natural Order is for the dammalaks and woylies and woggals and yongars and numbats and wombats. It's not for foxes. If I wanted to join the Natural Order, I wouldn't be here, you idiot!'

'Well, okay, that's settled. Don Canida, I am duty bound to honour your request. But my price is take-it-or-leave-it. No haggling.'

The voice outlined the conditions of the bargain.

Don Canida accepted them and left the way he had entered.

As he passed through the narrow passage back to the first cave, a chorus of shrill screams reached his ears. A strange smile stretched his jaw. Bargains are made to be broken. So what if he didn't intend to keep his side of the bargain? What can a solitary ghost bat do to him? He is Don Canida, all-powerful leader of the biggest family in the Kumakana; feared by all. The best thing he'd ever done was banish the ghost bats. He'd used their own curse against them. Oh he'd been sly, cunning and very, very foxy. He'd had them locked in a cave up north, guarded by his cousins. Like he'd really let them return? Those monsters would decimate his food supply overnight.

The entry to the cave was no longer covered. The curse was already in motion. He paused and looked at the dry stone, the curse of flowing blood. His distorted reflection looked at him as he passed the shiny surface of the stone of evil.

He squeezed through the gap separating the stones of profanity and censure and rounded the leading stone.

As Don Canida melted into the shadows of the Petrified Forest, a ghostly form emerged to the south and took to the skies, flying silently and rapidly into the forest.

Mundu Babill cut a solitary path across the trees, heading for the Valley of Lengthened Years and the Renewal corroboree. His family had long lived in the caves of the dead forest, contributing much to the fears that both animals and humans shared about the place, until Don Canida tricked them.

He rarely visited the Valley of Lengthened Years. Not that he personally shunned the work and efforts of the Gronups. But, truth be told, Mundu Babill had little call for cosmetic decoration and had no real religious calling. Nor was he particularly fussed about his food source, so long as it had blood coursing through its veins and meat on its bones. Decoration of his prey didn't matter because he didn't need to see them. He pictured the shape and surface texture by ultrasound. Consequently, it made hardly any difference to the ghost bat whether the Gronups were around or not.

He could see benefits for him if they weren't.

Although Mundu Babill was the Kumakana's only remaining ghost bat, this was a secret between Don Canida and him. His clan had invented the legends of the Gully of Six Curses to protect their habitat. Other animals of the forest called them vampires. This useful but entirely false identity ensured his privacy.

This is why his arrival at the Valley of Lengthened Years met with surprise. His reason for attendance was powerful. Don Canida's bargain meant that his days of loneliness would soon be over and the ghost bat would flourish in the Kumakana once more. To look his best, a little maintenance was called for. Moreover, Don Canida's curse had to be set in motion from within the Valley of Lengthened Years.

Chapter12

The Valley of Lengthened Years crosses the base of hills left behind long ago when the distant mountains were formed. The amphitheatre where Lavender watched the corroboree had been carved into the high wall of the northern bank of the valley. The performing area was a flat granite surface shaped by the valley winds, and smoothed by its rains over eons. A huge tingle tree rose behind it, dwarfing the rocky stage, its gaping centre providing the backstage green room, and dressing area for the performers. The stage director was a ruffle-headed royal spoonbill called Carker Barker.

Earlier in the evening, Carker Barker had received instructions from Babbildan Babbirra to include all the stories of the great beginning in tonight's show—an instruction he thought ridiculous. Impossible.

A huge cast was required to tell the great stories. There wasn't time to assemble them. Consequently, a lot of them had to double up.

And for what reason?

'A special guest,' Babbildan Babbirra had said. And the special guest had turned out to be a ... koolonger. An Enterer at that!

Carker Barker's wings fluttered and his crown ruffled as he

barked orders to the two pelicans coming off stage.

'Come on, come on ... Ret geddy for Bifficulty at the Deginning.'

The next act he'd had to make up on the spot.

'Now hare the well is Born Wro? He should be on stage.'

He cast around searching for his master-of-ceremonies, who was supposed to be providing commentary about the dances and songs so that the 'special guest' wouldn't miss the point.

'This guest may very well be vital to our survival,' Babbildan Babbirra had stressed.

Huh? How can an Enterer be vital? Especially one so young. This is sacred business—not the sort of thing any human should see.

Carker Barker shooed the next act onto the stage, swinging his long black bill wildly behind a gathering of *kulbardi*—magpies. Their role was to explain the meaning of the Arousal of Light at dawn. He barked loudly for Warn Bro to make the appropriate introduction.

He looked at his running sheet, the bowls of his huge bill clapping like castanets as he yabbered to himself.

'The widgis are stewing the dory of Struggles at the start— and they knould show ... Their clings've been whipped since bay wack.'

He grinned—a strange and awkward sight—and emitted a short laugh as, in his mind's eye, he watched a flock of great flightless birds reaching in vain for the sky. He was quickly brought back to the moment as the emus filed in from the backstage entrance. Carker Barker's demeanour altered in a snap and he nodded his approval. He looked at the next item.

Suddenly his crown feathers lay straight back and another fillip escaped from his splayed nib. He shouted at his talent coordinator, an old ring-tail possum given to finding dark corners where he could sleep off the effects of a long life. He moved slowly, and when he did, it was mostly on the wallaby track rather than where he ought to be.

'Hey! Fouthful yolly ... where're the woylies?'

He looked around sternly, grunted and snapped loudly several times in succession.

'I noo deed a wozen doilies for this.'

He shook his head and watched the retreating back of his talent coordinator skulk toward the exit. He consulted his list once again.

'Boo tizzy to hoe up shear doh nowt. Now. After that: Waiting— ah yes, the Numbing of Courishment ... cat'll be the thranes—'

'Yah lookin' for me Ca-ark?' Warn Bro drifted in from the dark behind the stage, the pupils of his eyes shiny buttons as he stalked forward. 'Had to take a nature break—if you get my meaning. Who's up for the story of Conflict?'

'Conflict? Wonflict's after Caiting. Why?'

'Well I just figure that's a good time to get rid of the guest. Scare her off, you know. Get her out of here. It's not right having an Enterer listen to our songs and stories. She's out there like she's takin' it all in. I think BB's makin' a big mistake. So here's what I reckon, right? If we make a big show out of Conflict, you know, make her think that's where it's all gonna end—for her that is—she'll get so frightened she'll go. And that silly 'coot who's looking after her will show her the door see. So you gotta get somebody really dangerous out there. Slimy. Ugly. Brutal. Ba-aad! And maybe if you get that silly 'coot in on the act, it'll be easier. Know what I mean?'

'Born Wro, you sing beautifully!'

Carker Barker suddenly felt a whole lot better. His mood lifted and he snapped and clapped Warn Bro onto the stage flicking his wings at the black bird's tail feathers. He fussed about rearranging his casting list, clacking and snapping to the rhythm of his thoughts: Nonflict arises over Courishment. And Wourishment comes of Naiting. And what's that yese thoung'ns lave to hearn. Waiting.

Wonaiea, in his earlier contact with Babbildan Babbirra, had informed the Yoolin-jah of Don Canida's diabolical plans. Now, with the excitement of being at a Renewal corroboree with Spot, Don Canida's plans retreated to the nether reaches of his mind. He'd barely left Lavender's side before being caught up in a string of games, guiding Spot through the local rules with the young woylies and the joeys. Once the woylies were called to their song—how youth and freedom leads through folly to discipline—he led Spot to the workshops.

The workshops in the Valley of Lengthened Years sit within the cavernous interiors of giant tingle trees. Wonaiea took Spot past a leafy clump of ferns and spiny balgas to a tree left of the ceremony.

A joyful Cedric whistled and slimed his way out of the tree as they approached it. He was positively glowing in a new suit of bright brown and orange. The brilliant sheen danced as his new scales reflected the moonlight in a writhing carpet of colours. As Spot pushed past him, his tongue involuntarily flicked in and out of his lipless mouth. Through unblinking eyes, he stared hungrily at the pup and his newly acquired Gronup riding top saddle before sidling off in the direction of the performing arena.

The tingle-tree cavern was abuzz. Spot stood in the entry, his little pink tongue pulsing across his bottom teeth, observing Gronups grooming and repairing the coats of their animals. He soaked up the atmosphere, his tail wagging ten to the dozen, excited little whimpers pumping from his throat.

Wonaiea directed the pup deeper into the tree, where fur was tinted, scales polished and feathers fitted with rainbows of interlocking barbs. Animals of all descriptions received wanton attention from swarms of Gronups toting fixers and combs and tints. Touch-ups here. Replacements there.

Eventually, Wonaiea found what he was looking for. Beneath a polished wooden wall of the tree, worn smooth by years of activity, a gang of Gronups attended to a young quoll about to receive the first of his spots.

In another secluded part of the corroboree, Jerramunga faced the strange gathering. He could hear the pulses and rhythms of the dances and songs through the trees. Sweat gathered around his collar and on the palms of his hands. The stings and aches of battle scars racked his body. His heart thumped hard enough to break out of his chest. But his spirit surged.

A small creature opposite him rose on a pair of long agile legs. A spaghetti tangle of fur flowed from a wild head, a pair of ears peaked from the top, tassels swept like antennae back from their tips. Jerramunga stared. The eyes that held him contained the wisdom of all the ages. He wanted to say something. He wanted to ask 'How did I get here?' and 'What's going to happen?' But the words wouldn't form. He tried to look away, to look at the other faces surrounding him. It was impossible to take his eyes from those before him.

If this was a Gronup, it was nothing like he expected.

His anxiety dissolved like sugar in hot cocoa. A flood of warmth replaced the butterflies in his stomach as his heart regained its steady silence and the fog lifted from his brain. A peaceful feeling rested gently on his shoulders.

The eyes smiled and released him. The mouth with its high arched lips and oversized grey moustaches broadened and moved.

'So, you have met Don Canida?' Babbildan Babbirra smiled.

Jerramunga nodded.

'Your bravery in saving the life of another is proof to us that your spirit is that of the great Ngungakatta.'

'Lavender!' Jerramunga blurted. 'I don't know where she is.

And Spot ...'

'They are safe ... at the corroboree,' Babbildan Babbirra told him. 'But there are more pressing matters. Don Canida is planning to ambush the animals as they leave the corroboree. His whole pack is preparing this very moment. They are out there waiting to destroy the Natural Order ...'

Babbildan Babbirra didn't need to finish the sentence for Jerramunga to understand.

'I knew I should've killed him,' he said quietly, gazing at the ground near his feet.

'It would have made little difference,' Babbildan Babbirra said. 'His is no ordinary line. If he had perished at your hands, another fox would have stepped up to take his place. Just as evil. Just as dangerous.'

Jerramunga's face clouded.

'But he'll destroy his own food supply. What's the good of that?'

'Don Canida has no thought or care about that. He will eat his own young if he has to.'

'What sort of mother would let that happen?' Jerramunga asked, more to himself than to the audience surrounding him.

Wollerta leapt to her feet and bounded into the centre of the group.

'He has a point. Maybe that's the key. Maybe Don Canida can be replaced by a female.'

The group erupted in a flurry of to-ing and fro-ing as one put a point and another countered.

'We need an army,' a voice called from the group.

'You already have an army,' Jerramunga blurted.

The meeting was suddenly silent and seventeen pairs of eyes burnt into Jerramunga.

'Pretty much an air force and navy too, the way I see it.'

Silence.

'Look, I saw what Squash and Stretch did slinging those gumnut missiles with their tails. And what that big kangaroo's mob did when they stormed through the bush earlier—you shoulda' seen Don Canida's face then—he fair shat himself! And then the emus and the snakes. Look, I reckon there are plenty of animals out there, big and small, who can do stuff. The only difference between you guys and Don Canida is that he's organised. You just gotta be organised.'

A murmur went round the group and grew quickly into a mild roar of excitement.

Koopoo addressed Jerramunga.

'What you say has merit. But how do we do this?'

'My grandfather reckoned there are always two parts to the battle. On the one hand, there is attack; and on the other, defence. He said you can only win if you do both in the right form. Don Canida thinks he's going to surprise you with an attack. But we know what he is planning so it's not a surprise. What we don't know is how and where. So the first thing is to get someone who can see well in the night and doesn't make any noise to fly around and report back on Don Canida's positions. The more we know, the more we can turn the tables.'

Seventeen heads nodded. The wedge-tailed eagle said, 'Ben Cubbin's crew would be best for that.'

Atnunga took her cue and faded quickly on the whistle of a wind that had suddenly sprung through the tree.

Kal Barri perched on a swaying branch above the performance area, his head cocked to one side watching Warn Bro deliver a rousing introduction to the dance of youth. Earlier, he'd waited for Mundu Babill to get him in and then, once inside, he'd sought out the crow.

'The wardong knows how to handle the situation,' he was told. 'He has debts to pay.'

Kal Barri had moved carefully under the cover of a dense cloud that momentarily blanked out the moon. Warn Bro had given him simple instructions.

'Stay hidden. I'll let you know when the koolonger's leaving.'

After that, Kal Barri could get to work on the second part of his mission.

He was concentrating so hard on his way back to his high perch that only by the slim side of a gum leaf did he avoid colliding with an escadrille of barn owls. They flew silently and quickly through the lower reaches of the trees. As he sat, willing his heartbeat to return to normal, a sight from the corner of his eye nearly made him fall off his perch.

A lift in the dance tempo below drew his eye. The band was

thumping and the entire arena hopping. Then he saw his daughter dancing with one of the dammalak youths.

A startled squawk caught in his throat. He bit down hard on an inflating balloon of anger and scanned the crowd. As far as he could see, she was the only one of his clan there. He stared hard at her, willing her to look up and see him so he could signal her to get the hell out of there.

But he was too well camouflaged. And she wasn't interested in looking anywhere other than into the eyes of the green and black dandy she was dancing with. That's when he noticed that she was sporting new colours: brilliant white stripes down the length of her tail feathers. A stroboscope of dark tips and striking contrast dazzled as she gyrated to the beat. There was no question—she had summoned her Gronup.

Kal Barri vigorously scratched his cheek with his left claw, his entire mission placed in jeopardy by a reckless daughter. And to make matters worse, he could see severe weather rolling in from the south.

The Gronups' workshops are not organised. The activities aren't grouped by colour or animal or marking. It's perfectly normal to find spotting next to scaling, and furring in the same place as feathering. The only ones who know the order of things are the Gronups, and if there is any particular organisation to it, it's their secret.

This is how Spot and Wonaiea came to be in the same workshop as Mal Aga, who was engaged in a heated discussion with a gaggle of male parrots. By sheer coincidence, Mundu Babill was in the same workshop. Had he not been, events may have unfolded very differently.

Mal Aga was copping a lot of stick from the rest of his clan. His cousin, Mal Acoota, held the floor. He had for some time—being one who enjoyed the sound of his own shrill voice. He babbled, squawking over the top of any other who wanted to get a word in. Twice he'd nearly sent the team of Gronups fitting his new pectals flying, waving his wing around like a traffic cop on point.

'You're a real dumb cluck Mal Aga. Talk about the *chuditch* among the chooks. You know what? If this nest-sharing thing takes off, our females will want to be out and about at nesting time. You think I'm kidding? I tell you, they'll expect to come with us. No more ducking off to the seed piles. No more racing. Next thing you know, they'll want *us* to share nest duties. They'll want to be liberated!'

Mal Aga was unfazed.

'Look Mal Acoota, what's the big deal? It's just temporary. Something to help out. Anyway, it was Atnunga's idea.'

'That'd be right. It's not like she's interested in anything other than her own ideas. More of her social engineering. And look who you're helping out. A gakkal-yakkal. That's the crazy thing. A gakkal-yakkal! What do you know about this cackle? Anything?'

'I know they're refugees from the east.'

Mal Aga stopped, suddenly thoughtful. He pivoted forward to

let a Gronup run an iridescent blue stripe down the outside of a tail feather. He spoke into the ground.

'I gotta say ... that pink and grey was pretty weird when he was watching Don Canida's muscle murder those quokkas. He took off like a bat outta hell straight after. Headed north. I didn't see him after that. And it's funny too, y'know, I was just about to invite him to the corroboree tonight, but something in my gut—'

He stopped and cocked his head to one side to see why everybody had suddenly gone quiet. Mundu Babill stared coldly down at him from above.

'Well ... you know what I mean,' Mal Aga mumbled, embarrassed by his gaffe.

'Yeah. And you know what I think,' Mal Acoota picked up. 'I think it's a plot. I think you're being used. And I think we're gonna have more trouble than enough from our females. They're gonna start gettin' high-falutin' ideas and changin' the rules. And we're gonna be in big strife, because that's gonna put our way of life at risk. Not to mention our nests.

'You'd better find that guy tomorrow and move them out. Or else you can forget about coming with us on the next cross-country seed rout.'

Mal Acoota swept his wing across the group. As he turned he came face to face with a breathless Dal Keith, a red capped parrot. He was a cousin of the dammalaks and a friend of Mal Aga's. Dal Keith's brilliant red crown was erect and his long tail feathers slightly fanned. He looked perplexed and clacked his beak several times without moving from in front of Mal Acoota.

'Well, what do you want?' the dammalak snapped.

'I came to tell Mal Aga that I just saw Mal Vern dancing with that young gakkal-yakkal female who came today.'

A chorus of clucking and malacking erupted.

'And that's not all. Her father is perched up a tree overlooking the story ground. I'm pretty sure he's hiding. He thinks he hasn't been seen, but you know me, I don't like crowds. I prefer to keep an eye on things from above, and I watched him.

'He waited till a cloud passed in front of the moon and flew down and waited in the shadows behind the stage entrance for Warn Bro. When he came out, they had a talk and then the gakkal-yakkal flew back up into the tree. He was watching his tail so hard he flew straight across the flight path of Ben Cubbin's stealth crew.

'I think he's up to something because he doesn't have his Gronup. All this sneaking around ... it doesn't make sense. I don't think the daughter's got anything to do with it because she's obviously called for her Gronup. She was getting some white stripes down her wings when I had my crown done. She came with Mal Vern but I don't think she knows the father's here because he nearly dropped off his perch when he saw her dancing there. How he got in is the mystery.'

Dal Keith paused to take a breath and looked expectantly at Mal Aga, who was shaking his tail feathers into place. The Gronups that had been working on them moved on to the next dammalak.

All eyes were darkly on Mal Aga. He shook his head.

'Why are you telling me?' he demanded.

'Well you're responsible for this guy aren't you?'

'That's exactly what I've been saying,' Mal Acoota squawked. 'And now's your chance to go and do something about him. Maybe we should all go and front him ... tell him to clear off.'

'I think we need to let Atnunga take care of it,' Mal Aga said softly. 'It's got nothing to do with me. I didn't bring him here.'

'Maybe your son did,' Mal Acoota snapped.

'If the daughter came with Mal Vern, and she doesn't know the father's here, then he didn't bring him. Besides, that gakkal-yakkal's Yoolin-jah of his clan, and only another Yoolin-jah could have brought him in.'

'Maybe it was Warn Bro,' Mal Acoota suggested.

'Maybe. But that'd be pretty difficult for him. He's been here all night and his song opened the portal in the tingle tree when the moon broke through. Others would have seen him. And if this guy doesn't want to be seen, it had to be someone else.'

'I think we should front him,' Mal Acoota urged again.

'Yeah maybe,' Mal Aga clucked. He turned to Dal Keith. 'Where was Ben Cubbin going?'

'Well that's funny too. There were a dozen or so barn owls in his squad and they headed out in full stealth. Seems to me they were on a mission.'

'Wonder what's goin' on,' another dammalak whistled.

'I think I know,' a voice rasped from above.

Mundu Babill hung upside down from the wall above the gathering. Two Gronups worked steadily applying light ochre tints to the new fur down his back. He'd heard everything, from the nest-sharing squabble to the speculation over the gakkal-yakkal. Having been raised in a nursery colony, nest sharing was perfectly normal to Mundu Babill. The trouble with these dammalaks, he thought, is they're selfish and too proud to know what's good for them. But his main concern was not their domestic accommodations—it was the idea of them fronting the gakkal-yakkal and creating an incident that could upset the entire banksia cart. He couldn't allow that. If his cover had been blown, it was up to Mundu Babill to do something about it.

News of a stealth flight of barn owls was worrying too.

With large radar-dish faces several times more sensitive to sounds than even Mundu Babill's huge foxy ears, their silent flight can be lethal. It was much too early for them to be leaving the corroboree. Hunting is banned during these hours. And what's more, they wouldn't normally leave in a large formation. He searched sonically around the chamber for a way to keep the dammalaks inside.

He couldn't risk being exposed. Not now. Not before he knew what was going on.

Cedric almost bounced round the grove that marked the entrance to the story ground. But his joyful mood was short-lived.

He was brought up short by Warn Bro.

'Aaah, Cedric,' the big black bird crowed, 'might I have a private word?'

Cedric squirmed to a halt. He normally had little time for Warn Bro, on the basis (so he told himself) that he detested scavengers. This big black bird, who was big as far as crows go, was a sneaky and unrepentant cadger—a bully who'd think nothing of pinching the last crumb from a starving fly lizard. He stalked around like a chook, head cocked in the air, bobbing like a snake poised to strike. Compared to this guy, the kookaburra's a saint.

An involuntary shudder rifled his backbone whenever he was confronted by a crow. He'd seen how they work. Being bailed up by Warn Bro put Cedric's suspicions on code red. He circled the crow in the shadows behind the stage entrance. Then he noticed that Warn Bro had shadowy company. His nostrils flared to their maximum, and his tongue investigated the odour of the air in rapid fillips. He looked for high ground and settled on a straggly dead branch on a wilted sucker. Not a good idea to be at a disadvantage in eye contact with Ma Lisse.

'Well I must say you're a pretty pair ... in a darkish kind of way,' he hissed. 'I 'spose your missus is out raiding the gnow's sand patch, Warn Bro—certainly wouldn't put it past the two of you—even though tonight is Renewal.'

'Actually,' Ma Lisse grunted, 'the sand patch is pretty safe tonight—it has, shall we say, a guardian angel watching over it. But we were wondering if you could do us a little favour.'

'I don't do favours.'

'Well, that's not what we hear,' Warn Bro a-arked.

'Oh. I thought you were too busy listening to yourself to hear anything.'

Cedric wondered what the crow had heard.

'Well now Cedric, my elongated friend, I think you spend too much time in low places. You can't possibly know what we more elevated folk get to hear. We mix more and get the drift of what goes on. I find that folk whisper things to us higher souls. Don't you find that Ma Lisse?' He shot her a knowing wink.

The fowl clucked her agreement.

Cedric twisted a little tighter around the branch.

'You see,' Warn Bro continued, 'there's a certain presence in this gathering tonight that a few of us feel oughtn't be here. And it's to our advantage to see that she's ... well, you know, shown the door. There's a big reward in it.'

'I can't help you,' Cedric said.

'We think you can,' Ma Lisse clucked.

'And if you don't, we'll be sure to let a certain four-footed landlord know how uncooperative you've been,' Warn Bro added.

'Why don't you do whatever it is that has to be done yourself?'

'Are you nuts?' Ma Lisse squawked. 'Interfere with the wishes of Babbildan Babbirra. What if we're seen? We'll be excommunicated. Banished. Fox food in a day.'

'So? It's the same for me.'

'Yeah, but you don't matter,' Warn Bro cawed. 'You're not on the endangered list and you're a low-life already. And you have more chance of not being noticed. For one thing, I gotta do a gig here. And Ma Lisse? Well, she's got no talent for subterfuge has she? She's a walking billbird. But you're made for it. And I mean you already get away with it don't you? You know ... the rent thing with "you-know-who".

'The way we see it, that little bargain puts you at something of a disadvantage. You already have the attributes to make Conflict seem natural. You're already in conflict. But us? We got choices. We can choose to let Don Canida know about your level of cooperation as I already said, or we could choose to tell your Gronup about your little deal. I notice Burra Baroona arrived tonight. Who do you think might be most interested? Don Canida or Burra Baroona? In the end it wouldn't matter ... it'd be the same outcome. Fox food. Conflict. It's a great story isn't it? I know I wouldn't miss an episode.'

By now, Cedric was wrapped so tightly around the dead stalk that it began to crack under the pressure. It was all he could do to raise his voice to an audible hiss. This new threat complicated matters enormously.

'You mentioned reward ... before ...'

'You know what?' Warn Bro said. 'I'm glad you reminded me. Yeah, reward. Well if we can do this successfully, you know, deliver the goods to the buyer before the moon shadows are smallest, he's promised to leave Ma Lisse's eggs alone completely—which you have to admit is a pretty big thing considering how much he and his boys like those eggs. And for me, well I get about the biggest feast you're ever likely to see laid on—I'll be like a bilby on the boronia path. I won't have to work a shift for days ...

weeks. Probably months.'

Warn Bro took a deep breath and his powder-blue eyes glazed in the light. He puffed his chest feathers and bent down to the dead branch that Cedric was choking and stropped his bill across it.

Cedric had seen Warn Bro work the shift many times.

He'd sit in a tree and wait for a victim to sit down to a hard-won meal—a quoll with a fresh kill splayed in front of him, say—and, with eyes that are sharper than the needle points of a dugite's fangs, Warn Bro spots him from a mile away and swings along to pay him a visit. Not too close. Just far enough away to be noticed but out of reach. Then he puffs his chest feathers and rubs his beak along the tree trunk like a butcher stropping a knife. Next, he breaks out in song—if you could call it that—attracting the diner's attention. Or putting him off his meal. Not wanting to be bothered, any self-respecting diner gets fed up and chases after Warn Bro to send him on his way.

But the sneaky crow's got it all worked out. He only moves a tree or two away, just a little out of reach, and then he just does it again. If the diner decides to move, Warn Bro's on his tail.

Cedric shook his head at the number of times he's seen it go on. Eventually Warn Bro lures the diner far enough away from his meal for his mate to swoop in and snatch it up. That's the shift. Then they go off and enjoy their meal.

'And me?' Cedric inquired, flatly, after he realised Warn Bro was not continuing. 'What's my reward?'

'Why, Cedric ... you get to live. In the same place. Under the same conditions. Maybe I can encourage Don Canida to forego your next rent increase. How's that sound?'

'Seems a bit lop-sided to me. What's he gonna do with the koolonger?'

'We don't know,' Ma Lisse replied.

'And we don't care,' Warn Bro added. 'So long as there are leftovers. He wants what he wants and he's willing to pay more than a fair price, so I think ... you know ... I think we deliver. Don't you?'

Cedric looked thoughtful.

'It's just ... from what I hear Don Canida's not going to be around much longer.'

He drew the tip of his tail across his throat to illustrate the terminal nature of his meaning.

Warn Bro looked darkly at the old snake, eyes blazing in the shadows.

'What exactly do you mean by that, Cedric?'

Ma Lisse clucked. 'Yeah, what do you mean?'

'It's just, I heard he is going to be taken care of,' Cedric said, quietly, swaying from one to the other. 'That's all.'

'By whom?' Warn Bro cried.

'Well ... I couldn't say,' Cedric returned. 'That'd be letting the cat out of the bag, so to speak.'

Warn Bro was stunned. It was possible that Cedric knew something. It may even be part of some dark scheme to eliminate Don Canida. Or was he just trying to divert attention?

'How do we know you're telling the truth?' he asked.

'You'll just have to wait and see, won't you? Anyway—' Cedric stretched his neck in the direction of the stage door and an agitated Carker Barker, who was looking urgently toward them, snapping his long bill like angry castanets. 'I think you're wanted.'

Warn Bro a-arked in exasperation. 'Look Cedric, I don't know what you're up to, but I've made arrangements. All you have to do is get that koolonger out of here during the story of Conflict. Okay? We can worry about Don Canida's future after that. Just get her out. Don Canida will be waiting to take her from just beyond the tingle tree.'

'Yeah. And I'll be watching you,' Ma Lisse clucked, nastily. 'You'd better remember that I've got friends among the kookaburras.'

'Don't be ridiculous, Ma Lisse,' Cedric retorted, unfurling from the dead perch and turning his head as though he had a shoulder to look over as he made off toward the corroboree arena, 'any friends you ever had are long extinct.'

Chapter13

 Lavender was dancing.

Her new friends jigged and bounced around her, swinging to the rhythms of the corroboree. A scaly goanna played a keyed instrument fashioned from tuned lengths of reed protruding from a hollow log struck by gumnut hammers and another one played a sedge-grass saw fiddle. A large bullfrog blew into a reed organ while a couple of kookaburras blew large horns and Ngo-lak Bungal sang.

She was in a new world with songs and stories that filled her mind with wonder—from the beginning of time to the birth of the new quoll kittens this very night.

The Gronups she'd met told her of life—how they watched and waited, studied and created. Without their art, the world would have no order or peace. The Natural Order, they called it—a ladder of life leading from the humble ant to the kings of the karri. The Gronup yoolin had all come to share a moment with her. They'd made her feel safe and warm—especially Wollerta, the old one with the silvery fur that swept down around a wizened old face, its crazed-earth features smiling as only a mother could.

'Everyone has a little good and a little bad within them,' she'd told Lavender. 'No creature is all bad, and no creature is wholly good. The secret to life is to know one from the other, and when to turn away from the path that leads you in the wrong direction. It is not wrong to head down the path—that's how you learn—it is only wrong to not turn back to the truth.'

'How do you know when you're on the bad path?'

'Listen to the spirits. They will tell you.'

'How do I know when the spirits are telling me?'

'You will know, Lavender Jensen. If you keep your heart open and your will free, you will know.'

'Will the spirits talk with me?'

'They already do. They are all around and within. They are the cause of everything and they have a reason for everything they do. If they see nature has left a hole, they fill it—like water fills the depressions in the river bed. If something is falling, they obstruct it the way rocks on the hillsides dam the streams. If your feelings are dark, they can brighten them—like the sun at midday. If your mood is impenetrable, they can get under it like the roots of the tree.'

At that moment a thunderclap shook the air. Lavender shivered at its roar. Wollerta smiled and continued in a kindly voice.

'That's the spirits talking. They make the world complete. They bring the thunder ... oh the shock! They gave Koopoo the spring in his step. He is the true leader of the clans, you know. And with the lightning, they brighten things so every creature can see one another ... so there are dark spirits and light spirits.

'The dark spirits are in the earth. They provide nourishment for everyone. And, in the Natural Order, they prepare everyone in their roles of providing nourishment to others. They make the plants come up from the seeds. And the light spirits in the sky make the flowers form their seeds. Together, the spirits complete everything.'

Another flash scythed across the sky. Wind whistled through the trees, increasing the thunder that followed hard on the lightning's heels. The ground rocked.

Wollerta laughed at the torment in the atmosphere.

'That's how the spirits transform things. The sky spirits and the earth spirits—always trying to reach one another. But they can't. The thunder never leaves the ground. The lightning never leaves the sky. The wind never penetrates the ground. It can uproot the trees, but the grasses merely bend to its power. So you can see that the mighty doesn't always have greatest strength. Sometimes the greatest strength is in the smallest things. The rain always falls from above. But the water comes from below. This, too, is the spirits trying to reach each other.

'When you feel warmth inside your heart, you are being reached by your sky spirit. And when you are feeling receptive in your mind, you are being reached by your earth spirit.'

'Does everyone have a sky spirit and an earth spirit?'

'Not everyone. There are those, like Don Canida, whose minds are closed. They cannot feel the spirits beneath them because they strive to seek their spirit above. They don't like the dark— they reject what they do not know. And there are those whose hearts are hard and cold—they nourish only themselves and care not for others, so they don't know their sky spirit.

'But you are special, Lavender Jensen, you have all spirits. Your heart is warm. Your will is open. You can light the way yet you know how to follow. There are many paths to follow. Trust your spirit and you will find the right one.'

'How come Jerramunga couldn't see the Gronups back there?'

'Most humans do not seek their spirit below; they seek only their spirit above. They look to the light and try not to see the dark. If you cannot see the dark, you cannot see Gronups. Those who do not cherish the Natural Order seek only the light. But if all the dark is vanquished by the light, the light will vanish too because, to see the light, there must be dark. That is why when darkness comes you can see all the sky spirits above.'

A seriousness crept into the Gronup's voice.

'But to see Gronups, you must see the darkness—not the light in the darkness, mind you—the darkness itself. Therefore, you must look below. The Natural Order is a dark thing and it exists to preserve all life on earth. All things must end and begin again—renewal is the secret to preservation. But if all the dark is removed, the Natural Order will be gone. The earth spirits will be gone. There will be no thunder, so there will be no lightning. There will be no wind, so there will be no rain.'

'Does that mean Jerramunga has a hard heart?'

'Not at all. It meant only that he didn't know where to look to find what he was seeking. He carries with him the spirit of Ngungakatta who once helped restore the balance to the Natural Order—a great spirit of both light and dark. Your friend is also special, for he can now see what he seeks.'

'Do you know where he is?'

'He is meeting with the Yoolin-jahs of the clans here in the Valley of Lengthened Years right now.'

Lavender's face brightened.

'Can I see him?'

'Of course.' Wollerta smiled. 'I will send someone to take you to him shortly. But meanwhile, there are other stories for you to hear.'

As Ben Cubbin's reports filtered through to the council, Jerramunga mapped the area surrounding the Valley of Lengthened Years on a cleared patch of ground and plotted Don Canida's positions.

A plan began to unfold.

The Valley of Lengthened Years is encircled by steep hills.

'Like a snake embracing a kangaroo,' Dan Daragan explained. Jerramunga worked the ground as the Nannup tiger continued.

'When Yurlungga first moved, it was from this place that he uncoiled and so he created the Valley of Lengthened Years in his first movements. He made the Kulwinkulkine follow his path, so when he stretched up this way, his tail could follow, 'ere see. So it loops around 'ere, cutting the gorge through these big hills 'ere at the eastern end. And 'ere, all along the valley, it comes an' goes, comes an' goes—you see?'

Jerramunga nodded as he plotted the course of the great river, fluting the soil with the edge of his hand to mimic nature's great undulations. He heaped mounds of earth to form the hills and riverbanks. The path of the great river coincided several times with the Valley of Lengthened Years' southern spine before it scoured southwards from its western end.

He stuck large sticks in the ground in an upside down V to mark the giant red tingle trees that provide the doorways to the Valley of Lengthened Years. He worked quickly, using crushed leaves to fill in the dense understorey that gathers at the feet of the giant karris. He marked all the hidden ravines, gorges and breakaways.

Where outbreaks of giant granite boulders loom suddenly enough to bring a trail to a complete halt, impassable to all except the most agile of creatures, he placed a stone.

From the advice of the yoolin around him, Jerramunga mapped the high ground and the low ground, the trafficked ground and the bad ground, the intersecting ground and the surrounded ground. He marked the obstacles, trails and water courses with lines and forest materials. Finally, using the seed pods of the Karri, he marked Don Canida's positions according to Ben Cubbin's reports.

They all agreed that the final mosaic was exactly how things were.

The fire started quite by accident. Although, for some time afterwards, there were those who persisted in the belief that it was a deliberate act.

Mundu Babill swooped down from his inverted perch high up the wall of the workshop and stood between the dammalak mob and the doorway, perching on the same raised section of the tree-cavern, but right way up (which was wrong way up for him). It was an awkward manoeuvre. He had to sweep forward with his wings, which became—on level ground, at least—de facto walking sticks, because his legs were not made for standing on. It was a struggle to keep balance on the edge of a narrow ledge.

Mundu Babill has about a third of the body length of Mal Aga but with more than twice the wingspan. He waved his wings around like a windsurfer in a high wind.

Mal Aga, who was in between Mundu Babill and the others, reeled backwards into Mal Acoota, pushing him into two or three birds that were perched behind.

Dal Keith froze with fear on the end of the perch. The dammalak mob crashed into him and pushed him over the edge. He fell, at first plummeting like a stone, but when he was no more than a feather's depth from the floor, he remembered he was a bird and made a miraculous recovery. His wingtip caught the container of pigment being applied to Spot's new spot and sent it sprawling from its scaffold.

Spot reacted instinctively, spinning nose to tail, catapulting Wonaiea from his back. The Gronup flew through the air toward Cecil Park, a young magpie receiving a brilliant white cape of wing-feathers as part of his pre-mating wardrobe. His brother, Cecil Plain, was with him. He had bustled in with a sensational nesting gift that he'd picked up from the Crow's Crossing shortly after singing the dawn chorus that morning.

It was Cecil Plain's second gift to him. The first was Lavender's earbuds, fantastic worm-like dangles that would make excellent early-bird training for future hatchlings. Cecil Plain's new gift was much shinier.

It was an old cigarette lighter which no longer had its original flip lid, and Cecil Plain thought it would be very attractive to Cecil Park's intended. Cecil Plain was showing it off, beaming as if he'd struck gold, when Wonaiea crashed into him. The lighter sailed high into the air, spun like a shiny penny in a two-up match, landed on its flint wheel, which turned and emitted a spark, lighting not only its wick, but also the highly flammable spot pigment oozing round the cavern floor.

Panic erupted inside the workshop as tails of flames lashed out in the confined space.

Mal Aga, being the speed king of the Kumakana, was the first out of the opening. He sent up the alarm. All the other animals and Gronups in the workshop were hot on his wing-tips, rushing the doorway as dragon puffs of smoke billowed from the aperture before them, snakes of blue-tipped flames licking at fur and feathers behind them. It was every bird, animal, reptile and Gronup for themself—fire was the least understood and the most feared of all things in the Kumakana.

Mal Aga hit the treetops at tremendous speed, heading for

a place downstream from the Pool of Many Reflections. He flew out of the Valley of Lengthened Years via a little known emergency exit near Willow Hollow. Had he not been in such a terrible hurry, he would have observed an unusual massing of cats more closely. As it was, it simply registered as unusual.

He turned right at a dense jarrah copse, dropping his altitude to just below the treetops and, agile as a wasp, slipped between branches and limbs, dodging clumps of leaves until he emerged at the other side of the wood with the river in sight.

He wheeled left.

The target of his search was a reed bed that lined the river bank. As it loomed into view, he dropped altitude to skim the spiny tips of the rushes, calling loudly until he was rewarded with a sleepy cronk. He banked right and bulleted along the shoreline heading for the sound, coming upon his target as he crested a rise in the riverbank.

Boo Ragoon's clan—more than a dozen pelicans—were asleep on their feet at the water's edge, well hidden among the bulrushes and reeds, their long bills tucked under stretched necks, resting like shooting sticks beneath their chests. Mal Aga perched precariously on a wildly swinging reed and shocked the great pelican from his open-eyed sleep with a loud cackle.

Boo Ragoon remained motionless.

He regarded the dammalak with a combination of concern and suspicion, a faint flicker in his huge yellow eyes the only sign that he had wakened.

'Fire!' Mal Aga squawked, his breath coming in rapid gasps.

'Fire in the Valley of Lengthened Years.'

Smoke was in the air, confirming his warning.

'That's bad,' Boo Ragoon croaked. 'Where exactly?'

He began to walk slowly up the embankment, flicking water off the end of his bill.

Mal Aga flew ahead, to the higher ground.

'Inside the workshop.'

'Any particular workshop?'

'The one where I get my feathers done.'

Boo Ragoon grunted again. 'That's bad. Has it spread to the outside?'

'I don't know—I came straight here as soon as it started.'

'How did that happen?'

'When it started I got out first and flew straight here—'

'No, dumb cluck! How did it start?'

'Oh. First Mundu Babill came at us and then Dal Keith fell off the perch and struck the yirri-yirri who went mad and struck Cecil Park, or was it Cecil Plain. No, hang on, I think when Dal Keith fell on the yirri-yirri, Wonaiea got sent through the air and landed on Cecil Plain and the yirri-yirri knocked over the spotting pigment which went all over the floor—'

Boo Ragoon cut him off with a snap of his long bill.

'All right, all right! The thing is, how do we get in there to bomb it?'

By the time Babbildan Babbirra arrived at the scene of the

fire, flames licked at the bark around the split in the giant tree's trunk but hadn't yet taken to its timber. It was mostly the oils in the pigments and the feathers and fur materials scattered around the floor and on the risers and ridges around the walls that were burning. Explosive pops signalled the combustion of pigment caches. Crackles and sizzles escaped the inferno ahead of the billowing smoke.

Babbildan Babbirra organised teams of bandicoots and numbats into digging parties. They lined up with their backs to the tree and dug frantically, flinging clods of moist earth at the flames.

As clumps rained down on the fire, Boo Ragoon arrived overhead. He had to over-fly the Valley of Lengthened Years, wheel around and approach with the moon at his back.

Atnunga had ordered a string of calls from strategically placed kookaburras to guide the pelicans through an opening in the forest canopy. Once beneath the treetops, things got a little trickier. There, they had to negotiate a maze of trunks and branches, keeping the wind at their tails, drop their heavy liquid loads on the fire and fly out without colliding with a tree.

Atnunga remained aloft to oversee the operation.

'The trick,' she explained to Boo Ragoon as he lined up his approach, 'is to fly between the trees and line up with that first fork branching out of the tree with the fire, and drop your water so that the forward motion carries it through the opening and then fly up between the fork and out above Willow Hollow.'

It was dangerous work for a bird with a wingspan bigger than the opening in the tree. Powerful wing flaps were needed to transport the heavy loads, and if the drop was timed wrongly, the updraft from the fire could lift the bird into the tree canopy. Such flying required great skills and bombing accuracy. Thirteen birds followed Boo Ragoon in a spread formation.

Boo Ragoon's load fell wide of the mark, soaking a group of onlookers. A roar of surprise and disappointment went up.

Atnunga ordered flight path adjustments.

The second bird came in lower. He too missed the target and soaked the digging crew on the approach side, wetting their soil, which added to the burden of their task and did little for their mood.

The third bird came in too fast. His load splattered against the tree trunk and dribbled down toward the flames, hissing and bubbling as it went. Kookaburra calls saturated the air, providing new range, speed and target drop details.

The fourth bird hit the target.

His load squirted through the opening and splashed down on the flames. A cheer went up from the onlookers, mingled with the loud sizzle of doused flames. Unfortunately, the target wasn't the only thing the bird hit. Chuffed by the applause for his accuracy, he was momentarily distracted and forgot to compensate for the sudden weight loss—he soared straight into a very solid branch and dropped like a stone onto the digging crew at the base of the tree.

Witnessing the entire event, number five dropped his load prematurely and soaked the bundle of bodies scrambling around below. The dumping helped revive the fallen bird, who fluttered around as he found his feet and scattered diggers in every direction with his huge bill and wings. It was a long walk back to the river.

The flames took advantage of the respite and began to gain ground. They licked higher up the trunk around the opening. The kookaburra calls steadied the next bird as he approached. They were joined by loud honking calls from Boo Ragoon, who had taken a perch in the top of a tree along the approach. He could see both the target and the entry through the canopy. He ordered the approaching bird to maintain concentration and keep his course steady until the target was correctly sighted.

'Use the energy of the heat rising from the flames and the sudden loss of weight for your climb,' he instructed. 'Feel for wind shifts and keep your wing steady as you release.'

The load splattered onto the fire.

Boo Ragoon kept up the steady stream of instructions as the great flying boats followed one another toward the inferno and returned to the Kulwinkulkine to reload. The hit rate continued to improve.

Onlookers had gathered to cheer the work of the gallant crews but victory was not certain.

Driven by the approaching storm, the rising winds fed the flames. They licked higher and higher up the tree trunk, clinging to new fuel as they marched. Pandemonium spread as wildfire might—smoke choked the air and the corroboree ground to a halt.

Feathering, furring, scaling, striping and spotting were all abandoned mid-stroke. Gronups downed tools and colours as animals headed out the doors of the workshops and crushed toward the exit. Dances and songs halted mid-step and Gronups suspended their ministrations. Fear mixed with the smoke.

Carker Barker the spoonbill was too busy arranging players and scenes for the next act to be aware of the impending danger. His first inkling came when the audiences vacated the gallery and the performers left the stage.

He protested loudly to anyone who would listen as, 'Potally unfrotessional hebaviour!' and went frantically in search of Warn Bro—who, of course, was nowhere to be found.

When he emerged from his stage door, the astonished spoonbill was swept along by a stampede of fur and claws seeking the way out. He gave up trying to return to his backstage sanctuary and rolled with the flow, continuing his tirade against the forces that were interfering with his art.

Mundu Babill had vacated the workshop immediately. But not entirely unnoticed.

Warn Bro happened to be taking one of his self-proclaimed well-earned breaks in the shadow of the stage door, chewing sagely on an old bone when the ghost bat flew past as though his wings were on fire. But for Warn Bro's acute eyesight, he would have missed the ethereal form altogether.

The crow watched the bat cut through the passage of the tingle-tree exit like a spectre. Curiosity drove him to follow, using the stealth of his dark form to hug the shadows.

Warn Bro didn't leave unseen either.

From his hidden perch above the amphitheatre, Kal Barri watched the dark shape of the bird lumber toward the exit tree, his wing flaps solid and purposeful. Although he didn't know that Warn Bro was following Mundu Babill, Kal Barri decided it was a sign that he too should follow.

As the gakkal-yakkal emerged from the cavern of the tingle tree, Ben Cubbin was returning from a reconnaissance flight and was directly in the pink and grey's flight path. To avoid a mid-air collision, Kal Barri climbed rapidly into the treetops. When he had recovered his balance, Warn Bro had disappeared.

Kal Barri perched on a branch and swung crazily in a rising southerly. He looked in every direction for the crow, when it suddenly dawned on him that he had left the Valley of Lengthened Years without fulfilling his promise to Don Canida.

The koolonger! He'd forgotten about the koolonger. The crow said he was going to take care of it, but the last Kal Barri saw, she was sitting at the corroboree deep in conversation with a Gronup.

And now he was on the outside with no way of returning.

Cedric seized his chance early.

His flickering tongue smelt the smoke before most of the other animals. He slithered up to Lavender and unfolded a story that he'd been asked to bring her to her friend. She willingly followed, thinking the snake was leading her to Jerramunga.

He led her eastward through the trees, away from the main entrance, giving wide berth to the inferno. They eventually arrived at the southeastern end of the Valley of Lengthened Years, where Cedric knew of a secret second exit portal. No other animals were to be seen.

Cedric concertinaed to a halt and indicated a yawning gap in another giant tingle tree.

'You are to go through here and when you come out on the other side, there is a path leading to the right. When you reach a fork in the path, turn toward the moon until you come to a willow tree. Your friend is waiting for you there.'

Unlike the golden glow that emanated from the split trunks of the tingle trees of the Valley of Lengthened Years, this huge cave was pitch black.

Lavender took a cautious step forward. She turned to ask the snake what a willow tree looked like, but he'd slithered away, melting silently into the shadows of the understorey.

She took a small step into the tree. The sounds of the Valley of Lengthened Years fell away, its light dissolved in the tree-cavern's darkness. She halted at what might have been the midpoint, unsure of whether or not to proceed.

The warm camaraderie of the corroboree was strong in her heart. It was driven by song, dance and stories that made sense of everything around her. And the snake seemed to be at the centre of so many of them—perhaps not this particular snake, but the snake nevertheless.

A thought occurred to her. The snake leaves a trail behind like a river, flowing this way and that, a trail with no beginning and no ending, flowing around obstructions, following the land up and down. There's no way of telling where the snake's trail might lead because it's shaped by the ground—by its undulations and obstacles.

She stopped at this thought, her heart skipping a beat or two while she caught up with it.

Where had he sent her? Why did he stop at the tree and leave her?

As the smack of silence gathered around her, she remained rooted midpoint between the entrance and exit of the giant tingle-tree cavern. Ahead, through the exit, the silver-blue light of the moon had turned grey from the menace of heavy cloud. Behind her, the soft golden glow of the Valley of Lengthened Years receded into a moon-tinted brown.

There were no shadows where she stood because no light reached her. There were no sounds except her breathing and the thump of her rushing heart. A prickly shiver ran up her spine; the kind that comes when you suspect you're being watched. She remained still, plumbing the depths of her surroundings with all her senses—her gut absorbing, detecting, ciphering and sending messages to her brain.

In the corroboree they'd said standing still was the only way to know what was moving. To have the earth beneath your feet, so you can allow your spirit to move around.

'Let your spirit explore,' Unkurta had told her, his avuncular voice resonant in her ears. 'Let it roam. Let it feed you with what you need to know.'

And Old Wonollee had said, 'To know when to keep still and when to move—that is the secret to life ... hrmph? Keeping still is in the heart; freeing your spirit, in the head.' He tapped his skull with a gnarled claw. 'These are not the same things.' She smiled at the memory. He sure had a wierd way of talking.

The dances and songs of the corroboree came with shocking clarity. She released her fears, breathing slowly to force her thumping heart to abate.

'Allow room for the circumstances ... hrmph? They will tell you what you need to know,' Old Wonollee had said. 'You must wait. You cannot change the circumstances. It is knowledge of the circumstances that makes you ready to move.'

Gradually, Lavender began to make sense of her surroundings. Her ears probed the silence, sifting for sound.

'Your spirit travels on the sounds,' Unkurta had told her. 'That's why songs and dances move your heart. If your spirit encounters danger, you feel it in your heart. If it encounters joy, you feel it in your heart. If it encounters sorrow, or freedom, you feel it in your heart. That's why it is so important to follow your heart.'

It was Burra Baroona, however, the one whose name and voice both sound like thunder, who said, 'Sound causes movement. So when it is time for movement, let it come from deep within your being, beyond your heart, deep down where your soul is kept.'

'Where is that?' Lavender asked.

'It is where you feel it most. Where you feel it first. And where you feel it strongest. You'll know it when you feel it.'

The words of the Gronups swam in her head as she sensed her way into the gloom.

Then a tiny sound reached her from the darkness ahead. It was so small, she wasn't sure she'd actually heard it. She strained further without moving, willing her heart to be still long enough to hear it again. And then it came. Faintly through the darkness. A low growl. Small, like a young animal, and just loud enough to hear that it was nearby. Somewhere within the cavern of the giant tree.

Lavender took a tentative step forward, the sensation of passing from one realm to another swept over her. She turned and looked behind.

The glow of the Valley of Lengthened Years was gone, replaced by the grey that filled the opening in front of her. Sounds now swept into the tree-cavern and resonated around the cone of the tree's interior. Bark flaps, rustles and wind howls drowned the songs of crickets and cicadas. The curious growl she'd heard faintly was now in full voice and menacing.

From somewhere ahead, outside the tree—but close—a shocking screech tore through the air.

'Aaieeaah! It's the evil spirit. Run. Run!'

The silhouette of two heads snapped away from the gaping hole in front of Lavender, pulling the unmistakable shapes of cat bodies behind them.

The surprise sent her heart into a flurry. She struggled to get her nerves under control. The growling she'd heard now turned its attention on her.

Her eyes searched the shadows, seeking the source. The smoky image of a young fox materialised in the gloom. It was trying to intimidate her with the deep-throated growl it had used to keep the cats at bay.

Lavender looked hard at the fox.

'Are you growling at me or those cats?'

'Cats!' the young fox snorted. 'That beast, Snowqueen and her Moggy Maulers killed my friends. I got away and she sent those two after me. The twins, they call them, because they are always together. They were going to get me too. Then, bam! There you are—are you really an evil spirit?—you are pretty scary.'

'Me? Scary? I was at the corroboree and I came out through this tree.' She paused and then said, 'What happened?'

'My mates wanted to get in on the action that my dad's got planned for tonight, you know. I didn't ... I don't think it's right and I said so, but, well they ... they thought they could be heroes or something.

'Anyway we came down here because my dad would have just sent us home with our tails between our legs ... he wouldn't approve, see. But my mates ... well, they wanted to, you know get even or something, especially after being humiliated by a lone yirri-yirri earlier. We knew that my dad wouldn't be down here, so we came but we didn't know she was here ... there's a big clutter of them ... huge clutter ... down near Willow Hollow and I think they're waiting ... waiting for something ...'

The fox ran out of puff, leaving Lavender bewildered. She'd had difficulty following the outpouring but the words 'Willow Hollow' got her attention. The willow tree was where the snake said her friend would be. Why would he be with the cats? Wollerta said he was at the corroboree.

The sensation of betrayal filled her heart.

'Snake!' she spat.

The fox looked up, surprised.

'I think Snowqueen's waiting for me.'

The young fox's hackles rose.

'You're with them? Then why did those two run like scared yellow feet when you appeared?'

'No, no! I'm not with them. I was tricked by this fat snake into coming here. I was at the corroboree. The snake said my friend was waiting for me at the willow tree. You haven't seen him have you?'

'Uuh, I don't think so.'

Lavender became thoughtful. After a little while, she rose.

'Well we can't stay here. And I don't know how to get back to the corroboree, unless I can find some Gronups.'

'Gronups? There's no such thing as Gronups, that's just a story.'

'They're real,' Lavender said, 'I was with them tonight. I met Wonaiea and Wollerta and Gubba Gubba and Old Wonollee and Burra Baroona and Arunga and Atnunga—'

'Atnunga? That's who the chitti-chitti keep talking about. They come around and tell me that if I join the Natural Order I'll get to meet the great Atnunga. My dad says it's all nonsense. He says he's the Natural Order—'

'Well, your dad's wrong. Atnunga takes care of the spirits of all those who use the wind. Anyway, who's your dad?'

'Don Canida, he's the—'

'Oh!' Lavender drew back in surprise.

'What?'

'I ... I've met him.'

'You've met my dad? No way. When?'

'He found me and my friend earlier tonight when we were lost and took us to the water hole. We ran away. Jerramunga fought him so Spot and I could escape. And now I've lost them both.'

The fox remained quiet a moment.

'Oh, I see. You're the one.'

'I'm the one what?'

'You're the one why my dad's doing what he's doing tonight.'

'What's he doing?'

'He's going to kill all the animals as they leave their corroboree. The whole mob is there waiting to ambush them as they leave. It's probably already started.'

'But that can't happen,' Lavender cried. 'We have to stop it.'

'You can't. It's too late.'

'We have to try. It would be a disaster. It would be the end of the world. You can see that can't you?'

'The end of the world's a bit of a stretch isn't it? But, like I said,

I don't think it's right.'

'We can't stay here,' Lavender said. 'Those cats will be back. We've got to try and stop this. I have to find a way back into the corroboree.'

She left the tree on the opposite side from the cats and stood quietly to absorb the sounds around her. The moon was now fully obscured by heavy clouds and a chilled wind whipped her hair into her eyes.

'We should head for the river,' the fox said. 'It passes near here away from Willow Hollow and close to the Valley of Lengthened Years. I think we'll be safe there because the cats don't like it, and I don't think my dad or any of his crew will be there.'

'Why don't the cats like it?'

'They don't like water.' The fox cocked his ear to the wind. 'They're on the move now—a whole clutter heading this way. We'd better get out of here.'

Lavender looked left then right. 'Which way?'

Wonaeia

Chapter14

 Mundu Babill found Don Canida in a copse of stunted trees and shrubs a short distance from the entrance to the Valley of Lengthened Years. He was sheltering from a foul wind. Had it not been for his radar, the ghost bat might have missed him.

'Well, if it isn't my almost distant cousin,' Don Canida said, raising himself to his full height. 'What news?'

'If I'm not very much mistaken, Don Canida, that tingle tree is about to spew a river of fur and feathers. I recommend you position your forces now.'

Don Canida's long incisors curved down wetly from his upper jaw, a pair of cutlass blades drawn and poised for action. The blood of vengeance, he anticipated, would taste like good wine—full bodied and fragrant.

A low growl brought dark shapes from beneath bushes. They moved silently toward the yawning tingle tree, where they formed into ranks several deep and dissolved into the shadows closest to the ground. Don Canida took a position directly in front of the tree entrance, behind his troops, from where he could observe all movement.

Warn Bro had followed the ghost bat and glided unseen and

unheard into a dark fork of a tree a little way distant. He watched with mounting interest as a huge troop of foxes gathered, deadly and ready to strike. All this for a koolonger seemed a bit much, he thought, and glided to a low branch in front of Don Canida. He strutted sidestep up the curve of the branch, his head cocking left then right, keeping the fox leader in the centre of his vision.

'What's going on, Don?' His caw drawled lazily into the wind. 'I thought you wanted the koolonger.'

The fox snapped back a growl, no visible signs of his surprise at seeing the crow.

'And where exactly is she, Warn Bro?'

'Don't you have her?'

'Now look wardong, don't play games with me. We had a deal ...'

'Indeed we did, Don. And I arranged for Cedric to bring her to you.' He lifted a notch in indignation. 'And I watched them leave, just after the fire erupted.'

Don Canida paced around beneath Warn Bro's branch. Warn Bro hopped in circles above the fox, keeping him in sight.

Don Canida seethed, 'You trusted that slimy son of a sea serpent with something as important as this? You stupid bird. They could be anywhere.'

'So ... all this is to make sure she doesn't escape?' Warn Bro waved his wing to indicate the waiting menace.

'Her and the rest.'

'The rest? What rest?'

The fox licked his lips wetly and tossed his nose into the

air. Mundu Babill, hanging upside down from a nearby branch smirked and answered for the fox.

'Warn Bro, you are so used to flying backwards, keeping the dust out of your eyes, that you can't see the moment when great good fortune smiles upon you. For someone who feeds off the misfortunes of others, you're not exactly tuned to the winds of opportunity are you? Don Canida has invoked a most awesome curse on the lords of the Kumakana.'

Don Canida turned and headed back to the shadow of his command post. His voice was hard and final as he spoke over his shoulder.

'When the sun rises on this ground you shall have the pickings of the finest the Kumakana can offer. You shall feast like you have never feasted before. And there will be a new order in the Kumakana. My order!'

'You've got to be nuts,' Warn Bro squawked, choking as the words came from deep in his throat. 'You're intending to massacre every creature that comes out of the Valley of Lengthened Years?'

'You got it in one, bird. Now get lost or get killed.'

For the first time in his life, Warn Bro was stunned into silence. Although a bird with an extraordinarily keen eye, he had failed to see it coming. He looked at the ghost bat hanging in the tree.

What is this creature's magic? What mysterious powers lie at the bat's claw-tips? Until now, he'd assumed his powers were mere superstition—folklore to explain his solitary existence. He stared into the mocking face. A streak of lightning split the sky, reflecting off the ghost bat's razor-like teeth; a reflection of alarming brilliance.

'I suppose the fire was your doing?'

'Well ... only in the most roundabout way. Still, I have to say the timing was most fortunate. I always say, timing is everything.'

'Seems to me you're beating the rhythm of a bad drum here, Mundu Babill.'

'Aah, the things you don't know, my feathered friend. Don Canida has invoked a curse—one that I daresay will live long into the future histories of the Kumakana. When the sun rises, a new order will prevail, with a new guiding spirit.'

'That's very curious Mundu Babill. What about your Gronup?'

'Why should I care about my Gronup? I have little time or use for a Gronup. Under the new order, I'll have all the care and attention I need. Not to mention blood sacrifices.'

Lightning once again split the sky and Mundu Babill's wide mouth showed bright white teeth around a bright red tongue anticipating the oncoming assault.

'If I were you, Warn Bro, I'd stick around and collect the leftovers because there's going to be plenty.'

The crow shook his head and stropped his long beak against the branch of the tree. He could faintly make out the form of Don Canida crouching low in the bush. He looked back in the direction of the portal to the Valley of Lengthened Years, and turned again to look at Mundu Babill, hanging upside down from a branch above him.

Mundu Babill sensed the big bird's nervousness as he flitted along the branch before swooping off toward the tingle tree. The ghost bat called out after him.

'You can't stop it wardong.'

His screeching peals of laughter followed Warn Bro into the night.

When Kal Barri realised he'd lost Warn Bro, he flew back in the direction of the Valley of Lengthened Years entrance. The ghost bat's screeching laughter surprised him. He swerved suddenly and collided violently with Warn Bro at the portal entrance. Both birds, stunned and entangled, plummeted to the ground. The foxes hiding inside the tree's portal were swift and brutal. A silent cheer went up from surrounding bushes.

First blood had been drawn.

Mundu Babill swooped quickly, gathering Warn Bro's warm but lifeless carcass in his powerful claws and took off across the trees to his home in the Valley of Six Curses. The first kill of the night belonged to him. For him, eating crow was nothing to be ashamed of.

Inside the Valley of Lengthened Years, there was a crush to escape the fire.

Old Wonollee held the massing crowd at the exit and called for calm, assuring all that the fire was being brought under control.

Strong winds blanketed the valley with smoke, shrouding a large portion of the crowd. He raised himself before the throng. As his voice rained down, the crowd quietened.

'We have seen lightning burn wood before. Rain is imminent, it will quell the fire and stimulate new wood. What the fire has consumed will be replaced. Let us all look forward to a good storm ... hrmph?'

He drew in his cheeks as his face turned grave, furrows braced his brow.

'We will face danger tonight.' He pointed. 'Out there are enough foxes waiting to slaughter us all. If we leave now, we will perish. Because he will not join the Natural Order, Don Canida would see it destroyed.'

Every animal, reptile and bird before Old Wonollee knew the preservation of their future depended upon their faith. Old Wonollee's message—that there had to be either an ending or a beginning—made it clear. It was up to them and how they reacted.

He laid Jerramunga's plan out before them, organising the clans.

'Like a living carpet of spines, the echidnas will rumble forward and prick the snouts, feet and underbellies. Hrmph ... drive them back.

'The dammalaks, kulbardis and wardongs will provide air support ... hrmph? When the dammalak's zip between the fox's ears, they will turn their heads and herd them. As the kulbardis swoop in and bombard them with heavy objects and, from a height, the Wardongs lob clods of muck, they will force them back under cover.

'Squash and Stretch will lead the artillery from the trees, blitzing them with volleys of gumnuts and prickles. Hrmph ... Don Canida will be isolated. Juna Dana will trample his command positions, and Koopoo's mob will deal with any foxes remaining.

'The dugites and tiger snakes will slither down the forest side and fan out with the echidnas. A wedge of cranes will marshall them inward ... hrmph ... they will strike on the ground with their clawed feet.

'Our objective is to drive Don Canida to the Pool of Many Reflections. Where fate will decide the outcome. Hrmph!'

Within minutes, the crowd was transformed into an organised and lethal army.

Simultaneously, a thought occurred to Wonaiea, Spot and Jerramunga.

'Where's Lavender?'

Wonaiea studied Plain Jane who was standing on a rock, stretched on her rear legs, her neck craning in every direction.

'I thought she was with you,' he said.

'Well, I had to duck off for a little while ... claws and whiskers ... you know. And when I got back, she'd disappeared. No-one saw her go. Ooh ... I'd hate to see anything bad happen to that koolonger. Have you seen her?'

Nobody had.

The question pulsed through the crowd like a Mexican wave, but nobody remembered seeing her after the story of the Folly of Youth. Plain Jane grew agitated. Jerramunga stopped organising.

Spot ran around in circles yapping.

Wonaiea made a snap decision.

Catching a powerful whistle in the upper reaches of the giant trees, the little Gronup melted from the crowd and began circling around the Valley of Lengthened Years, each circle bigger than the previous one. It wasn't long before he spotted her, running furiously through the dense bush along a slim serpentine trail toward the river.

He reported back to Jerramunga.

'She's outside the Valley of Lengthened Years between Willow Hollow and the Pool of Many Reflections!'

'Outside? How did she get outside?' Plain Jane screamed, bewildered by the sudden turn of events.

And then a more horrible thought pushed the question from her mind.

'Wait! If she's heading for the Pool of Many Reflections, and Don Canida's mob is forced down there, she could be in danger. Wonaiea, you have to do something.'

'What can I do? We are not allowed to interfere, Plain Jane— you know that. Babbildan Babbirra made that perfectly clear.'

'Well you have to do something!' she screeched at him, stretching her neck and arching over the Gronup like an axe waiting to fall. 'Somebody has to do something!'

Wonaiea mounted Spot's shoulders and stood to meet Plain Jane's gaze.

'I didn't say we weren't going to do anything,' he said evenly. 'But there is more you should know.'

A flash of lightning, followed instantly by an ear-shattering peal of thunder, split the sky.

'She's travelling with a fox—Don Canida's son.'

A loud 'oooh' went up from the crowd. Before he could continue, another lighting-thunder couplet shook the ground. The smell of ozone lingered before being blown away by a powerful gust of wind.

Wonaiea continued.

'And there's more. A bunch of Snowqueen's heavies are chasing them. They're not far behind.'

Spot had heard enough.

With Wonaiea mounted on his neck, the puppy sidestepped Old Wonollee and bounded recklessly through the exit portal.

He felt the hot stink of a fox's breath before he saw the animal.

As the gaping jaws swooped toward his head, he sprawled headlong beneath the fox's forelegs. The jaws snapped shut a whisker away. Spot rolled right and sank the spicules of his front teeth deeply into the flesh behind the fox's nearest ankle. The fox yelped and collapsed as the tendon severed. Spot zipped out through the back legs.

The second fox came in fast, zeroing in on Spot's path. But the feisty little pup ran rings around the fox. The bigger animal found its tail gripped excruciatingly between its own jaws. At the lip of the tree, Spot turned sharply left and hugged the base of the tree as he made his way around. Two or three foxes bolted toward him.

Inside, Jerramunga wasted no time.

He ordered the waiting army into action. A spiny river of echidnas flowed through the tree portal, blanketing the ground. The two wounded foxes received severe punctures in exposed parts of their bodies, helpless against the jagged ground force. They limped to safer ground. The foxes chasing Spot were brought up short as the spiky foot soldiers oozed from the base of the tree.

Waves of possums—ring-tailed and brush—scaled the trees with their arsenal of stinging and dangerous missiles. Squash and Stretch took a small band to follow Spot.

'*Malak-malak-malak-malak* ...' Mal Aga's war cry trailed loudly on the wind as he led the charge of the dammalaks.

In waves, the squadron followed him, zeroing in on Don Canida's front line.

The confused foxes turned tail.

Mal Aga flew close enough to his first victim to scare the ticks off his ears, skilfully avoiding the gleaming incisors. As he pulled out of his dive he saw two foxes latch onto Spot as he ducked and weaved through the undergrowth, Wonaiea rode him like a cowboy on a bronco. Mal Aga spearheaded a pursuit, bearing down on the lead fox with such speed that the green and black blur could hardly be recognised as a bird. He clipped the fox's left ear with his claws, drawing blood. The stinging blow brought the fox to a halt. His mate, perilously close behind, ploughed headlong into his backside, sending both into the spines of a balga bush.

Spot shot away, his legs motoring, barely contacting the forest floor. He took obstacles in his stride, leaping, swerving and ducking. His pulsing tongue showered Wonaiea with a fine spray of sticky saliva. He cared only to reach his target and bring her to safety.

Lavender and Junior were making steady progress. Their path had been drawing them toward the river. As they entered a heavily wooded section of marri and sheoak trees, it turned left, parallel to the watercourse. A stormy wind rose at their backs, screeching and screaming its ferocity through the valley. Junior regularly checked for signs of pursuing cats. They watched a large formation of cranes fly above them, the leader trumpeting instructions to the flock. The young fox wondered aloud where they were going.

'Perhaps they've left the corroboree,' Lavender said, struggling with an eye-level branch from a prickle bush.

'What's it like?' the young fox asked.

'Well, it's ... amazing.'

She didn't quite know what to tell him.

'The animals all gather together and tell their stories and dance. The birds sing and everybody eats and drinks and talks to each other. All of them celebrate who they are. They get new fur and feathers and scales from their Gronups. And they tell stories about their ancestors. It's really fantastic.'

'What sorts of stories?'

'Well you know ... how the dammalak got the golden ring around his neck?'

'No, I don't know.'

'Well that's the sort of story they tell. Or how the kangaroo got the spring in his step.'

'Oh.'

They plodded on in silence for a while. Lightning grew more frequent, lighting the sky every few seconds with a flourescent rage. Clouds piled high and pressed upon each other. The wind screamed through the trees. Lavender was sure that the heavens would open any minute.

Were the sky spirits angrily smothering the earth? Or were the earth spirits shutting out the sky spirits?

Gubba Gubba had told her how the waters come to smooth things out. There is always tension before it arrives. The trees become angry and thrash about in the wind, calling for the water. The water holds back, waiting for the right moment, teasing the trees with trickles and spits.

'They have such different natures, the wind and the water,' the Gronup had said. 'Goodness though, they need each other so much. Water brings the life to the trees, but it is dark and deep, sometimes hidden so far in the depths of the earth that only the trees know where to find it. The wind spreads the life of the trees across the earth, carrying water with it. But it is invisible to all except the trees. The trees show us where the wind is, and where the water is. If we had no trees, we would have no wind and no water.'

'So how did it?'

'Huh?' Lavender was brought back to the moment by the young fox's question. 'How did who what?'

'The dammalak. How did it get the golden ring around the neck?'

'Oh that. Well, they say that long ago, when animals were men and men were all friends, a dark wind blew up one time and brought dark spirits. The wind grew stronger and stronger and gathered up the whole dammalak clan. They were taken to become the slaves of the dark spirits. They had to work for the dark spirits and could only eat what the spirits gave them to eat. They couldn't go where they wanted to. Husbands and wives were forced to live apart. Whenever babies were born, the dark spirits took them away.

'One day, some of the dammalaks ran away with their children, but they were caught by the dark spirits and taken back, and chains were put around their necks. They were never allowed to roam without the chains so they couldn't go far. The dammalaks rattled the chains trying to summon the rains to rust them away so that they'd be free. This made the dark spirits angry, and they called upon the winds to bring fire so they could make more chains. But the winds brought the rains instead and washed away the dark spirits. The dammalaks in chains also got washed away, but the remaining ones were free. They were given wings by the wind and the Gronups gave them the golden bands around their necks to remind them of the sacrifice of those who were chained up.'

'Wow!' puffed the young fox. 'Is that true?'

'I don't know. It's the story they told.'

'Come to think of it, when you listen to the dammalaks talking, it always sounds like they're rattling chains.'

They laughed.

'This corroboree sounds like really good fun,' he said as they skidded down a short incline.

'It can be a bit scary.'

'Yeah, I suppose. But not as scary as those cats.' The young fox shuddered. 'Nor that yirri-yirri we met earlier.'

'What's a yirri-yirri?'

'Uh ... it's a dingo pup. When I was out with my friends we came across one tearing through the bush with a yellow thing in its mouth—'

Lavender cut him off.

'That must have been Spot. He's my friend. He's not scary, he's just a pup.'

'Well, I tell you, there's something funny about him. I told those other guys to leave him alone, but they just kept on teasing him. They were going to kill him and take him back to my dad, but he beat the daylights out of them. I swear, I've never seen anything like it. He must have been possessed.'

Lavender was impressed. And was about to say so, when a noise ahead in the bush stopped her short.

She stood perfectly still for a moment, and then eased her way back into the safety of a huge karri trunk. The young fox stood still, tail in the air, hackles raised, nose high and ears forward.

He strained to catch a follow-up sound. Moments passed and no sound came. Lavender began to wonder whether she had heard anything at all and was about to ask her companion when a movement from a branch in front caught her eye. She held the bone she'd been carrying all night in front of her like a wand.

The cat fell directly onto the young fox's back and was followed immediately by a second one falling just behind the first. Junior yelped as claws ripped into young flesh. He spun around desperately trying to throw the offending animal from his back. The second cat leapt for the young fox's neck but missed its mark and went hissing headlong into the ground. But the first cat remained firmly attached to his back.

Lavender could sense the Maulers gathering in the branches above them. She lashed out at the cat on the young fox's back with the bone, swiping its face. Stung, the enraged animal let go, hissing and spitting at the girl.

She swung it again. The bone whistled a deadly scream through the air and the cats scuttled out of range. Junior retreated to the relative safety of Lavender's legs. More cats dropped from the branches and joined their colleagues, fanning out to surround the two hapless travellers. En masse, they moved toward them with slow purposeful menace.

Junior hastily licked the nasty scratches on his back and rump and readied himself for the coming onslaught. He bared his teeth, hackles raised like tines on a garden rake. The cats advanced, closing in from the flanks. Lavender pointed her bone and swished it through the air. But the cats were determined, buoyed by their numbers and no longer scared of the weapon or its brutal sound.

Suddenly the bush to Lavender's right erupted and a small brown animal shot out in front of the cats, synchronised with a spectacular flash of lightning. The violence of its appearance and its ghostly form scattered the cats back into the bushes and up the trees. The hero was none other than Spot, with Wonaiea riding high on his shoulder.

He went after the nearest of the cats, yapping furiously to chase them back into the trees. Lavender followed him, the long thin bone in her hand flying left and right stinging the ears of screaming cats as they fled. Junior was right behind her.

Wonaiea grinned at Lavender as Spot turned round and licked the girl sloppily on the ankle.

'We don't have time to hang around,' the Gronup said. 'We have to go.'

Spot led them into the bush, Lavender and Junior moving quickly to keep up. When they came upon small clearing with a rocky overhang that gave shelter from the wind, large drops of rain had begun to fall. They stopped to let Lavender catch her breath. She gave Spot a pat. Spot looked warily at Junior, who looked sheepishly back at Spot.

'That's the yirri-yirri I saw earlier,' the young fox said, quietly.

Lavender smiled.

'Yeah. That's Spot. And that's Wonaiea on his back.'

Junior looked.

'I don't see anyone on his back.'

'Wonaiea is a Gronup.'

'Well I can't see anyone except ...'—three pairs of eyes followed the gaze of the young fox—'... my mother.'

A bolt of lightning lit the sky. A furious gust of wind blew rain into the shelter. Immediately in front of them were the angry eyes of Bella Canida. And perhaps a dozen others behind her.

Don Canida's battle wasn't going well. His front line had been savagely routed, driven back by the tide of echidnas, bombarded by hordes of dammalaks and kulbardis; and splatter bombed by a murder of wardongs. Using claws unique to his line, Don Canida had retreated to the fork of a tall wandoo, from where he watched mobs of emu run wildly among his command posts and kick the living moonlight out of the troops stationed there. Beaten foxes all over the theatre were turning tail.

One pack darted toward the hills, only to be turned back by a writhing mass of dugites, rearing and hissing at the retreating foxes. Others fled upriver and were greeted by a wall of cranes, standing on one leg, with the other raised like a raptor claw and the sails of their wings turning them into formidable apparitions. They too were driven back into the pack.

Eddie Vulpré had devised an effective counter-attack and was making some progress. He'd organised his team to carry short waddies in their mouths, which they used to scoop under the echidnas and overturn them. This exposed their soft underbellies to the lethal fangs of pack members following the waddy wielders, who pounced on them. Don Canida barked orders to other foxes to follow Eddie Vulpré's lead. But the confusion was too great for effective communication and they had little chance to regroup before the possums launched their punishing assault. Gumnuts, sharp sticks and balga spines whip-flicked from their tails struck with stinging accuracy.

By the time Koopoo led his clan into the fray, the foxes were bunched and retreating toward the Pool of Many Reflections. Don Canida fervently exhorted his troops to hold their line, but it was hopeless. Before long, he too was besieged with a hail of missiles from the possums. A cluster of balga spines exploded in his face, blinding him momentarily. He lost his footing and sprawled unceremoniously down the tree. He picked himself up, narrowly escaped a tail whipping from a young boomer and fled in pursuit of his troop. Two of his bodyguards were not so lucky. They were kicked into the trunk of a mighty karri and left dead at its foot.

Casualties among the foxes climbed rapidly as Koopoo and June Dalup kicked and scythed every fox they encountered. The storm intensified with great streaks of lightning as it bolted unrelenting across the sky, amplifying the action of the battlefield. Monstrous thunder pealed through the ground and bounced off the valley walls. Rain bucketed from sodden clouds.

And through it all, the animals herded their quarry.

A squadron of quolls, wedge-tails and crows mopped up, devouring the dead and dispatching those with no chance of recovery. Foxes with non-fatal injuries were herded to the Clearing, heavily guarded by young kangaroos and emus.

Chapter15

The remnants of the fire sizzled in the rain. Babbildan Babbirra retreated to the meeting chamber, head to foot in mud and soot. Exhausted pelicans bee-lined for their reed-bed harbour and a well-earned rest. Mud-covered, soaked and sooty bandicoots dribbled to the workshops for claw and paw repairs.

The fire was left to die alone.

Responding to the summons, the Gronup yoolin materialised into their positions at the altar as the sounds of the forest filtered through.

Babbildan Babbirra willed them to silence.

'We have won against the fire,' he announced. 'The young Ngungakatta with his clever battle plan has outfoxed the foxes.' He permitted himself a small chuckle at his joke. 'There is to be a serious reckoning at the Pool of Many Reflections and the outcome will be impossible to predict—but one thing troubles me still. What has become of the wallagudgal?'

The gathering was silent.

Old Wonollee shifted in his position. His words were a door gradually opening.

'Hrmph ... Wonaiea spotted her. What Wonaiea spotted, the

yirri-yirri saw in his mind. They were last seen tearing through
the opening in the tree like a bat from hell. They set the battle in
motion.'

'Does no-one know where they went?'

Atnunga took up the commentary.

'Some of Don Canida's foxes pursued them, but Mal Aga sent
them off. He lost sight of them after that.'

A shock of thunder shook the ground, its lumpy waves pealing
off into the distance. Burra Baroona took it as his cue.

'They are travelling toward the Clearing. She is there with the
yirri-yirri and Wonaiea. But they are in company.'

Gubba Gubba's finger followed a line in the altar.

'They have taken shelter from the winds and the rain. There is
the presence of young fox with them.'

Atnunga excitedly swirled her hands over her place at the
altar, gushing.

'But they are facing a gathering of older foxes—separate from
Don Canida's skulk.'

'They are mothers,' Wollerta announced, flatly.

'Are they in danger?' Babbildan Babbirra's eyes shone like a
pair of full moons.

Gubba Gubba shook her head slowly.

'Hard to say. They are between the rock and the fox, like the
waters of the ravine. But the young fox is with them—in the
middle. Wait! The koolonger has success in her heart—her spirit
has survived great adversity this night.'

'We should help!' Arunga, the youngest sister, exclaimed.

'Impossible!' Unkurta was firm. 'Events must take their course.'

'But we can lend joy to her heart,' persisted the younger sister. 'To give her the firmness and strength she needs. From that alone, she will see the Way.'

Babbildan Babbirra cast a grave look into Arunga's eyes. 'Then you must attend to it, younger sister. You, Atnunga and Gubba Gubba. Her heart must have joy. But she must see the way ahead and deal with the danger in her own way. If she is unable, then nature has its way and there is nothing more we can do.'

Bella Canida stared at Lavender Jensen.

'What are you doing with my son?' Her voice had the edge of a slow-moving glacier.

Lavender stood still, shivering from cold, exhaustion and fear. She forced the fear into her boots. And ignored the cold. The angry eyes that she looked into were mirrored by at least a half dozen more pairs bunched around those of Bella Canida. Her exhaustion multiplied their menace.

'And where are the others?' Bella Canida asked, lowering her head and sniffing the ground as she expected to find their tracks.

Lavender looked at Junior, and then back at Bella Canida and her company. Junior stepped forward to speak, but was immediately silenced by his mother.

'They have been killed by the cats,' Lavender offered.

'And you were responsible for that?'

'No,' Lavender shot back. 'It was before. The cats've been chasing us, trying to get us. We got away. They're probably still following us.'

'You'll pay for this,' snapped one of the other vixens. 'You led our sons into a trap. It's you the cats want. And you caused their death.'

The foxes closed in on Lavender and Spot.

Junior leapt between them.

'Wait! What she says is true. Snowqueen's mob attacked Bruiser and Greaser and the others before I met Lavender. They were waiting to trap her but we stumbled onto them because Greaser wanted to be part of Dad's operation tonight. He thought he'd be a hero if we went to the Willow Grove. She saved me when she came through the tree opening.'

Bella Canida stopped the other foxes from advancing any further.

'Through the tree opening? Where did you come from?'

'I was at the corroboree with the Gronups. A snake called Cedric said I was to meet my friend near a willow tree, but it was a trick.'

'I know Cedric, he's about as slimy as a crow's gizzards,' Bella Canida said, her tone slightly softer. 'I've heard of these Gronups. The chitti-chitti come around preaching their virtues all the time. Don Canida doesn't believe in them. I'm not sure they even exist.'

Lavender brightened a little.

'Of course they exist. There's one right here.'

She indicated Wonaiea sitting on Spot's shoulder.

'I don't see anything,' Bella Canida insisted, echoing Junior's earlier words.

'Well he's right here.'

Lavender reached down to let Wonaiea sit in her hand and held him forward.

'Let her see you,' she said to the Gronup.

'I can't,' he replied. 'To see a Gronup you have to let go your beliefs. You have to accept the way of the Natural Order.'

Lavender repeated the Gronups words.

'What is the way of the Natural Order?' one of the foxes asked.

Lavender was hesitant.

'It's ... like, the forest has a proper way of life. You enjoy what it gives you, and hunt those who are there for your food. And you get hunted by others who you are food for. It means that you can celebrate life as it comes and goes and no-one rules everyone— it's like there's a proper order that means everyone has enough. That's the Natural Order. It's simple.'

Wonaiea beamed at her.

'How can that be?' another said. 'Who could possibly hunt us?'

'Well there's the wedge-tail, dingo, the Tasmanian devil and Nannup tiger ...' Lavender recalled the stories of Struggle and Difficulty at the beginning. 'The trouble is, a lot have been hunted away by my kind, but if you joined the Natural Order, I'm sure they'll come back.'

'I still can't see this Gronup,' Bella Canida repeated.

'Maybe you just need to use a little imagination,' Lavender said.

'Imagination? What's that?'

'It's … it's seeing something in your head … something that's not really there.'

'That doesn't make sense—how can you see something that's not there?'

Lavender struggled for a way to explain.

'It's like pictures of things you want to see.'

'If they're not there, how can I see them?' another vixen demanded.

Wonaiea was also quizzical.

As were the three Gronups observing from a short distance away.

'This is the thing Burra Baroona mentioned earlier,' Atnunga said to the other two. 'He said the koolonger already has it. Had you experience of it before?'

Both shook their heads.

Arunga the younger sister shared her thoughts.

'Perhaps it's like a reflection. You know, when you see the image of the clouds in the lake. The clouds are not really where you see them, they are somewhere else. Maybe imagination is a bit like that.'

'Maybe your head is in the clouds, little sister,' Atnunga said.

Lavender took another tack.

'Some of you lost your sons tonight,' she said, with a careful measure of compassion. 'You're never going to see them again because they're dead, right? What if you close your eyes now and try to remember what your son looked like last time you saw him. Perhaps you can recall the scent. Can you do that?'

Several of the vixens concentrated a moment. Within seconds, one issued a short bark of exclamation.

'Yes! I see him! I see him! Plain as if he were standing right in front of ... no wait, he's in the den ... Oh he's just a baby ...'

One by one the others caught on.

Bella Canida was stunned.

'What can I imagine?' she asked.

'Well how about Don Canida,' Lavender suggested. 'He's not here right now—maybe you can see what he looked like when you last saw him.'

Bella Canida closed her eyes as her tongue quietly pulsed across her lower jaw.

'Yes,' she said promptly, 'I believe I can see him.'

'Okay,' Lavender said, 'now can you see how things might be if everything was completely different? As if you didn't hunt an animal in the forest just because it's there—just because there is a scent—but only when you are hungry? And let's say you only hunt large and medium animals—not babies—see yourselves doing that!'

They all closed their eyes and let their minds wander. Lavender continued.

'Now look at my hand, and see the little guy sitting there.'

Junior was the first to react.

'I see him. I see him,' he yapped.

It took a few moments, but before long all eyes were on Wonaiea glowing in the girl's hand, grinning.

'Now you're getting the picture!' he exclaimed enthusiastically.

'And the young Ngungakatta?' Old Wonollee asked loftily.

Gubba Gubba, Atnunga and Arunga had returned with the news of Lavender's extraordinary accomplishment.

'He's with Dan Daragan at the Pool of Many Reflections,' Unkurta replied.

'The wallagudgal and her companions are also there,' Atnunga said.

'And the female foxes?' Babbildan Babbirra asked.

'Yes, Yoolin-jah, they are there.'

'Then we must join them,' he said brightly. 'But before we do ... what is the potential of this thing, imagination?'

Burra Baroona's voice boomed in the chamber.

'It is like the lake of the mind. I can see its usefulness. But beware—there is a dark side to everything that is as yet unformed.'

Unkurta reached back into the recesses of his mind to consider the import of the discovery.

'Imagination must take more from space than it does from nature. Ours is the realm of nature. We have spent our time mimicking nature and representing its myriad movements without considering that there may be an alternative. The wallagudgal has shown us the possibilities of an alternative.'

Next to him, Arunga continued.

'The way to know the future comes only from looking into the past. When life is complete it leaves only history. In the end, all we are is stories. The Natural Order simply repeats the stories, perhaps the wallagudgal shows us that new stories can come from the old.'

From directly across the altar, Burra Baroona beamed at her.

'Your words are wise, Arunga. Every life has both beginning and ending, otherwise it is not a life. That is nature's way. But as we all know, an ending is not without its purpose—a new beginning. This thing—imagination—may give us endless possibilities for new beginnings, but it must not alter the fact.'

Babbildan Babbirra looked around the gathering, satisfaction reflected on his face.

'There is new hope,' he said. 'This imagination can generate untold influence. We can use influence to regulate the masses. We see it all the time. That is the purpose of the bush.'

All heads turned to the Gronup leader. A discombobulate feeling permeated the chamber. Babbildan Babbirra saw the confusion and made to explain.

'Nature gives us rain, right?'

Heads nodded.

'But the grass that grows is influenced by the amount of rain.'

More nodding.

'Nature gives us wind, and the winds influence the bushes— how they move, how their seeds are dispersed to all corners of the earth.'

He checked that everyone was with him. He leapt to his feet.

'The bushes compete for the water, and when one bush dominates, it is because it consumes more water—less remains for others. You see? Don Canida is like a bush with too much water.

'The Enterers use imagination to influence how wind and water reach the essences of life. If we influence the way they use imagination, the new beginning arises. Gubba Gubba's oracle is fulfilled!'

The room was silent.

'And now we must go to the Clearing and call upon the spirits to make a judgement about the events of this full moon.'

Cedric had avoided all contact since ushering Lavender through the portal at Willow Hollow. He left the corroboree concealed among the dugites, but deserted before the hill-climb to retire to his tree-stump residence at the Clearing. More than anything, he craved sanctuary. So he surrendered to creature comforts with the knowledge that tomorrow the sun will surely rise. He didn't know that his home, once a sacred birthing place in the Natural Order, would be at the centre of what was to come.

'Don Canida!'

Koopoo stood in the narrow neck of the Clearing. Don Canida was among his clan, all of them contained within the clearing and surrounded by the animals of the Kumakana.

The fox came forward, accompanied by Eddie Vulpré and followed by a string of lieutenants.

'Koopoo,' he said, with supercilious confidence, 'is this a showdown?'

'It's a reckoning.'

Koopoo stretched out in pentapedal lopes, then stood and leaned forward, poised like a cobra.

His eyes met the fox's.

'Do you and your clan want to continue to live in the Kumakana?'

'Are you planning to stop us?'

Don Canida signalled to his mob to fan out around him.

'If that's the way it must be.'

Koopoo raised himself and emphatically repeated: 'Do you want your clan to continue to live in the Kumakana Forest?'

Don Canida bared his teeth and stepped forward and to the side. Several of his companions turned around to face backwards. Others moved to the opposite flank.

'Are you suggesting you can stop us?'

The foxes began to form up into groups inside the Clearing, facing the emus and kangaroos at the perimeter.

'It's been done before,' Koopoo stated, turning to follow Don Canida. 'But it doesn't have to be like that. Not if you agree to join the Natural Order.'

'The Natural Order is a fundamentalist myth. The law of the jungle is the way to survival. I could never subject my family to a way that would ruin their future. It's not as if there aren't animals in the Kumakana who haven't prospered from our way. Have you seen the way the wardongs live around here? Or the snakes?'

'Maybe. But what about those who did live around here once, but don't now? They've got no new seed. Their Gronups are gone. What about them, Don Canida? How many more can we afford to lose before the Natural Order is destroyed altogether? Your way and the Natural Order cannot exist side by side in the Kumakana. The Natural Order, Don Canida, is the way it will be.'

As if to emphasise Koopoo's point, lightning and thunder met simultaneously at Cedric's home for the third time in the tree stump's history. This time, it combusted spontaneously.

When everyone's sight returned from momentary impairment, a torch raged before them, handfuls of gossamer fingers clinging to the air they seared.

Cedric was lucky to escape alive.

Thrown from the inferno by the power of the explosion, he was scorched from nose to tail-tip and landed heavily by the water's edge, where he sizzled for a moment or two before slithering painfully into the reeds.

Don Canida took advantage of the distraction and made a desperate attack on Koopoo's flank. Koopoo's flesh tore in the grip of Don Canida's teeth, the pain striking every nerve in his leg. He twisted quickly away and pivoted on his opposite leg. His massive tail whipped in a vicious arc, leaving the fox sprawled on the ground, panting.

But his recovery time was remarkable.

Blood dripped from Koopoo as he bounded forward, sat back on his tail, took aim and double kicked Don Canida across the arena into his waiting deputies. Three foxes rounded on Koopoo. Two launched a frenzied run-past flank attack. Koopoo wasn't put off his mission. He dispatched each fox with powerful, expert strikes.

Koopoo faced Don Canida again. Several more foxes materialised at his side.

'What about it, Don Canida?'

Don Canida backed off sideways, casting his eye over the foxes waiting for his direction.

The crowd, watching in silence, was awed by the events. But as the battle intensified, the silence melted, and small chatter erupted among the crowds at the perimeter. Congratulations were murmured for various things—births, deaths, furrings, featherings, scalings. Nobody mentioned the fire or the battle.

A lone voice rang out from the river side stunning the crowd into a renewed silence.

'We will join the Natural Order.'

It was Junior Canida. He'd arrived with his mother and her companions—Lavender, Spot and Wonaiea, escorted by the cranes.

Don Canida was flabbergasted. 'Are you challenging me, Son?'

Junior moved forward, facing his father.

'I have seen the Gronups, Dad. They're real.'

'Gronups are no more real than wombat wings. You're young, Junior, it's difficult to understand—'

'What's to understand? If you'd succeeded tonight, you would have stolen the future from your own children and their children. The law of the jungle doesn't work in the bush. What will we eat when the food runs out? If you destroy the Natural Order, you destroy us.'

Junior appealed to those around him.

The vixens commended him. Lavender beamed outwardly, but inside, turmoil raged. She was on tenterhooks. Things could go either way. Best to support the change, she thought, while Spot and Wonaiea kept their eyes on things. The foxes in the scattered mobs began to take notice. Each fox grappled with what they saw—a number of vixens supporting Junior, all at odds with Don Canida.

Koopoo took it all in.

'Looks like you've had your day old man,' he said, his disrespect poorly shielded. 'Junior's on the right path.'

'Junior doesn't know the path he's chosen.'

Don Canida advanced toward his son and circled around him, slowly pausing at the first flank to say into his ear, 'If he will not follow me, then he has no path.'

He looked at Lavender and addressed Koopoo across Junior's back.

'Clearly he has been fooled by this koolonger's magic. She has used that special magic to trick him, the magic of her heart.'

He turned to Bella Canida.

'The legend, Bella, from the old country—the heart of the child—remember how the wolf got the magic? Do you remember that legend?'

'Yes, Don Canida, I remember the legend. But Junior already has her heart. So do I. And so do those around me. We didn't have to take it. It was given freely. You would have deprived anyone else from sharing that heart tonight. I can't let you do that.'

Junior pronounced his father's judgement. 'You are banished. You may leave by crossing the Kulwinkulkine.'

Bella Canida and her companions closed round Junior.

Gathering numbers of foxes came in support of Don Canida.

'We are not done,' Don Canida said, as a wall of foxes separated him from Junior and the vixens.

Behind the wall, Don Canida moved quickly, tearing into Koopoo from the side as a small leash of his thugs struck from the opposite flank. The great kangaroo went down in a violent mass of fur and blood and mud. Don Canida was about to make a final lunge for Koopoo's jugular when a sickening thud from the other side of the kangaroo stopped him.

Jerramunga had waded in, a hefty branch in hand, which had made deadly contact with the head of a fox mauling Koopoo's flank near his tail. Another blow from the waddy left a second fox with a dislocated foreleg.

'You!' Don Canida snarled, backing away.

Jerramunga headed round the fallen kangaroo, his club whistling menacingly through the air.

'None other, fox. I suggest you take your son's advice.'

Two foxes, practically flying through the air, struck Jerramunga in the middle of the back, driving the wind from him and pitching him forward into the jaws of an advancing Don Canida.

Don Canida gripped the boy's waddy arm and sank his teeth deep through the flesh, twisting his head sideways to bring Jerramunga screaming in agony to the dirt. The foxes behind pounced, each seeking the soft flesh of the neck.

Meanwhile, Koopoo had recovered enough to stand, and he leaned back on his tail and fired a double-footed kick, lifting both foxes simultaneously into the air. They landed at the feet of a mob of young boomers, who wasted no time in finishing their leader's work. As Koopoo rounded again on Don Canida, the fox tore the top of Jerramunga's ear from his head, spat it at the kangaroo, spun quickly around and grabbed Koo Tea roughly by the scruff of the neck, held him for a few seconds for the crowd to see, and bolted for the river.

Koopoo reacted instantly and made to bound after the fox but collapsed as his legs gave out from under him.

Lavender had no second thoughts.

She leapt from a small rocky groin that jutted out into the river's flow, hoping to head the fox off at the water's edge. Don Canida dodged and then used the cover of a paperbark to slip into the water, carrying the kidnapped joey in front of him. Lavender returned to the rocks and made for the end where she dived into the stream.

Swimming had long been her strength and she ignored the icy shock of the water as her powerful strokes drove her further out into the stream to head off Don Canida. The fox turned toward the other side. Koo Tea's nose vacillated through the surface as

Don Canida strained to keep out of Lavender's reach.

Spot reacted next.

With Wonaiea riding shotgun once again, he dived into the water and swam to Lavender's assistance. Don Canida, swimming strongly and carried by the middle-river current, was now within reach of Lavender, who was steadily treading water.

'Hold your breath,' she said to Koo Tea, and reached out pushing Don Canida's head beneath the surface. She watched as the joey blew bubbles. She lifted Don Canida's head above the water.

'Release him, Don Canida.' The fox only shook his head.

'A little longer this time, Koo Tea,' she said, and once again submerged the head of Don Canida.

Don Canida fought against the need to breathe and tried to twist his way out of the grip. He suddenly released the joey and ducked beneath Lavender's sinking pressure. He snapped at her and struck out for the opposite bank. Spot swam straight in and grabbed the joey by the scruff of the neck, and dog-paddled like fury toward the shore and the joey's waiting mother.

Lavender again lunged for Don Canida, the current and movement taking them closer to the rocks. Don Canida shook himself loose and scrambled up a rock worn smooth by the river's symphony and time. Lavender floundered in white water, and the increasing pressure of the stream drove her mercilessly onto a rocky outcropping. Her feet found a fallen tree branch wedged between the rocks. She stood as Don Canida slid from the smooth rock back into the water and she raised her hand high above her head as the fox was pushed into the tree.

Lavender brought her hand down hard and fast, embedding the bone she held deep into the fox's neck. A stream of blood mixed with the foam, turned it creaming-soda pink, as she pushed the body away from the fallen branch into the rush of the Kulwinkulkine.

Panting heavily from the exertion, she climbed across the rocks to the shore.

Relieved silence fell upon the Clearing. The fire in the old stump had burnt out, reshaped one more time by nature, regaining its mantle as a sacred birthing place.

Dotty, the bandicoot, given that she now, 'had one in the pouch,' volunteered to be the first to use it. Spot—her partner—had deserted on the news.

'Gone,' she'd said to Plain Jane, earlier, 'to do his duty; fulfil his part in the Natural Order. But that's the way with all the males,' she sighed. 'We love 'em to death.'

The gathering began to disperse.

Koopoo limped away after calling a council of elders so work could begin on the details of admitting the foxes to the Natural Order. Junior Canida went with him while his mother led the clan back to their dens.

Boo Ragoon announced his retirement from the fire brigade. Mal Aga was elected to a new position on council, promising his mates that he would make good the damage caused by his rash agreement for nest sharing with the gakkal-yakkal family.

Plain Jane fussed over Lavender as she settled back into the old tree stump, wet and exhausted. Babbildan Babbirra appeared, holding the bone Lavender had used to kill Don Canida.

'There is a place for this at the entrance to the Valley of Lengthened Years,' he said. 'It will be set into a rock as a symbol of the great magic you brought to the Kumakana.'

Lavender smiled at him.

'I thought it was magic,' she said, 'it's what caused the landslide at the breakaway.'

'No,' the Gronup said, 'it contains no magic. But you ... well now that's a different story. With your magic of imagination ... Yes, indeed, that's a different story.'

Picking up a song line left drifting on the wind, he disappeared.

Jerramunga and Spot, who was once again carrying the yellow ball, joined her inside the shelter of the stump.

The boy was badly bruised and deep gashes from his fight with the foxes lined both arms and his shoulder. But his smile was as wide as ever.

He held his hand out to her.

'I think this is yours.'

And he dropped dangling strands into her hand.

Lavender reached out and touched Jerramunga's hand.

'You got it back for me.' She squeezed his hand. 'And thanks for saving my life.'

He grinned.

'Thanks for saving mine.'

A serious look came over her. 'I guess this is secret business, right?'

He shook his head slowly from side to side.

'Can't tell a soul.'

And he bent to Spot and mumbled something incoherent.

The next thing she knew dawn had broken and she woke to the song of a magpie overhead.

'The dawn chorus,' she said.

The magpie chortled.

Spot, who had fallen asleep on her lap, wagged his tail and nosed the yellow ball toward her, as though he wanted her to throw it for a game of fetch. Jerramunga roused himself with a stretch, peered out of the gap in the old stump and grinned at Lavender.

'I know which way to go,' he said.

She didn't argue.

Rather, she smiled, stood, took his hand and said, 'Let's go.'

APPENDIX

Word List

balga	zanthoria tree
Bibbulmun	the people of Australia's south-west
bilby	type of marsupial
buddung	the sound of a jump
chiriger	blue wren
chitti-chitti	willy wagtail
chuditch	western quoll
chukkup	discuss
dammalak	Port Lincoln parrot (twenty-eight)
dugite	brown snake
gakkal-yakkal	galah; pink and grey Major Mitchell cockatoo
gnow	mallee fowl
Gronup	small mystical forest creatures that provide spiritual ministry and grooming services for all the animals in the Natural Order
karri	eucalyptus of the southwest forest of WA
koolonger	children (male and female)
koomborlie	brother
kulbardi	magpie
Kulwinkulkine	the longest and largest of the rivers that run through the Kumakana Forest
Kumakana	the old name of the forest; place of great beginnings
kwenda	bandicoot
mardo	yellow-footed antechinus
murna	sound of any living creature in the woods

numbat	small ant-eating marsupial, also wee-oo
Nyungar	Indigenous man of the south-west
potoroo	small rat-like kangaroo
quokka	small rat-like kangaroo
twonk	talk
waddy	heavy club
wallagudgal	spirit that is unclaimed by either heaven or earth; a pure, innocent spirit
widji	emu
woggal	carpet snake; python
woondah	bull roarer
woylie	small kangaroo, kangaroo rat
yaller-yaller	converse; to talk
yantamurra	afterglow of a falling star
yay	greeting, hello
yirri-yirri	pup, especially dingo pup
yongar	kangaroo
yoolin	tribal counsellor; elder
Yoolin-jah	chief of tribe
Yorgah	Indigenous woman of the south-west
Yurlungga	the creator spirit

The Characters

Arunga, youngest sister Gronup council member (yoolin) the joyous, reflective one, represents the lake

Atnunga, elder sister Gronup council member (yoolin), represents those who use the wind and wood

Babbildan Babbirra, most revered Gronup council leader (yoolin-jah), the bright, represents light

Bella Warra, pigmy possum

Ben Cubbin, barn owl

Boo Ragoon, pelican

Burra Baroona, eighth Gronup council member, and younger brother (yoolin) represents thunder and those who use the earth

Burra Coppin (aka Burra C), black-faced hairy-nosed wombat

Bella Canida, fox, mate of Don Canida

Bluey, feral cat, current boyfriend of Snowqueen

Bruiser, young fox

Carker Barker, ruffle-headed royal spoonbill

Cedric, snake, carpet python (woggal)

Cecil Park, young magpie, brother of Cecil Plain

Cecil Plain, young magpie, brother of Cecil Park

Chad Stone, blue wren

Cornelius, fox, member of Don Canida's gang

Dan Daragan, the Nannup (Tasmanian) tiger

Dal Keith, red capped parrot

Dotty, bandicoot

Deary Ree, mallee hen

Don Canida, leader of the foxes, direct descendent of European grey foxes brought by mistake to Albany port in 1830s

Djit Arning, frog

Eddie Vulpré, fox, member of Don Canida's gang

Gloves, fox, member of Don Canida's gang

Greaser, young-adult fox

Goo Malling, freshwater long-neck tortoise elder

Gubba Gubba, middle sister Gronup council member (yoolin), who represents the flow of water and ministers to those who use running waters

June Dalup, emu elder

June Dana, emu

Junior, young-adult fox, son of Don Canida and Bella Canida

Kal Annie, female gakkal-yakkal (galah), mate of Kal Barri

Kal Barri, male gakkal-yakkal (galah), mate of Kal Annie

Karra Katta, red-tailed black cockatoo

Koopoo, yongar (kangaroo), Yoolin-jah of his clan

Koorda, female yongar (kangaroo), mate of Koopoo and mother of Koo tea

Koo tea, Koopoo's joey

Kul Yannobbin, musk duck

Kul Bellup, musk duck

Mal Aga, male dammalak (parrot), mate of Mal Ala

Mal Ala, female dammalak (parrot), mate of Mal Aga

Mal Acoota, dammalak (parrot), cousin of Mal Aga

Mal Vern, dammalak (parrot)

Ma Lisse, gnow (mallee hen), fowl

Mum Darda, pigmy possum

Mundu Babill, ghost bat

Naraait, gnow (mallee hen)

Ngo-lak Bungal, white-tailed black cockatoo

Ngungakatta, ancestor of Jerramunga

Plain Jane, kwenda (bandicoot)

Preacher, chitti-chitti (willy wagtail)

Red Cliffe, fox, member of Don Canida's gang

Rusty Steyne, fox, member of Don Canida's gang

Snowqueen, feral cat, leader of the Moggie Maulers

Stretch, possum

Squash, possum

Tiltili, gnow (mallee hen)

Toota, gnow (mallee hen)

Unkurta, father Gronup council member (yoolin), representing Heaven, strength, and the creative powers of the spirits

Warn Bro, wardong (crow) yoolin

Wal Pole, quokka

Old Wonollee, eldest brother Gronup council member (yoolin), represents stillness, mountains and lofty views

Wonaiea, mischievous Gronup

Willie Abrup, chitti-chitti (willy wagtail)

Willie Ams, chitti-chitti (willy wagtail)

Willie Ton, chitti-chitti (willy wagtail)

Wollerta, mother Gronup council member (yoolin), representing the breadth of the Earth, devotion, nurture and caring

ABOUT THE AUTHOR

Born in Narrogin, Western Australia, in 1953, Kevin Price
spent his formative years on a farm in the West Australian wheatbelt.
He attended Narrogin Senior High School and later received a
BA in English and Creative Arts and a Graduate Diploma of Education—
both from Murdoch University. He describes himself as a writer, teacher,
and student of story. Kumakana is his first novel.

www.ingramcontent.com/pod-product-compliance
Lightning Source LLC
Chambersburg PA
CBHW030629020726
47493CB00006B/1625